This Way North

Olly Williams

First published in The United States by Holland Brown Books, LLC 2008

632 East Market Street, #2
Louisville
Kentucky 40202
USA

www.hollandbrownbooks.com

ISBN 13: 978-0-9797006-0-6
ISBN 10: 0-9797006-0-4
Library of Congress Control Number: 2007931984

This Way North / Williams, Olly
1st Edition

Typeset and Printed in Great Britain by CPI Antony Rowe,
Bumpers Farm, Chippenham, Wiltshire

This book has been printed using paper from sustainable forests

For Lisa

The animal in man, the jungle in nature, is never far away.

Hugh Steadman Williams, playwright

Prologue

Sunlight streamed through the dense canopy, diffusing rays of golden late afternoon light through the Alaskan spruce forest. Already there was a chill in the air, the high country resting under a good dusting of mid-November snow. Lower down the valley the bull moose moved carefully along the creek, pausing after each step to listen for any noise that would betray the presence of danger. His summer coat was nearly gone now, the last strands of his light pelt replaced by a new, thick, oily, chestnut brown winter hide that glistened in the dappled sunlight. He was looking for the last of the new shoots and shrubs on the low ground; soon all would be seized in winter's icy grip and he would be forced once again to survive the long winter months on coniferous tree bark and low-lying willows. Despite his inbuilt awareness to danger, he had little to fear in the forest.

Standing six and a half feet at the shoulder and weighing 1,600 pounds, the Alaskan bull moose was a formidable adversary for any predator, including wolf and bear. During the past five years of rut he had triumphed over all the other bulls and had sired many young. Now thirteen years old, he was approaching his prime, and judging by his great size he had many mating seasons left in him. But still he sensed danger – that was his nature. Earlier in the year he had stood his ground and fought off a pack of timber wolves. Refusing to turn and run away, he had thrust his formidable rack to and fro, keeping the wolves at bay. In a confrontation that had lasted many hours, the wolves had eventually retreated and then run, yelping, tails between their legs as the bull gave a victor's chase. They knew there was easier prey to find; it was not their day.

Having spent the early part of the afternoon feeding in the lower creek, the moose followed the tree line up a steep rise and began to feed on a fresh area of young saplings, leaving a tell-tale browse line along the forest's perimeter. He was, if anything, a creature of habit and followed the same trail day after day, making only the occasional detour into the thick scrub if he spotted a particularly succulent willow on which to feed. By last light he had stepped gracefully across the snow line, making a neat alternating walking pattern, his huge half-moon hooves leaving their unmistakable imprint in the fresh snow. A light wind carried messages of passing through the valley and across the forest. The bull moose tasted the air, standing perfectly still. Grunting as if to reassure himself, he pushed deep into the trees and began walking in ever-decreasing circles, clearing away the light dusting of snow before bending his great legs and resting in his new bed. Never completely at ease, he lay still and drifted off into a light sleep, for that was the lot of a solitary moose. Too deep a sleep and it could be your last. Tonight at least, all seemed well.

The hunter had picked up the fresh moose tracks shortly after dawn. The spoor was probably only minutes old, judging by the way the night's icy crust had been stamped cleanly into the permafrost, leaving soft and fluffy snow beneath. The hunter gently laid his large framed pack by a tall spruce and began to track the moose carefully, carrying only his rifle and knife. Hugging the tree line he hunkered down low, almost creeping, alert and listening for movement. Despite the moose's immense size, he knew from past experience how these animals could melt into the forest and if spooked remain hidden, sometimes indefinitely. It was this characteristic that made moose such a challenge to hunt. For the first time that year the hunter had the feeling he was being watched from the tree line, and it made him feel uncomfortable.

In search of new quarry the hunter had ventured further than before, landing his floatplane on the Great Bear Lake and crossing the Kuskokwim range on foot by a low mountain pass the previous day. The enormity of Western Alaska stretched out before him, a vein of new life totally undisturbed by man, two million square miles of roadless wilderness. The hunting was still good here, wilder than his native Wyoming, and in the crisp morning light the hunter knew it would be his day. He could feel it. From within the forest, eyes were on him. He waited, perfectly still, listening, his eyes closed, his breath held, but he could hear nothing, not even the familiar sound of raven in the muffled snowscape. An eerie silence engulfed him. The moose tracks had led him further than he had wanted to go without his kit and now he wondered if he should quickly retrace his footsteps and recover his equipment in case the weather turned.

As he opened his eyes and once more turned toward the large spruce tree, the bull moose walked out into the open, as if defying his presence, only yards from where he was standing. Barely believing his luck, the hunter slowly brought his trusted Heym Express rifle into his shoulder and pushed forward the safety catch. Many safaris in Africa had taught him well. In close cover he always hunted with the gun loaded and cocked, safety catch on, since he often needed to take a snap shot. Hunting dangerous game alone and without back-up in Alaska was no exception. Closing his left eye, he aligned the iron sights at the huge musculature of the bull's shoulder and, exhaling gently, squeezed the trigger. The heavy rifle jerked violently upwards, as the delayed report of the .505 Gibbs round echoed around the valley. The moose staggered backwards and then, for a brief while, stood motionless. The hunter deftly worked the bolt from his shoulder and aimed once more, this time keeping both eyes open, looking for signs of a charge, his adrenaline pumping. But a second shot was not necessary. It rarely was with the .505. In slow motion the moose tried to kneel and then crumpled sideways into the snow, emitting a low, deep grunt. Past experience had taught the hunter to hold his ground and wait, keeping the rifle aimed at the dying animal. He waited, and he waited some more.

After a few minutes he carefully approached the moose from behind and prodded its open eyeball with the muzzle of his rifle. No reflex movement, no retinal dilation. The moose was dead. The hunter immediately set to work. First he felt for the space between the moose's forequarters and, pushing and turning his blade vigorously into the moose's soft chest region, he punctured and bled out the beast's heart. Next he made a shallow incision along the moose's stomach to clear away the hair and skin. Placing his finger on the flat top-strap of his knife, he worked along the underbelly, cutting a clean and bloodless line. Warm steam gradually began to waft from the open cavity as the hunter positioned the moose's head above his body on the gradual slope. He heaved the moose's lifeless body downwards and, delving into the steaming hulk, pulled hard from within the abdominal cavity, easing the stomach and large intestine out on to the snow. With his boot he kicked the huge stomach and offal to one side and set about field dressing the animal. He deftly cut around the moose's foreleg joints, then, taking the massive head in his hands, he made a deep incision in the neck and cut out the windpipe. Next he began to saw through the sternum with the serrated part of his knife and managed to cleave open the chest cavity. Then he broke the hindquarters, splitting the thighs at the saddle, and began to pull away the skin from either side of the flanks. As he worked he began to sweat and as he began to sweat he started to get cold. He was grateful for the warmth of the dead moose but he was conscious of the time it would take to prepare the massive beast for the long walk out. After an hour he was nearly finished and stood back to survey his handiwork. The butchered moose stared lifelessly up at him, the head and rack sitting neatly above the folded and bloody cape. The two thighs, ribs and saddle lay nearby, the deep purple meat set like rubies in the glistening snow. He would leave the rest of the beast as food for ravens, foxes and the odd lone wolf. In this harsh winter habitat nothing would be wasted.

It was now late morning and the best of the day's light was beginning to fade. By three it would be dark and the hunter knew he would need to make camp and hang the meat in the trees before nightfall. Looking toward the mountain pass he noticed dark snow clouds forming. There was spindrift coming off the highest peaks and the wind on the higher ground would make a bivouac on the pass impossible. He knew the weather was beginning to deteriorate and decided to make a sheltered camp in the nearby forest. He would tackle the pass the next day and fly out that evening.

Leaving his trophy in the snow, he quickly collected his pack from the tree line and strapped the moose's great head, rack and cape on to the rucksack for his first load carry into the woods. Despite his good fitness he found the going hard as he pushed on through the deep snowdrifts down the slope, keeping his eyes peeled for a suitable clearing in which to pitch camp. The adrenaline of his hunt still coursed through him and soon enough he found his rhythm. After no more than twenty minutes the snow began to get thinner underfoot and the going less tiring. The spruce trees became denser and the valley got darker. The hunter stopped. He could have sworn he had heard a sound, the breaking of a branch underfoot. He knelt down on one knee and looked into the dark low forest. Yes, he saw it again, a movement, a deer maybe, or a raven. Taking off his pack, he quickly walked toward the trees and peered once more into the impenetrable depths. As he strained his eyes trying to make out movement he thought he could see the outline of a wooden structure, a cabin.

He could see it clearer now; it was definitely a cabin, not thirty yards into the trees. Walking up along the line of spruces he soon found a small game trail that led into the forest. He pushed the branches aside and entered its mass, straining and pushing against the sea of pines and spruces. The hunter was amazed at how the dry brown needles crackling under his feet were barely touched by the snow on the surrounding slopes, and by the thickness of the cover of the forest canopy. He had heard of hunters sheltering under pine trees during winter storms, using their branches as one would use a tepee, but here, crawling into the cover of the forest would be enough to escape the driving snow and wind. He pushed on into the depths of the wood.

The hut stood on wooden tree stumps, a primitive structure, but practical and solid. The clearing looked to have been cleared by hand and was big, at least twenty yards square. The stumps of the felled pines showed the tell-tale signs of a manual saw blade: they stood uneven and rough. Whoever had cut this clearing had done so without a chainsaw. The hunter guessed it must have been made many years ago by a trapper wanting to live out an undisturbed, solitary existence.

The hunter called out, "Hey! Anyone home?"

There was no reply. He walked up to the door – there were no tracks, and any earlier ones would have been covered by the fresh snowfall that day. The door had no handle, and he gave it a good push. It opened with ease and the hunter gingerly went inside. The interior was sparse. In the center of the room were a single chair and table; a caribou skin lay by the stone hearth. There was no glass in the windows, which were just two small openings covered with fur flaps as makeshift shutters. In the corner by the door was a large moose pelt covering some kind of structure. The hunter couldn't help his curiosity. He lifted the skin back and laid it on the floor. Underneath stood a beautiful antique sled, its runners perfectly polished and its five wooden slats oiled and well smoothed. On the sled lay a thick, tightly strapped roll of felt with a small tin of what smelled like wax and a pressed metal flashlight. How strange, thought the hunter, for on closer inspection the sled appeared to have been made in Germany, the old Germany, bold Germanic text crudely stamped quite clearly into the right-hand runner. It must have been an old family heirloom used for transporting kills along the trap line, he thought. Without further delay he replaced the pelt as he had found it.

Tired now, he sat down on the lone wooden chair and noticed a roll of fabric on the floor. Again it was felt, a roll that was probably no more than a foot long. The hunter unraveled the roll and could make out the rusted impression of a large knife, an oxidized sepia stain defining the blade's outline in the thick fabric. He began to feel uneasy. He was in a stranger's cabin and that person had a big knife. It was time to leave. He had let his curiosity run away with him far enough. Without looking behind him he made his way back through the narrow line of trees and out on to the open slope. He collected his rucksack and made his way hastily to collect the meat. He had decided he would now try his luck further up the valley so he would not have to travel so far in the morning. The dense forest and the cabin had given him the creeps. He didn't want to meet its owner, not tonight at least.

Soon he was over the last rise and powering his way toward his cache of meat. As he approached he noticed ravens.

"Hey! Get away!" he shouted.

The ravens jumped and cackled and flew a few yards away, watching him intensely. He knew he had been stupid not to carry all the meat with him, but he had anticipated the possibility of not finding an appropriate site for a camp and returning. What the hell, so long as he didn't lose the meat to a wolf or wolverine, the odd raven could only do so much harm in the twenty minutes he had been gone. But he was mistaken. Before him only the ribs remained and these had been half-consumed by the birds, their tell-tale footprints surrounding the kill. But the hind legs, ravens couldn't have taken those. The hunter was visibly shaken. He started to fear the worst. Only a bear, wolf or wolverine could have made off with his prize cuts. Christ, how stupid he had been. He paced to and fro until he saw them . . . unmistakable tracks in the snow. At first he feared a winter bear, unable to sleep and brought out of his den by the smell of the kill. But on closer inspection he realized these were not bear prints, they were something much more sinister. They were human prints, primitive hand-made snowshoe prints.

The hunter froze in his tracks. Just as he had felt earlier in the day, he now knew he was being observed, watched by someone or something close by. The hairs on his neck began to stand up and he felt a cold trickle of sweat roll down his back. Grabbing his pack, he swung it over his shoulder and checked the chamber on his rifle. The big Heym was loaded. He raced up the slope trying to retrace his tracks, which were beginning to be covered by light snowflakes. Time was against him but now all he cared about was getting out of the valley. He was shaken, really rattled, and his mind was racing. Who lived in that cabin? Who was following him? And why had his meat been stolen? As far as he knew no one could survive in this area without re-supply from civilization, and whoever was living out here was at least 200 miles from the nearest settlement in any direction. He had not seen any evidence of a mooring or floatplane on Great Bear Lake, which if his flight maps were accurate was the only suitable lake large enough to take off and land on in the whole region. As he came to the crest of the snowfield he passed the spot where he had laid his rucksack before stalking the moose. The tree was larger than the other trees, its bark covered in the thick lichen that indicated the purity of the Alaskan air.

The hunter couldn't quite put his finger on what it was that made him walk around the tree, especially in light of his rush to get away from whoever it was that had stolen his moose meat. But as he walked slowly around the mossy trunk he noticed that a patch of bark had been recently removed. He crouched down and brushed aside the lichen. A word had been carved in the trunk, the trunk of a tree that grew in a valley of a million similar trees. True it was slightly larger and it stood at the head of the snowfield, reasoned the hunter, but by the law of averages . . . a billion to one, no, a trillion to one . . . It made his head spin.

He began to read the carved letters out loud to himself. "N-E-M-O," he said in a slow, low voice. "NEMO," he repeated.

★ ★ ★

Part 1

Jack Wyler

All men dream: but not equally. Those who dream by night in the dusty recesses of their minds wake in the day to find that it was vanity: but the dreamers of the day are dangerous men, for they may act out their dream with open eyes, to make it possible.

Lawrence of Arabia, Seven Pillars of Wisdom

Chapter 1

Jack Wyler glanced at his Rolex. It was 6:50am and he felt strangely drained. For the past week now he had struggled with his 5am wake-up call. Normally he was raring to go, but today, already halfway through three new business plans, he was having trouble focusing, as if his mind and body lay elsewhere.

His office was warm and quiet. The surrounding wood paneling and ornate corniced plasterwork gave the room a solid, expensive feel. A leather and chrome Eames desk and matching pair of Arne Jacobson egg chairs were the only furniture in the large airy space, in addition to a Stair-Master placed discreetly and unused in one corner.

Jack stared at the painting in front of him. His new acquisition, a large eight-foot-by-four-foot Jean-Michel Basquiat "door panel" painting framed in a perspex box. It leaned against the largest of the paneled walls, a primitive centerpiece dominating the room. The work had struck him with its rawness and naivety. There was something in the nature of the line, a crudeness and simplicity that knocked him off his feet, the shocking pinks, the dirty greens and the dark sinister skull-like head, totemic and crowned with wire. The painting bewitched him and drew him in.

Jack swiveled his chair to the left and caught his own reflection in the floor to ceiling mirror. He studied his face, dark brown eyes narrowing to a penetrating stare. Already the tell-tale haze of stubble was beginning to shadow his square jawline and rugged chin. He had forgotten to shave, and he smiled fakely, a suave, smarmy, left-brow-raised, eye-catching smile, "Ah, Mr Bond," he joked. "Nah," he muttered to himself, turning away from the mirror. Not this morning, he couldn't pull that routine off today.

Jack spun back around to look at the Basquiat that he had wanted since first seeing it at auction four years before. He wished he had bought it then. By the time it appeared again at Sotheby's on 72nd and York in early 1999 it was held on a reserve of over $330,000, a good $100,000 more than on its previous outing. The bidding had become heated and Jack, always a bull, had gone all the way. Hans Groub, a Swiss gallerist and recent bidding adversary, had backed out at $405k. Jack had seen the infamous Groub a lot recently, from a distance at the auctions mainly, going well into seven figures for the big boys, the abstract expressionists. Now he was bidding against him again, the most powerful dealer on the East Coast. The adrenaline felt good, the knowing nod, other bidders falling by the wayside. What a trip it was to go for it, to be able to afford such a work. But for Jack it was the principle more than anything else. Jack Wyler hated to lose, and after all, it was his thirty-fifth birthday present to himself. He felt he deserved it.

Annie, Jack's long-time personal assistant, arrived at 7am sharp and set about her daily tasks. "Coffee, Jack?" she asked.

"Yeah, sounds great," Jack replied in a low voice. Spinning away from the painting, he stared once again at the screen. "Fucking computers," he muttered under his breath. "Second time this morning I've been trying to log on. Is the server down, Annie?"

"No, I checked it with the techies on the way up. It must be your laptop, have you tried re-booting?"

Jack sat back in his worn Eames chair and gazed into space. Maybe he was overly drained due to his recent bout of intense recurring dreams. They were vivid and exhausting, an affliction he had suffered since childhood. They were such strange dreams, so much space, mountains, some type of wilderness, and he was moving through it fast, flying through it, high above the valleys and over the snow-crested ridges. Christ, he had woken up this morning as exhausted as if he had just done a ten-mile run.

Daylight flooded into his office through the large bay windows in front of his desk and reflected off the polished aluminum picture frames that lined the office walls. Jack loved gazing at the view from his office, straight out over the Hudson River, the water shimmering in the early morning light. Sometimes when he was in the depths of a deal he barely noticed it, and then again on days like today it could be a bit of a distraction, but a distraction that was somehow a necessity. Jack often wondered how people could work without the view or the light – he knew he never could. His other great diversion was his paintings, the art that kept him sane, as he was so fond of saying.

Jack's art collection was diverse, but centralized around a core of primitive painting and art photography. The works were not monumental as a rule – Jack's preference was for modesty of scale, objects of beauty that could travel. It was not exactly a given criteria, and the new Basquiat door panel had broken the rule, but size was certainly an important consideration. To be able to take them with him if need be – it was part of Jack's semi-nomadic nature, the result of a childhood spent traveling, a hand-me-down from his parents' philosophy about ownership and possessions. "Have just enough, take with you what you need, get rid of the rest." Jack Wyler had broken most of those rules, like most poor kids made good, and he had a lot more than he needed. But deep inside, in his subconscious, he knew this philosophy to be true about himself, despite all the gear, the beautiful things.

The works had not been hung anally, more by line of sight, "salon style", in order of size and personal choice, with Annie darting left and right to Jack's impatient call. The first work to be hung had been a small Tapies footprint painting delicately rendered in ochre and glutinous Chinese ink on handmade paper. There followed a series of mistakes, what Jack liked to refer to as his "bull market acquisitions" driven by uninformed tips at work. He had made a loss on Warhol's original Ali set due to discoloration. But after several wrong moves he had made a serious decision, informed by his belief in the market, to "pay up for quality". The result was a major acquisition of a small Cy Twombly painting, *Untitled no. 6*, graphite and black on battleship grey linen, scrawled and impatient, the lines eager to run amok and off the small canvas. Then there was the Joseph Beuys; a mordant ink drawing entitled *Stag with Human Head*, iconic, delicate and spiritual. Jack had a special love of Beuys, a love fostered as a child by his mother and, like good DNA, carried into adulthood. Several photographs by Cartier-Bresson, the haunting image of the old Matisse, a large Olly & Suzi African photograph of lions lounging regally at the waterhole entitled *The Last Supper* and Peter Beard's bloodstained crocodile photo-montage, all hung in well-spaced order around the room.

Other lesser-known art works were stacked neatly around the desk and the room, as were mementos of Jack's many foreign trips: a shark's tooth from South Africa, a tiger claw from Nepal, a pair of crocodile skulls from Lake Turkana in Northern Kenya. Two images of Jack held pride of place on his desk: a crumpled photograph of him and his old man hunting in Alaska and another taken three winters before on Canada's Ellesmere Island of a weathered and frost-bitten Jack with his two best friends, Bob Anders and Jim Williamson, after completing a grueling 400-mile dog-sled circumnavigation of the interior icecap.

Jack was a man of extremes. Extreme work and extreme play. His passion for collecting art was matched only by his love of endurance travel. His biggest buzz came from the challenge, physical or mental, the mind-set of a champion athlete winning at all costs, testing himself to his limits, living outside his personal comfort zone. But this morning, tired and drained, it seemed to Jack that this was the one thing missing ... the passion. Until today, it had appeared that three more years as managing director of research at investment bank Klein, Loeb & Silvers (KLS) was achievable, so long as he took it one day at a time. But now, staring from the computer screen to the new painting and back and anticipating the 450 daily emails that were waiting for him (when the gods of technology felt it appropriate to let him get online) he was troubled. Something had begun to gnaw at Jack and the more he studied the dark nuances of the Basquiat the more uncomfortable he felt about his life.

Annie slipped quietly into the office and put the coffee down on his desk. "Are you okay, Jack? You seem a bit subdued this morning."

"Yeah, Annie, think I might take a bit of a walk. The Basquiat's speaking to me, Annie, you know, distracting me. I've got a clear morning until eleven. Could you take any messages? I'm on the cell if you need me. I've got a strange feeling it's about to wake up."

"Get some air, we'll see you later. And Jack, I'd better not catch you talking to those paintings, I mean, you're getting as bad as your mother and her flowers."

Jack gave her a weak smile and mouthed, "You're fired," winking as he walked past her desk. Annie shook her head and went back to her computer as Jack grabbed his cashmere overcoat and his phone and walked down the corridor to the elevators.

Outside in the street there was a nip in the air and Jack walked briskly north, crossing Canal Street and heading into the cobbled pot-holed streets south of Houston. Whenever he felt a bit low he went to SoHo, grabbed a coffee and browsed the last remaining downtown art galleries on Broadway, Wooster, Greene and Grand. Immersing himself in the New York art scene was like stepping into another world and helped take his mind off the pressure and pace at work. Looking at art helped him relax. He could lose himself in the work; conceptual, sculptural, performance or paint really didn't matter. What did matter was that there was something else out there for Jack to believe in, and here in the heart of SoHo he was able to reaffirm that there was life outside banking, a concept that many of his colleagues didn't understand.

Part of Jack's newfound dilemma came from a dawning realization that only one of his new investments, a life-science business called Microstem, was of any real interest to him. Aside from the kudos and substantial cash rewards he gained from the majority of the recent KLS internet and dotcom Initial Public Offerings (IPOs), it was in the area of medical research that Jack found a creative focus beyond his investment methodology. Financial services, e-commerce, retail fashion sales and online banking just didn't get him excited beyond the initial deal process and cash bonus rewards they could eventually yield. Having been raised to understand aesthetic, creative and natural world values, part of Jack's disaffection with the pace of his investment banking lifestyle lay in the daily absence of important or engaging business concepts.

Nearly all the recent and successful business models that landed on his desk followed the same formula: strong management team driven by top-line industry-specific Chief Executive Officer (CEO), Finance Director from a big five accounting firm or city bank, big brand marketing head and aggressive sales force. Then came technology, one of the critical pillars in any dotcom or technology business equation. The Chief Technical Officer (CTO) would be a veritable computer and network genius poached from Microsoft, Oracle, Cisco or Hewlett Packard. His core team would consist of designers, programmers, techies, net-heads and ex-hackers from the private sector, guys who would work through the night and solve the problem and keep the site online 24–7. The business team would be selected on their experience and designed to ensure investor confidence in the proposition and the four critical areas of successful new economy business methodology: management, marketing, distribution and technology. Investors would be looking for players who could operate well outside the tramlines of big business, equity driven risk-takers with credentials and credibility who would thrive on the manic pace of a dotcom start-up environment.

Next came the proposition. These varied greatly in length and structure but ultimately had one unifying factor. Whether they were selling content, products to consumers, or services to businesses, their business plan assumptions dictated that they would all be profitable within twenty-four months, burn their cash reserves slow and sell their products high. The estimated time to market from concept to trade sale would also vary, but none would take more than eighteen months, the stormy seas of any dotcom investment time-line. Many of these internet start-ups had received their first round of funding in late 1998 or early '99, an investment rush from small venture capital firms famous for funding many a business concept on a sheet of A4 paper. There was a wall of money out there for the next big online idea, but what worried Jack now was not the ability to grow the businesses and attain institutional funding from the large pool of willing KLS clients, but the sustainability, integrity and broad public interest of the propositions.

The current internet mantra went as follows: "Content is king and to him that supplies and ringfences the content lie the riches." But as Jack walked the streets and galleries of SoHo on that cold winter's morning he considered another idea: What if content was not king, what if content was just content? Billions of terabytes of undifferentiated, uncensored information, some valuable, most useless. What then? What if the research assumptions made by 99 percent of Jack's portfolio of investments were wrong? What if the world did not make the speedy progression to shop, talk, buy and communicate online? What if the market couldn't sustain its current growth? As a market analyst, Jack understood recurring cycles: boom and bust, peaks and troughs, the bull market and the bear. But with this understanding came his questioning... could exponential growth be sustained? Did people believe enough in the new economy? Would consumers trust new and unestablished brands? Could the internet engage, inspire and build the brand loyalty enjoyed by old-world blue-chip businesses, institutions, shops, service providers, schools and colleges? Could it solve the big problem, the promise of a human experience, something you could touch and feel, something real? There were just so many questions, and this morning, for Jack at least, too many doubts.

Jack stopped outside his favorite gallery, Groub at 131 Wooster Street, and breathed deeply. It was not like him to concern himself with the ethics of the market. He understood the nature of the beast, which after all he had been instrumental in growing. It was just that it all seemed more confusing now. Walking the few blocks uptown had helped shift the barrier that had been hindering and stagnating his thoughts. Although the questioning process was full of so many variables, it was the process that mattered. Maybe now he would be able to pinpoint his concerns. Maybe his little early morning panic attack would blow over and he could get back to what he knew, calling stocks as he saw them and researching tomorrow's winners today. He hoped so.

★ ★ ★

The huge frosted glass windows and doors of the gallery radiated exclusivity. Jack faced the opaque wall and read the bold black letters: "Art of the Primitive". He pushed the heavy door and walked inside. The gallery's interior was beautifully lit by a large dome skylight and was perfectly symmetrical, the four large walls providing an acoustic void, perfectly silent, where you could hear the smallest sound and where whispers would carry. The walls were painted a brilliant white, giving the large space a feeling of peace and spiritual clarity, as if it was a place of worship. Paintings, drawings and small sculptural plinths were sparsely displayed around the gallery.

In the center of the space was the only large work in the show. A glass case stood on the grey concrete floor. Inside was a dark wooden sled with polished runners, on which was placed a rolled length of felt and a square tub of fat. A metal flashlight and an old razor blade rested on top of the installation. Jack was visibly excited. Although he was familiar with the work as a multiple from catalogs and books, he had never seen the original handmade prototype before and had never heard of it being exhibited in a private gallery for sale. The artist, Joseph Beuys, was one of Jack's favorites and he had recently bought his small ink drawing for a steal. As Jack understood it, Beuys was one of the most innovative and important artists to emerge from the ruins of war-torn Germany and gain respect and prominence on the world stage.

Beuys represented a "shamanic" view of the world, and his many installations, sculptures and drawings had transcended the confines of the contemporary art world, standing as metaphors for primitivism and man's place in the natural world. Renowned for his belief that everyone could be an artist, Beuys had striven to break down the barriers of the general public's perception of art as something alien, aloof and unattainable. To do so, he had conceived a cunning plan, the objective of which was to democratize the ownership of conceptual art by creating the culture of the multiple-editioned work.

Working in a variety of unusual materials – felt, fat, rusted metal, bone, wood, stone – Beuys created a series of iconic and often familiar objects. Film canisters, paper bags and sleds were in turn signed, stamped, developed, branded and marketed at affordable prices in large editions to a hungry public. In much the same way that lithographic printing had been used for distributing editioned two-dimensional art works, Beuys was able to penetrate a wide new audience with his objects and sculptures. Through his utilization of film and televisual media, Beuys further spread his unique brand of art by staging a host of unconventional actions, happenings and media savvy performances.

It was his "life as art", his full-time commitment to changing and challenging people's perceptions of art, the environment, Nature, diverse

17

materials, beauty and death that made him possibly the most important German artist of the post-war period. The other German greats, including Gerhard Richter, Georg Baselitz and Sigmar Polke, may well have disagreed, but regardless of the critical climate and the trends and snobbery inherent in the German school, Beuys refused to be boxed, branded or pigeon-holed. Besides, Jack reasoned, upside-down paintings, technique-intensive photo-realism and multimedia abstraction, they could keep it!

In this significant work the sled symbolized the journey, a natural tool for natural travel, a vehicle of the tribe. The felt, the fat and the razor had a more personal and historic pertinence. Obvious metaphors for warmth and life, the felt and the fat had formed the basis for a series of dreams, hallucinations and events in the formative years of the young artist's life. Jack knew the Beuys story like local folklore.

In 1943, the twenty-three-year old Joseph Beuys, a World War Two German fighter plane navigator, had been shot down on a mission over the Crimea. Beuys survived the crash but the pilot was killed outright. The remarkable story of Beuys' survival in the depths of the Russian Taiga has undergone many variations, but his own version is the most compelling. Near death and in a hallucinogenic stupor, nomadic Tartars drag Beuys from the wreckage. He is cut free with old razors from his harness and, unable to walk, laid on a large sled covered with animal skins. Having survived a night in the wreckage at minus 20, with substantial burns, Beuys drifts in and out of consciousness due to his hypothermic state. The Tartars cover him in a thick layer of fat and wrap him in felt blankets to shield his burnt limbs from the air. Beuys then spends a period with the nomads recovering and only regains his full faculties in a military hospital some weeks later in Kiev.

Regardless of the factual interpretation of the story's details, Beuys had undergone a traumatic ordeal that was to inform his artwork throughout his life. This was what most fascinated and inspired Jack. For him, Beuys was proof that creativity and art could represent something tangible within his own life experience.

The dream element to the shamanic work of Beuys was a key factor in Jack's obsession with the artist. For as long as he could remember, Jack had had dreams of almost spiritual clarity but devoid of any specific message or conclusion. As a child, he had tried on countless occasions to unearth their meaning, which invariably involved him analyzing their key elements of physical flight, the wilderness and wild animals, but to no avail. One particularly vivid recurring dream in his youth was of himself flying, arms outstretched, at low level over the forest floor, close enough to see animal tracks. The dreams led him nowhere; Jack never reached the destination of his flight, and the scenery never changed.

Perhaps it was the transient nature of Beuys' drawing, the floating, flying figures, primitive icons, men, women and animals depicted swimming free of perspective in the confines of their scale and medium, that had first caught Jack's attention. But as often with great art, literature and poetry, Beuys' work touched an unspoken chord and expressed a sentiment in Jack's subconscious that he couldn't begin to explain. Beuys provided Jack with a channel for his dreams and aspirations. Beuys' art spoke to Jack but it also challenged him. This morning, more than any other, Beuys caused Jack to assess his own life.

Jack stood transfixed, staring at the installation, for what must have been over half an hour. His habit of "zoning" into a work of art, a landscape, a place of beauty, had at times worried his mother and close friends. Combined with the intensity of his regular pattern of dreaming, at eleven years old he had been taken by his mother, Laura, to visit a psychotherapist in St Paul on referral from the family physician. After a simple series of examinations the consultant had assured her that since the dreams were almost entirely peaceful, and as the less frequent occurrences of daytime conscious contemplation, his zoning, caused no behavioral unpleasantries, she should not worry. The therapist's conclusion was astute and disarming. He concluded that Jack was a particularly bright and sensitive boy and if anything his moments of peace should be encouraged. The therapist assured Laura that the eyes and the brain needed rigorous use and exercise to develop to their full potential. The brain, she was told, needed constant stimuli for it to grow. Looking, thinking and analyzing, even at Jack's young age, could do no harm, the therapist concluded. On the contrary, he would most likely grow into a brilliant student.

The longer Jack studied the art work the more his mind raced about his job, his travels, his friends, his family and his trips into the wild with his father. The sled, its very form, its representation as an object, conjured up such imagery and emotions that even Jack, the bright investment banker, was taken aback.

Before his talent as a financier had been discovered, Jack lived for the adventure of being on the road and in the bush. Weekends and vacations were almost always spent in the backwoods of his native Minnesota, canoeing, skiing and hunting with his old man. As Jack got older and his proficiency and bushcraft improved, he and his two best friends were given the freedom to explore the surrounding wilderness, sometimes for days at a time. Early on, Jack's father laid out some simple ground rules. Plan your route and stick to the plan, trust your compass; just because you are lost doesn't mean your compass is broken. Carry enough food and extra clothing for twice the journey time and check in on the VHF radio twice a day. Simple rules, but rules that would keep him and his friends safe in the wild.

Long weekend forays into Minnesota's backwoods with Jim and Bob led to trips further afield hunting moose and caribou with his dad in Canada and Alaska, week-long dog team trips into the Quetico National Reserve, summers spent trekking in the Yukon and most recently, the Ellesmere Island traverse on dog team, a serious undertaking even by his father's standards.

But today, as Jack stood confronted by the seminal Beuys, he wondered what he had ever really achieved. What had he truly experienced outside of his father's death? If he was brutally honest, all he had felt was the rush, the adrenaline, moments of fear but nothing tangible. He certainly hadn't stood on the proverbial edge, he hadn't undergone a baptism of fire and he was unscarred by deep wounds of trauma. When all was said and done, who was he? Another banker with a love of travel, a Wall Street high-flyer with a taste for expensive art and far-flung destinations. Jack didn't like the answers he was getting.

"Excuse me, sir," came a quiet voice from behind him. "May I help you in any way?"

Jack turned around suddenly, startled. "Thank you, no ...I ...I was just enjoying the work," he replied awkwardly.

Hans Groub, the gallery owner, was a short man, exquisitely dressed in a stylish, dark grey Yohji Yamamoto suit. "You seem quite captivated by *The Sled*. Are you familiar with the work of Beuys?" he asked, a subtle Swiss-German accent to his near-perfect English.

"Yes, I love his work. First time I've ever seen the real thing. It's surprised me, I guess."

"Yes, it can have that effect. I have had the original – the prototype so to speak – in my collection for many years and decided to show it quite impromptu."

"When did it go on display?" asked Jack.

"Tonight is the opening, so it is its first outing today!"

Jack felt a tingle shoot through his body. What a strange coincidence, today of all days, he thought.

"Mr Groub, I have enjoyed your gallery for the past two years. I'm Jack Wyler." Jack stretched out his hand.

"Mr Wyler, I remember you from the Sotheby's sale last month. I believe a large Basquiat now dominates a space in your home, no?"

"Yes, that's right. You have a good memory. Has this piece ever come up for auction?"

"Only once, in 1970. After that I have been quite protective of it. I just haven't been able to part with it, until ... "

"It's for sale now, I trust?" Jack quickly replied.

"Possibly ... I really don't mean to sound vague, but I want it to find the *right* home."

Jack knew the game. Flatter the prospective client, dangle the work, get a bite and hike the price. But he sensed Groub's sincerity.

"Maybe we should talk then, Mr Groub, later on this week, perhaps?"

"I would be delighted. Let's say Friday, one pm lunch at Lola's. Or is lunch a problem? What line of work are you in, by the way, Mr Wyler?"

Jack was a little taken aback, and for the first time in years felt slightly embarrassed to answer. "I'm in banking, a bit boring really."

"Not at all, Mr Wyler. It would appear you do your profession a service by having a nose for an important work. So many financiers seem to be throwing money at poor work these days."

"Poor work?" replied Jack. He was intrigued.

"Yes, and it's not restricted to bankers, Jack. In fact most collectors I know seem obsessed with building what I call clichéd collections – they want something big, something to endure, but they rarely have the courage of their convictions to rigorously pursue a single artist with early examples, complex works as well as the most notable career pieces ... how shall I say? With an intellectual understanding and commitment to an artist's life's work ... "

Jack was taken aback – it was as if Groub was in some way challenging him to react by casting aspersions on the solid concept of a varied diverse collection. He laughed weakly. "Yeah, I guess that's about the truth of it. But Mr Groub, surely there's nothing wrong with building a varied collection?"

"Oh, far from it," replied Groub. "It has been my good fortune to facilitate and nurture that particular obsession with my diverse clientele. All I am saying is that it is a shame that the desire for a fine collection is for so many confused with the pursuit of an 'assortment' of works, much like an assortment of Swiss chocolates."

Jack could feel himself losing this debate with such a wise adversary. At the same time he was enjoying sparring with Groub. "But surely it's the intuition and nose of the individual collector that should be the key driver in his or her decision to buy or not to buy – not the pursuit of a singular artist's entire life's work?" he countered. "Surely the risk factor is way too great from an investment perspective? That's a bit like backing the wrong horse, so to speak – for instance, I would never advise a banking client to invest solely in one particular stock."

Groub studied Jack for a moment – the kid had brains, there was no doubt about that, but this one deserved the full treatment. After all, he was young enough to be influenced, to be educated.

"Well, you are right and you are wrong. The nose, the instinct that you talk of, yes, I agree that is paramount, but tell me, why do so many collectors obsess over the name, the brand of the artist? And to follow in your equestrian line of argument – what end is there in having a stable of average racehorses – average examples of great artists' work – a Rauschenberg, a De Kooning, a Twombly, a Beuys and a Basqui..." Groub winked at Jack – he could tell from Jack's reddening complexion that he was getting to him.

"Look, Mr Wyler, I'm partly joking with you. For the most part, your Basquiat for example – now that is a great work, in fact it's possibly one of his finest – a museum-worthy example for sure – hell, you beat me to it – you clearly know what you like and I respect that. It's just that the truly great collections are driven by more than a nose for a singular work, and certainly more than the market value in the Wildenstein catalog. Great collections are driven by amazing and outrageous concepts; they are driven by individual ego, passion and total commitment. They defy fashion and laugh in the face of market trends, ultimately great collections, and by this I also mean great collectors, have the courage to stand alone and eventually their collections act as a magnet, a magnet for more great art. A good example would be the Basquiat – a noteworthy work in anyone's books. Now imagine this set into context, used if you will as an indicator to an artist's direction, a turning point even, a sentinel for a new emerging body of work."

Groub's argument was mesmerizing. Jack was captivated.

"Now imagine you have the commitment, and the funds, to structure the piece in context, like a perfectly formed story, with a beginning and middle and an edifying end – now we are getting close to the point of a true collection, eh! And I tell you what – you build one of those and every one takes notice – curators, national museums, international touring shows. You see, a true collection must be shown, it is not just for personal consumption, it is an obligation and a responsibility that I myself have been avoiding with this sled piece and the other unique Beuys works in this show – MOMA have been twisting my arm for years and now, well, I cracked – it was time, I guess."

Jack stood dumbstruck. Of course the venerable Groub was right, the posture of his collecting methodology had indeed been driven by a desire to attain examples of the key brand names and with far too few exceptions his collection slid well into Groub's description of an assortment, but Beuys – surely this was his true passion, yet on reflection he only had one small work in his collection. It was as if ownership of the multiple had diluted the need for ownership. True ownership of Beuys came from understanding him – maybe this was what Beuys meant by art for all? Art that could be taken with you, in one's mind, a philosophy rather than a tangible object.

"Okay, okay – I concede, Mr Groub – now that you put it so eloquently that maybe my collection is indeed somewhat of an assortment."

Groub smiled kindly – Jack had just been elevated to the next level.

"Oh please, Mr Wyler, I wasn't meaning to offend, far from it..."

"No, it's okay," replied Jack, laughing. "To be honest, your candor is much appreciated, and anyhow you have probably saved me a whole bunch of cash in the long term."

"To whom shall I send my invoice then?" offered Groub.

Both men began to laugh. Jack stole a glance at his Rolex. With a respectful tilt to his head and a slight smile he held out his hand. "I'm afraid I've got to run – it's been a pleasure, Mr Groub."

"Indeed, Jack, the pleasure has been all mine. Please call me Hans. I so look forward to talking further. Till Friday then..."

Jack shook hands with the elderly dealer and made his way swiftly to the corner of Prince and Broadway to hail a cab. It was 10:58am and he had an eleven o'clock meeting downtown. For the first time since joining KLS four years earlier, the persistently punctual Jack was going to be late for a board meeting. The thought made him smile. "I should do this more often," he said to himself.

Chapter 2

Jack's success in Wall Street and his newfound wealth was a mere consequence, the result of a focused mind. By February 2000 he had already banked over $10 million. Although not extraordinary wealth for a thirty-three-year-old Wall Street financier, his rise to substantial fortune had been unorthodox to say the least. In less than two years he had developed into a brilliant market analyst. Having seen the potential in technology and internet stock as far back as 1996, he had gone for broke, enlightening the board of his investment bank KLS to a fresh concept. While the tech sector was studded with potential stars, the "real" riches just waiting to be capitalized on rested with a small handful of emerging Fortune 500 companies, the stock of which had climbed to previously unheard-of heights.

Based in the KLS's research department on the ninth floor, Jack had been made director within six months of joining his new department. After a year and a half as director of technology research, he had hit Wall Street fame by accurately predicting the highest ever share target of $300 for musicjungle.com, the online CD retailer. The stock broke through it less than a month later, gaining 120 percent. The markets went into frenzy for the stock, which fuelled huge fees for the investment banking department of KLS. Companies eager to reach comparative post-IPO valuations lined up for the "musicjungle" treatment. The *Wall Street Journal*'s lead internet journalist, Elliot Schafner, declared: "In Jack Wyler, KLS have a very refined tool. Mr Wyler has demonstrated he possesses a realistic assessment of growth rates in emerging tech companies. Unlike others, he makes tough but accurate calls using common sense in the irrational world of internet stocks."

A week after the article was published Jack was summoned to the tenth floor. The CEO, chairman and partner board were impressed. In September 1999, at thirty-two, Jack was made a Managing Director (MD), the youngest partner in the firm. With headhunters around every corner, it was the only sensible option. KLS were not going to lose their man to the competition. From his new lofty perch, he would work alongside Lane Connor, the CEO, his brother Peter, the CFO, and his direct boss Lou Jacobs, KLS's infamous senior internet/electronic commerce analyst. Jack's package included a further estimated $10 million in stock options as part of the ensuing KLS partnership payout. Everything he touched was turning to gold. In Wall Street speak he was "cutting cheddar".

Jack had come the hard way to all the right places. In high school in Minnesota, he had scored highest in the state on his SATs and been awarded a Seymour Scholarship to Johns Hopkins University, where he majored in Philosophy and Anthropology. Throughout his four years at university he achieved a 4.0 grade point average and graduated Summa Cum Laude. Rebelling from the academic influences of his degree tutors and refusing to apply to postgraduate courses, Jack decided against the need to study any further and spent the next three years on the road, traveling the length of the Americas, from Punta Arenas in southern Chile to Point Barrow in Alaska.

Having grown up in the backwoods town of Ely in Northern Minnesota, Jack had a rare quality that made him as at home in the wilderness as he was in the city. His father, Joe Wyler, had been a park ranger of the Quetico National Preserve and on his retirement, aged fifty-eight, had traveled to Alaska with the teenage Jack to hunt moose and barren ground caribou. Jack's mother, a deeply religious and quiet soul, had taught history of art part-time at the University of Minnesota in St Paul and had fostered Jack's passion for contemporary art. Her faith was hers alone and existed well in a house full of atheists. For Laura it was her way of dealing with her own life. Jack, when he wasn't chiding her, had a certain respect for her beliefs and could never reconcile how seldom she made mention of them around his father, a disbeliever of biblical proportions. Laura didn't put pressure on any of them but lived by her own standards, a quiet calm influence, supportive and loving to the last.

Although the Wylers were not well off, Jack and his much younger sister Holly had not wanted for a thing and had the happiest of childhoods, complemented by an even mix of creativity and the great outdoors. Neither Laura Wyler nor her husband had ever been motivated by money, far from it. Both of them along the way had been offered drastically improved incomes by the university and the park service respectively, but in this they shared an uncommon resolve. They were happy and they had enough. Despite their religious differences they were so similar, joined in the belief that it was the quality of life that mattered, beyond all else. After all, who knew what life was going to chuck at them. They could be hit by a truck and then what? No, they both agreed, enjoy what they had, their health and their children. Best keep life simple.

Arriving in Alaska after nearly two years traveling north, Jack worked the oilfields in Alaska's Point Barrow for a while, crewed as rookie on a crab boat for two summers out of Dutch Harbor and took work where he could find it on the road. After his second season fishing he had met Lucy, the daughter of a salmon cannery boss, and had become smitten. It was about this time that his father started to feel a faint trembling in his right hand. Having recently retired, he put it down to his body unwinding after years of hard physical work and a certain amount of stress. But the tremors didn't get any better. Dr Louis Peterson referred Joe to a specialist neurological unit in St Paul. The prognosis was not good. Returning home after the first examination Joe, never a man to mince his words, took his wife in his arms.

"Honey, I have an incurable brain disease. How 'bout that?"

Joe did not suffer long. As is often the case with Parkinson's disease, the damage had been done long before his recent diagnosis, with over 90 percent of the cells having died over that past year. Joe's condition began to deteriorate quickly. They say that fighter pilots, firemen, combat troops and all those who have led a hard active life age dramatically in the first years of retirement. Joe was no exception. The active retirement syndrome did nothing to help the disease that saw Joe tremble uncontrollably from 6am until the drugs cut in an hour or two later. For the first five months the inertia created by the lack of motor control kept him relatively active, but with the onset of winter he started to slow down. His wife would find him stooped and still on the porch, staring into space. He didn't last long and he really didn't want to put the family through years of pain. Joe Wyler died in his bed one crisp fall morning in 1994. He had simply decided enough was enough.

Jack took the news hard. Laura had God, while in Jack's eyes the Lord was a poor substitute for his old man. Had it not been for his father's death, he might have married Lucy, stayed in Alaska and worked the south-eastern fishing runs. It was not to be. Jack returned home to Ely, Minnesota, immediately, promising to return to Lucy once all the funeral arrangements had been made and he had had some time with the family. He should have taken her home with him. With his mother and younger sister now in need of support, Jack, in an act of great but reluctant cowardice, wrote Lucy the hardest letter he was ever to write, and broke her heart. As solace he partied hard, trained harder and found his way to

Wall Street and a fresh start via a brief spell in Minneapolis' downtown business district, where he discovered he had a talent for predicting stock fluctuations. His old high school friend Bob Anders had introduced Jack to his bank, Aslop & Co. in St Paul, and Jack joined the Minneapolis office a week later as a trainee analyst.

Jack's first year at Aslop's, his baptism to the world of private investment banking, was an eye-opener, and he loved it. Working alongside Bob was not only a blast, Jack had his very own mentor, an old friend to show him the ropes and the pitfalls. "Read between the lines, Jack," Bob would constantly say. "Nothing is quite what it seems in investment banking, remember that, okay?" And Jack did. He was a fast learner.

Bob had a certain calm, an inner peace. Jack had always been somewhat in awe of his confidence, his natural athletic prowess and ability to apply himself to anything and do it well. Bob had a confidence that came from knowing what he wanted out of life. If he was wise for his age, astute even, it was probably on account of not having gone to college. He had made the choice himself. Somewhat uniquely his folks had wanted what he wanted, and although the college route made sense to most of Bob's peers, his parents hadn't applied the pressure. From their standpoint they knew he had the self-discipline, intelligence and good, down-to-earth common sense to cut it his way.

A talented athlete, Bob had played on the high school football team with Jack and like his two friends he graduated in the top percentile with college grade SATs. Like both his friends he was naturally bright, but for some reason he couldn't see the point in wasting any more time with formal study. He wanted to get on the wage ladder early.

For a while he was hungry for it and the money was good. From a personal development perspective he had always been a voracious reader, eager to fill his mind with new concepts and ideas, so not going to college hadn't seemed an issue. At Aslop's, although being conscious of the stigma of not having a degree, he had absolutely no problem with it, no proverbial "chip". Bob had simply gone a more direct route than Jack, joining Aslop's as an office junior from high school and taking his trading exams within two years. Having found his niche early in life, he had left most of the new graduates at the starting blocks.

Bob in short order developed into a solid, shrewd investor and took the time to pass on his hard-earned lessons to his friend. But Bob was a different animal from Jack. On the weekends he was happy to spend time with his long-time girlfriend and high school sweetheart Teresa, who in turn spent most of her time trying to match up Jack with her friends. Jack had no complaints, and when he wasn't out on the town trying to impress the girls he spent most of his time crashed out at Bob's large townhouse getting fed and getting his ironing done. Jack liked his friend's domestic set-up, although such security was not for him. He had known Teresa since high school too, and so hanging with his friends was like an extension of his youth, his family even, before all the problems and the death of his dad.

Bob was such a good bouncing board for Jack's ambitions, his plans and more importantly his adventures. The one major advantage of working in St Paul was that on weekends Bob and Jack could still get out on short expeditions, although these were rationed to two a month by Teresa, who missed having her two boys around. Jim Williamson, Jack's oldest friend, the third musketeer, rarely made it, having created a new life for himself in New York City, but once or twice a year they got away, all three of them, and that was what Jack lived for. Boys on tour, carefree, on the road.

Getting away from the city, even for the night, into the woods north of their childhood home in Ely, into the Quetico and Boundary Waters, gave perspective to Jack and Bob's desk-bound weeks. Away from the city they talked endlessly about high school, about growing up together, and about Joe. Joe had been a role model for the boys, the ultimate outdoorsman, a super-dad with the pick-up and six-gun to match. Both Bob and Jim had spent their lives in awe of Joe and somewhat jealous of their friend for having such a cool old man. He had taught them it all, everything they needed to know about the bush, fire building, shelter, protection, navigation and survival. And when he died, they had all three felt it, a tremendous space and gaping hole in their lives. Joe's death broke their hearts and they promised Jack, they promised each other, that they would always be there for one another. Whatever happened in their lives, however rich or poor they became, they promised each other they would always be there together to get back to basics, get back to the woods, in memory of Joe, the old days, the best years of their lives.

★ ★ ★

After a successful year at Aslop's, it was clear to Bob and his team that his young protégé was ready to move on to greener pastures. He had become a lynchpin in Bob's investment team, and if Bob was honest Jack was far hungrier than he was and struggled with the small city mentality. High risk, high reward were not sentiments shared by Bob's bosses and it soon became clear to all concerned that Jack had outgrown his position. In Aslop's, promotion was dead men's shoes, Rotary Club membership, the country club mafia. Even Bob had begun to feel the frustration of kowtowing to the conservatism of the senior management. It had made Jack's decision to move on easier and Bob had been both glad and sad to see his buddy leave. They both agreed it was for the best.

Three regional interviews and a trip to NYC later, Jack landed *the* plum job for a budding analyst. He was given a small advance, advised to take a holiday and started at the head office of New York's second biggest investment bank, Klein, Loeb & Silvers, in September 1996. Bob and Teresa were blown away, and somewhere deep inside Bob knew he too should make the break while he still could. Jack had inspired him, and if he was honest he was more than a little bit envious of his ambitious friend.

Jack adapted to life in the Big Apple well. His outward-bound childhood had given him a gregarious way with people that made him both popular with the guys and of great interest to the ladies. Since his buddy Jim was working as an assistant movie producer in the city, he got a crash course in the city's wild party scene, nearly missing his induction to KLS due to a crazy night and the ensuing hangover. His academic qualifications made the work of market analyst a joy, since his focus on primitive history had led him to assimilate facts and keep trends in context. As he would rather prophetically state in a press interview: "If you have an understanding of the psychology of man since his emergence in the Rift valley ten thousand years ago, if you have any sense of global market history, you will understand that predicting whether a company is going to succeed or fail depends on a variety of factors. These factors are influenced mainly by the market, the economy and current events, in a nutshell, the entire fiscal landscape. Unless you are a survivor, a brutally competitive and a "winner-take-most" business, by the inevitable drop off of this current boom you will most probably merge, go bankrupt or quietly fade away. Generally this sentiment can be extracted or at least sensed in the first meeting with the business. I guess that is my talent, identifying what the market wants and who is best positioned to provide it. Moreover I try never to let a business get personal or to have too many preconceptions. That's precisely the reason I operate in my own universe. Although corporate finance is involved with the road show of our successful businesses, I cannot let the investment banking wing influence my research. In that we are independent, at least on my watch!"

If Jack's background was a tad unconventional for a budding Wall Street banker, it was ruthlessly effective. Thanks to Bob's intuitive schooling he had learned to read people, he could analyze market statistics, he could sift through business plans in quick order and differentiate hype stock from solid growth. More importantly and even more surprisingly he had a spooky way with numbers. Due to his streetwise understanding of the human psyche, he knew what made people happy and what made them scared. Jack's philosophy of investment could be described as the ability to identify and corner a growth market based on solid research, in much the same way as a hunter corners his prey by sound bushcraft. It was second nature to Jack. He was a natural.

But as with all extremes, the excesses of success were starting to take their toll. The past twenty-four months had been a whirlwind and Jack was beginning to feel the pressure to keep his remarkable track record performing. While Jack was the diligent one, careful not to back the wrong horse, his direct boss, Lou Jacobs, was the man with his pedal to the metal. Having been quick to notice the lead taken in first-stage internet investments by small venture capital outfits, Lou had been pivotal in turning the larger cogs that ground the investment philosophy of KLS New York toward second-stage internet investment at least a year before Jack joined the company. Lou's passion and drive were of a completely different nature to Jack's more refined methodology. Lou, in close collaboration with Lane Connor, had realized that while maintaining the official status quo and publicly observing the strict "Chinese wall" between research and the investment bank, he could build KLS considerable banking fees by spinning the IPO whirlwind in his favor. The spin lay in his ability to influence the market with his regular appearances on CNBC *News Watch* and *The Money Hour* on NYB1 – the financial community's number one business radio show. Technically his public persona and image was an independent one, Lou Jacobs as opposed to "KLS's lead internet analyst", which therefore alleviated any legal obligations to restrict stock tipping. The reality of his weekly appearances was of course another story altogether. Everyone knew who Lou Jacobs was. The man behind '80s giants KKR's numerous takeover bids, the research guru who had stood in the wings during Berkshire Hathaway's relentless climb and the man with the ear of the great Warren Buffett. In the four years he had been with KLS, his personally authored research documents had influenced over twenty internet IPOs and he was privately known to have an impressive portfolio of personal investments. His relationship with Lane Connor was one of the closest and most publicized in Wall Street. Two twice-divorced, workaholic market makers with a passion for fast women and fast cars. Due to Lane's role as chief executive there was no problem with such a close association, since technically Lane ran the ship and was not involved with the stock promoting of KLS clients.

Companies born a year earlier were now receiving substantial tranches of second-round investment from the KLS coffers and loyal institutional clients. With Lou's team's guidance, these fast growth businesses were completing IPO and attaining NASDAQ or NYSE listings sometimes within eight months of their second-stage finance. The problem lasted only until the internet boom, when IPO was restricted to companies with a minimum of six years' trading records and fully matured business practices. Using Jack's analogy of the IPO process as a "bread oven", traditionally people in the public markets were used to buying fully "baked" companies. However, the businesses that KLS, together with numerous VC houses, were now rolling out had mostly only been in the oven for ten minutes. The problem was, of course, that KLS, amongst others, was offering them as cooked, which in Jack's eyes was untrue.

Since March 1999, Lou's research had resulted in a managed portfolio of new investments that had cost KLS just under $100 million in second- and third-round investment. The net return on equity held for the funding was, at current market valuation, well in excess of $6 billion. The markets had gone haywire and KLS had been quick to capitalize on the gold rush, thanks of course to Jack's team's research vision and Lou's aggression and drive. Success case studies were numerous. Under Lou's tutelage three of Jack's recent investments had, at the year of their birth, received no more than $15 million in funding respectively. By IPO they each had market valuations worth over $450 million, their founders and senior management rich beyond belief. KLS, with a minimum standard contract holding per investment of 20 percent (that was the deal, take it or leave it), were printing money, with an average return on these three ventures alone being in excess of 600 percent.

For the first eight months in Research, Jack had lived on coffee and adrenaline. History was being made, a new information life-blood was taking the world by storm and there was no turning back. Established companies and brands that ignored the internet and online services would, by Lou's assessment, lose 40 percent of their market share to new web-based business within twenty months. The old economy was crumbling, and Lou Jacobs and his team were relishing the kudos that their "told you so" investment methodology had spawned.

As Jack's first tipped investments began to go public and the "proof of concept" was acknowledged by the senior partner board, he was given more freedom and more power as Lou withdrew from KLS front man to public business media guru. It now seemed to Jack that his new life consisted solely of meetings and contract negotiations. He was no longer watching, analyzing and marking the markets; he was being instrumental in creating them. Although Lane and Lou were constantly applying the pressure to out-perform past IPOs, Jack began to sense he was not being given the appropriate tools to carry out correct research and make reports. In addition, he had started to be gravely concerned that Lou was bridging two distinct business areas that formally had a huge conflict of interest, namely the banking and research divisions. Just before Christmas 1999, Lane crystallized Jack's concerns by sending a directive: "We are once again surveying your contribution to investment banking. Please provide complete details of your involvement, paying particular attention to the degree your research played a role in originating banking business."

The ramifications of Lane's memo were proving extremely detrimental to Jack's workload. His team began to feel the need to justify overt bank-related commercial relationships by drafting lengthy reports to secure their employment positions. The staff were fully aware that any hesitation in complying with the CEO's directives would result in a speedy sacking. The day after the memo hit Jack's desk he asked Annie to draft a confidential note to Lane. Although Jack always asked Annie to draft all his official memos, he was anxious for this one to be kept in secure hard copy. Annie, loyal as ever, knew not to ask any questions.

Dear Lane

In response to your recent memo and on behalf of my team, I must say I have some grave concerns about the broad ramifications of your directive. As you know, I am fully enforcing the rule that there is to be a clear and defined separation between the banking and research divisions at KLS. This current memo would seem to contravene that stance. I regularly watch Lou Jacobs on CSNBC *Business Hour* and want to make clear my concerns that an overt public stance, as he is known to make, must not be used to recruit new investment banking clients for KLS due to incorrect stock analysis. It is also my understanding that he is not paid for any business that may or may not be forthcoming.

My concerns therefore are twofold; that my credibility will be undermined by the ambitions of others, namely Lou Jacobs, and that I see my role of calling stocks as I see them, without influence from the banking wing, as presently under threat. Lou seems to have called a number of recent stocks that in my professional opinion are "junk", to say the least. The only rationale for such calls is that the banking division will continue to get their substantial fees, until of course the stock drops and we are left with considerable egg on our faces, not to mention the onerous responsibility of knowingly losing our clients' money.

I hope you understand the delicacy of my memo and perhaps we could discuss this privately. At the moment my team seems somewhat distracted due to the need to justify their existence in a commercial banking business context. For the record, no analyst on my watch will be giving "buy" rating to junk stock or for that matter be involved with the practice of stock spinning. I hope this doesn't sound too crude, but if this were ever proved to be the case, the whole of KLS's credibility in the tech sector would be as stable as a powder keg.

I trust you take my points as valid and we can keep this between ourselves until we have talked them through.

Kind regards
Jack Wyler

For any mere mortal the memo would, politically at least, have constituted professional suicide. But in the KLS universe Jack was no mere mortal, and Lane realized he needed to pay special attention to his young, ambitious director. Furthermore, Lane had suspected that Lou had, for some time now, been operating outside the boundaries of strict professional guidelines, but due to his huge commercial worth he had turned a blind eye. On more than one occasion Lou had told Lane personally, "The whole idea that we are independent from banking is a big lie."

The problem was, of course, that Lou was right. Internally, the entire tenth floor knew it. Sure, corporate finance and other wings were separate with clear mandates, but senior management – well, they knew the score. However, in the midst of the frenzy, with too many people getting rich, the bank's partners, the venture capital firms, the clients, there was no one yet willing to blow the whistle, no one until Jack Wyler. He would need handling correctly. Lane and Lou would take care of that.

★ ★ ★

The pace of Jack's life continued to ramp up. High-powered lunches, dinners, working breakfasts used to build business relationships and engage with the management of the numerous new businesses, led to research trips, lectures and weekend workshops. Although he rented a beautiful apartment on the park, Jack was never at home. After the dinner meetings ended there was the after-hours entertainment to be attended to, and who better to lead the charge than Jack, the golden boy. Hard liquor, the club scene, lap dancing and the occasional line of coke made up at least four nights of any given week. None of his numerous amorous relationships over the period of his move to the city had stood a chance. The minute he was asked, "Jack, can we stay in tonight?" or "Jack, why are you always working?" he moved on. There was no time for going steady and Jack made a decision to keep his business life simple by avoiding a private life. There was just too much to do and too much choice for a firm commitment.

The strategy for the new economy venture capital investment model was simple. The second-stage investors sniffed out the solid performers based on risks and reports taken by the smaller first-stage venture capital firms. From these business models, the venture outfits partnered with the investment banks and their analysts weeded out the wheat from the chaff. They eliminated the greatest risk propositions, giving successful prospective investors the "feel good" handshake and standard fancy dinner at Nobu. Once the businesses were set to sign, Lane was wheeled out to engage with the respective investment propositions. He paved the way for the notoriously aggressive KLS corporate finance department to get the deal done, with Lou on the end of the telephone to smooth out any contractual issues and front the deal for the CEO.

Throughout '98 and '99 KLS had something to sell and everyone wanted in. Morgan Stanley, Lehman Bros, Goldman Sachs, J.P. Morgan, Warburg Dillon Reed and Merrill Lynch just couldn't match the success and pace of capitalized new investments of Lane's investment banking team. If you had the cash there was no better place to vest it and success seemed to be a sure thing. Of the 110 million blue-chip-stock-holding Americans, 70 million had bought or transferred their stock portfolios to technology and internet stock within a twenty-four-month period between January 1998 and February 2000. Lou's research department (with Jack as second in command) were to a great degree responsible for this shift. Technology was now the new blue chip stock, with Microsoft, Cisco, Dell and Oracle forming the pinnacle of the Fortune 100 companies. The KLS research teams had drafted the definitive investment studies for all new business areas. Whether it was e-learning, internet recruitment, online banking, business to consumer (b2c) or business to business (b2b) investment portals, KLS were leading the field with their research and the world was watching.

But Jack, by the end of '99, was starting to feel the stress that the lifestyle and newfound respect had awarded him. The situation with Lou and Lane had not been fully talked through, and he was growing ever more concerned about the state of the tech bubble that was growing larger with every successful IPO.

★ ★ ★

At thirty-three years old, Jack had been fit and active for much of his adult life, religiously working out, some would say in the extreme. He had a heavy frame, and at six foot one and 220 pounds he was immensely strong. Although he would like to have been nine or ten pounds lighter he carried the extra weight well, and with his dark hair and strong features he was quite a presence, whether in the boardroom or the gym.

In his first three years at KLS, Jack had lived by the high school football mantra, "Don't hoot with the owls if you can't fly with the eagles", training hard and partying hard. He had run more than seven regional decathlons and trained obsessively for an average of ten hours a week. For the bulk of his adult life Jack had top and tailed his average eleven-hour working day, from 6:30am till 5:30pm, with an hour-long training session. A stickler for punctuality, he believed a fit body led to a fit mind. He needed to be sharp and always on time. Time was money. He ran for five miles before work in the mornings, showering at work, and would be in the gym by 5:45pm on a working day. Free weights, jumping rope, Stair-Master and a swim on Sundays to "de-stress", as Jack called it, were the drill, the routine.

As '98 turned into '99 and internet fever took its grip on the ninth floor, Jack's religious training routine began to suffer. Within a short period he had cut back to two sessions per week and these did not follow his traditional balls-to-the-wall routine. He was driven by another goal now. Before the internet, he had figured on a solid career with a great lifestyle. He enjoyed his work, so what was the rush to retire? His training and his passion for art and traveling kept him sane, and on his director's salary and bonus there was plenty of recreational time and money to fund his passions. He got eight weeks' vacation a year, and had, until the internet gold-rush, planned a six-month sabbatical to train for a major Arctic expedition that had been a driving obsession since the Ellesmere trip with Bob and Jim four years before.

Now there was a different goal on the horizon, to work out his three-year contract, which would ensure full vesting of options in the partner payout, and retire. But a further three years, at his current pace, was no mean feat. Ethically, Jack had concerns about the rumors of client kickbacks, stock flipping and ultimately the manipulation of initial public offerings by KLS and their partner VC firms. Too many young companies were being advised and encouraged to go public too quickly, and that weighed heavily on Jack. From a stress perspective, two partners on the ninth floor had had breakdowns in the late nineties, and burn-out for executive directors was not uncommon, even for financiers in their early thirties. Jack just hoped he could hang in there. But this was what Jack did. He kept it together and he kept his cool. He was a survivor.

Chapter 3

Jack's cab pulled up outside KLS a few minutes after 11am. Abraham Williams, head of KLS' security, opened the door for him. Abe was a bear of a man with a smile and open manner to match his great bulk. Three knee operations had finally seen the end of a promising football career plagued by injuries as a rookie line backer for the Cleveland Browns. But Abe had taken it all in his stride; besides, the money was excellent and there was no shortage of kind words and respect from his new paymasters, even if they were a bunch of overpaid rich white boys!

"Good morning, Mr Wyler. How are we today?"

"Late, Abe, and you know what, let 'em wait!" replied Jack, winking at Abe.

"Absolutely – now you're talking!" boomed the huge doorman.

Taking the elevator to the tenth floor, Jack walked purposefully down the long corridor and entered the main meeting room without knocking. Annie as always was in hot pursuit. Invigorated by his brief visit to the gallery, Jack felt his old self. Lane Connor sat at the far end of the room with, next to him, Peter, who was observing Jack with a fixed gaze. Although there was only five years between them, Lane and Peter looked almost unrelated. Lane was clearly the lover of the family, a good-looking man with a permanent tan and a shock of silver hair, swept back Gordon Gecko style. He had a voracious appetite for younger women, which was reflected in the brazen appearance of his numerous secretaries. Despite being the wrong side of fifty, he was wearing well, his slight but trim build giving the accurate impression of a man disciplined and well-kept, to the point of being almost vain.

Peter, on the other hand, was almost bald, his hair cut to a tight crop accentuating his porcine features. At university Peter had taken to playing rugby and, being somewhat squat and solid, had ended up in the front row. For the uninitiated, this pugilistic position had resulted in a phenomenon called "cauliflower ear". While common in thirty-something British males, it was much more rare on Wall Street since boxers are the only other sportsmen to suffer this unfortunate condition and boxers rarely make it to the highest echelons of investment banking.

If Lane was the ageing playboy, then Peter was the stressed-out family man with three kids, two ex-wives and high blood pressure. But Peter was also the fighter in the family, a savvy, aggressive financier with a quick wit and an even quicker tongue. Lane could charm anyone, even giving the impression he liked you, but with Peter there was no lying, he just couldn't mask his feelings.

On the far side of the desk sat Benjamin Small, a director from Corporate Finance, a choirboy of a man compared to his alpha male bosses, with pale blue eyes, high cheekbones and a cleft chin that looked like it had been cleaved with an axe. Small had the nervous, jittery persona of a man constantly on the edge of his seat, unsettled, frail and skittish. Worse still, his inability to relax and his annoying habit of fidgeting when others were speaking gave the impression he wasn't listening, which was far from the truth. Small was listening too hard, analyzing every comment in his highly charged brain and computing the ramifications of his responses with such precision that he put chess masters to shame. The brilliance of his deductions was, however, often lost on those around him, since he had the unnerving habit of responding to almost every question with his own well-thought-out query. Client board meetings would often go on for hours, accompanied by Small's incessant biro spinning, unless, of course, Jack was there. Then things moved at a faster clip.

Startled, Small looked up as Jack walked into the room, his eyes wide, his pale blue pupils dilated, his yellow notepad clutched to his narrow chest, the signature spinning chewed pen at the ready. Lou's absence was as conspicuous as ever.

"Sorry to keep you, gentlemen," offered Jack.

"Not at all," replied Lane. "I was enjoying a second's respite from the phone."

Jack poured himself a coffee and grabbed a couple of cookies.

"It's been a good quarter, Jack," said Lane.

"Yes, Lane, but we're predicting a slow-down over the next twelve months. That's my feeling anyhow."

"Yes, I've been hearing rumors to that effect from research. I want to see our new tech and life science business IPO pre-April, Jack. Can it be done?"

"That depends on the sales team and whether we can add sufficient value, I guess, Lane," replied Jack, sitting back in his chair and shooting Benjamin a subtle smile. "Six of the ten businesses are on track, so if we pedal to the metal I am confident we can push all the buttons. It's really an issue of whether we should drive a business like Microstem along the same timeline as Lou's dotcoms."

"The devil's always in the detail," sniped Benjamin, smiling weakly at Lane. "We have to be realistic and give accurate assumptions, the lowest common denominator, so to speak. I for one would want to really understand the bottom line with their cashflow assumptions, Lane. I mean, this is critical, is it not?"

"If that was directed at me, Benjamin, do me the courtesy of looking at me," Jack said coolly, a distinct menace in his voice.

"No, no, Jack, please. I'm not wishing to dampen your enthusiasm and passion for the deal. It's just I have grave concerns about the viability of Microstem's current management to give investor confidence and meet the aggressive timelines pre-quarter one. Do you not agree?"

Ben had edged forward in his chair and was looking straight at Jack now. Lane watched the two carefully. It was common knowledge that there was bad blood between Jack and Ben, but he quite enjoyed the sparring. It helped the board see both sides of the propositions and also helped distract his too ethical warriors away from other more sensitive matters. Ultimately a well-worked-through argument provided a critical element in the final analysis and the deciding factor in any decision to move ahead or stop funding.

Lane intervened. "Jack, I want you and Benjamin to work closely together on this. I understand your differences of opinion on some of the ongoing investments but I will not have these businesses flagging. Our total investment to date in Microstem is north of $5 million. I just won't accept that money cannot buy us a good return, worst case excellent trade sale and a good exit. Let's focus, gentlemen. I want it done."

Peter, a man of few words and even less patience, stood up without excusing himself from the table. He made his way to the door and as he reached for the handle he stopped and turned to Jack. "I need you on Friday, Jack. Lunch, twelve thirty. The Israelis from Mediotech are in town. Let's say Odeon, the usual table. We have to give them the handshake thing. They're sticklers for the research, Jack, really keen on our work. Bit of a bore, I know, but they're important clients."

"What about Lou?" offered Jack, the color showing on his face. "After all, he drafted the Israeli tech docs, Peter. I just added some preliminary stats and to be honest I wasn't that impressed."

Peter shot Jack a hard stare. "Well, I would appreciate it, Jack, if you would keep your opinions to yourself. There's a lot resting in that business for the whole of the investment bank. Besides, Lou can't make it, Jack. That's why I want you there."

"Okay, Peter, keep your hair on, I'll be there," replied Jack, hiding his anger but enjoying the look of rage on Peter's face. "Hair on", that was a good one!

Jack was next to leave. "Benjamin, let's discuss this later. Five pm, okay? Lane, let's catch up."

Checking his watch, Jack hurried to his office. "Annie, I need the number of Gallery Groub."

"No probs, Jack," replied Annie, without taking her eyes off an email she was reading.

"No, Annie, just give me the number now, thank you," Jack said curtly.

Annie looked up, slightly surprised, "Yes, of course, Jack." He must have had a big night, she thought.

Kicking the door to his office closed with his heel, Jack sat back in his Eames chair, donned his headset and dialed in the number with agitated speed.

"Gallery Groub," answered a bored female voice.

"Yes, may I speak to Mr Groub, please? It's Jack Wyler."

"I am sorry, Mr Wyler, Mr Groub is out of town until Friday."

"But what about the opening tonight, surely he'll attend?"

"No, I am afraid he has had some pressing business that will not wait."

"Do you have a cell number for him, then?" asked Jack.

"I am afraid Mr Groub doesn't have a cell."

"How about email?"

"No, I'm sorry, he's traveling and doesn't use it anyway. He's a bit old-fashioned, I'm afraid."

"Well, how do I get him a message then?" Jack was starting to get annoyed.

"He should call later in the week. Can I get him to call you?"

"Yes, okay, please tell him it's Jack Wyler."

"Thank you, Mr Wyler. If he calls I will be sure to pass on the message."

Jack hung up. "Brilliant, the one man I want to communicate with is so far out there he doesn't have a cell or email. Lucky bastard."

Annie knocked on the door. "Shall we run through the week, Jack? It's starting to look very busy."

"Yes Annie, just keep Friday free from one pm. I have an important engagement that can't be moved."

"But Peter has just popped me a reminder about Friday lunch, twelve thirty at Odeon. He seemed to really want you to be there."

"Leave that to me, Annie, and keep this between us, okay?"

Jack sat with Annie for the next hour assigning and planning the week's meetings, conference calls and team briefings. Annie Harper had been with him since '96 and was an invaluable asset. The truth was she was more than an asset; she was critical to Jack's success. Her diligence and care of Jack's affairs meant that his diary was never compromised, clients were always happy and the workload was well balanced, intricately planned and finely executed. But it was her loyalty that Jack most valued. And it hadn't come at a price, like so many of the other incentivized PAs on Wall Street. Indeed, Jack made sure she received a good Christmas bonus, expensive birthday presents, the occasional flowers when he had behaved like a prick, but her loyalty and his trust had been earned by a daily regard and respect for each other. That and the fact she was also from Minnesota; although she came from the twin cities and not Upstate, she was from Jack's patch. She was a single mother and treated Jack like a second son. After all, it was thanks to him she had kept her job when the rest of his equities team had been let go on his ascendancy to Research on the ninth floor. That she came with the package was part of the deal. Moreover, he trusted her, and Annie enjoyed the prestige of working for such a bright man, even if she wasn't entirely sure about his taste in art, which she found rather strange. In stark contrast to Lane and Lou's more glamorous PAs, there was nothing spurious about their relationship from a sexual standpoint. Annie was in her mid-forties, short and plump although not unattractively so, with warm brown eyes and a great sense of humor. In Annie Jack had found his professional confidante and Annie her charge, even if he was sometimes a bit brash and certainly swore too much for her liking.

At one Jack brought the meeting to a close. "Annie, please make sure Small is in here five pm prompt. He's going to get an interview without coffee today, I can tell you."

Annie smiled to herself. "Good," she thought. "I dislike the little shit too . . . hateful man."

★ ★ ★

Getting into the trenches with fast growth businesses was what made Jack tick. From a research standpoint it was a critical process to evaluate value and strength. If he had been a soldier he would have had that rare gift that allows high-ranking officers a respect and love of their men, based on integrity and leading by example. If he requested that all the employees work through Christmas, they knew he would be there. If he asked them to work nights he would also be there burning the midnight oil, fine-tuning and crafting the deal, looking with trained eyes for chinks in the various business plans, management team and growth strategy; the stable of any fundraising push. It was Jack's attention to detail and understanding of the market that made his investments so attractive to the market as a whole, the energy and ethical simplicity of his vision filtering down from investor to office manager in equal measure. Everyone involved with the KLS technology investment portfolio was tuned into Jack's work ethic, ethos and overall understanding of fast growth, "high risk high reward" investment methodology. Everyone that is, except Benjamin Small.

Benjamin had recently been recruited to the KLS corporate finance division to take a contracting lead on media and creative-based propositions. Having a background in television-related finance gave Benjamin the necessary acumen to understand, structure and aggressively ringfence intellectual property and distribution of the various KLS online media investments for the shareholders. Although not an accountant by training, Ben, as he was generally known (aside from to his mother and Lane, who both preferred the formal tone of Benjamin), had a specific passion for fine-tooth-combing numbers and more often than not questioning every assumption. Lane had liked Ben's focus and attention to the math and his constant challenging of the bottom line. Having a media-specific mind on board was critical for KLS with the huge amount of dotcom and digital streaming investments currently maturing in the portfolio.

It was this focus, however, and lack of lateral thinking that were in part responsible for Ben's complete and total inability to think outside of the box and see the bigger picture. What's more, he did not possess a creative bone in his body. Again, this flaw in Ben's skill set was not of great concern to Lane. With Jack's team and of course his own not insubstantial ability to see the wood through the trees, Lane was eager to have a pure processing mind to get the deals done, without himself or Jack losing any goodwill with the respective investments. In short, Ben was a fantastic scapegoat, a necessary evil that would act as a focus of complaint and contempt from the various investments and their respective managers and founders. Ben's role within KLS (and Lane's personal agenda) was the personification of "good cop, bad cop". The only person who knew this of course was Lane

Connor. But KLS was his ship, and if there were occasionally small ripples on the seas through which he was steering then it was better that he could control them, even if Ben's employment and rather annoying presence were more often than not the cause.

But Ben's ability to get people's backs up was beginning to play a damaging role in the progress to market of at least two of the KLS investments. As with the majority of second-stage start-ups, positivity combined with morale within the business was critical to success. One poor hire or difficult personality within such a small team could have terminal consequences if not weeded out. Having to deal with this type of negativity from the top level and beyond was a recipe for disaster.

The markets had over the past two years been so buoyant that all Jack's team had to do was replicate the dotcom formula and cash out. This ability to raise capital, trade sale and IPO business born only months earlier based on their impeccable track record had enabled KLS to be slightly more daring than most investors. KLS backed propositions in new and dynamic areas of capital growth, ranging from nanotechnology and the life sciences to fine art sales and e-learning. Although the formula of management structure and fundraising were similar, the founders of such businesses were invariably conscientious and unwavering in their respective knowledge and expertise.

Jack's daily work was involved with getting into the mindset of such entrepreneurs, adding investor-driven objectivity and selecting the top performers and minds based on their reputation in their respective fields. He helped them to lay a hugely commercial veneer to often non-commercial motivations. It wasn't that these businesses were not hungry for the capital. They all were. It was just that their founders were not always motivated by wealth.

A classic example of this was the biotechnology firm Microstem. Professor Johan De Blevis had approached Jack after a personal introduction from the Dean of the University of Pietermaritzburg in South Africa. In 1997 De Blevis had developed a "neuro-stimulator program". In a three-year trial his team had succeeded in partially regenerating and reanimating, via cerebral reintroduction of nerve controlling "mother cells" (the dopamine-generating brain cells essential for control and movement), the partially severed limbs of apes. The basis for his ongoing research was the advancement of stem-cell technology as a whole, with a specific short-term focus on Parkinson's disease and Alzheimer's. But De Blevis' ambitions did not stop there. Combined with a long-term radical electrical pulse (EP) therapy (which would be used to jumpstart tissue nerve endings and reinvigorate the muscle memory), De Blevis believed his tri-mix program (surgical regenerative stem-cell engineering/DNA grafting, parallel pharmacology and the advanced EP therapy) could successfully treat paraplegics and quadriplegics, as well as all manner of physiological motor and neurological traumas.

From a research perspective, Jack's assessment of the Microstem proposition and the financial ramifications were nothing short of eye-watering. From a personal perspective Microstem represented everything he had wanted to achieve for his old man, a real raison d'être, a balance to the fiscal excesses of his somewhat shallow existence. But it was De Blevis himself who had struck Jack. The modest, mild-mannered founder and CEO of Microstem was a man of such high caliber that on their first meeting Jack had noted him to be the most inspirational scientist he had yet encountered.

De Blevis' track record was impeccable (praise for his doctorate on regenerative engineering had appeared in every medical journal of the day), and this labor of love provided him with a foundation for future research, a base from which to launch his vision. It was this vision that had sold him to Jack then and there in the first meeting, the outrageous, gigantic depth of vision that dared to challenge all previously held research on neurodegenerative disorders; to take out Parkinson's, Alzheimer's, all predatory neurocancers from the human DNA, to cancel them, kill them, to literally re-engineer the mechanics of stem-cell research.

From the outset Jack had been blown away, too excited to sleep even, and within a day of meeting De Blevis he knew that he too had the skills, the acumen, the vision to make Microstem a global brand, a byword for revolutionary medical change. With this one seminal meeting Jack realized that his life within KLS had a point, an ethical focus for his endeavors. Jack knew what he needed to do. De Blevis, this short, balding genius, would become his personal project. How proud his father would have been to see it if he could pull this off. Jack could feel it, he would make it happen whatever the cost, however hard the road.

From its initial conception Microstem had one major challenge, long-term research capital. Although a common story for fledgling biotechnology businesses, De Blevis had been fortunate enough to enjoy a modicum of security in the form of an ongoing apartheid government grant. Although not enough capital to grow the business fully, the money had allowed De Blevis and his skeletal team to conduct the initial trials of his thesis, the results of which De Blevis believed would allow Microstem to attract new investors, as proof of concept.

Within the space of a few months of the South African free election of Tambo Embeke, the University of Pietermaritzburg's research budget was decimated in favor of a regional blood-testing program and De Blevis was left without a job, a laboratory or the ability to continue with his life's work. He had returned to his family home on the Cape and spent a long summer thinking his options through. Jack Wyler's card had sat in his wallet long enough, and although somewhat wary of working with venture capital, he had liked the passionate young director of research and made the call.

It was all the opportunity Jack needed. On returning to New York City after a summer spent traveling, he worked up the proposal for the board of KLS. With every day he spent working on the plan with De Blevis, the business got more and more under his skin until his passion for Microstem became nothing but evangelical.

In De Blevis he knew he had found his man. A man who could, if the structure and finances were made available, change the medical landscape forever and contribute toward healing the wound left by his father's untimely death. Jack felt he owed his old man that much, and now nothing was going to stop him. Within a month and with over three further visits to Johannesburg to meet the Microstem team, Jack had laid out the proposition to KLS.

Lane had loved it; the bottom line was massive and the board agreed. They would let Jack run with it. De Blevis was ecstatic, his research team attaining institutional funding of over 5 million dollars. Within two months of the deal being signed De Blevis had moved with his family to New York, bringing with him a team of doctors and professors so astounding that their reputation grew to cult status in medical circles and beyond within a twelve-month period. The *Lancet*, published in the UK, and the *American Medical Journal* had described Microstem as "the most innovative and groundbreaking research outfit in the history of regenerative neuro medicine". However, De Blevis and his team, while motivated by success, were not motivated by the money, a concept Lane had found hard to understand.

Due to intellectual property ethically owned by UP under De Blevis' prior employment, fifty percent of the assets of the business were owned by the university and diluted by the 36.5 percent that KLS had agreed to invest. The founders and employees owned the remaining equity. De

Blevis was paper rich, running a business with a value day one of close to thirty million dollars, a good salary with a bright future. What motivated him was the work; with millions, without millions, that was what De Blevis did ... he wanted his place in medical history. It was that motivation that Jack had bought into. De Blevis was one in a million. Jack could smell it.

★ ★ ★

By December 1999 De Blevis and his team, with Jack's guidance and KLS's financial support, were beginning to make history, the first successful trials of the tri-mix program being complete within six months. Yet within a further three-month time frame Ben and his minions in corporate finance had begun to take an increasingly aggressive stance with the new business; and Ben's constant interference was beginning to make De Blevis mad.

Jack had conducted his meeting with Microstem on a Monday morning; what he hadn't known was that KLS's corporate finance had agreed to run the larger CFO role themselves until De Blevis had recruited a full-time finance director. The finance meetings with De Blevis and his senior staff had taken place every Friday afternoon. The effect of the "good cop, bad cop" routine was starting to wear thin on De Blevis, who spent most of the weekend frantically trying to compile data for delivery to KLS to ensure funding support for each and every month. Lane had structured the management of Microstem that way. Jack buoyed them up and Ben cut into the nitty gritty. What Lane didn't anticipate was the negative effect these milestones were having on Microstem as a whole, a sword of Damocles approach that could, if not checked, stifle their creativity and ruin their chances of success.

De Blevis had called Jack late one Friday in despair. He'd had enough. Jack came immediately and sat listening to him, the anger and frustration evident in this normally quiet and composed man. After half an hour with the directors of Microstem, Jack was beginning to understand the full extent of the damage Ben was causing. Critical equipment had to be acquired to meet the test deadlines, digital operating systems programmed and structured, smaller components designed and a full nanotechnology team recruited.

Yet Ben, behind Jack's back, had threatened to put a stop to their monthly funding until all the cashflow forecasts and board actions were adhered to. The founders themselves were being pressurized by corporate finance to get the final business plans completed for prospective treatments within their first months of trials. In Jack's mind this was sheer lunacy, akin to asking a racehorse to pull a junk cart. What did Ben think he was doing meddling with Jack's baby? What were Ben's team of fifteen chartered accountants and finance MBAs doing asking medical research professors to draft business plans or pressurize the managers in place to do those jobs? Had Ben forgotten the chain of command?

That afternoon Jack did his best to firefight with the rankled management of Microstem and make good in the wake of Ben's earlier morning visit. However, with April's IPO push looming and the critical commercial partnerships still not in place, Jack knew something had to be done to ensure this didn't happen again. Ben was directly undermining Jack's hard work and now he was in for a rocketing on a nuclear scale. Jack was going to enjoy every minute of it. As far as Jack was concerned Ben was off the business.

★ ★ ★

Jack walked briskly through Tribeca back toward Wall Street. The more he thought about Ben the faster he walked, beads of sweat breaking on his brow despite the winter nip in the air. It felt good to walk, to really push the pace, to get some cold, fresh air into his lungs. After a mile or so Jack turned a corner and was hit by an intoxicating rush of wind, rich in oxygen and ozone, the force of which took him by surprise. The gust had a familiar smell; it tasted of the north, of mountains and wild places. Jack hadn't tasted that smell for many months. Winter was coming, and with it all the things that made Jack happy: familiar memories of skiing, Christmas with the family and the Minnesota snows. The familiar north-east wind had cleared his mind briefly and Jack forgot about Ben, KLS and the impending problems at Microstem. For a moment at least he relaxed. Looking up toward the sky he breathed in deeply, closed his eyes and exhaled, the cold bracing itself against his face. He could be anywhere, he thought, except for the familiar wailing of a police siren and the occasional hoot of cars racing downtown.

The mountains stretched out in front of him, white, clean; he could taste them, feel their pull. He strained his eyes closed and pushed himself deeper into the senses of the wind, the touch of the north. The cold air fused with his mind, massaged his brain; God, how he needed it, the peace, the moments away from the pressure, frustration and anger he felt at work.

Even here downtown he could escape, but only for a second. It wasn't enough...

As Jack opened his eyes he fixed his gaze on the twin towers of the World Trade Center, the commercial pillars of the American financial engine of which he and KLS were a small but critical cog. They loomed high and impervious to the wind and the weather, their massiveness a triumph of the American dream. Jack felt professional pride to have been involved with the current high-technology boom, but at the same time he felt torn by deeper feelings that set him at odds with the investment banking infrastructure, designed to exploit the economic opportunities the new economy had yielded. Jack wondered whether investment capital, despite mounting profits, could ever be used to nurture business that did not fit the regular "burn low, sell high" commercial models. Did KLS need to pressure the business to reach market too quickly? In the case of Microstem, couldn't the founders be afforded the time to fully capitalize on sound research and the benefits this added time would bring? Why did this business in particular have to be processed in the same aggressive time-frame as the other KLS propositions, when the full return on such an investment would be so much more important, not to mention lucrative, if allowed to grow organically?

Jack lost the vision and was back to his questioning again. He needed to maintain the escape for a bit longer but there was just too much going on inside his head. He would have to be satisfied with his brief moment away, but he tried once more, closing his eyes, breathing deeply, trying to inject himself back into the mountains...

"Hey, Jack! What the fuck you doin', man? Look like you're losing it, man, don't tell me you're doing that zoning shit again!" called a slim, scruffily dressed man emerging from a taxi.

Jack spun around, slightly annoyed at being denied a second entry into his inner world.

"Jim, what are you up to, what you doing down here?" he replied, a broad smile breaking across his face.

Jim Williamson walked over to Jack and gave him a big, friendly hug. "Haven't seen you in weeks, man. Where you been? Yeah, I know, working like a mad dog. You should chill out with me more, man. I've been landed with these French models for the next week, man, and I just can't cope on my own. Know what I mean?"

Jim was the most incredible womanizer Jack had ever met. At slightly over six foot, slim and strong, with long blond hair, Jim had the boyish, cheeky looks of an oversized high-school dude. His informal manner, warm personality and uniform of baggy black jeans, thick woolen sweater and dilapidated biker boots gave Jim the complex formula that meant from Monday to Saturday he never slept alone, never paid for it and absolutely never had a steady girl. Jim was able to chop and change his women on such a regular basis that Jack had long since given up counting. Whether they were Prada-clad Italian models, uptown super-bitch art dealers or downtown grungy movie stars, they all had a thing for Jim. He was, to quote Robert Palmer, "simply irresistible".

"What brings you this far south, Jim?" asked Jack.

"Just going to the Beuys opening at Groub, some awesome work, man. They say he has the first sled, cocktails too! Kicks off at six pm. Can you make it man, he's your hero, right?"

"Yeah, I saw the sled earlier today, believe it or not. I got a thing on at five but I could possibly make it by six-thirty. You up for a drink after? I've got something I want to pass by you, man . . . "

"Let's do it. See you in the scrum!"

They hugged again and Jim jumped back into the cab. Jack smiled as he thought of Jim's wardrobe and crazy lifestyle. Shit, he has fun, Jack thought as he headed south toward the growing shadows of the twin towers.

Invigorated by his walk, Jack took the stairwell and jogged slowly the nine floors to the technology department. Just before opening the fire door to the warm office he stopped, adjusted his tie and breathed heavily, trying to catch his breath. Jack glanced at his watch. It was 5:02. Late again, he thought. Twice in one day.

Annie stood in the corridor, sorting mail. "Jack, I've just received a message on your voicemail from Small. He can't make your meeting. Said something had come up. I think he's in with Lane. Do you want me to rearrange?"

"No, Annie," replied Jack, his face hardening. "I'll deal with this."

Entering his office, he threw his coat over his chair and sat down on the sofa. He was too incensed to think. His mood darkened. Unable to sit still, he paced back and forth, finally stopping in front of the Basquiat. The skull mesmerized him, its awful grimace matched only by his own rage. Suddenly Jack spun around, as if woken from a trance. Annie was watching him from the doorway, choosing her moment to speak.

"Jack, are you okay? I've got Lane on the phone. He was wondering if you could join them in the boardroom. Seems important."

"Tell him I'm there."

Without another word, Jack carefully squeezed past Annie and walked swiftly down the corridor. Lane sat at the far end of the boardroom, a calm but stern look on his face. Benjamin sat nervously next to him, playing with his ballpoint. Jack took the far end of the table, a confrontational stance that clearly annoyed Lane immensely.

"Jack, for God's sake, what's the matter? Join us this end! We've got important decisions to make here. I'm not looking for a punch-up, just a resolution to the problem."

"Sorry, Lane, I just do not expect to be blown out by a colleague at such short notice."

"Jack, I really must say, I thought for the good of the company it was important to come to Lane directly with my very real concerns about Microstem," bleated Ben.

"Ben, you report in to me. If I feel it's worth bothering Lane with, I report it in to Lane, that's how this works. We had a five pm to discuss Microstem. I've spent the good part of four hours of my day trying to right the shit you created this morning. Why the hell didn't you inform us this morning about your visit?"

"I had to look carefully at the projections and balance sheets before I made my concerns official. It's serious, Jack, and I'm convinced you're not viewing that business objectively. You're too involved."

"Involved? Listen to me, Ben! That business is *the* most important, and, if I might be so bold, only truly valuable business we've got right now. Fucking right I'm involved! I've been nurturing it for over a year and you have succeeded in undermining most of my work in one hour! What do you think you're playing at?"

"Listen, Jack," said Lane. "Ben is convinced the business is at least twelve, if not twenty-four months away from concluding final tests on the nerve stimulator. The complementary pharmacology is even further behind. How can we IPO that business if we haven't got the product or patients? I had no idea we were that far behind."

"I have always been transparent about my belief in the nerve stimulator project. It's cutting edge, Lane. De Blevis' team has proved it in rodents and recently in primates, and they are the best out there. You know full well you can IPO business on a sheet of A4 at the moment. This business just needs a bit more care. It's the capital potential and proof of concept that attracts an aggressive public offering. Shit, Lane, that's what you taught me! And in a way, I agree with Ben. It does need more time . . . with zero negativity, that's all. My point is that if Ben and corporate finance paint all propositions with the same formulaic brush, then we will lose the support of the founders on this one. Trust me, Lane. Ben's asking De Blevis and his team for sales forecasts, equipment expense spreadsheets and manpower status reports, not to mention threatening to stop funding if all board minutes are not observed. The guy's a fucking genius and we're asking him to wipe our asses. We've got guys who crunch data all day, who write business plans with their eyes closed. Why aren't we doing it, Lane? I just don't see the logic."

Jack was starting to see red but Lane was not going to be dictated to. "We are not an incubator, Jack. These propositions have had their first round of finance. We are there to capitalize on the second and third round growth, massively, Jack. We're in the 'making shit loads of money' business, remember that. We're an investment bank, Jack, not a charity. If any business becomes a drain on our resources, we will lose our momentum and focus. That's not our model, Jack, and I won't let it happen. I will not have you, Ben, any department head giving too much of yourselves to a specific project. I don't care how emotionally involved you are."

Jack sat back in his chair, looking straight at Lane and Ben. "Well, gentlemen, here goes in language we all understand. Microstem needs twelve months of full KLS support and funding. You can forget our other recent dotcom IPO strike prices; 300 mil, 450 mil, that's a joke compared to the billions Microstem will attain on capitalization. After looking at the ramifications of AZT, Viagra, and recent other 'wonderdrug' case studies, we will make billions on this if we play our cards right. Historically, surgical, medtech and drug advances are among the most significant inventions of our time. Microstem's solutions could, with our support, cure Alzheimer's, motor neurone disease, Parkinson's … Do you have any idea how huge that is? I propose we parachute in two full-time financiers to make it happen and let the founders, especially De Blevis, focus on what they're good at. We keep the six board meets in the diary and let our joint finance and their CFO oversee and delegate the full funding tranche. I am suggesting we deposit the remaining funding of approximately 1.5 million and a further five million to see De Blevis through to next winter. I will take an enlarged role in the project and everyone will answer to me. You will have my head, Lane, but I want Ben off the business. No IPO pressure. That's the deal."

The room was silent. Ben sat, eyes wide, staring at Jack and Lane intermittently. "I don't believe I'm hearing this Jack, you have got to be kidding. I mean, this is not what we do, I just..."

"That's enough, Ben!" snapped Lane. "If you would excuse us, I need some time with Jack."

Ben grabbed his pad and sped to the door, his bottom lip quivering. "You're putting me on the spot, Jack, that was out of line what you just did. Don't make me make a quick decision on this one, Jack, because the answer will be a no."

Jack laughed aloud. "Yeah, okay, Lane, hard ball is it? Let's not forget who helped put this department on the map. Sure, you and Lou saw my potential and promoted me but I came up trumps, didn't I? Don't tell me that wasn't solid performance on *musicjungle*, a real market leader. But let's face it, seventy percent of the rest of the tech market is hype, Lane, it's just not real. Before me Lou was instrumental in creating that hype, pure and simple; you know it, I know it. Sure, he has called his share of winners but do you really believe his mantra, that the internet will become the most pivotal tool in our commercial lives? The reality of that situation is at best years away and he's forgetting the human factor, the whole physical experience of human interaction... Lane, trust me. Microstem isn't virtual, it's real. This technology could change the medical world. It's not some buy and sell dotcom and we can't treat it as such. Even the best of our other biotech businesses can't touch it for vision and proof of concept. It's leagues ahead of the pack. Remember our meeting with KKR last November? Remember what their chief analyst said as they gave us over a hundred million in investment capital? Well, let me remind you ... 'Invest in projects that exist beyond just the internet; in something you can touch and feel. Something that will really have relevance.' I am asking you to trust me, Lane. Jesus, I've proved it before, haven't I? I've tried to add some objectivity, haven't I? Fewer companies, more value... how many times have I said that? On how many occasions?"

Lane studied Jack. He knew Jack meant business but he didn't like to be pushed around. After all, KLS was his ship. "As I said, Jack, we are not here to support businesses indefinitely and your research has to cover a wide market. I can extend the timeline to July but I need results by May, that's three months away. If it's looking promising then I will sanction a further three months of funding capital, but I want Ben *on* the project, Jack. He sees things numerically and that's vital in the months to come, I sense things are going to change quarter two."

Jack looked stunned. There was no way this was going to happen.

"Numerically fuck, Lane! He can see as many numbers as he wants. Listen here, Lane. Ben is killing the business, he doesn't see anything at all, he just processes by the book. Fuck knows why you hired him, he's completely unable to visualize or add value."

"For your information, Jack, I didn't hire him, Peter did. And he stays, okay?"

"If Ben stays I'll have to consider my position moving forward in KLS, Lane. I am deadly serious about that, Lane. Really, I am. Combined with the Lou situation and the banking boys pressurizing us to boost their stocks, well it's getting dirty, Lane. Oh, and another thing while we're on the subject. I haven't managed to so much as talk to Lou in well over two weeks. He's never in the office, Lane. He's too busy being quoted and courted by the fucking media. It's a total fucking joke, it really is. As to what he is currently tipping, well . . . "

Lane stood up and turned to Jack. This was what CEOs did, they diffused bombs, and it was time for Lane to turn this around. "Don't throw it away Jack, not over this. I suggest you reconsider your position. And as for Lou, he's put in more time and earned us more credibility in the tech sector than the whole of your team put together. I will ask you not to forget that, Jack."

Jack stood in front of Lane, fizzing, he was so mad. "Lane, I feel this like it's inside me. Small will screw Microstem if you let him. He can't help himself. And Lou, if he continues the way he is going Lane, well, it's tantamount to fraud. You know that, don't you? Some of the reports he is currently authoring are so way off the mark they are misleading investors simply to promote companies our bank is doing business with. It's fucking wrong Lane, it's criminal, especially in light of the fact that he's privately trashing the stock he's publicly hyping. I'm serious, Lane. He even emailed me the other day right after he had made a big thing out of Peter's beloved Mediotech on *News Hour*. You know what that email said? I'll tell you, he called it 'a piece of shit, based on a poor technological platform'. I mean it doesn't get any more fucked than that. How do you explain that Lane, eh?"

"You let me worry about Lou. Don't forget you're a partner in this firm, Jack. Your opinions are yours alone, in fact that's all they are. I want you to remember that you are in a very privileged position here and have access to things . . . well, things certain members of the financial community are not privy to. When you lead the pack there are a lot of people gunning for you. I will ask you to be discreet on all these matters, since you quite clearly are not looking at the big picture here. As for Ben, we shall see, Jack, but for now he stays."

Jack faced Lane. "Are you threatening me, Lane? I sensed a little 'cosa nostra' just then."

Lane sat down and turned his back to Jack, looking out of the window. Without turning around he sighed and took a deep breath as if worn out by the exchange. "No, Jack, it's not a threat, it's just a reminder that you're a part of this firm, a key figure in the research department and any heat will affect all of us, including you. Don't think you are above it Jack, it's what you signed up for. It's how Wall Street goes round. It's why you earn so goddam much money. You wouldn't earn that digging ditches or putting out fires, you know. What's gotten into you, Jack? You used to be a team player, what's gone wrong?"

"Let's just say I'm starting to see things in a different light. As for the responsibility thing, I'm well aware of that, Lane, and you can save the lecture on corporate loyalty. You don't have to worry, that's why I'm coming to you and you know what . . . how I feel right now, well I'm not so sure I wouldn't be happier doing something completely different. But if that's the final word Lane, then so be it."

Jack made his way to the door.

"For God's sake, Jack, you're a partner in this bank, you've got responsibilities to the shareholders and to the board. You can't chuck it in over this, it's your career, it's your life, man."

"No, Lane, it's *your* life. I'm not so sure it's mine any more. I guess we need some time to think this thing through, eh . . . "

"Well, Jack, I suggest you take a few days. You really don't want to do anything rash; the ramifications could be . . . complicated, to say the least," added Lane in his fatherly tone.

"I'll do that, Lane. I think I need a bit of time . . . "

Without looking back, Jack closed the door and left Lane standing alone in the boardroom. Then he went back to his office and collected his coat and phone.

"Annie, I might not be in tomorrow. Sorry to dump this on you, but could you cancel my meetings for the rest of the week. If Microstem or De Blevis need me make sure they call my cell."

"Yes, sure, Jack. If you don't mind me saying, you need a good rest tonight. You look stressed."

"Yeah, Annie, it's been a bit of a day."

As Jack sped uptown, Lane sat fuming at his desk. Jack was now a serious problem. Opening his mailbox, he began to draft a memo to Lou. "Lou, we need to talk. I think we have got a situation brewing with Jack – possibly terminal. Lane."

Chapter 4

Jack jumped a cab uptown to SoHo, where a large line had formed on the street outside Gallery Groub at 131 Wooster. Tall blonde models with clipboards and headsets waved in over-anxious clients and blocked the entry of the less desirable. Jack stood patiently at the back of the line. After a few minutes he was summoned forward. A particularly beautiful girl escorted him into the main gallery, which was filled with New York's rich and famous. Well-groomed waiters were serving champagne cocktails and caviar canapés and the whole gallery was buzzing with the heady intoxication of affluence and success.

Jack was amused to see that no one was looking at the art. All the beautiful people were studying each other, their conversations being conducted with their backs to the various paintings and sculptural installations. He made his way toward the centerpiece of the show and stood, a slightly odd figure, in the middle of the room, studying the sled in its perspex case.

"Jack, you showed up!" shouted Jim from a far corner. "Get your ass over here and meet Mikaela and Natasha, they're huge movie stars from Moscow!"

Jack knew only too well that everyone Jim knew was a "huge" star of some sort, his powers of description being limited to either "awesome" or "huge". He was in no doubt that he had already been described as an awesome financier who was hugely rich, etcetera. But that was Jim, and he was after all hugely successful with the ladies, which was clearly all that mattered to him tonight.

"Ladies, it's a pleasure to meet you. I do hope scruffy here is looking after you."

The girls laughed.

"Jack, what do you think of the sled? Man, it rocks."

"Yeah, I love it Jim, really."

"Pity it's sold, man, I could have seen that in your apartment, dude."

Jack turned to Jim, the shock visible on his face. "It's sold? Where do you get that from? It's only just been shown."

"Groub's assistant, Helena, told me. You better ask her, I . . ."

Jack turned and walked toward Helena, Groub's glamorous assistant.

"Helena, hi. I believe we talked on the phone this afternoon. I met with Mr Groub this morning. The sled . . . I've just been informed it's sold, is this true?"

"Yes Mr Wyler, it's been put on reserve – Mr Groub instructed me so earlier on today. I don't know any more about it than that."

"But Groub's away. Did you tell him I called?"

"No, I am afraid he hasn't called yet, but I'll be sure to pass it on."

Jack smiled weakly and headed back to Jim and the girls. "I'm fucking blown away by that, Jim, I'm shocked, man. I was talking to Groub only this morning about the sled, I just don't get it . . ."

"Don't sweat it, man, your time will come. Anyhow, stop bitching, dude, and let's party."

Jack grabbed a tray of drinks and Jim proposed a toast. "To a big one, guys and girls!"

"Yeah, why not?" agreed Jack, winking at Mikaela, the tallest of the Russian girls.

Jim, famous for his inability to stay in one party, bar or club for very long, led the evening's tour: Café Noir, Tunnel Club, Hogs & Heifers in the Meat Packing District and ending up at Florent, Jim's favorite late-night haunt. By 4am Jack, Jim and the girls were totally smashed. Jack and Jim sat slumped in the corner of the diner, a girl in each arm. Jack had acquainted himself with the beautiful Mikaela, whose hand rested keenly on his thigh. He stared at the ceiling, his head resting on the back of the corner sofa, a drunken smile on his face.

"Jim, I did something really stupid today. I think I nearly quit KLS."

"Cool, man, means you might not be so uptight," Jim responded in his normal laid-back drawl.

"No, seriously, Jim, I gave the big man an ultimatum. Either he trusts me on a deal or I leave."

"Dude, you've needed to get out of there for fucking ages, man. That shit can kill you . . ."

"Jim, this is serious, man, a real career-breaker. I mean, I'm starting to get soft, Jim. I've got a bit too involved with a business on a personal level, I . . ."

"It's got to be personal, man, or you just won't have the passion for it. Listen to me, Jack. Sure I don't earn your kind of dollars, but you don't need it all, man. Look at me, I mean, I got all I need, right?"

Jack looked at Jim. If it weren't for his boyish good looks he would look perfectly at home in a bread line. His biker boots were worn down, nearly falling off him, his black jeans were faded and his signature Norwegian sweater threadbare and shapeless. Jack knew the reason Jim always ate at Florent. He could just about afford the burger and fries, and the bulge in his back pocket could be attributed to the ten or so credit cards that provided him a lifeline in between movies. But with a babe on his arm and the freedom to wake up when he pleased, Jack would have been lying to himself if he was not a little in awe of Jim's somewhat bohemian lifestyle.

"Fuck, Jim, you look like shit! But then look at me, suited and booted and nowhere to go."

"I tell you what, dude, we should get out of here for a while, Jack. Let's do a trip, man. It's been over two years, man, and I need a break from this shit too. I need my cold dose, something really tough, man, I don't know."

"You're right, I should take some time off before I do something rash. Where do you think? Canada? Alaska? I know this really desolate..."

"You boys like to travel in cold places, yes?" interrupted Mikaela. "You visit Sredny in Siberia. My brother, Viktor Sedov, Russia's top polar explorer, now he runs the meteorological station there. Only Viktor and his family and many polar bears."

"Sredny, where is that?" Jack was intrigued.

"Siberian Arctic island. Last land mass to Pole. You fly there from Khatanga and Norilsk, out of St Petersburg..."

"Have you ever been there yourself, Mikaela?" asked Jack.

"Yes, for Easter time. Viktor had first child so I went to see them. Beautiful wooden house overlooking the pack ice, open water never come to Sredny, always ice-bound, I think you say."

Jim and Jack glanced at each other, broad smiles breaking across their faces.

"Ice-bound, I like it," thought Jack, resting his head against the soft skin of Mikaela's shoulder. "Maybe we could talk to your brother?"

"We shall see, Jack. I'm not sure if you are worth it yet," jibed Mikaela in her sexy broken English. "You'll have to do better than buying us a few cocktails, if you get my drift... I'm not sure if you are man enough to meet Viktor. I mean, I haven't seen what you are made of yet..."

"Do you sense a physical challenge, Jim?"

"Dude, I think we are in for an all-nighter. Yes, I'm sure of it. I hear there is a drunk front coming in from the east..."

★ ★ ★

Tuesday brought with it one of the worst hangovers Jack had ever known. Jim and Natasha lay intertwined on Jack's sofa, with a trail of clothes, shoes, underwear and vodka bottles sprawled around the apartment. Jack awoke to find Mikaela draped over him, her beautiful raven hair covering his chest. Jack tried to reach the glass of water on the bedside table without waking her but as he moved Mikaela stirred.

"Jack, bastard, you passed out on me! I was just getting going, I . . ."

"Darling, you're a wild, sexy thing and I was just too drunk. Do you want water?"

"*Water*? I Russian! Vodka, Jack, I want a vodka!"

"You're nuts, baby, but if that's what you want . . ."

Jack walked naked across a designer rug toward the open-plan kitchen. His apartment was massive, a huge rectangular central reception room forty feet by sixty feet with high ceilings and aged oak flooring, brushed steel furnishings, minimal, sparse, barely lived in. Of the three bedrooms only one had ever been used, on the odd occasion when Jim needed to escape the continual stream of foreign women who used his modest apartment as a permanent home from home.

Jack preferred to sleep in the main open-plan area, and hadn't even had the linen curtains fitted. He was always up at first light anyhow, and from his position on the top floor of his parkside apartment noisy neighbors were not an issue. The view across Central Park West was mind-blowing, a swathe of leafy green, interspersed with rocky outcrops, hundreds of tiny people dotted across the crisscross of footpaths and cycle tracks, greens and lakes, an enclave of foliage in a vast metropolis. The panorama was clearly reflected in the rental price. In the three years he had lived there he could have bought an entire house in Ely, but he liked to keep it loose. Ownership was not an issue to the Wylers, Laura had seen to that; it just wasn't in their DNA. Anyhow, Jack didn't see the need to own a city pad, since he had no intention of living in New York forever. The apartment was a stop-gap, a calculated tax-efficient expense, part of Jack's bigger plan; cash out, retire, keep his assets liquid so he could up sticks and travel. For the time being it suited him fine.

Stopping at the door on the far side of the apartment, Jack crouched down to pick up the mail. A beautifully embossed white envelope lay on the doormat, "Gallery Groub" tastefully printed on the front. Jack pulled up a stool and eagerly opened the envelope.

Dear Mr Wyler

I have taken the liberty to enclose a photograph of the original Beuys sled. I hope you do not mind or in anyway take the gesture to be pushy but I have taken the liberty of placing the work under reserve pending our lunch meeting on Friday.

Yours sincerely,
Hans Groub

Jack stood up and walked over to Jim. "Wake up, man, you'll never guess what! Helena was right, the sled is under reserve, man, but for *me*. Can you believe that, Jim? Groub is a clever old bastard."

"Dude, it's a bit early for me to take this in," murmured Jim from under the duvet. "Maybe in a few hours, man. I mean, respect my sleep, dude."

"Sleep? How can you sleep? We've got work to do, man. Mikaela, why don't you grab the first shower? I think we should all have some breakfast, then let's buy the maps. I want to take a look at this Sredny place."

★ ★ ★

For the next two days Jack surfed the web, read and gathered as much information as he could about the region. Alone in his apartment, he pored over a single flight plan of the Severnaya Zemlya archipelago. It had taken Jack most of Tuesday to locate any cartography of the region, since Sredny (the only inhabited island) had been one of the last northern listening posts for the former USSR and maps were not readily available to anyone outside the soviet military. Harry Lewis, who ran the Explorers' Club of New York, had made a few calls and discovered a lone map in the depths of a deceased member's plan chest, which had recently been delivered to the society, a term of the will. As fate would have it, Harry had made another treasure of a discovery; none other than Viktor Sedov's expedition journals from his epic solo crossing of the Arctic Ocean in 1968.

Jack held the manuscript in his hands, feeling its weight; lifting it to his nose, he smelled the well-thumbed pages, sensing for hints of Viktor's remarkable journey, a waft of salt, an echo of the creaking polar ice. These pages had been there, day in, day out, a site-specific labor of love and survival. Carefully wrapped and unwrapped every night of that huge adventure, pen and ink, perfect Cyrillic script, very few crossings out. To his eyes, of course, it was all totally illegible, a different alphabet, words from another world. Jack opened the robust leather folder and stared at the opening page. It was simply illustrated with an original faded color snapshot, probably taken on a self-timer with a mechanical Practica SLR delicately placed on an improvised tripod out there on the ice pack. There he stood, the young Sedov, long hair tied in a single plait, wide brim ski goggles pushed rakishly high on his forehead, a large muscular arm bent in a relaxed salute, shielding his bright piercing blue eyes from the glare of the Arctic sun.

Jack could tell, even with his down jumpsuit on, that he was thin, painfully so, his face gaunt, angular even beneath his overgrown beard, the result of months of physical torture. But despite his evident weight loss, he did not appear frail or weak. Viktor Sedov after 104 days of constant polar travel was still strong, indomitable, Jack could see that, a powerful walking machine, forward all the way. It was in his eyes, lupine almost, piercing and focused. After all, the man had done it, the impossible – he had made it across that ocean alone.

The critics had said it could never be done, that crossing, foolhardy in the extreme. Pah! No one could make it in one season and without re-supply, without drop-offs and caches, or without wintering over at the Pole as Wally Herbert and the Brits had done it. From Canada to the Pole and out again, all the way, till the ice back in the '70s became sea and the summer melted it all from under him.

The Inuit elders had said that no man could survive the bears, out there on the ice, across the great Arctic sea. To cross that ocean you would have to become the bear, eat his spirit, gorge on his meat. And that is what Sedov had done. He had become the bear. Lived subsistence, from the land, the seals, the bears and occasional fish. He had not made the mistakes his father's generation had made out there, hunting polar bears on Wrangle Island. They had died as a result of their feast. The bear's liver had seen to that, resulting in hypotoxemia – death by vitamin A, a toxic overload to the digestive system. For Sedov the liver had made great bait for the fish, the ammonia-rich urea liquefying and melding with the undersea current, sending messages of fear and weakness, an animal in distress, to the voracious passing Arctic cod beneath the pack. He had used all of the beast, the meat, the sinew, the bone and, most importantly, the fur for bearskin pants, lining for his parka, insulation for his sled.

Back in the '70s Harry's volunteer research team had transcribed highlights of the notes for the inaugural opening of Viktor's US tour. The translation was on cheap paper, not the well-worn heavy gauge, rough hew of the original Russian pages, but still legible, if slightly faded. The notes had been a gift from the young Sedov on his first visit to the States in 1970 and marked the launch of his US lecture tour. As with the British team led by veteran polar explorer Wally Herbert, who had successfully crossed the ocean in two seasons in '69, Sedov had managed the feat alone, in one winter and unsupported, a remarkable feat of human endurance.

The crossing had taken 104 days. Viktor had had the canoe built into his bespoke sled in preparation for his treacherous finale, canoeing over 150 miles of open ocean and finally coming to rest on Sredny in June '68. The triumph of his gargantuan undertaking was, however, short-lived, overshadowed in '69 by the lunar landings. But Viktor wasn't bothered. His had been a higher mission than attaining a world first. Viktor's raison d'être was of a purer kind, that of physical endurance, a personal test. Moreover, it was a serious biophysical experiment. His daily blood pressure readings and blood work had resulted in one of Russia's most conclusive studies on the effects of extreme cold on the human metabolism. It was to be in the area of medical research that Viktor Sedov made his mark. Mother science had been his taskmaster and it was to science that Viktor had dedicated his life.

Viktor had walked to the Pole twice in his life, crossed the Arctic Ocean in one season and covered over 40,000 miles on dog-sled. His discoveries in the pursuit of knowledge and science in the Arctic had given him his career, his freedom to travel, an export of mother Russia's virtues. Intelligence through hardship that even Stalin would have approved of. Khrushchev certainly had done. Sedov had been awarded the order of the Soviet Union with oak leaves and clusters. Professor Viktor Sedov was free to travel and when he was ready he could choose his posting, anywhere; money would be no object, and protocols would be sidestepped.

After sabbatical in the USA and social honors in Moscow, Viktor's choice had surprised even his closest friends. After the lecture tour in 1970 he had seen all he wanted to of the west. He wanted to be back in his Arctic, the place that had given him so much. A place where he was free and happy. He wasn't rich. Even if he had fully exploited his national fame, to Viktor money alone would have constituted false gold. After all, there was nowhere to spend it. Viktor had chosen Sredny, the polar laboratory and accompanying meteorological station overlooking the jagged and broken sea ice, a posting to which open water would never come. It was a good posting, a great place to see out his years. It felt like home.

What intrigued Jack about Viktor's choice was Sredny's extreme remoteness. At 83 degrees north, the archipelago's northern tip, Cape Artchisky, was barely 600 nautical miles from the Pole and constituted the major jumping-off point for all of Russia's North Pole attempts. Having previously traveled to Alert on Canada's Ellesmere Island (the other staging post for polar trips), Jack was struck not only by the similarity of their relative geographic, climatic and polar latitude but also by the great difference in the surrounding sea ice conditions. What Jack discovered was that Sredny's ice was much more sled-friendly than its Canadian counterpart, the reason being that the ice surrounding Sredny was so new. Ice on the Canadian side could form into fissures and ridges over 100 feet high in stretches of over forty miles, making ice travel impossible to all but the most hardened and experienced traveler. The Canadian pack ice had been compounded over millennia, an average pressure ridge being in the region of 100 years old. By comparison the ice on Cape Artchisky was, due to constantly changing floes and currents, barely older than five years at the most. The ramifications for Jack, Jim and Bob's expedition meant that they could island-hop, circumnavigating the archipelago in a faster and potentially safer fashion. Ultimately the sea offered an attractive alternative to scaling the treacherous 8,000-foot glaciers, cathedral crevasses and mountain ranges prevalent in the northern interior. The main concern when traveling either by ski or sled on the pack was, however, not the prospect of falling into the sea.

Ice so close to shore was many yards in thickness. The true danger came in the form of polar bears, the largest concentration of roaming and denning bears in the Russian Arctic. Jack had contended with bears before in Ellesmere, but other than the normal paranoia that accompanies travel in polar regions, he had only ever had a single sighting of a bear and that was at a good distance. In Canada, he and the team had carried shotguns loaded with "cracker" shells, designed to scare the bear if an advance was imminent. The real trick to being safe in bear country lay in the precautions taken with food storage and camp hygiene. The trouble with extended journeys on the ice meant that after a few days you yourself started to smell like food. Due to the frequent storms it was often necessary to eat in the tent, an activity that was sure to attract a hungry marauding male. But like most predator–human interactions, the bears were the ones who invariably came off worse in any situation. Jack pondered this point and remembered a book he had recently read by a young Norwegian about the tragedy of human–bear interactions in the wild.

Perr Brovig, a young Norwegian polar explorer, had killed three bears in the 1997 push for the Pole. It was a particularly warm year, with an abundance of open water leads being found close to the Pole itself. Perr had encountered his first bear in the ice rubble close to the Canadian shoreline, at extremely close quarters, and had been lucky to get a shot off at the young charging male. Once through the infamous pressure ridge zone, he had the constant nagging fear of being stalked and took his twenty-fifth day on the pack to retrace his steps for over five miles. He had found fresh bear prints no further than 400 yards behind his tracks. Waiting in the snow for an hour, petrified, cold and hungry, Perr waited until the bear made a move. It had been lying close by, hidden by a small ice fissure. Unafraid, it walked straight toward Perr and was shot three yards from the exhausted explorer's feet. Perr was now beside himself, disillusioned with his quest and genuinely morose about the killing of his favorite animal.

After a further fifteen days and now close to the Pole, Perr stopped to fix a ski binding unaware of a third bear only yards behind him. As he went for the shotgun on his sled, the bear charged. Again Perr was lucky, but as he later wrote in his autobiography *Without Limits*: "A piece of me had died out there on the ice. I sat for many hours crying next to this beautiful animal, the still warm bulk steaming in the morning light. Who was I to be here, to take a bear's life for my self-serving aims? I vowed I would never return."

The story of Perr and the bears had a great effect on Jack. For him it posed an important moral dilemma about the very nature of his passion for exploration. Would the wild not be better off without man's interference? But if left alone, who would tell the world of the great wonders and who would be there to protect it from future harm? Had Peary, Shackleton, Amundsen, Herbert and Hillary not pushed the envelope and discovered what lay at the Poles and highest mountains, and had Aldrin and Armstrong not landed on the moon, would the planet be a better place? Jack didn't know, but in his heart he thought not, for the simple reason that exploration and scientific research had shown so many the beauty and wonder of the natural world. In Jack's mind the experience was worth sharing, whatever the cost.

★ ★ ★

By Thursday Jack had amassed a good body of material on Sredny and had formed, in his mind at least, the core of a trip plan. Having Viktor as guide was the icing on the cake. Jack could barely believe he would be traveling with such a great man. But somewhere in the back of his mind he believed he could drive the pace. Maybe it was raw arrogance or a steely inner confidence, but deep down inside he knew he could have achieved the Pole, endured the months of hardship, hack it, if he had had to. As a result Jack decided to lead the trip, with Viktor as guide and adviser for the first-ever traverse of the northern arrowhead, the tip of the Sredny archipelago. The mountains were far too problematic for a line-of-sight approach. The team would contour the land by dog-sled on the sea ice. It would be a first, Jack's first, that was important, part of the competition he felt constituted the very essence of any expedition. It was not enough for the team to have an experience, it had to be balls against the wall, extreme, a bit of danger, and he would need to show Viktor he had it. Besides, Viktor was no spring chicken, he'd had his day. As far as Jack was concerned he could just sit back and enjoy the ride.

★ ★ ★

For the past week Jack's cellphone had been unusually quiet, but he put it down to good diary management by Annie, who was notorious for keeping clients at bay when Jack was stressed or over-tired. Having had a few days off from the office and with the Arctic trip on his mind, clients and the board off his back, Jack was looking forward to his Friday lunch with Groub. Although he was delighted not to have lost the sled to another collector, he felt Groub's note somewhat presumptuous, especially since they hadn't discussed price yet. Maybe that was what made Groub such a great dealer.

A few months earlier Jack had watched a documentary about Groub's handling of his clients. Not only was Groub able to move a large percentage of his works, he was incredibly selective about the prospective home of a piece. The credentials of a prospective client went well beyond the normal prerequisites of having enough cash, or even, in the case of his numerous recent Basquiat consignments, being offered twice the going amount by an over-zealous collector. It was all about the prestige of the potential collection; would the work sold lead to a consolidation of the artist's work? Would a sale result in more sales and would the "right" people own that specific artist's work? Groub's skill was therefore to be focused in the placement of the piece, the highly complex matching of client to art, a skill at which Groub was the undeniable New York master.

In light of this, Jack the collector felt honored to be courted by Groub, deemed worthy to own such an important work . . . well, that was counting one's chickens.

Jack settled back in his old leather armchair and picked up a well-thumbed copy of *We Walk This Way*, the new definitive biography of Joseph Beuys. Although the sled was not pictured in the book, Jack read for the umpteenth time the account of Beuys' interaction with a coyote in Gallery Rene Block entitled, "I like America and America likes me". Beuys coexisted in a confined space with a coyote, armed only with a shepherd's crook and felt blanket. The black and white photographs depicted the entire duration of the performance, the coyote at first wary then indifferent to the artist's presence. By the end of the week the coyote would sneak up and try to steal the felt blanket, and it even engaged in a tug of war with Beuys.

Although the coyote was not wild, in the sense of being taken from the wild, it was a wild animal, with instincts completely different from that of a domesticated dog. Jack had read earlier that a coyote and fox, wild dog and jackal, have completely different DNA from that of a dog. A wolf, on the other hand, has identical genes. This is a crucial point to grasp in deciphering man's complex relationship with the dog and the primordial hunting relationships between early hunter-gatherers and the wolf.

Jack had, in stark contrast to Beuys' city-bound interaction, heard of a trapper in the far north who, having broken his leg, had been forced by frostbite and hunger to feed on a caribou kill at the same time as a pack of wolves. A week later, recovering in his winter camp, the trapper had heard a scratching on the door of his cabin. Cocking his revolver, the trapper carefully opened his door to find a large male wolf sitting on the porch. Without a sound the wolf gently pushed past the bemused trapper and lay down by the fire. The trapper sat next to the exhausted and injured wolf and stroked him until he fell asleep. The wolf died in the trapper's arms later that night.

Compared to the story of Perr and the bears, Jack was intrigued by the message of Beuys' performance and the true story of the Alaskan trapper. It was the connection between the man and the wild that fascinated him so much, the primal coexistence of man and beast. For Jack, Beuys the shaman, the instigator, fired his imagination. Jack knew that he had to learn more about Beuys, but moreover that he needed that sled, if nothing more than to give his life a new meaning. Yes, his acquisition of the sled would mark a new beginning. It was time to move on. It was just the symbol he needed, an investment . . . an investment in his future.

★ ★ ★

Jack and Jim had breakfast and went through all the plans. Jim would be in charge of equipment, a skill he had so refined that he had barely spent a penny on expedition gear in ten years of trips. Jack would make all the travel plans, book the flights, fix the insurance and delve into the route details. They both decided they should liaise with Viktor as soon as possible so that he could organize the dog teams, internal helicopter flights and a good guide. In his haste to plan the trip Jack had somewhat neglected Mikaela, whereas Jim had been keeping Natasha busy.

Jack switched his cellphone on. Jim watched in disbelief as Jack first excused himself and then went straight to the point. "Mikaela, it's Jack. Sorry not to have called you this week. I've been a bit tied up. Listen, I'd love to see you again. Maybe tonight? We could go out with Jim and Natasha. Yes? No? I really want to see you. Oh, also, maybe we could talk to your brother when you come round . . . shall we say eightish?"

"Man, you don't fuck about do you, Jack? I mean, you've got to do better than that if you want her help, dude," jibed Jim.

"What's wrong? You can talk! Who else have you been seeing this week? I bet you're in double figures by now."

"I don't know what you're talking about," replied Jim, a cheeky grin breaking across his face. "I've only been seeing Natasha, man. That is, when I've been seeing Natasha."

Jack and Jim started to laugh.

"What are we like? I just want to get laid and you, Jack, there is always an angle, right? Man! We will go to hell, man, I swear it."

"Bullshit, Jim. That's the way it goes, we are all after something. We all use each other. They use us too, man, don't forget that, and another thing . . ."

Jack's phone rang mid-sentence.

"Jack, it's Annie. Just had a call from Lane and Peter. They need you in for an urgent chat before your Mediotech meeting at Odeon. You still have that in the diary, Jack?"

"Annie, what are you talking about? I told Lane I needed some time. That lunch was to help Peter with a pitch. You always knew I was tied up on that lunch. I was just going to pop in and do the handshake thing, and that was before our little tiff on Monday."

"Jack, Lane is really on my case about this. He was insistent you turn up."

"Well, tell him I can't. A few days off means a few days off. I'll need more than two hours' notice to turn up. What's he thinking, Annie? Tell him to get Lou. It's his baby anyhow."

"Lane said the same about you, Jack. And Petra tells me Lou is traveling for the next two days. We've tried that one. He really turned on her in such a nasty way when she asked him too. Such a rude man. Lane, by the way, classed a few days as two to three. He was trying to get you in last night but I told him I couldn't get hold of you. I didn't want to disturb you in the evening."

"Listen, Annie, it's not happening. I've got a very important lunch today, so it's out of the question."

"Well, Jack, you're the boss. I just think Lane will blow on this one. I hope you are aware of that."

"Annie, tell him I'm out of town for the day. I'll call on Monday. It'll be fine, I promise." Jack turned his phone off and put it inside his jacket pocket.

"Thought you'd got KLS off your back, Jack. Looks like they still got a hook in you, man."

"Of course they have Jim, you dick!" snapped Jack irritably. "I'm a fucking KLS director, but can't they just let it be for more than a few days? They've got five hundred other employees to choose from. Lane, I mean, fuck him! I wonder if he can't stand on his own two feet sometimes. He always gets others to either do the deals or fire people. Well, I tell you what, he's on his own tomorrow. And Peter, I really don't give a shit about his deals. Fucking corporate finance, bunch of number-crunching monkeys."

"Relax, man, you're not going. You're going to swagger around with Groub, buy the sled, and we are doing this trip, okay? Anyhow, you got bigger problems. You got to handle Mikaela tonight. She's an animal, dude, hope you're feeling fit!"

Jack got the check and left Jim on the phone calling chicks and doing deals. It was midday by now and he thought he would get a bit of air and walk uptown to Lola's. This was one meeting he did not intend to be late for. Half an hour later he arrived at the restaurant. Being slightly early, he decided to read a paper at the table. As the working breakfast crowd was beginning to leave and as Jack waited at the bar for his table, Benjamin Small was collecting his overcoat from the cloakroom. Jack, unaware of Small's proximity, turned to the barman and ordered a bellini, his favorite aperitif. As Benjamin made for the door he thought he recognized the solidly built man at the bar. Shooting a quick look, there was no need for a double-take. It was Jack Wyler, sure enough. Benjamin quickly put on his coat and slipped out the door, leaving Jack alone at the bar, blissfully unaware of his presence. Once on Seventh Avenue he hailed a cab downtown.

"Odeon restaurant, Tribeca, as quick as you can."

★ ★ ★

For the first time in weeks Jack was beginning to enjoy himself. The bellini went down a treat and he ordered another. It was his first time in Lola's and he found the atmosphere intoxicating. A pianist played Cole Porter tunes and crooned softly in the far corner of the bar as he sat and watched the toing and froing of people going about their busy lives. Sitting in a public place, observing, watching and relaxing, was not a familiar exercise for Jack. He couldn't remember when he had done it on a working day. He probably never had.

Through the milling of diners and waiters, the impeccably dressed maître-d' approached Jack. "Mr Wyler, your table is ready. Mr Groub is already awaiting you."

Jack was led through the bustling dining floor to a large oak door at the rear of the restaurant. The maître-d' ushered him into a smaller room and up a flight of stairs to a beautifully decorated private dining room, the walls hung with exquisite pen and ink works on paper, all framed identically in boxes.

"Mr Wyler, so glad you could make it. I hope you don't mind being away from the hordes. I thought it would be appropriate if we had some privacy to discuss Herr Beuys."

"No, this is fantastic. How have you been?"

"Good. Well, it was a shame to miss the opening, a very poor example to my employees and a disservice to my clients, but unavoidable in the circumstances."

"I do hope everything is okay. Was it a personal family matter?"

"Oh, God, no, Mr Wyler, nothing so mundane. A new work has

become available, very important, extremely so – I just had to make sure its acquisition was secure."

"Please, please call me Jack."

"Yes, of course, Jack. And as for me, Hans is much better, yes – how formal we can be. So, Jack, before we get to business, what would you like to drink? Some '88 Krug, perhaps? I find it a perfect tonic for the Friday blues . . ."

"Yes, it's my favorite, but Friday blues? I have never heard of Friday referred to like that before."

"Well, what is there to look forward to? One just gets warmed up, business is good and then two completely irrelevant days when people don't want to do business or even pick up the telephone. How frustrating the weekend can be!"

"I can deduce from that you rather love your work."

"Of course, Jack. Surely you love your work too, no?"

"Well, I guess I have been more enamored with it. I am having second thoughts at the moment, though. I'm seriously considering where to go from here . . ."

"Well, Jack, you are young. I am sure you will be successful at whatever you turn your hand to . . . I, however, only really had one choice."

"How's that, Hans? Your skill sets could be applied over a broad range of financial, commercial markets. I mean, you are a market leader, are you not?"

"Yes, Jack, I suppose I am, back home in Switzerland at least. It is just that wasn't my chosen vocation. Did you know I was a painter in my youth?"

"An artist. Really?" Jack was impressed. "That's awesome, Hans. I have never heard that."

"Yes, believe me, not too many people know. I do not like to publicize my failings."

"But why were you a failure? Surely it takes some time to be recognized?"

"Well, early on, I had a very influential tutor as a student in Düsseldorf. If anything, he taught me that it was creativity rather than the practice of painting and sculpture that was of importance. Everyone can be an artist, he used to say."

"But surely a good tutor is supposed to show you not how good he is but how good you can be."

"Yes, that's the problem really. He wasn't a good tutor, he was a great tutor, and he did, he taught me that my talents lay elsewhere, in promoting and understanding not just the financial value of art but also the necessity of art. I guess I took him rather literally on that one. You see Jack, I studied under Beuys for four years."

"You were taught by Beuys? My God, Hans, that's incredible! What was he like?"

Jack sat and listened to Hans Groub's account of his student days with Joseph Beuys, from attentive pupil to principal collector. Over a thirty-year period, the young Groub had established himself as one of the most important dealers of abstract expressionism in the world. Leaving Europe in the early sixties, he went to work building relationships with the New York School. His business model was unique. Once Hans had courted the artists and their direct representatives by personally buying a number of important works by each of the New York School, he established a trusting relationship with the artist directly, and taking individual works on consignment shipped the works, on a Swiss import carnet, to Zurich. Each consignment was then offered exclusively to a number of the wealthiest industrialists in Switzerland as a solid investment based on their growth over the last ten years (from mid '50s to late '60s).

Dealing principally in the works of Rothko, Klein, De Kooning, Twombly, and later Tapies, Schnabel and more recently Basquiat, Groub established a total stranglehold on the market. If you were a Swiss and wanted to collect, you had to go through Groub. European exclusivity deals with the majority of New York's galleries followed, based on the performance and reliability of Groub's collector base. He set up an exclusive travel business that enabled enamored collectors to travel (first class, of course) to New York, where they would spend two days with the artist in his atelier. This not only led to guaranteed sales (paintings often being shipped still wet) but also resulted in a greater understanding of the work, and the honors started to roll in. The National Arts medal followed, as did prestigious invitations to sit on the board of the Guggenheim and the Museum of Modern Art.

But for Groub, his success was to be channeled in one direction only. His great wealth empowered him with the means to indulge in his life's passion – the collecting of works by his master, Joseph Beuys. Unlike his success in the placement and sale of the New York painting school, from the '50s to the late '80s (a period in which Groub drew a direct line in ascendancy from De Kooning to Schnabel, in much the same way as

71

boxing enthusiasts drew the line of lineage from Mohammed Ali to Mike Tyson), Groub's astounding collection of the works of Beuys was never intended to be sold. It was purely for his own indulgence, an eccentric passion for the work and teachings of the man who was Groub's lifelong mentor until his death in 1986.

After two hours of champagne and deep conversation, Jack, now quite drunk on Krug and fine wines, got to the point.

"So, Hans, you've built this incredible art collection that you clearly never intend to sell – why do you want to sell me the sled? Surely such a significant work is the centerpiece of your collection?"

"A good point, Jack. I last allowed the prototype sled to be shown at Documenta 9, the Art Olympics, so to speak, in Kassel, Germany in 1992. Beuys had helped the Documenta come to fruition in the early '50s as a statement of rebirth and reconciliation in a depressed and ruined Germany after the war. Documenta 9 was the first Documenta that Beuys did not attend – he had died five years earlier. You see Documenta really is a bit like the Olympics, as it is only staged every five years. I therefore felt, since Beuys had departed on his greatest unknown journey, that the sled would be rather appropriate. I guess in a similar fashion to the Vikings' kings who were buried with their longships for a voyage in the afterlife. As to me selling the sled, well, that would also be completely out of the question and would, as I have explained, negate every principle I have upheld with regards Beuys' work to date."

"But if you don't intend to sell me the sled, why are we having this conversation?" asked Jack abruptly, the confusion apparent on his reddening face.

"Because, Jack, Beuys gave me the sled as a symbol of my new journey in the world as a dealer. Now I want you to have it as something to be enjoyed, and when the time is right to be passed on, that is my only condition. I hope I make myself clear, Jack. I will give you the sled but you must never sell it, not ever. Do we have a deal?" Groub held out his hand. "Shall we shake on it?"

Jack was speechless. "Hans, I don't know what to say, I'm . . ."

"So say nothing and shake on it, Jack. I have been looking for many years for someone to enjoy this work. I must come clean, though, Jack. I had a good friend check you out, professionally so to speak, a person who will, I feel, be a good friend should you need him in the future. I do hope you don't mind, Jack. It's just that I had to be sure, although my gut instinct told me you were right when I watched you studying the sled in my gallery. Of course you have been on my radar for some time – I observed you bidding for various works and then for the Basquiat. I couldn't help myself. Sure I wanted it, but when we cut away from the pack at 360K, well, that was quite something. You needed that work Jack, just had to have it, eh? It's a hard piece after all, no? Very dark, most challenging, seminal early Jean-Michel with fire in his belly, no money for canvas. Christ, the man started to cut up his apartment for material on which to work, now that's dedication, that's commitment, Jack. In a sense I knew that work would lead to you being here in a roundabout sort of way. I just knew you should have it. My KLS contact just confirmed what I felt about you, the signs and signals so to speak, your intensity and sensibility, that told me, despite the fact we hardly know each other. I believe you will be a most fitting keeper."

Jack was stunned and slightly annoyed. Check him out, for what? How dare he? But he kept his feelings hidden. Listen, came the voice, listen and don't be so predictable ...

"But what if I hadn't come in today or any other day? I just don't get it, Hans. I came into your gallery, did I not? You didn't lure me in." Jack was confused, his face flushed.

"Well, let's just say I knew it would only be a matter of time before the sled spoke to you. The spirit of it, how shall I say, it coerced you in, yes Jack, it was just a matter of time."

Jack turned away. Hans was getting to him, something strange, intoxicating. He sat for some time and still the voice reminded him to keep from blowing it. Hans sat next to him in silence as Jack had his "moment". As he closed his eyes he felt it, as clear as anything he had ever felt, a simple feeling of calm. And then he knew for sure that this wasn't a ruse, he could let his well-honed corporate defenses down. This was real, genuine generosity, parental, philanthropic and rare.

Finally Jack took Hans' hand firmly in his own, tears welling in his eyes. Groub smiled and then embraced Jack.

"It's okay, Jack, it's okay. I'm glad you are moved. He has had that effect on me and will continue to do so for ever."

★ ★ ★

As Jack and Hans Groub said their farewells uptown at Lola's, another meeting of minds, downtown, was just beginning. Lane and Peter sat alone in the boardroom at KLS, a steely silence hanging over the room. Peter sat staring into space, his complexion similar to that of the grey-stained, lime table. In fact everything about him was grey apart from his mood, which at this moment in time was decidedly black. Lane sat somewhat uncomfortably staring out of the window, fingering his shock of grey, rather long, lank hair, backwards in a slow, repetitive, well-practiced rhythm. Even his subtle permatan seemed to have faded a few tones to reflect the ominous mood of the room.

"Well, Lane, that was a total goat fuck. I can safely say we have just lost the Israeli business. I can't fucking believe it. I mean, Jack was briefed about that meeting on Monday. Don't you have any control over the man? Lane, he's your boy for God's sake."

"Give me a break, Peter!" snapped Lane. "Don't be so melodramatic. I warned you about our little discrepancy. I mean the man hasn't taken more than two days off in over three years. There is no way I thought he wouldn't show. I left how many messages with Annie and besides, this isn't something I can't put right with a phone call. Worst case I will fly out there myself and get them back on board."

"Well, as far as I'm concerned, Lane, Annie has just got fired. We can't tolerate collusion on deals like this, Lane. She's fucking gone."

"I can't say I agree with you on that one, Peter. If you sack Annie, Jack's fucking out of here. He's hot-blooded enough right now. I suggest you leave him to me. I'll have him on the case early next week. Just leave it to me."

"Listen, Lane, I left him to you today and look what happened. You can't fuck about in the sector right now. If we don't sign their portfolio of tech investments by April we could lose out on over two billion dollars, Lane. That's the complete Israeli tech sector deal up in smoke and two years of my time."

"If it's so much your deal, Peter, why was Jack's no show such a big drama? Sounds to me as if it's Jack's deal!" replied Lane provocatively.

"Jack's deal! You're kidding, right? Benjamin and his corporate finance team structured the whole contract, built the models and placed the finance."

"But Jack engaged with the founders, Peter, didn't he? He was the one that made how many trips out there and it was his research team that initially highlighted the value in Israel's technology businesses and brought it to you, if my memory serves me. That's also the reason why we had such a fucking appalling result today. Because Jack wasn't there to hold their hands, Peter. I mean, when are you going to wake up to the fact the boy is good, Peter? And he's got you chasing your tail, hasn't he? Just leave him to me, I will get him back on side."

The voicebox on the table bleeped twice. Peter picked up the phone and listened, his eyes narrowing.

"Well, Lane, Benjamin has some info for us apparently. You okay with him joining our happy little meeting?"

"Yes, okay, get him in. Let's hear what the little shit has to say."

A moment later Benjamin Small entered the boardroom, his file and palm pressed into his chest as if he was carrying the world's greatest secret. "Lane, Peter," he began in typical, slimy corporate fashion. "You would both be surprised to know I saw Jack drinking cocktails in Lola's twenty minutes before our lunch meeting with the Israelis. Didn't you say Annie said he was out of town for the day, Lane? Well, I can confirm he wasn't, not today at least."

"You really are a brown noser, do you know that, Ben?" commented Lane as he adjusted his seat.

"Sorry, Lane," said Ben, visibly taken aback. "I thought you would appreciate that intel, I mean, he was supposed to be . . . ."

"Yes, Ben, we are all aware of where he was supposed to be, but he wasn't, was he, and there's nothing you can do about it now. Also, Ben, I'm intrigued about why you didn't remind Jack – I mean, if you were there and all. Maybe he forgot. I bet you were thrilled to be able to catch him out and report in, eh? Well, the laugh's on you, I guess."

"No, Lane," growled Peter, annoyed by Lane's assault on his chief financier. "The laugh's on you, Lane, because you are the CEO and will have to explain this cluster-fuck to the board. I hope for your sake, Lane, and for the good of KLS you reign in your boy or it could well be your head on the block, and mine."

"Not to mention yours too, Benjamin! How ironic. Ha, ha," replied Lane, a perverse glint in his eyes.

"No, gentlemen, I don't think it will come to that. I have just the incentive to keep young Jack in check. You see, unlike the rest of you, he actually gives a shit about one of our investments; I mean really gives a shit, beyond capital profits. Yes, Jack needs to build this Microstem deal, he really believes in it. He wouldn't want anything to happen to that business. You see Peter, Microstem, well now, that really is his baby . . . isn't it?"

★ ★ ★

Jack decided to keep his cellphone off for Annie's sake more than anything else. If she couldn't get hold of him she was in the clear, and besides, he didn't want to ruin his mood with KLS bullshit. Jack walked downtown via Paragon, the outdoor outfitters, on 19th and Madison. He climbed the stairs to the second floor and checked out the new line in GoreTex jackets, down salopets and wind-suits for the forthcoming trip. He collected the new North Face and Patagonia catalogs and tried out two full expedition systems. Jim would need all the equipment lists to make his extensive orders, and anyway, Jack enjoyed looking at new kit. There was nothing more enjoyable, since it was not only justifiable, good kit was essential for his safety and the overall success of the trip.

Before leaving he looked at the technical equipment displayed in glass cabinets at the checkout counter and spotted a new programmable Global Positioning System with updated global mapping software. On Sredny they would be north of the magnetic Pole and would need GPS over a compass. He had had experience of navigating in the Arctic with a compass before, and the complexities of the geographic offset required to make a correct bearing were just too much of a drag. He bought the best one in the store, plus a beautiful custom pocketknife with a cream and green, fossilized mammoth bark ivory handle. Jack had always liked knives, and a solid pocketknife that could be opened with one hand was essential when dealing with frozen ropes and tangled dog-teams at sub-zero temperatures.

Rather than walk around town with his new-found literature, Jack decided to pop in on Jim and get sorted out for the evening ahead. Anyhow he needed to tell someone about his amazing lunch, and Jim would be green! Jim was finishing off a lunch meeting himself in his regular hangout, Café Noir. The two talked about the trip and all the technical kit needed. Jim planned over the weekend to put together a full inventory of non-shippables for Mikaela to fax to Viktor: dogs, harnesses, sleds, walled tents and the approximate weights for the helicopters which would drop and pick up the three of them after the trip ended. There was one main problem: team member number three, Bob Anders.

Jim had been tasked with getting Bob on board but as yet had not been able to pin him down to a firm commitment. Bob's role in the trip would be critical for a number of reasons, none more prevalent than the overall safety of traveling over the ice and crevassed sections of glacier at the end of the trip. Three people ensured the possibility at least of pulling a team member from a lead by acting as a securing belay if the sled and dogs were to fall through into the freezing sea. Bob, Jim and Jack had made most of their previous expeditions together since their early trips to the backwoods in Minnesota, and there was no way either Jack or Jim wished to change a winning combination. Besides, Bob was so capable, so calm. As nothing was broken, why fix it?

"Jim, give me his cell number, I'm not having Bob passing up on this one. I mean, it's a no brainer, isn't it? I'm paying and all he has to do is get a pink ticket from the wife and turn up."

The phone rang and connected to Bob's voicemail. Jack left an abusive message accompanied with a spattering of derisory remarks from Jim. Jack ordered a round of drinks and got to the task of looking at departure dates, ice conditions and ambient temperatures.

★ ★ ★

Unlike Jack and Jim, Bob was happily married with a beautiful three-year-old daughter and another one on the way. Teresa had never had a problem with him going away with the boys, but she couldn't lie about the fact that she had been relieved their trips had slowed down of late due to Jack's pressing work commitments. Inspired by Jack joining KLS, Bob had moved to the city in 1996, but Aslop's New York did not prove to be quite the "cash-cow" that KLS had been for his friend. In fact, Bob had fallen into a bit of a rut with Aslop's, missing out on two promotions in just eighteen months.

Traditionally Bob had taken a long-term view of the market and remained cynical of the high-tech sector, probably to his detriment in the current climate, but he was relatively content to offset any disaffection with the current trends and his conservative firm with a heightened passion for his young family. Bob was, as far as bankers go, relatively content with his lot and managed his stress well with a hard fitness regime that gave his long week a manageable structure. For the most part, Bob enjoyed his life and earned good money. In a sense he was glad not to have the hectic lifestyle of a Wall Street high flier, being acutely aware of how difficult it would be to spend time with his family. Most of his friends at Morgan Stanley, Goldman and Lehman Brothers only saw their kids on Saturdays and Sundays, their traditional 6:30am to 7:30pm working weeks ruling out any possibility of spending quality time with them. Bob managed to organize his client meetings around a later start and he often managed to get home to his downtown apartment in the afternoons to make calls and send emails. It was a matter of priority and a certain lifestyle. Unlike Jack,

Bob was in no hurry to retire by forty; fifty-five would suit him fine, so long as he had time to enjoy watching his children grow up and get into the wilderness for a yearly trip with the boys.

★ ★ ★

By mid-afternoon Bob was organizing his desk for the week ahead, having just completed the numbers on an internal memo. As he left his office he switched his phone on to let Teresa know he'd be back early. Before he could complete the call his cellphone vibrated into life. Bob smiled as he listened to Jack's message and thought he might pay an impromptu visit to the boys, a quick cocktail to celebrate yet another uneventful week at Aslop's. Jack and Jim were into their fourth tall one, still deep in conversation about the ins and outs of wearing drysuits for the duration of the sea ice section of the trip.

"All right boys, which one of you two thinks he knows about sea ice?" barked Bob from across the bar.

Jack and Jim looked up to see Bob laughing at them.

"So you've decided to come and see your friends, have you, you old bastard? Get over here! Louise, a whiskey sour for the guy with a libido problem!" shouted Jim to the waitress.

"Hey, a bit more respect when addressing the silverback, okay? At least I'm not firing blanks – you two still practicing, are you? You pair of seedless fuckers!"

The three men cracked up laughing and gave each other a hug.

"How's it going, Jack?" asked Bob. "What are you doing hanging out with this reprobate on a Friday? I thought you KLS guys weren't let out till after dark!"

"Nah, I've taken a bit of a break this week, Bob. It all went off with the CEO. Think I might have gone a bit too far and missed a big lunch today with the guys from Mediotech. Still, that's all boring crap. Now check this out. Guess what I got given today?"

"Go on, let me guess, another dose of the clap," responded Bob.

"A blow off Mikaela," joined in Jim.

"Both wrong, boys. Hans Groub, you know, the big art dealer. Well, we did lunch today, hence why I blew out the Mediotech meet. Anyhow, the guy gave me Beuys' sled, man, he fucking gave it to me!"

"What, for the trip? That's saved you a bit of cash," said Bob.

"No, dick-wad! *The* sled! You remember that artist I collect, Beuys, the one I told you about, Bob, who crashed during the war?"

"No way, man!" chipped in Jim, his mouth agape. "You're joking! That dude doesn't give anything to anyone, dude. Word has it he's the wealthiest and toughest dealer on the east coast."

"Straight up, man, it's fucking mine."

"So what you going to do with it? What good is a sled if you can't use it?" said Bob.

"Use it? It's fucking art, Bob, seriously important sculptural art. I'm going to put it in my apartment with a fucking huge alarm around it and enjoy it, man. It's awesome, dude!"

"It is, actually, Bob. I mean, where have you been? Doesn't your wife let you out, Bob?" said Jim.

"Well, actually, boys, wrong again. She's fine with me going on the trip but I can't leave till March the first, is that cool? I'm owed some time off but I have a deal to put to bed this next month."

"Fucking cool, Bob. You're not shitting us?"

"No way man, straight up, I'm on."

"Okay, Bob, here's the deal . . ."

Jack and Jim talked Bob through the logistics and trip plan. Mikaela and Natasha arrived a couple of hours later. Soon they were all very drunk, due mainly to Mikaela's insistence that if she was going to organize for Viktor to be their guide on Sredny, they would all need some training in Viktor's favorite hobby – shooting vodka. Bob cut away at 9pm, staggering to a cab and on to his wife. Ten minutes later he arrived, somewhat sheepishly, home. Teresa took one look at his expression and shook her head.

"Well, I guess the trip's a goer then." She knew him too well.

★ ★ ★

Jack felt more relaxed than he had done in years. He had just had the most extraordinary meeting of his life, he was out with his best friends, he was off on another trip, KLS were temporarily off his back and, more importantly, he realized he was getting more and more into Mikaela. That night, Jack, having learned from his experiences earlier in the week, didn't get too drunk. He had learned it was quite impossible to out-drink Mikaela and he wasn't going to miss out on the sex this time around. She was so hot, in a way he hadn't experienced before, a different feel, a different smell, and an active, aggressive partner whose sex drive was probably greater than his own. They made love all night and after a brief sleep Jack lay awake just happy to look at her body, feel her warmth and her breath on his chest, caressing her slim back with his fingers.

Jack couldn't remember the last time he had been happy to share space and sleep with a lover. Probably not since Lucy in Alaska, and certainly not with the majority of the bimbos he had dated since arriving in the city. Mikaela was different, though, she was from another place, another culture, far removed from the stuffy pretensions of the girls on Wall Street. She was so alien, unsafe and wild. Sure, her looks helped, she was gorgeous, but there was something about her nature that was untamed and didn't want to be either. Mikaela had hunger, real attitude, but she was so hot too. Jack would have to keep a check on this one. He didn't need anyone getting too close, but despite his rules he couldn't help himself. She was starting to get under his skin, he could feel it.

Saturday slipped lazily into Sunday. Jack made a point of keeping his phone switched off and his mind free of KLS-related stress. On Sunday afternoon, after three previous attempts, Mikaela finally talked to her brother on Sredny.

"Very good news. Brave polar explorers most welcome. I will organize everything," came Viktor's upbeat reply.

They were on their way. Jack was ecstatic and called both Jim and Bob. That night Jack took Mikaela out for dinner to celebrate. Sitting alone together at the table, he proposed a toast: "To you, baby. Thanks so much for organizing all this with Viktor. It's quite unreal really, to be getting out on to the ice with such a guy. I mean, he's a legend, Mikaela. Until the other day, well, I had no idea, the polar ocean, in one season..."

Mikaela, a serious look on her face, cut Jack short. "Jack, baby, he's my big brother, that's all. Sure, when he was younger he made the news with all his expeditions, but now, Jack, he's just the sweetest guy. He will make it safe for you but look out for him too, Jack, okay? He's not quite the man he used to be. The problem is with you men, you don't always see yourselves as you really are and he doesn't see what I do, Jack. He's too close to it, the danger, and he's not getting any younger – he's what, fifty-five now, crazy fit, but still, he's fifty-five. That's old in Siberia, Jack, real old."

Jack could sense Mikaela's concern; she clearly didn't like the ice or the cold, but he also saw her fear, the fear of losing a loved one. Jack smiled and took her by the hand, his large hands cupping her cool, long fingers.

"Baby, listen, it will be fine, okay, I promise. It's no big deal, two weeks is all, trust me, Viktor's the man, okay, that's a fact."

"I just hope you find what you are looking for and come back to me safely, Jack. Come back to me safely, okay?"

Jack smiled back fondly but in the back of his mind he was concerned about Mikaela's words, "I hope you find what you're looking for..." Deep down he knew what she meant and her astuteness bothered him. Beautiful, intelligent and perceptive, now that really was a challenge.

★ ★ ★

Jack woke early on Monday and decided to call Annie. The events of the past few days had helped recharge his batteries and anyhow he knew he couldn't dodge the inevitable showdown with Lane any longer.

As expected, the news from the front wasn't good. Annie briefed him about the Friday meeting and that she had learned from Lane's PA about his meeting at Lola's. In a sense he was glad he had been rumbled. It would make his position clear to the board. He had a life outside of KLS and so long as he did they couldn't get to him, or so he thought. Jack arrived at the office a tad after eight. The last thing he wanted was a summons. After all, he wasn't a kid and Lane's fatherly tone was beginning to wear thin. Jack knocked on Lane's office door.

"Come in, Jack."

Jack walked up to Lane, looking him straight in the eyes, and held out his hand. They shook and he sat down, this time next to Lane. There was no point in shouting at each other from opposite ends of the large desk.

"So, Jack, as I'm sure you have heard by now, we had a cluster-fuck of a meeting with the Israelis."

"Yes, Annie briefed me."

"You really dropped me in it with Peter, Jack. I mean, he had briefed you on the importance of Friday a week ago."

"Yes, Lane, but we agreed I was to take some time."

"Yes, Jack, a few days, not the whole week."

"Listen, Lane. I missed the meeting because I had another appointment I couldn't cancel, okay, that's the facts. If you were badly prepared, well that's not my call. You must have known I wouldn't be there."

"Actually, Jack, I thought you would have made it out of loyalty and professional responsibility. You are still a direct..."

"Don't give me that, Lane. If you missed the point of our heated debate last week, let me remind you. I really was serious about being unsure of my position."

"Yes, well, have you reached any further conclusions, this matter aside?"

"Well, actually I have, Lane. I've thought about it a lot as it goes, and without doing anything 'rash', to quote you, I've realized I need a break to recharge the batteries, I guess. I want to get away for a few weeks or so . . ."

"A few weeks! Jack, do you know what is happening at the moment? We're trying to take Microstem and the other pre-IPO businesses on a roadshow. We're trying to add shareholder value, including our own holdings. We're trying to make money here, Jack, remember that. The next few weeks are critical in preparing the sales team and I want you to lead this push, Jack. I really don't see how you can realistically take a break now."

"Well, Lane, I need to do this now. Look, I can get Microstem straight over the next month and then disappear for a couple of weeks. I'll be back late March to walk them out in April. I think I spelt it out that Microstem need more time to refine their drug tests, so marching them out April and May should give us more time to have the initial trials of the neuro-stimulator. Before I go I'll brief their CFO and our corporate finance to the format of the funding docs and the detail of the executive summary. It will leave us ample time, Lane. And there is one more thing: I want to take Microstem out myself. I am happy for corporate finance to conduct the model and line up the meetings but I want in on their pitch and I don't want Small anywhere near it, Lane. I want him off."

Lane studied Jack intently. He was biting, Lane knew that, but this time his timelines were badly wrong. He needed to lay down the law but at the same time he needed to keep Jack committed. Lane sat back in his chair and breathed out deeply.

"Okay, Jack, here it is. You've got Microstem. As per our last meeting, I'll agree to funding from our coffers until April thirtieth guaranteed. Small is off the project but Peter will take an enlarged role from corporate finance and oversee deal structure. If he chooses Small as his number two that's his prerogative but I'll ensure Small is out of the trenches and has no contact personally with the business. You will report directly to me on all issues, okay? We have a very important shareholders' meet on the fifteenth of March and I need you to present on Microstem. That will require you taking at least a week to prepare the documentation and get Microstem all cued up. De Blevis should also make an appearance but the timing and his role I will leave to you. So as long as you set the timeline and deliverables with Microstem before you go, I am happy for you to take leave as of Wednesday. By my calculation that gives you about a month to get your head focused and geared for the push. By the way, Jack, that's the deal, no negotiation, okay? That meeting is firm, no changes."

Jack knew he was on the spot. The offer to run the Microstem deal was on the button, he couldn't have hoped for more, but the main problem was the timing. Not the Microstem schedule – that would be a breeze. The departure times meant Bob would be off the trip. If Jack made the trip after the fundraising, the sea ice would be melting and spring-summer would have taken its hold of the high Arctic. Jim would be no problem, the dude was super-flexible, but Bob the family man was not. He had made that clear due to work commitments until the first of March. If Bob was to come he would have to postpone the trip for a year and he knew he just couldn't handle that. He needed this trip. He had to do it for himself, if for no more reason than to take him out of his tired corporate existence, and now Lane had handed it to him on a plate. Fuck it! he rationalized. Bob could make it next year, and anyhow Bob didn't need it like he did, not now at least.

"It's a deal, Lane," replied Jack after collecting his thoughts. "I really appreciate you trusting me on Microstem. I won't let you down."

"I know you won't, Jack. Enjoy your break ... where are you planning to go? I bet you've already bought the tickets!"

"Not quite Lane, but yes, I have a pretty good idea. Off to the Arctic, a dog-sled trip, you know me."

"What's wrong with sun and surf? Well, whatever turns you on I guess, just make sure the Keyman insurance covers it. I don't need you getting hurt out there, Jack. We've got a lot to do when you get back!"

"Don't worry about me, Lane. I'm always okay, you know that." A hint of arrogance in his voice.

"Well, good luck, Jack. Now get the hell out of here, some of us have work to do, like getting the Israelis back on board!"

Jack walked out of the office. Turning the corner he jumped and did a slam-dunk in the air.

"Yessss!" he shouted to himself and reaching for his phone he pressed Jim's cell on speed dial.

"Pack your bags, Jim ... we're going sooner than you think."

Jack had to hold the phone away from his head as Jim was heard howling down the phone, then there was a brief silence. "That's awesome, dude, you jammy fucker. But one problem, Jack, what about Bob?"

"I'll deal with it, Jim, I know he'll understand. I mean, he's got a family; what have we got to lose, nothing, right?"

There was a brief silence. "Only our lives," replied Jim soberly.

"Get a grip, Jim," scoffed Jack. "We've never had a drama yet, and I don't intend to start now!"

Chapter 5

Before Jack could get away he needed to tie up some loose ends, and top of his list of priorities was Bob. It felt wrong to do the trip without him, especially after all his help at Aslop's. Jack owed Bob big time. The problem was Jack had no options, it was either go now or postpone for a year, and he couldn't cope with that, not now he had geared himself up for it. Bob would understand, he always did, but still, he was not looking forward to the phone call. Contemplating Bob's despondent response, Jack began to dial.

"Bob, it's Jack, how's it going?"

"Cool, Jack, what's up?"

Jack hesitated and Bob knew immediately from the silence.

"Listen, dude . . . I'm afraid we've got a problem. It's KLS, they need me to . . ."

"Hey, Jack, it's the dates, right? You've got a problem with KLS? Listen Jack, whatever the reason, I understand, dude, fuck, this trip's your baby, man. I was just on for the ride."

"But Bob, let me explain. I . . ." Bob cut Jack off. He already knew, from his friend's tone, he knew him so well, and although he had so wanted to go on this trip he also knew there would be no changing Jack's mind. When Jack wanted something he went for it. Bob had noticed that more and more with his friend, since working at KLS, the power thing. On the whole it didn't bother him, after all, he had made his decisions, got married early, had the babies . . . but still, it was a shame. He decided to put a brave face on it.

"Seriously, Jack, listen, everything's fine. Teresa will be really excited, so I get some brownie points there, big style. We'll get away in the summer, anyhow. Really, Jack, I knew we might have problems due to my inflexibility in Feb. We'll do another one soon. To be honest I was pleased with the offer, I know being attached doesn't help when these things come up at such short notice."

"Fuck, Bob, don't be stupid man, you *are* the team. You're always invited, you know that. Well, you sure have made this easy on me." The relief was evident in Jack's voice.

"No sweat, Jack. Listen, just one thing, make sure you listen to this Sedov guy. I've done the research on him. You'll be in great hands, just look out for Jim, okay, look out for each other. You shouldn't do this without a third man, just in case."

"No way, Bob, absolutely, no, we're a three or it's a no go. Hey, we can't do it without Viktor anyhow, he's got all the dogs, all the logistics ..."

"Well, Jack, you take care, man. Give us a call when you get back, I can't wait to see the photos..."

"You're on," replied Jack.

"Expedition debrief on me. Caviar, vodka, the works, that's a promise, okay!"

Bob was such a bud. Jack knew that despite his kind words he would be destroyed by the news. But Bob had taken it so well; that's a true friend, he thought.

★ ★ ★

Jack spent most of Tuesday and Wednesday going through the plan with Jim and liaising all the logistics long-distance with Viktor. The man was completely unfazed by their new start dates. From the Russian side all would be arranged. They would arrive on the seventh of February, the following Monday. Jack and Jim had a week to make it all happen.

Jack's next call was with De Blevis. He spent all Thursday with the Microstem team. At first De Blevis was concerned about the workload needed for the March fifteenth meeting, but with Jack's two top analysts working on the model, Peter lining up the meetings and Annie in coordination and support, Jack assured him all would be fine. He wanted De Blevis to concentrate on the proof of concept. It was, after all, the medical trials and test results with all relevant statistics that would provide the KLS team with the potential assets to take the business to the next round. Although KLS were now actively looking for a partial exit from the investment, Jack knew that they would continue support only if another investor could shoulder a portion of the hefty responsibility of future funding. Jack was convinced that with the Microstem team on cue and the successful trials results presented personally by De Blevis, it would be an easy sell.

Next came Groub. Jack had received a note from his assistant, Helena, setting out the delivery times for the sled. He put her in touch with the apartment concierge and alerted his insurers of the new arrival. By Friday all would be covered. The sled would be installed by Groub's shipping firm on Friday at 3pm. He couldn't wait. As Jack was about to leave his apartment his cellphone rang.

"Jack, it's Hans. Helena told me everything is arranged for Friday's delivery."

"Yes, Hans, it's all sorted. I'm so excited."

"I can imagine, in fact I know exactly how you feel. Listen, I was wondering if you would like to join me for dinner with some rather special clients. Sunday night, about eight pm?"

"That sounds fantastic, Hans, only there's just one problem. I leave for this Arctic trip on Monday and I was planning on spending the evening with my new lady."

"Please bring her. I would love to meet her, she's most welcome."

"Really, Hans? Are you sure?"

"Eight pm, then. I'll have my driver pick you both up. Say seven thirty, okay?"

★ ★ ★

Jack arrived at Mikaela's apartment shortly after dark. She had had a casting that day and was getting out of the tub when Jack pressed the bell to her apartment. Mikaela buzzed him up. With only a few days to go before his trip, Jack found himself wanting to spend as much time with Mikaela as he could. Something had come over him, a strange feeling of impending doubt and anxiety about his imminent departure and a sense of forthcoming loss being far away from her. It wasn't that he had never fallen for a girl before. There was Lucy, but by the end that had got so safe, so conventional and so very predictable.

Mikaela, though, was different. For starters he hardly knew her. Lucy, Jesus, he had dated her for over three years. Now he just wanted to be with Mikaela – there was nothing awkward about it, it felt so natural. Jack didn't even feel the need to talk all the time, to push the conversation; it was as if he had always known her. But the whole relationship was no more than a few weeks old, the honeymoon beginning of something new. Admittedly Jack had gone in hard that first night with Jim in the gallery. Sure he had been attracted to her, she was drop-dead, but if he was brutally honest, right then and there she was a lay, a hot as hell lay. How wrong he had been, judging her like that, "Russian teen", a good fuck. Whatever he had first felt, he didn't feel it any more. And it was more than the Viktor connection, more than just using her for the sex or contacts for the trip. He even surprised himself, and Jim for that matter, because he could feel himself slipping, all his old rules beginning to crack. He was falling for her; her intuition, her inability to tell a lie, her passion, her looks, the whole package and that ass. She was too much, and here he was leaving her for more than a month to sit in a small tent on ice with Jim and a crazy Russian. The absurdity of that final thought made him laugh; what a prick he was.

As Jack took the elevator to the fifth floor he had a crazy idea. Why didn't he take her along, at least as far as the meteorological station? She could see Viktor and his family again and wait for him to return. At the end of his trip they could have a romantic few days together in St Petersburg. He would find out, away from the city, away from his world, if his feelings for Mikaela were genuine. They would have shared something, got away from it all, traveled, argued, laughed; besides, she would love it, seeing her brother again.

Mikaela was waiting for Jack on the landing. She was dressed in a large white dressing-gown, her hair wrapped in a toweling turban. As Jack got out of the elevator she gave him a wicked smile.

"So you have come to rescue me from my terrible day. I swear, I cannot bear another casting in this city, not ever, it was so shit. They gave the part to this horrible short blonde. I mean, what do I look like to you, am I not beautiful enough?" Mikaela opened the dressing gown and stood naked before him.

"You are sensational, baby, and if I have it my way you never need to do another casting again. Now get inside before you get a chill."

They kissed tenderly in the hall to her apartment and Mikaela jumped up and wrapped her long legs around Jack's waist as he walked her through to the bedroom. He laid her gently on the duvet and rolled over next to her, taking her passionately in his arms.

"Darling, I have an invitation for us both. Dinner with my friend the art dealer Hans Groub on Sunday night."

"But Jack, that is your last night before you go to Viktor. I wanted you all to myself."

"Honey, it will be great. Hans has some very interesting clients he wants us to meet and besides, he is very excited to meet you."

"Whatever you want, Jack, but make sure you save midnight onwards for me, okay? I want a good few hours to give you a real goodbye present."

"Goodbye, I do hope not. I think you mean bon voyage."

"What is 'bon voyage'? Anyway, the facts are clear. You are leaving me for a cold, dark place; I will never forgive you!"

Mikaela, play-sulking, turned away from Jack.

"Well, baby, that is what I was just thinking about. How would you like to come with me, to Sredny? I'll pay for everything, you can stay at the met station with Viktor's family and when we get back we'll go for a long weekend to St Petersburg together."

Mikaela looked at Jack, shocked. "You kid me right? I thought you just want me for my body! You really want me to come with you?"

"Seriously Mikaela, I would love it, and Jim could bring Natasha too."

"Don't play with me, Jack," replied Mikaela, tears welling in her eyes. "You really want me to come too?"

"Darling, look at me, do I look like I'm joking?" Jack pulled a stupid face and took her in his arms. "I want you to come with me, okay, I really do. What do you think?"

★ ★ ★

When Jim heard the news, he was less than enthusiastic. Going on expeditions had, until Jack's recent spontaneous outburst, been all about getting away from everything, especially his overly complicated love life. Now with Mikaela and Natasha so completely over-excited, he was on the spot. The Russian element to the trip had got him excited for a number of reasons, including of course the opportunity to party and maybe pick up some chicks in St Petersburg. Not only had he heard crazy stories about the over-abundance of willing ladies, he had always loved discovering the wild and steamy side of a foreign city, unhampered by a clinging woman. He wasn't going to have any of it. If Jack wanted to screw his time in the pussy capital of Eastern Europe that was his problem, but he, Jim, was not going to be dragged into it.

After a heated debate with Jack on the phone he made his position clear. Mikaela was welcome but Natasha was not. Furthermore, Natasha was officially dumped. Jim felt this would make the situation clearer. It did, and with it Jim broke yet another heart. As for Jack, he was unfazed by Jim's reaction and totally unrepentant. Anyhow, he reasoned, it was better not to lead Natasha along. He knew that Mikaela was open-minded enough to enjoy some R&R with the boys and he also knew she would prove a critical link in guiding Jim to the best clubs. A local was essential in getting the most bangs for your buck and so their first argument of the expedition was solved. Mikaela would have a role in the trip after all. On reflection, Jim was ecstatic!

By Sunday afternoon both Jim and Jack were packed. Viktor had helped push the visas through at the Russian Embassy in Washington and all was set at the Russian end. Jack and Mikaela hardly left the apartment except to eat the occasional meal. The fact that Mikaela was now coming on the trip had done nothing to abate Jack's desire to spend time alone with her. If anything her presence was like a drug: the more he got, the more he wanted. Jack had sometimes wondered over the past few years if he had been missing out by not having a regular girl, someone waiting for him at home. All the other directors were either married, had long-term girlfriends, mistresses or both. The hypocrisy of the affairs always bothered him. He couldn't see the point. Why not keep it simple and remain unattached? That way no one got hurt, and to Jack that had seemed the most logical path. He didn't need the commitment, or so he thought, or the hassle; he was far too selfish for that. Getting out on the town with Jim or some of his more laid-back colleagues at KLS was how Jack liked it, until now, until Mikaela. The thought of being without her, dare he admit it, would have left him feeling empty and unfulfilled. How shit changes, he thought. He owed Jim for this one, for sure.

The sled had arrived on time and by Saturday morning it had taken pride of place in Jack's living room. It rested inert inside its perspex case, homage to a bygone age. When not packing his bags or making love, Jack stood naked admiring his new present. It hardly seemed real to actually own the original, and he wasn't afraid to admit that it looked slightly out of place in his apartment. To say the sled dominated the room was an understatement. It overwhelmed the apartment and seemed to emit a powerful energy, a force Jack couldn't begin to comprehend.

Turning up for dinner at Groub's empty-handed bothered Jack. He had just been given the most amazing gift and Jack felt he needed to repay the compliment, if nothing more than as a gesture of his gratitude. But what to give the man with everything? After several moments contemplating this problem he had an idea. A year earlier Jack had acquired his first Beuys, the small drawing called *Stag with Human Head*. At $35,000 he had paid over the odds in a private sale, but it was perfect and he had wanted it. The only problem was it was now the weekend and it lived in his office downtown at KLS. Getting into the office was not such a problem, he had his ID card and digital key and besides, the office was open 24/7. It was more that there wasn't anywhere he would rather be less, especially the day before his trip. It was one of those strange, hard to define feelings he occasionally got, similar to the feeling he would have returning to university during the summer vacation. Still, he rationalized, it would mean the world to Groub, and therefore he decided it was definitely worth the effort.

Mikaela was lying on the couch watching a movie when Jack appeared dressed in his tracksuit and sneakers.

"Where do you think you are going?" she chided.

"For a quick run, baby. I will be back by five and then we can get ready for dinner together. Maybe you could bathe me!"

"Well, hurry back, Jack, I'll miss you. Run quickly!"

It was dark and cold outside, and as he began to jog Jack's breath came in short, misty plumes. He ran along the southern perimeter of Central Park, crossing to Seventh Avenue at Columbus Circle and 68th Street. He ran with the traffic until 14th Street and then cut through the West Village to West Broadway and on to Canal. He hadn't done this run for over five months and it felt good to stretch his legs again, especially in light of the fact that he was going to be cooped up on planes for the next few days. Normally he would spend months preparing for a trip but he felt confident about his fitness, especially since he had a week in Khatanga and Sredny to tune in and acclimatize before they left for the ice pack. Jack had always been good in the cold, and the few extra pounds he had been carrying for the last few months would come in useful working on the sleds ten hours a day, at minus 30.

Three-quarters of an hour later, he arrived, sweating heavily, at the KLS building. Abraham was on duty again.

"Mr Wyler, what a surprise. Popping in for a bit of weekend work?"

"No, Abe, just have to collect something for a trip on Monday. I won't be long." Jack really didn't feel like elaborating, especially since Abe could talk and Jack wanted to keep his movements as low key as possible.

"Take as much time as you like, it will be peaceful on the ninth floor, no one else is in. Guess everyone had a big night on Saturday!" Abe laughed.

"Guess so. Well, yes, must hurry."

The ninth floor felt strangely quiet as Jack walked through the corridor leading to his office. All the lights were on but the office felt like a different place without all the noise of his team going about their daily work. No Annie to keep him in check, no Lane to report in to and no Benjamin Small to piss him off. What a perfect working environment, he mused. Jack had to admit he preferred it. It was a good thing he was going away.

The Beuys drawing hung to the left of his desk, one of the four recent acquisitions that for Jack had symbolized the direction of his collection of originals, small and wonderful. The Tapies, Twombly and Basquiat would need to be rehung now the Beuys was gone, but the works still looked magnificent. Jack pulled open his bottom desk drawer and took out the piece of carefully folded tissue paper that he used to keep his unframed drawings and prints in. He wrapped the small work in the tissue and fastened the neat package with a single strip of tape. Emptying a card file from his desk, he placed the drawing in the file and turned to switch off his desk light. Sitting in the dim twilight of the darkened office, Jack closed his eyes. It felt good to have a few seconds alone, away from the three pillars in his life, his newfound feelings for Mikaela, his best friend Jim and the professional engine that fueled and constituted his work at KLS. Here he was sitting in the only neutral space he could find and quite coincidentally it happened to be his office, the one place that for over two years now had driven him to near distraction. The irony was not lost on Jack. He began to relax.

He was outside again, running, jumping free, but the streets were far behind him and the trees were all around. He wasn't scared though, just glad for the moment of time away. In the forest he heard feet rustling, the sound of footsteps treading heavily through thick crusted snow. There was another sound too, the shushing of a sled, laden down, cutting deep tracks. To Jack the sound was unmistakable, a sound from his childhood, and then it was gone and the footsteps were lighter now and barely audible. The forest began to melt away.

Jack slowly opened his eyes, and as he got up from his comfortable leather chair he heard a sound, the faint padding of footsteps walking away from him down the passage.

"Abe, is that you?" he called.

There was silence. How strange, thought Jack, remembering that no one else was supposed to be on the ninth floor. He picked up his ID card and the file and walked down the passage to the elevator; there was no one to be seen. Jack pressed the large orange button and waited. He must have been hearing things, he concluded, the heating system, or maybe the elevator shaft or something, large offices can be noisy places. He stepped into the elevator and pressed the button to arrive at the ground floor, the doors closing to the digitized sound of a bell. Jack watched the floor numbers, 9, 8, 7, 6 ... and felt a slight churning in his stomach as the elevator glided downwards. Checking his appearance in the mirror, he immediately froze. The mirror to his left was slightly fogged, and crudely drawn into the misty glass was an algebraic equation, "K=K", followed by the words, "We walk this way." The interior of the elevator began to close in on Jack, the faulty, flickering diffused halogen bulb in the ceiling adding to the claustrophobia he was feeling. The single small mirror made the elevator feel so much smaller than it really was, and Jack felt his head spinning. Staggering back against the metal rail, he held on, his knuckles whitening, as he waited for the elevator to arrive at ground: 5, 4, 3, 2 ... the LED numbers flashed slowly in succession as it moved ever downwards.

Finally the doors opened and Jack jumped out and raced across the checkered marble lobby to where Abe was sitting at the central reception desk. He was sweating profusely now, and Abe jumped back when he saw the crazed look in his eyes.

"Abe, who the fuck just came down in the elevator? I mean, that shit has just really freaked me out!"

"Now hold on, Mr Wyler. I haven't any idea what you are talking about, honestly. There is no one on either the seventh, eighth or ninth floor today and I haven't seen anyone come out of that elevator for over two hours."

"But that's crazy, Abe. Are you sure? Listen, some fucker just scared me half to death by writing a message on the mirror in the elevator. I heard their footsteps from my office on the ninth floor."

"I am afraid that just isn't so, Mr Wyler. As I said..."

"Listen Abe, I'm not arguing with you. Come over here and take a look for yourself."

Abe hurried over with Jack to the elevator. The mirrored walls were crystal clear, no sign of any moisture or condensation anywhere to be found.

"Mr Wyler, if I may be so bold, maybe you yourself leaned or breathed on the glass. You were sweating pretty heavily when you arrived."

Jack, head hung low, just stood silent for a while. This was all getting a bit much for him.

"No, Abe, I really did see that writing ... but yes," he said, taking a deep breath, "maybe you are right. Maybe I am a bit whacked out. It's just I know what I saw..."

"Listen, Mr Wyler, why don't I get you a taxi? You probably pushed it a bit on your run. Just take a seat and I'll get you a glass of water."

"Thanks, Abe, yes, a drink would be great. Maybe I'm coming down with something. It's just I could have sworn I saw . . ."

Ten minutes later Jack's cab arrived. He thanked Abe, took the file under his arm and walked to the taxi. He slumped into the back seat and nodded appreciatively at the big doorman, who waved him off.

"Got to have too much money to imagine shit like that. There's another one headed for a burnout!" Abe shook his head, smiled and ambled back to his desk.

★ ★ ★

The journey uptown took forever and Jack had time to compose himself before arriving back at the apartment. The last thing he wanted to do was frighten Mikaela. Rationalizing, Jack concluded that he was probably a bit dehydrated from his run. He had also zoned out for a while in the office, so maybe he had got it confused, maybe he had imagined it all. But this was different, there was a concrete message, he could still see the letters "K = K We go this way." A rhyme of sorts, but what did it mean? If the experience had been imagined and was in fact a part of his earlier dream, this was a first. Never before had Jack experienced such lucid detail and never in the form of words. No, this really had to have happened. He wondered if he should mention his afternoon's experience to Groub; then again, maybe not. He definitely needed a bath though, a relaxing, long soak. He needed a bath with the lovely Mikaela and a good meal. Everything would be just fine after that. There had to be a logical explanation, there always was.

Less than an hour after his experience in the elevator, Jack sat somewhat on edge, dressed in a simple grey suit, studying the sled. The felt roll sat to the left of the five wooden seat slats, firmly bound with an oiled leather strap like an emergency blanket on a stretcher, the tin of fat and an old pressed metal flashlight precisely positioned for use on the journey. The sled was ready, ready for a trip it would never make, a survival situation it would never encounter. How ironic, how sad, thought Jack. He checked his watch. It was 7:25. He shouted for Mikaela.

"Darling, are you all set?" A hint of tension in his voice.

"Calm down, baby. What do you think?"

Mikaela stood behind him dressed in a little black number. Her long legs went on forever, the shimmering velvet hugging her full hips and large breasts.

"Wow, you look edible."

"Maybe later, if you are a good boy. Now where is this car?"

The drive uptown took no more than fifteen minutes, the traffic having dissolved into a steady stream of downtown weekend congestion. It had started to rain, a cold biting rain, and Jack was glad to be chauffeured and not have to compete for a cab. It was always such a fight in the rain.

Groub's house at 25 East 73rd Street was built in the grand style, a magnificent example of a post-colonial brownstone. Jack could tell Mikaela was a bit uneasy; she had never been to such a grandiose house in the city. The huge wooden door loomed large and intimidating as Jack rapped the heavy bronze figurine to announce their arrival. Mikaela squeezed Jack's hand and reached over to kiss him on the neck.

"Jack," she whispered, "don't leave me alone tonight, I am not so good with people I don't know, you understand." Jack gently squeezed back in recognition as the door slowly began to open.

Jack and Mikaela were escorted to the first-floor drawing room by an elderly, distinguished butler and were soon seated on a magnificent Harry Paw sofa, sipping chilled vodka martinis. "Herr Groub will be down in a short while. Please let me know if I can get you anything," offered the waiter. Jack smiled politely, while Mikaela took another gulp of martini.

They felt a bit like schoolchildren being taken for tea at a fancy restaurant by their grandparents. The décor of the rooms was sumptuous, antique mainly, and the walls were covered with some of the finest abstract expressionism Jack had ever seen: De Kooning, Pollock and a huge, almost jet black Rothko. It was almost too overpowering, but Jack liked the feel and despite his own modest upbringing felt strangely at home. Besides, so many places were too minimalist these days, too bare and cold. Groub's house radiated color, nostalgia and warmth. The house smelled of history, oil paint, freshly waxed wood, aromatic spices, fine things.

Hans Groub entered the room from a small hidden door to the side of the Rothko and threw up his arms on seeing Jack. Accompanying him were an elegant older-looking couple, probably in their early seventies.

"Jack! And this must be Mikaela. How wonderful to see you both. Jack, she is so beautiful."

The old lady quickly chastised Hans. "Hans, for God's sake, she's blushing. How can you be so rude?"

Groub first made his way to Mikaela and gave her a kiss on both cheeks. "I'm sorry, my dear, I have an eye for beauty, I can't help myself. Thank you for brightening up our evening. And Jack, well, it is great to see you again."

Jack and Hans hugged and then he introduced his friends.

"Mikaela and Jack, may I introduce you to my oldest clients, Nelly and Ingvar Soderstrom. We have been friends now for over...well, shall we say longer than we all choose to remember. Jack, Ingvar is almost as passionate about our mutual friend as we are. Isn't that right, Ingvar?"

"I can only guess we are talking about Beuys. Yes, you keep all the best work for yourself, apart from the elephant – that is mine and whatever happens you will never get your hands on it, not ever."

"Really Ingvar, such venom. Well, we shall see," chided Hans, a glint in his eye. "How rude of me, let's have dinner. Jack has informed me of the trip that you are off on tomorrow, so I will not keep you long, just a quick snack."

Hans led the way through the main hall to a pair of large oak doors. As he reached for the handle one of the waiters opened the doors revealing a massive dining room and a long dining table. The room was less cluttered and had a sparser feel; no paintings adorned the walls, and the only decoration in the entire room sat on a shelf above a simple sandstone fireplace. A small white polar bear, carved from whalebone, stood on its hind legs. It couldn't have been more than ten inches tall but it was the most beautiful carving Jack had ever seen.

The five of them sat grouped together at one end of the table, Jack finding himself between Nelly and Hans. Mikaela sat opposite Nelly with Ingvar to her left. They formed an odd if not cozy group in an altogether massive room. Nelly and Ingvar made a handsome and distinguished couple; both silver-haired, they had the well-kept, bronzed appearance of a man and wife who knew how to enjoy their well-heeled retirement. Fun-loving, sporty and outgoing, they both appeared much younger than they really were.

"Jack, Ingvar was a banker too, many years ago."

"Really, Ingvar, who were you with?"

"In my youth I traded in commodities, but I ended my days in senior management running an investment bank, Klein, Loeb & Silvers. I believe you are familiar with the business."

"Familiar, yes, you could say that, Ingvar, I am an MD."

"Yes, I know, Jack, Hans gave me the lowdown. How are you finding it? How is that old shark Connor treating you?"

"You know Lane?" replied Jack with surprise. "Well, he's just fine. I, on the other hand, as Hans may or may not have informed you, am due a bit of a break. It's been a crazy couple of years."

"Yes, I know. As a shareholder I have enjoyed the recent returns, but Jack, man to man, this massive tech growth, how long can it continue?"

"Well, it's a good point Ingvar, I've been asking myself those same questions recently and it's my job to build that sector. That's part of the problem for me – I am a little concerned we may be due for a downturn."

"It's good to hear you are questioning the whole process, Jack, that's a good thing."

"Process, Ingvar? I am not sure I'm with you."

"Well, that's what it is. It's a game really, you know that. How much can you make? How much can you take? The Lanes of this world are a dying breed, you know. When he first started at KLS it was rumored he would get home at eight pm, put the kids to bed and return to the office. He's had three wives but still he drives that business like a battleship. He's been through two major recessions and he hasn't lost his drive. In my day we had our share of ups and downs but in the fifties and early sixties trading and investment was conducted at a slightly more reasonable pace."

"Yes, Lane is driven, I'll give you that."

"Hans tells us you also have an eye for art."

"Well, I'm a beginner really. But I have to confess I love Beuys, and Basquiat for that matter."

"Beuys was an example to us all. There we were either pretending to be artists" – Ingvar winked at Hans – "or like myself busy trying to buy it all up. From an investment standpoint he was bold enough to challenge and change a lot of things."

As the waiters poured the wine and served the first course, a game terrine, Mikaela, intrigued by the conversation, hesitantly spoke up.

"What did Beuys challenge? I thought this man made things, made sleds, planted trees . . ."

"Yes, he did, my dear, but what he really made was waves. He rattled the art world but not just with 'shock of the new' sensationalism. He went deeper than that. He took them head on, in their souls and in their pockets, so to speak. Well, Jack, let me propose a toast to you both and to my old friends. To us all, to our journey and to the spirit of Herr Beuys."

Jack and Mikaela looked at each other, a bit puzzled. They were both beginning to wonder if they had been invited to some age-old ceremony, a séance for the artist. Mikaela for one had begun to feel slightly uncomfortable.

"So, Jack," continued Hans, "I have a little present for you, something to represent your survival and a token of good luck with your expedition."

"No, Hans, really I think you have given me enough. Anyhow, I have something for you. Mikaela, is it in your bag?"

Mikaela passed the small, framed drawing to Jack.

"How kind, Jack, but please, my gift first."

Groub pressed a small, white buzzer next to him on the table. Within seconds a waiter walked across the room, a short roll under his arm.

"Jack, from me to you. Good luck in the Arctic, my friend." Hans took the covered roll from the waiter and presented it to Jack. "I feel this belongs with the sled. It completes the package, so to speak."

Jack sat dumbfounded. Another Beuys. This was getting embarrassing.

"Thank you, Hans. Okay, we open them together." Jack passed the framed work to Hans. Carefully, Jack unwrapped the package, revealing a dark, tightly rolled felt cylinder. At one end he observed the hilt of a steel blade. A strand of leather kept the felt roll bound together. Slightly puzzled, he looked to Groub. After three cautious turns, Jack revealed the contents. Inside rested a large, worn, rusted and beautifully forged blade.

"Actually, Jack, it's supposed to be kept rolled up. Joseph called it 'Samurai', the knife as weapon, as man's first tool, hidden within the felt of our soul. It's powerful, no?"

Jack was, for the second time that week, speechless.

"Oh Jack, don't be so moved, it's nothing really. It belongs with you. Now, what have we here?"

Hans used his table knife to cut open the tissue wrapping. A broad smile broke across his face. "Oh, well, Jack, this is wonderful, a real gem. *Hirsch mit Menschenkopf*," he muttered under his breath. *"Stag with Human Head."*

Jack was impressed. Hans really knew his stuff.

"You see this, Ingvar, this is one of the Secret Block drawings," said Hans, proudly holding up the work to his friend. "A secret block for a secret person in Ireland. One of the most important collections of his drawings ever assembled, it catalogs his drawing from 1936 to 1976. I think this piece was made circa 1955. There were exactly 456 works in the block. After it was first shown in '76 I attempted to buy the entire collection but was unsuccessful. It's taken me over twenty years to track them all down and this one had until today slipped through the net."

Jack was slightly taken aback. He had no idea what an important work he had bought. He was rather proud, though, that it was such a good piece and moreover he was relieved that Hans had liked it.

"So, Jack, we both appear to have done very well. Thank you very much for this work, it is truly beautiful."

"No, Hans, it's nothing. I mean, you have already given me so much."

"But Jack, as I say again, you were meant to have the sled. Beuys would have wanted it that way. After your sled he made the multiple of fifty sleds, a large production. The concept revolved around his theory that everyone was an artist, that the work should be exactly what it was, a vehicle for the communication of ideas. Yours, though, is rather different. It is the first and to my mind, the prototype. Very few know it even exists. You understand it better than most. Anyhow, you know what it means."

"He is right," added Nelly. "From what I can tell you are more in touch with Beuys than we have ever been. They say he speaks to you, to those that can really see. I personally have never experienced his power but Hans tells me you do."

"Sorry, Nelly, speaks to you? What do you mean?"

"Yes," joined in Mikaela, "what do you mean?"

"I think what she means is that the power of the work speaks to those who are open to it," concurred Hans. "But let us eat. I think we need to have some wine and warm food before we bore our guests to death."

They sat in silence as the meal was served. Jack's mind raced. What did Nelly mean, "he speaks to you"? Beuys' work had been known to communicate with people in a mysterious and spiritual sense. Jack felt the blood draining from his face. The elevator, Jesus, what if that was . . . no, the thought was too out there. It had to have been a prank and there was a reasonable explanation. There had to be.

As they finished the entrée, Hans addressed the table. "Jack and Mikaela, we were wondering if you would care to see Ingvar's latest acquisition. He has asked me to store it for him. It's what he calls his 'Elephant'."

"Sure, Hans, we would love to, right, Mikaela?" Mikaela gave Jack a subtle open-eyed glance. Jack took her hand in his and reassured her with a kind smile. "Yes, let's see this elephant of yours, Ingvar, I'm intrigued."

Ingvar and Nelly rose and took Jack by the arm. Hans led them into the rear corridor and along a broad open hall. A third set of doors led into an even grander room. Hans stopped Jack and turned to him. In a low, knowing voice he winked at him and whispered, "As Beuys used to say, Jack, 'we go this way.'"

Jack, eyes wired, took Hans by the arm. "Forgive me Hans, did you say, 'We go this way?'"

"Yes, Jack. Are you familiar with that phrase?"

Hans looked knowingly into Jack's eyes. He could read the confusion in Jack's face. He smiled kindly. "It's okay, Jack," he said reassuringly. "It's okay."

Hans continued to open the doors with both hands. A huge mammoth skeleton stood in the center of the room. Its bone structure was massive. The tusks, as much as ten feet long, curled elegantly to the floor, the enormous cranium and honeycombed frontal lobe armor looming above what would have been trunk and forelegs. Daubed in red paint, thick and large across the skull, was inscribed a simple equation, "Kunst = Kapital".

Jack suddenly felt ill. "K equals K, for fuck's sake! What's going on?" cursed Jack, confused, under his breath.

"You see, Jack, this was the challenge Beuys offered to all of us," added Ingvar, "to everyone, even us bankers, the whole world ..."

As Ingvar began to explain the intricacies and importance of the installation, Jack stood alone in the room. The temperature dropping, it was now close to freezing and Jack began to shiver, not violent shaking but a slight and constant trembling. The words were larger than he remembered them and daubed in an ochre paste along the length of the cave wall. Despite the warmth of the fire and the flickering of the flames that danced against the cave walls, Jack could sense he was not alone. The fear of what lay deeper in this primitive dwelling did nothing to abate his shivering. Somewhere in the depths of the cave he could sense there was another life form, maybe many more life forms, their hidden bodies generating a sense of rhythm as they breathed in and out, asleep and menacing. Jack held his nerve. He knew he had to, and slowly he brought himself back round to the place he knew, to the room. Once he had decided he had seen enough, the shaking began to ebb and Jack clenched his fists together close by his side, a reassurance that he was back from the other place.

Groub and Mikaela stood close by talking together and Ingvar was still explaining the work, his full lips moving as he spoke in muted silence while Jack stood and watched, waiting for his senses to return, the signs of normality that he knew would return any second ...

"Kunst equals Kapital, art equals money, creativity equals value. It's a hell of a concept for a world driven by industry and commerce," added Hans, "to put art at the top of the tree. Well, you can see why he was often described as mad." Groub paused for a second, as if to contemplate the profundity of his assessment, "Yes, it's a hell of a thing, even if I say so myself."

The remains of the evening passed pleasantly enough and Jack felt himself relax into the conversation. He had learned that if his moments were to go unnoticed by all but his closest and dearest, he would have to remain calm. Practice had made him expert at that, but Jack was far from over the experience. And now he knew that Groub knew, he must have known. There was a powerful force at play, something Jack had never felt before in his lifetime of zoning and dreaming; a powerful force that had crossed the line from his imagination to affect his reality.

As Jack walked out into the cold spring night, Groub took him by the shoulder. "Jack, I don't want to bore you with any fatherly advice but be careful out there. Beuys used to tell us, be careful what you hope to become and even more careful what you wish for, you may just get it!"

Jack, taken aback, turned to Groub. "Thanks, Hans. I'm not quite sure what you mean but I'm sure I'll find out soon enough."

"Good night, my friend, I'll be seeing you."

Chapter 6

The spring pack spread northwards from the land for an eternity. It was solid, rigid and indestructible, a sea of concrete, frozen and buckled, a crisscross of ice rubble, low, waist-high walls and flat ice paddy fields stretching for over 800 nautical miles to its epicenter at ninety degrees north, the Pole, and then beyond, down again, to the lower latitudes of the ice pack, as far south as Hudson Bay and the eventual sway of the open ocean. A white topping to the earth's crust, the realm of the Arctic sea ice and the Siberian north. The pack was an awesome spectacle.

Jack, Jim and Viktor looked up as the thud of the approaching chopper gradually filled the air. They waited in the freezing cold, crouched down low, hugging each other, turning their heads away from the swirling cloud of snow dust that consumed the air. Soon the helicopter was hovering above them. The second the huge rubber wheels hit the ice pack Viktor gave them the signal and they bundled into the sparse interior of the Mi8. Within seconds they were airborne, flying low over the ice pack that surrounds Sredny on the archipelago of Severnaya Zemlya.

Their journey had already taken four days. Flying from New York to London and then on to St Petersburg, Jack, Jim and Mikaela had joined Viktor and his wife Ursula at the Russian Polar Institute for a full trip briefing. The first meeting in St Petersburg had been emotional, Mikaela beside herself with joy to be reunited with her only sibling. Viktor had been equally moved, his tall rangy frame enveloping the euphoric Mikaela in a true Russian bear hug. The kisses didn't stop. Jack and Jim were moved too, to be met by the great Soviet explorer and to be grabbed, hugged and beset with kisses from this dark bearded giant of a man and his beautiful wife – tall, elegant, minimalist, a woman for whom over-indulgence and luxury were unknown values.

It was quite a welcome. Jack was struck by how youthful Viktor still was. He had kept himself in good shape, an impressive figure of a man, despite over thirty years of Arctic wear since his groundbreaking achievement on the ocean. The months of fierce sunlight, brutal cold and tough living had aged his skin and weathered his face, but even at their first meeting Jack could tell Viktor had a wonderful childlike quality to him.

It showed in his electric eyes, the light blue irises crackling with energy; he was continually joking, his spirit always high, a man never down, a man for whom nothing was too much trouble. If anything Viktor looked better than he had done in the faded photo in his journal from 1968. Then he had been so drained, so thin, withered almost. But now he seemed massive, six foot four, broad shoulders, long rangy arms, in fact quite the wrong build for a polar explorer.

The thing that struck Jack the most was Viktor's hands: massive dinner plates, his fingers split and calloused from years of running the dogs, chopping wood, working in the cold. And Jack liked him, they both did. Jim and Jack knew they were in good hands, literally, strong hands of stone, hands that would take you by the arms and hold you safe till danger had passed. But Jack was uncomfortable with the contradictions he was feeling deep inside. The sense of security he got from Viktor and a niggling feeling of danger, the danger of being reliant on someone stronger than himself. Viktor was a different build of a man, his physique all sinew and bone, probably not as heavy as Jack or as well muscled but far stronger. Viktor's was the type of strength you are born with and that's built on year upon year; tempered steel to Jack's rough stone.

Needless to say they had all hit it off immediately, and after a couple of days R&R (and a serious amount of vodka courtesy of Viktor) they had flown to Norilsk in northern Siberia and then on to the remote fishing town of Khatanga. There they had rested for a couple of days and prepared their equipment for the long journey north to Sredny.

Walking about the town in the late Arctic twilight, Jack was struck by how harsh and unforgiving Siberia was in the grip of winter. The temperature ranged from minus 20 in the day to minus 40 at night, and the cold was accentuated by the bleak, derelict buildings and soot-blackened snow of a small industrial town. The interiors of the buildings were surprisingly warm, though, and the people extremely friendly. Many of the town's native population were descended from the Dolgan tribe of nomadic reindeer herders that traveled and lived on the surrounding tundra. Jack was sure Joseph Beuys would have liked it here; the nomadic people a distant relation to the Tartars of the Crimea. Local indigenous trade revolved around fur clothing, hats and mukluks (native reindeer-skin boots), and a huge array of carved bone trinkets. Needless to say both Jack and Jim spent a few hours bartering for fur ruffs and hats as they prepared and adapted their wind and down clothing for the trip north. They made their final checks, tested their specially insulated walled tents, cookers, fixed ski bindings, dog harnesses, and repacked their rucksacks and sledges.

After a short delay due to bad visibility they flew north once again to Sredny at 80 degrees north. They would be based here, at Viktor's northern camp, the remote meteorological station, for three days, doing test runs with the dogs on the pack while keeping a vigilant eye out for marauding polar bears. Mikaela was glad to be away from the city. With only two commercials in six months, her debut in American cinema had not been quite the whirlwind tour she had hoped for. In Moscow and St Petersburg she was quite well known. Her latest picture, *Lost Worlds*, directed by Sergi Alitaloliov, had been well received and had even premiered at Cannes, but the international euphoria had been shortlived. Five castings later Mikaela was still without a new project and her so-called agent hadn't called her for two weeks. Life was so much simpler here, and anyway she had missed her brother like mad. Mikaela was enjoying being in Russia with Jack. Now she was on her turf, able to dictate the way, open doors, show him all the things she had wanted to but either couldn't afford to, or hadn't the knowhow to, in New York. Moreover she needed to see how he liked it in Russia, her beloved Russia.

Aside from Jack's passion for the galleries and museums in New York, even the Metropolitan couldn't compare to the splendor and opulence of the Hermitage, the State Opera, the Kirov ballet and the Imperial Tsarist architecture of St Petersburg. Jack appeared to like it; every view had made him stand and stare in the way he sometimes did – Mikaela was pleased that she had begun to see his strange ways. It made her happy to see him so moved, even in Norilsk and Khatanga, without the culture but with the views, the desolation of Siberia, the people, the Dolgan, the skins, the reindeer. Jack was inquisitive, not spoilt and narrow-minded like so many of the other men she had dated in the city, who were all too often the product of too much family money, the Ivy League and the "frat house" bubblegum culture.

Jack was different, there was no doubt about that, and he was handsome, strong-minded and strange. Natasha had warned her about these types, the wealthy bankers, after their first night together. But Mikaela knew, after she had quite literally drunk him under the table, that she could tame him. For the first time since arriving in America she had met a man who was interested in more than just sex. It wasn't that she held sex as a lower priority; it was just that she was so good at that game. Before Jack she had always got want she wanted from men, Natasha even accusing her on some occasions of being a bit of a whore. But Mikaela knew the truth. If she had been born a man she would have been one of the guys, a player, a stud, and God, was it was fun, mutual fun. And anyhow, she got so bored with most of the others, one-race horses. After sex there was so little to say. She played on that sometimes, the "Russian teen" routine, the bimbo, the MTA ("model turned actress"). It was a perfect cover, very believable, so much so that she sometimes felt herself slipping into it with Jack. She used it as a protective cover that bought her time to stand back, see the real issue and analyze the situation. This is how she coped with the judging, the games, the infidelities, the abuse, all the lies and crap she had to endure on her climb up the ladder since she had arrived in St Petersburg as a fifteen-year-old model.

Jack, for all his eccentricities, intrigued her. In New York he had had something she needed, not just the money and the security but the potential of true companionship. She even wondered if he might be the one for her, but now in Russia, back home, away from the role-play of New York, she didn't know for sure. It was too early for that, but if he played his cards right, anything was possible. Her only concern lay in the fact that from the day they had landed back in Russia she could no longer suppress her yearning to be there, not just a fleeting visit to the family but to live, to raise a family there. And what of Jack? It was too early to say, but what would be in it for him if they were to take it any further? How could he leave everything he had in the city and his career? But she filed her reservations, put them away into a small compartment in her subconscious where she placed the things that troubled her, a place she kept to herself, hidden and secret.

Mikaela was so excited to see Jack's face when he first saw the met station. She held an image of it in her mind when she was in foreign countries, her prized picture postcard. This place was special, and Jack was the first man she had ever brought here. It was her place. The met station was beautiful, perched on a spectacular granite outcrop of high ground overlooking a natural harbor that had only been ice-free four times in the past fifty years. Often covered in a thin layer of verglass, the old wooden lodge with its pink sidings and pale green shutters looked as if it had been pulled straight from the set of *Doctor Zhivago*. It was a great place to unwind, and as always Mikaela was glad to be staying inside away from the terrible wind and freezing temperatures. A short walk to the sauna and back was quite enough of a reminder of the severity of the high Arctic cold. Why Jack and Jim wanted to sleep on the ice she couldn't understand, and as for Viktor, his daily snow bath was enough to make her stay hidden under the warm down duvets indefinitely. Yes, she loved Sredny but from the safety and warmth of the fireside. That was the way it should be.

Over the next two days Viktor, Jack and Jim ventured on to the ice on foot, being careful to look for signs and tracks of polar bear. On their second evening, Viktor organized for a chopper to fly them across the ice-bound islands looking for bears and they spotted their first two, which were running free across the pack. Jim, his mechanical 16mm camera at the ready, filmed from the open chopper door but they were thwarted from landing on two occasions due to unsafe ice conditions. It wasn't until the following night that they were able to land successfully on the pack, close to a huge male. For Viktor it was critical that all explorers who visited Sredny had a good understanding of the bears. There was only so much one could learn from a book and training video, and he was intrigued to see Jack's and Jim's response to being on the pack with a large predator.

The chopper circled around the large male polar bear. Quickly they gathered their kit and cameras and secured their clothing, as the pilot gave Viktor the thumbs-up to get out. The helicopter hovered just feet from the surface of the ice as, one by one, they jumped down on to the snow below. Once on the ground, Viktor made them form a small group and they huddled together as the chopper lifted off, leaving them alone on the pack with the bear. As the sound of the helicopter faded in the freezing air, they stopped and waited. From ground level it was hard to see the bear because of a small ridge of ice blocks spread out in front of them, leading to the open water. Cautiously they moved forward, intensely aware of the speed and agility of the predator they were now stalking. Although the bear was a good eighty yards away and hidden behind the ridgeline, all three knew that he could close that distance in under five seconds.

★ ★ ★

Jack and Jim had assimilated a lot of facts about the polar bear during hours of talking and drinking around the fire with Viktor at the met station the previous night. Viktor's talk had started out as an informal lecture – he had wanted to stress the power and dynamics of this awesome predator. In his broken English, he had painted an intimidating picture. Jim and Jack sat like children listening to his words of wisdom.

"So, yes, the great ice bear, 'Biely Medvied' we call him, Russian for polar bear. Where to begin? Have no illusions, these bears in Sredny are big, seven to fifteen hundred pounds, and can run at nearly thirty miles an hour over short distances, faster than my sister's Skoda."

Jack and Jim laughed nervously.

"On hind legs males stand up to ten feet tall and can kill seal of similar size with single blow. Remember they can pull the seal out of the water with their jaws, dragging it for many hundreds of yards. And in case you think you can escape them if you fall in, forget it! Polar bears are just as at home in the water as on the land. I once sighted bear swimming out a hundred miles into the open sea. They are classified a marine mammal you know, *Ursus maritimus* I think you say in Latin. Unlike southern cousins *Ursus arctos*, brown bear, polar bear does not enter into yearly winter sleep, so they are out there guys, trust me. They are built for this cold, made for it. Bear has huge wedge-shaped frame and hollow conductive fur, allowing for excellent thermal protection from these coldest Russian temperatures. I bet you don't know color of skin, Jim, what you think?"

Jim, already feeling somewhat freaked, looked to Jack for help. "Black," mouthed Jack.

"Yes, very good Jack," winked Viktor. "Fur is white, skin is black – to retain heat, you see. Now why are Medvied so dangerous to us? You know why? Well, I tell you, the cold, yes, harsh environment is what makes them so dangerous to man. During winter months bear never stop hunting. They need to generate huge amounts of energy and enormous reserves of fat to survive the winter here in Sredny, and therefore cannot afford to be choosy hunters. Remember that, guys, they do not care, they cannot afford to. What about seals? I hear you say. Yes again, seals are preferred prey because high in fat, but bear is not selective, opportunist by nature ... So if you remember one thing, remember this. We make good meal for hungry bear, trust me. I have not read this guys, I have seen it on pipeline in seventies, several times, they will kill us if we give them chance. They will stalk us, bite us and eat us on this pack. He is unique, this bear, unique. Only predator on earth that kill man for food with regularity. Just don't give them opportunity, be safe and look out for each other."

★ ★ ★

Armed with Viktor's advice, they continued to move cautiously toward the ridge, Viktor monitoring the ice rubble with his binoculars for signs of sudden movement. He signaled for them to crouch down, keeping their eyes on the ridge, and wait. After no more than a minute the bear peered around an ice fissure. He was facing them, sniffing the air. Jim wound the 16mm and started to shoot footage and film, Jack sitting prone with a 300mm camera lens aimed at the bear. The bear seemed curious. After watching the three for a short while he rounded the ridge and began to approach their position. Then he started to run. Viktor shouted over to Jack and Jim and ordered them to stand firm. The bear was now at full tilt, running in their direction, and Viktor could sense that his two clients were starting to feel on edge. Suddenly the bear switched his direction from right to left and slowed down to a lope. He circled them and soon his objective became clear. He was heading to the open water inlet fifty yards to their left. They watched and waited as the bear moved slowly toward the water's edge then crashed into the icy water, swimming across the short section of open sea. He looked tired and lay for a while on safe ice, watching the three of them intently, his breath steaming in the golden light. He began to roll and play on the ice, cooling himself on the frozen surface of the pack.

The whole experience had made Jim nervous. The bear's sudden turn of speed had jolted him, awoken him to the danger. Viktor could tell, but it was hardly surprising, Jim looking over his shoulder for reassurance from his experienced guide. Viktor called it the "polar bear pirouette", an automatic reaction to being in the presence of such an unpredictable and well-camouflaged predator, to being on the food chain. The impulse to stop, to catch one's breath, the heart rate to quicken, was a result of man's pre-programmed primitive DNA, the muscles' distant memory of an age when we were the hunted, out on the primeval taiga.

Unaware of his biophysical response to imminent danger, Jim was having an encounter without walls, safety moats and electric fences, a zooless experience of predator watching, and it made him excited and nervous. Jack, on the other hand, stood transfixed. Viktor was intrigued to watch him from a safe distance, his old Russian 7.62 Nagan bolt-action rifle resting in the crook of his arm just in case the bear took a closer look. But Jack didn't look back as Jim had done; he just stood there watching the bear as it ran across the ice field not eighty yards in front of him.

★ ★ ★

The whiteness was real, Jack knew that, but what felt strange was the water, all around, on top of the ice so as to let him stand firm, standing on water. The dogs were there too. All of them, straining and yelping, and

108

Viktor, he was close by, and for Jack that was enough to keep his anxiety at bay.

The bear was absolutely massive. He stood, panting heavily, happy just to wait and watch. Somehow Jack wasn't scared, just alert, alive. The bear gave him a certain focus and then he saw it, the black water. He wasn't sure if the water was above him or below him, but it was there, moving, slipping across the ice. The bear wasn't fazed by the icy dark liquid, the sea bear, *Ursus maritimus*, had no need to be, but for Jack it represented a deep terror, a fear of a medium, a substance, that he couldn't control. And then he felt solid again and able to move, but as he turned to find Viktor he had a premonition, a moment when everything went black, the water, the sky, a dark charcoal pitch black, inky and dead. But the feeling didn't last long and soon everything came back, the light, the wind, the smell of ozone, and he breathed again, slowly, and opened his eyes.

★ ★ ★

Viktor's beard was moving, and now he could see the joy written all over Jim's face, elation at the experience they had just shared with the bear. But for Jack, as the words and sounds came into focus once more, there was a worry, a very real fear about the expanses of water, the trip and all that he wanted to achieve. The journey, this way north, circumnavigating Sredny's northern arrowhead, worried him now; hell, it wasn't the bear, that was just a catalyst, a sign, a trigger. His fear came from a more powerful intuition. It was the elements, the simple element of H2O, all that ice, all that water and the hope that the water would remain in a frigid state.

Now two days in, Jack yearned for the trip to begin for no other reason than for it to end, for it to be over, so he and Jim and Viktor could have a laugh about it all, all those silly thoughts and all the insecurities. He wanted to be held by Mikaela, to have it all on his terms, his life, Microstem, all his money, his friends and a lover who meant as much as he knew she could mean if only he let her, and he wanted it after the trip. He would make it right with Mikaela, really commit, he promised himself. The bear, the ice pack, the overwhelming reality of Siberia had got to him in a moment, faced him with something, as the sled had done, and his other art work, the dark menacing totemic image of Basquiat's skull painting, the death's head.

It was now well past midday and the light had turned a rich golden orange. As the bear settled by the water's edge, six seals surfaced but the bear remained unfazed. He knew these animals and they had spotted him, too far away to be of any threat, but a menacing presence just the same. The water steamed and created illusions of fire as the sun dipped low on the horizon. All three men were transfixed. The bear was now completely relaxed, lying forward on his forepaws, switching his attention from Viktor's team to the seals. Both Jack and Jim realized then that human–bear interactions did not get any better than this. To watch a predator in the wild, in its natural habitat, was a truly wonderful experience. They had intruded far enough into the bear's hunting domain and Viktor signaled for them to retreat to the safer ice to await the return of the helicopter. As the three men moved away they watched the bear approach the water, once more silhouetted against the haze of ice, sea and sky. Again he swam, crawled, lay and played in the snow, giving them one last magical memory. As they flew back that night the pilot circled the bear for the last time, and as the chopper banked away toward camp they watched him bounding across the ice, a magnificent free animal running wild.

Viktor was pleased with them both. Jim had kept a lid on his fear and Jack, it was as if he were in another world; and in some ways he was, they both were, a world away from what they had known, including the Ellesmere trip that Jack had been so eager to push as qualification for the Sredny plan. Viktor had shown great interest and it wasn't for him to burst Jack's bubble, but he knew that they had only modest experience of the sea ice. Most of their past Arctic trips had been conducted on land. But they were good men and fit and they had come from northern states and hence were no strangers to the cold. For that he was glad. They had the best kit and had lived out there for short periods. They would be able to look after themselves, maybe even look after him, not that they would need to worry about him, Viktor Sedov, the great Russian polar explorer.

They had passed his first test. On the trip ahead they would have to coexist with the bear, sharing space and time with this magnificent creature, and control their fear, day in day out. Viktor had wanted Jack and Jim to understand the bear's speed and respect its space. If his little induction course had made them think a bit, put the wind up them even, that was a good thing. Besides, Viktor smiled to himself, it had been fun watching their reactions.

Jack sat in the rear of the helicopter and gazed out of the window at the pack ice below. Pulling his fur-trimmed hood over his head he felt warm and safe, much safer than he had done on the pack, his kit next to him and everything he needed to survive. At that moment in time he felt complete. His life was beginning to make sense once more, even if the incident in the elevator had rattled him somewhat. The truth was it had been too long since he had felt this way, alive again; it was good to be in the wild once more, a real breath of fresh air.

Back at the met station Viktor's wife, Ursula, had prepared them all a magnificent farewell dinner. Viktor wanted them to have a good meal before they set off the next morning. A man running dogs in the high Arctic required a huge amount of energy, between 4,000 and 6,000 calories a day. Sheer exhaustion, poor sleep and high dehydration meant that in reality it was very difficult for the three to eat and drink the right amount. Viktor knew that they would lose at least fourteen pounds each over the course of their journey. The most critical ingredient for such a relatively short trip was taking in fluid. Dehydration results in irrational behavior and in severe cases can lead to exposure, shock and death. While the most common result of low fluid intake in the Arctic is bad circulation and cramp, this in turn can result in frostbite. They would have to drink at least six pints of water a day and this was pushing the minimum requirement. Viktor's job would be to ensure, at nearly every rest stop throughout the day, that Jack and Jim got the stove going and made coffee. The added morale of a warm flame and a hot drink was invaluable and helped give emphasis and punctuate the stages of their working day. It was this daily rhythm running the dogs that Viktor wished to establish, and it was this rhythm, as the Alpinist Reinhold Messner once said, "one foot in front of the other", that would define their success.

That night Jack didn't sleep well. His moment on the pack was still with him but he kept it to himself, the great bear and that fear of water. For all the obvious reasons Mikaela wanted to be close to Jack, and as far as he was concerned, for all the right reasons, he could not reciprocate her affections. Not now at any rate, not before he was off on the journey, it would make him weak, her touch, he would be taking her with him in his brain and he needed to focus on the job at hand. It was her immediate presence that bothered him, the fact that there had been no clean break from his feelings for her, no tearful goodbye at the airport, no closure. She was there in his tuning-in space and he was to blame, since he had invited her there. Why had he done it? Out of a sense of duty, out of respect for her family or for Viktor, or was it something more selfish, the warmth of her body, the sex? He didn't know. Yes, he really liked her, she made him feel great, but now he needed to be alone and there was just no way out of it, not without hurting her feelings and creating a scene. That was the last thing he wanted, but his body language, tense and irritable, he couldn't hide it.

Mikaela sensed Jack's unease. Without a word she rolled away from him, hugging the side of the small double mattress. She had wanted to be closer to him than ever that night, to tell him something intimate, something important, to make it a special night. But now, feeling rejected, she turned cold. Jack lay on his back and sighed. He knew instantly he had messed up.

"Darling, are you awake?" There was silence. "Baby, please ..."

"Why, Jack?" replied Mikaela in a quiet voice. "Why did you ask me here if you don't want me, why?"

Jack closed his eyes.

"Baby, it's not you, please understand that, it's just this trip. I guess I've never been with anyone the night before. I'm sorry, darling, really, it's just we've got our work cut out for us and I can't help thinking about it, that's all, darling. Come here, give me a hug."

"No, Jack. You want a hug, you hug me."

Jack took Mikaela in his arms. There was nothing left to say. He held her until he fell asleep. Mikaela lay staring into space, the tears welling up in her eyes.

★ ★ ★

Jack awoke to the excitable, shrill yelping of the dogs being fed. It wasn't yet light but Viktor had been hard at work for an hour. Mikaela lay fast asleep, having stayed on her side of the bed all night, and Jack slipped out of the room being careful not to wake her. Grabbing his down parka and Alaskan bunny boots, he shuffled down the dimly lit hall and kicked Jim's door.

"Dude, D-day! Better get up."

Jim groaned, half asleep, "Okay, I'm there."

Jack kicked the door again.

"Jim, NOW, buddy! I'm going to help Viktor. Get the coffee on, okay?"

Jack grabbed the flare pistol that lived on the Bakelite phone stand in the hall and pushed the door sleepily with his shoulder. On a past trip to the Arctic Jack's host had handed him a flare pistol every time he went to the can, saying, "When you are caught by Mr Bear with your pants down taking a crap, it sure beats a grin!"

The guide was right; it was better to be safe than sorry. The dawn temperature whipped against his warm skin as he stumbled out of the lodge door. Fifty yards away in the dim half-light Jack could see Viktor, ladle in hand, pouring the warm steaming seal soup into the battered tin dog bowls. This was a morning ritual, an essential part of running dogs in the north. Whatever the weather, the dogs needed their morning feed. The soup, although not thick in meat, comprised all the essential nutrients and fluids to keep the team fully hydrated and running all day. This process took over an hour from the lodge with running water. Out on the ice, preparing enough melted snow alone could take over two hours. Mixing twenty-eight portions of frozen seal meat and dried nutrients would then take a further half an hour. It was a cold but rewarding chore.

Jim joined Jack outside. Together they walked through the deep snow to Viktor.

"So guys, are you ready? It's going to be a good trip; I can feel it, very cold. This is good."

"Yeah, Viktor, about that cold, could you turn it up a notch?"

They all laughed.

"Jack, Jim, we need to leave in an about an hour. Drag your kit out here and wait for me inside. When the chopper arrives we'll load up together."

The rotor wash of the Sikorsky Mi8, the Arctic Land Rover, sent dull bass reverberations throughout the lodge. Mikaela sat in the warm kitchen, her nose buried in a large mug of hot coffee. She could feel the bass of the rotors pass through her. It made her stomach tighten. She didn't want Jack to go now, not like this. As Jack opened the door to the kitchen she looked up and ran toward him. She didn't say a word. She just clung to him. Jack closed his eyes.

"It'll be fine, darling, okay? I'll be fine," he whispered gently in her ear. "Now help me check the room, I always forget something."

Jack and Mikaela walked together down the long dark corridor to their small room. Jack gave the room the once-over and noticed a small envelope on his pillow. Mikaela smiled as Jack leant over and picked it up.

"Is this for me?"

"Yes, a peace offering. I find in an old bookshop. I hope you like. I thought you could take it with you, for luck ... "

Jack carefully peeled open the envelope and inside found a postcard. It was an original invitation to Beuys' show at the Frankfurt Kunsthall in 1972. In the photograph Beuys sat on a bench, his head bowed into the depths of a luxuriant wolfskin coat.

"Darling, that's so sweet of you, I've never seen this before. Where did you get it?"

"Oh, a friend told me where to look. It reminds me of you in your Arctic gear. Please take it. It will bring luck."

Jack opened his parka and put the postcard in his inside pocket. "Yes, baby, I won't let it out of my sight. I promise."

It was getting light now and as they pulled their sled bags across the snow the icy spindrift filled the air with tiny frozen particles, making it hard to breathe. The huge chopper hovered overhead and slowly, defying all laws of gravity, descended on to the solid pack. The dogs were going mad, a mixture of excitement and fear combining to make them almost unmanageable. The curved forged hook of the snow brake jolted back and forth with each jump and pull of the fourteen 180-pound dogs. These were not lithe southern racers; they were sturdy Alaskan malamute stock interbred with the strongest of all sled dogs, Canadian Eskimo dogs. Viktor had built a reputation for breeding the strongest non-indigenous dogs in Siberia. The dogs had run Viktor's teams in Antarctica until their recent ban, and his lead dog, Gregor, had made the 850 miles with Viktor to the Pole in Viktor's second successful bid in the mid '90s. This was dog travel from another age, Inuit style.

The harness and leads were designed to fan out across the pack, since narrow forest trails that required the two-by-two harness lay over 1,000 miles to the south. From a safety perspective the dogs were freer to swim if the ice gave way, and with regard to bears, they could engage a large male and surround him, keeping his attack at bay while their driver got off a well-aimed shoulder shot. Their fur was hollow, and due to their waxy double coat and solid build the dogs needed no shelter from the elements, even during the worst blizzards. Thousands of years of harsh Arctic winters had forged the dogs' lupine DNA and metabolic cycles, able to cope with temperatures under minus 70 and wind speeds of 150 miles an hour. In the severest storms the dogs would just curl into a ball, their noses slightly raised, and let the snowdrift form around them. Their heart rates would slow down to the lightest of beats and their peripheries would shut down to concentrate the flow of life-giving blood to the brain and heart. Their body's core would remain warm and their raised noses would act as chimneys that once lowered would provide a frozen airway to the harsh world outside.

In 1986 Viktor's team had been forced to sit out a blizzard that lasted over eight days. Emerging from his tent, weary and racked with hunger and guilt, Viktor stood in the pristine Arctic landscape without a dog in sight. As he sat on his sled, bent double with grief, one by one the dogs had forced their way out of their icy tombs and, with tails wagging, howled for joy. Every single dog had survived without food and drink for a week. They had simply shut themselves down. They were an Arctic phenomenon.

As the three heaved and crammed their kit into the rear of the chopper, Mikaela and Ursula stood on the porch and watched. The two gang-lines of dogs yelled and strained vigorously against their anchors as one by one they were untethered and led patiently into the tailgate of the Mi8. Once inside, Jim was given the responsibility of hooking each dog up to a makeshift anchor-point in the chopper. Within half an hour twenty-eight dogs, three ten-foot sleds, three explorers, 600 pounds of equipment and supplies and two pilots were looking toward a nervous engineer for the thumbs-up. It is an old tradition with Soviet combat chopper pilots that the engineer gets to fly on all missions, just to make doubly sure he and his team have carried out the correct hour of maintenance per hour of flying time. Often flying in total whiteout and in severe wind chill, there was no room for mechanical or electrical failure. If the chopper came down there would be no rescue, since there was only the one serviceable chopper on Sredny.

Watching her man leave on yet another expedition was a familiar experience for Ursula. It wasn't that she didn't worry, she did, it was just that she knew it wouldn't do any good. As the rear door of the chopper started to close, Viktor, Jim and Jack waved farewell to the two girls. Mikaela felt an awful wrenching in the pit of her stomach. Why had she been so insensitive toward Jack that night? Why hadn't she told him her secret? She wished she could have the night again. What a fool she had been. Standing there in the spindrift and wash of the ascending chopper, she understood what he had been feeling. She was alone, cold, and without the security of knowing everything would be all right. She would have to wait for that feeling to return. Ursula looked over to her and smiled.

"Everything will be fine. Viktor will take care of them. They are big boys. Now come here and let's get out of this cold."

Ursula turned, put her arm around Mikaela and they hugged. Mikaela, her head resting on her sister-in-law's shoulder, watched the chopper disappear across the frigid sea toward the warm glow of the horizon.

★ ★ ★

The chopper flew on a westerly heading for about half an hour. The island of Ostrov Shar was situated to the far west of the archipelago at 80.5 degrees north and 92.5 degrees east. The small outcrop of frozen, rocky tundra represented a stable platform for hooking up the dogs and allowed the team the chance to set off from land. A gentle slope led across the first five-mile stretch of frozen sea to the first night's camp off the Kuybysheva peninsula on the mainland. Jack planned for the team to make the traverse of their objective, the arrowhead-shaped landmass, in five legs.

Contouring the land in stages and then making "bold line of sight" advances across the frozen sea, Viktor estimated that they could reach the expedition's mid-point of Cape Architsky in a seven-day push via the western Libknekhta peninsula. To plan a traverse of the land mass would require, for the main part, traveling at least five miles out from the coast to avoid the bulk of the pressure ridges, but this made the final advance to land more difficult and dangerous. Cape Architsky represented the meeting points of all the ice shelves both west and east, joining at a crushing northerly pinnacle. Once navigated, Viktor predicted easier conditions, with north-east winds to their backs taking them south-east toward Lokot and Lyuksenberg and the Asian coastal buffer zone. If all went well they should complete this ambitious traverse in just over two weeks, but Viktor had allowed enough provisions for three. He would carry the HF radio and a heavier load. They would make a call each day at 4pm to the met station when they made camp.

Once all the equipment had been loaded on to the tundra, the chopper quickly departed. Viktor wanted it that way. He was well aware of the security that the chopper offered and the sooner Jack and Jim were thinking for themselves the better. As the dogs strained and howled on their anchors, Viktor got a brew on and started to fill a large tin with snow. Jack and Jim struggled with the harnesses and packing straps but within an hour the sleds were loaded and ready. Viktor, tin in hand, inspected each sled in turn and then kicked each one on to its side. They watched as he checked the towlines and karabiners for stress, then carefully sipped the warm water from the bowl and, crouching next to the upturned runners, dribbled warm water on to the metal struts. Carefully he polished the runners with a leather mitt until they were coated with a mirror smooth verglas. Jack was impressed, and by now he was getting cold.

"Viktor, you are an artist. I once saw Inuit do that in Grissefjord on Ellesmere. Do you think it really helps the running?"

"I'm convinced of it. Anyhow, it is a ritual I always enjoy! Let's get

116

moving, guys. I want to reach Kuybysheva by four pm. Five miles is plenty for today."

Viktor crouched down by Gregor, his lead dog, and whispered in his ear. Without a word he unhooked the anchor and began to jog next to the team. After no more than fifty yards he cracked his long Inuit whip and hopped on to the sled. They were off. Jack brought up the rear, with Jim in between. It was good to be moving, and as the sun climbed in the spring sky Jack was aware of a perfect silence, bar the crystal shushing of the sleds across the firm snow. For him this was what it was all about, oneness with the environment and a communion with the ice. They made good going. The ice was firm, and even in the overflows there was no sign of the dreaded open water leads. So close to land they were not expected, and to save on space and weight the dry suits and flotation bags had deliberately been left behind. Viktor had made this decision because of their relative proximity to the various coastal spits that would form the five checkpoints on the journey. But the possibility of falling into the water was always there, representing a dull nagging fear that couldn't be totally put aside by any of them until they were all back on firm land.

There is a saying in mushing circles that unless you are the lead dog the view never changes, but from Jack's perspective he was glad to have Viktor running point. At over 100 yards ahead Viktor looked like a crazed fly fisherman, a bearded shaman hurtling across the Arctic wastes, his whip floating in a slow rhythmic arch above the dogs' heads as he steered the team skilfully across the ice. Jack smiled to himself behind his thin polypropylene balaclava. Joseph Beuys would have enjoyed such a journey.

Two hours on and the dogs were running well. Jack's lead dog was attentive and strong, although his right wheel dog seemed to be taking it a bit easy. Jim's team was also strong, and as the sun began to dip once more toward the west, Viktor began to slow the pace and soon stopped. Both Jim and Jack followed suit and kicked in their anchors.

"Whoa, boys! Whoa!" cooed Jack as he brought his team to a halt.

It was getting cold, and Viktor pulled out his down parka from the sled bag and quickly zipped it up. In his other hand he produced a small bottle of vodka.

"So guys, we are here, camp one. That wasn't too bad, was it?"

Jack and Jim looked at Viktor in disbelief, surveying the campsite. There was nothing but desolate sea ice for thousands of yards.

"Really, Viktor? But it's only ..."

"Four pm, yes. Time flies when you are ... I propose a toast to our trip and of course to new friends."

"I'll drink to that, Viktor. What do you think, Jack?" asked Jim.

"Absolutely," replied Jack. "To us!"

An hour later the two dome tents were erected and the dogs had nestled down for the night. Jack and Jim sat drinking warm soup with Viktor, all three crammed around the roaring Coleman stove. Viktor deftly tuned in the high-frequency radio and rolled the large dial until the static died away, pressing the handset receiver inwards "Viktor to met station, over. Ursula, can you read me, over?"

Ursula's calm voice replied, "Yes, Viktor. How is it out there?"

"All is fine . . ."

Jack and Jim discreetly looked at each other and got up to leave, sensing this was Viktor's time. Spending so long away from home on the trail, they both figured he enjoyed his evening chats with the missus.

"Hey, Viktor," said Jack quietly, "great day, man. Please send my love to Mikaela. I'll speak to her some other time, if that's okay . . ."

Viktor smiled and nodded his acknowledgement.

Jim and Jack had both spent enough time together under canvas not to warrant endless hours of banter. Often on trips they didn't talk much at all. Having squared their respective sides of their tent before dinner, they quietly slipped into their bags and pulled out their books. After all, that was what tent life was all about, sleeping and reading. By 8pm they were both fast asleep.

That night they all slept well. The relief of having started the trip, of it simply being under way, swept over Jack and he began to dream, the type of vivid dreams you have after an extreme experience and can only remember at a later date. Jack woke only once to take a piss in his pee bottle and then slipped back into a deep, warm sleep. Although they were lying on nothing but sea ice, Jack felt secure. After all, he was with his best friend and in the hands of a sound guide. Moreover, Jack understood it out there, and to some extent he knew that this was what he was cut out to do. It was this knowledge, the knowledge that he carried everything he needed to survive in his head and on a 100-pound sled, that gave him his certain sense of security. It was the complete yet simple nature of his Arctic existence that comforted him; it was perfect.

He woke early, to the gentle blowing of the wind on the taut fabric of the dome tent. He lay awake for an hour staring at the ceiling of the tent, listening to the wind, deep in thought. He had left so much behind: his apartment and office crammed with paintings and the detritus of his hectic city life, and the irony was that in so doing he had come away with all that he needed in a bag on a sled, even if it was only for the next few weeks. Maybe he needed to cut away some of the crap from his life, clear out all the "stuff", box it up, store it, give it away...that was what he needed to do. Then he could piece his life back together again. It would be a start.

Jack loved the early mornings. Back in the city it was the only time he had when the phone never rang; it was his time. He could hear Viktor open his tent and crank up the large double Coleman stove. Then he heard first Gregor and then the whole team yelping excitedly as he unzipped the frosted zip of the outer tent door. Food was coming.

"Gregor, yes, we run well today, okay, my boy? You show these youngsters how it's done, okay?"

Jack smiled as he listened to Viktor stroking each dog in turn. He was the team coach before the big match. It was time to break trail. Jack couldn't wait.

★ ★ ★

From their first night's camp at Kuybysheva they made good going despite the mounting easterly wind. After three nights and around sixty miles they hit the land spit of Karla Liubknekhta and took a rest day to enjoy the high temperatures and rest the dogs. Jack and Jim had both led on alternate sections and Viktor had been impressed by their aptitude for navigation on the GPS. On day four their next passage led them out on to the pack over fifty miles from land, as Viktor followed a north-easterly heading to the mid-point of Cape Architsky. The evening transmissions relayed without a hitch, since they had been traveling on the westerly arm of the archipelago and there had only been low ice fissure elevations between them and the met station on Semelya 200 miles to the south. The weather had been fantastic, but as they headed out for the long two-day push to Cape Architsky, Viktor noticed that the barometer had risen rather alarmingly. The weather was changing, high pressure followed by a low, and raised temperatures. On this section of relatively exposed ice they might run into trouble and, more importantly, into open leads.

Viktor sat silently for a while alone in his tent. Both his clients had impressed him. Although they were relatively new to sea ice travel they had taken the testing snow rubble sections in their course with a good sense of humor. They handled the dogs efficiently and seemed to be squared away well, but it was their confidence on the possible open sections that worried him most. If they came across shulai, rubber ice, he just hoped they would trust him.

In '92 Viktor had been stranded on a large broken section of ice without his sled as his clients refused to follow him across the short section of undulating grey ice. Viktor, never a man to take a risk with a client, had tested the conditions and had been satisfied that it was safe enough to traverse on skis, but his clients were having none of it. In the forty-five minutes it had taken him to convince them to come across, the lead had opened considerably and fresh running seawater had flowed over the rubber ice. The detour had taken Viktor two days and cost his clients the Pole. It was a risk that came with the territory. The only problem was that on his Pole trips he carried dry suits. Worst case he could swim the sections with his dog team and float the sled across, but due to his earlier decision to save on weight that was not an option now. Viktor cursed himself; he should have remembered that if one thing was guaranteed in the Arctic, it was that nothing was guaranteed. The fuck-up factor, Murphy's law, call it what you will, Viktor now had to deal with the consequences. He hoped for their sakes he was wrong, but somehow he could sense that a drama lay ahead.

Both Jim and Jack had no such misapprehensions and were now, four days in, finding their pace. They were raring to go. Having spent many a spring skiing and mushing across the frozen waterways of Minnesota's boundary waters reserve, they both felt confident and secure on overflow sections of ice, knowing full well that the ice beneath them was many feet thick. The problem was that the ice on which they were now traveling was a different creature altogether, a constantly moving, undulating and unpredictable cocktail of fresh water and sea ice at the mercy of the ocean's currents. Even sections many feet thick could be crushed open by opposing forces of undercurrent, lunar gravitational pull and severe gusts of Arctic surface wind.

Viktor realized he needed to shatter their illusions, and after a quick breakfast walked over to their tent. Despite his warnings, Jack was convinced Viktor was being over-cautious. After all, they were only a day and a half away from their midpoint and the ramifications of a barometric change would surely take a few days to register on the ice's stability. Viktor remained skeptical, and for the first time in the trip he and Jack agreed to differ. If Viktor was breaking trail surely it would be all right, and if they did hit a lead, reasoned Jack, they would cross that bridge when they came to it. Surely speed was now their best friend; since the ice was getting weaker they needed to travel faster to Architsky.

Not only did the weather affect the stability of the ice, it affected the dogs too. The first four days had seen ideal running conditions of around minus 20. Although a potentially dangerous temperature for unprotected areas of human skin, the ice was firm and the top crust thick. The dogs' metabolic engines raced and burned at a perfect equilibrium, helping them maintain a good thermal consistency even at flat-out running speeds. They were not too hot, cooled by the frigid air, and not so cold that they would need their protective paw covers – even huskies could get frostbitten and blistered feet. But after only an hour on the trail the dogs were showing signs of over-heating. By midday the thermometer had climbed to just under zero and combined with the bright, reflective surface of the snow and the high sun it was hard to believe they were traveling across the Arctic Ocean. As the dogs started to pant and struggle harder in the melting crust, Viktor slowed the pace and they stopped to remove layers of fleece and down. The dogs frantically ate snow and licked at the ice surface, desperate to rehydrate.

"This is really very strange, guys," shouted Viktor. "I haven't seen this kind of heat for many years. We will have to go carefully now, okay. Keep an eye out for leads and cracks. If the dogs go in, make sure you cut the tow-rope to the sled. They will be fine and we will have to help them back up on to the flow. If you go in, whatever you do don't panic, keep moving, keep buoyant and do whatever you have to do to get out. I will be there but keep an eye out for each other, okay? At least if you do get wet it's warm out, but understand this, you will be fighting for your life regardless. Just get those clothes off, get the tent up, get the stove going and get into your bag with each other, okay. I've had two dips and I re-regulated fine both times. No one has a heart condition, do they?"

Jack looked over at Jim. "Fuck that for a game of soldiers, Jim. Stay dry, okay?"

"Most definitely, dude!"

Jack noticed a look on Jim's face, a look he hadn't seen before. It was pure fear. The stark warning from Viktor had got to him, really put it up him, that and the heat, the pace they were setting, it all amounted to expedition stress, a stress there was no walking away from. Jim had always been so carefree, but maybe they had been in the city too long, had too much security, become too soft. Whatever the reason for Jim's nervousness, it worried Jack, since he was generally so reliable, so unflappable, so laid back.

Viktor's warning had the desired effect and as they set off toward the Cape there was a noticeable change in their movements. They were under no illusions: they were traveling on thin and ever-changing ice. For the next seven hours they made slow progress. Viktor was taking no chances and both Jim and Jack were grateful for his constant vigilance. They moved in a slow procession, Viktor stopping regularly to scan the horizon and take careful bearings on his large screened Garmin 75 GPS as they crisscrossed from solid section of pack to six-inch-deep overflow. Overflow always worried Jack: the foot of clear meltwater resting above many feet of ice took great nerve to cross, just in case it was an open lead and the light was playing tricks as it sometimes could. The most dangerous overflows were layered, the three-foot-thick ice being pockmarked with thermal holes leading to open sea beneath. Generally the overflows started to degrade well into the summer, but with high spring temperatures, nothing was certain. At the end of the day, judging the sea ice was down to experience, and that was a waiting game, it couldn't be rushed.

By 4pm they had made sufficient progress to be able to stop. Viktor was a stickler for routine and seemed to be able to set camp, crank the Coleman stove and get his HF call in simultaneously. But the ravages of the heat and the constant stress were beginning to take their toll on Jim, who by now was seriously dehydrated. Jack had been keeping an eye on him for most of the day, but the pace had been numbing and the overflows had meant that much greater attention was needed to keep to the trail. Jim sat on the side of the sled, his cheeks flushed red and his mouth dry. Jack felt his forehead and knew he was starting to go down. His exertion had led to dehydration then to heatstroke, his sweat glands having dried up on the trail. Now he was burning up, his pulse was high and Jack noticed that his speech was beginning to slur. Jack knew that in severe cases heatstroke could lead to loss of consciousness, cardiac arrest and coma. He needed to get Jim out of the elements, out of the unforgiving sun, let him rest up and administer fluids quickly. He got the stove going as Viktor came over to discuss the day.

"Hey Jim, you did well today. Tomorrow we make Architsky and then we will have the wind on our backs, much colder, I promise."

Viktor looked at Jack as Jim lay on his bag, eyes closed, a faint grin on his face.

"Hey, Jack, let's leave him to rest, I want to show you something."

Jack followed Viktor outside, sensing he wanted a quiet word.

"Is he okay? He looks, well, pretty fucked, I suppose, heatstroke maybe."

"No problems, Viktor, he'll be okay, just had a tough day, that's all. I think he's taken all that weak ice crap too seriously. At least you got him off worrying about the bears!"

"Yes, Jack, but it is a real danger, you know that, don't you? We need to clear the Cape tomorrow. We'll never make land otherwise. The pressure ridges are over twenty feet in some places from here in. If we can clear Architsky then it's a breeze, the ice build-up drops dramatically. We could probably camp on land tomorrow night and take another rest day, but we need to really go for it. I've told Ursula that we'll check in later tomorrow, maybe even the next morning, so we can make the camp on the far side of the Cape. Is that okay with you, Jack? I mean, you know his limitations better than me. We could chopper him out today, absolutely no problem with that."

Jack was somewhat taken aback and slightly insulted. Jim would be fine, he assured Viktor. He wasn't having him taken off the ice, since that could compromise the purity of the expedition, no way. They would do it together, they would show Viktor; Christ, they weren't tourists – they had put in some bush time over the years and they had never had a drama yet. Jim would be staying with him; after all, he would never forgive him. Evacuate? Not in a million years.

"Yes, I hear you, Viktor, but I know him, really don't sweat it," replied Jack somewhat defensively. "We've done a lot of this before, Viktor, okay? Trust me. He just needs to get enough fluid down him tonight and he'll break trail all day tomorrow. He's that kind of guy. There is just no fat on him, all high-twitch muscle. He has days like that on all our trips. Personally, I put it down to a severe lack of pussy myself. The boy just can't live without it."

They both laughed, tensely.

"Good, Jack, I like that. He seemed strong until today. It's just easy to go down out here. Hell, it could happen to me tomorrow. Just keep an eye on him, you're the boss."

Viktor walked back to his tent shaking his head. He hadn't seen that in Jack before, the pride thing, and that niggled him. Sure, it was his trip, he was paying and he had planned an interesting first, the Arrowhead, but pride, it could be a killer, combined with the competitive nature of exploration. That was why he had chosen to go solo on all his major trips.

He hated the rivalry and buzz of competition within a group. It all seemed so futile, egotistical and pointless. In reality, theorized Viktor, one is born alone and one dies alone. Who better to compete against than oneself? That way at least when Murphy reared his ugly head, you only had yourself to blame, only your own life to lose.

★ ★ ★

That night the wind picked up to near gale force and Jack slept lightly, listening to the sound of the guy ropes playing in the sudden gusts and the sporadic dull creaking of the pack. Even the sound of the dogs and Viktor's loud snoring had been drowned by the wind. Periodically, Jack woke and helped his friend sip the Kool-aid that he had prepared earlier. The sugars made it more desirable to drink than plain water and helped restore Jim's energy. He was glad of the long night, as he knew Jim needed to rest. Despite his defense of his friend, Jack had to admit he had been struck by how quickly Jim had gone down. At least he had a good ten hours of rest ahead of him. He would need it.

★ ★ ★

In the twilight hours the bear came, floating by, coming to rest in Jack's dreams. Ironically, Jim had forgotten about his previous nemesis, while Jack was now traveling with that great animal. The strange thing was that in his dream the bear wasn't a threat, he was more of a guide, a sentinel. He was huge, standing well over fourteen feet on his great hind legs, pillars of muscle, on the edge of the floe. The water though, that was another matter. It lay before him, menacing Jack in his warm bag, all around him, just outside the tent, lapping against the snow valance. Furthermore, he was alone in the wild and unable to move, unable to act, cocooned in his bag. It was as if he were a spectator in the dream, unable to affect the outcome or influence events, the water and the bear and a loud snoring and farting presence that existed somewhere deep inside the tent.

★ ★ ★

By morning Jim seemed stronger and for once Jack was relieved to hear him fart loudly.

"Fuck, Jim, you're an asshole! I babysit you all night and that's how you repay me!"

Jim, still hidden in the depths of his bivi bag, peered over the lip of the GoreTex hood, a glint in his eye. "Hey, dude, think of it as breakfast!"

"Don't, Jim, I'll puke!" snapped Jack.

After a quick coffee and one of Jim's favorite nut bars, Jack unzipped the tent door.

"Time for the morning cable," he announced. "I'll bring you back a piece if you like, Jim."

"No, I'll pass, Jack," replied Jim as he disappeared back inside his voluminous down bag.

Outside the sky was grey and foreboding and the wind blew in a constant forceful gust. As Jack stumbled out on to the pack, he gasped. But it was not the strength of the wind that had taken him aback. It was the inky black water that lay only feet from the tent's door. As he stood staring wide-eyed across the pack, the full horror of their predicament confronted him. Viktor was nowhere to be seen. His tent was gone. The dogs were gone. The open lead was so wide that the pack was many hundreds of feet away. Jack stood silent, staring out across the still water.

"Jack, for fuck's sake, dude! Zip up the tent, man. I'm freezing in here."

Jack didn't reply.

"Jack, er, hello man, are you there? Earth calling Jack..."

Jack, still facing the lead, knelt and carefully reversed into the tent's outer compartment. He crouched motionless, silhouetted by the bright light of day. And there he stayed, transfixed by something, something real yet utterly unimaginable. Turning to Jim, he at last managed to summon up the words to speak.

"Jim, I think you had better take a look outside, man. I think we are in shit, Jim, seriously big shit ..."

★ ★ ★

Jim, now fully awake, spun around in his bag and lay in the tent's opening. Together they stared at the water. It was dangerously close to the tent, lapping gently against the turquoise wall of the berg. The ice edge was firm, though, and was raised above the water level by over a foot. Behind them there was a good solid section of pack but this lay at least thirty yards to the south. For the time being they were marooned, resting on a berg no more than forty feet in diameter. To the north there was now only open water and, far more ominously, no sign of Viktor. He had vanished, and deep down they both knew he was gone.

The wind had been so strong and loud they hadn't even heard his calls for help, if indeed he had even managed to call out. The lead had probably cracked right under his tent, no more than twenty yards from theirs, and he wouldn't have even made it out of his bag. The dogs too, tethered to ice screws and secured by karabiners to Viktor's laden sled, wouldn't have stood a chance. It just was too terrible and tragic to contemplate. The radio was gone, the rifle, the ammunition and all twenty-eight dogs. They had no skis, only snowshoes, the flare pistol with five flares and enough food for no more than ten days. Worse still, they were more than 250 nautical miles from the met station, with no GPS. Jim had his compass, but navigation above the magnetic North Pole required a complicated geographic offset that they had only used once before.

At least it would be possible, since Jack had packed the spare map and had marked all the camps each night. To reach Ostrov Shar, their starting point, they had over five days of dog travel, well in excess of ten days by foot and then a further four days to cross the channel back to Zemelya. A total of twenty-three days of man haul, weather permitting, with no open leads and no polar bears.

After discussing the options they agreed that they needed to move on fast, divide up the loads and repack. The sled bags could be dragged on their trays and they both set to work, fixing harnesses out of spare 8mm rope and karabiners. They had one other option. They could wait . . . wait for a chopper that might never find them, for help that might never arrive. The survival handbook dictates that if you are lost in the wild, you should seek shelter and wait by your plane, jeep or camp. But out there there was no fixed location, no last refuge. The moving pack can shift seven miles in a single day, and with leads, overflow and changing wind there was no guarantee there would even be any pack left in the next few hours, let alone the next day.

When Ursula didn't receive her call from Viktor again she would wait, probably another twelve to twenty-four hours, before alerting the chopper, a total of over forty-eight hours of not knowing. No, it was better they moved on, tried at least to head for the security of land. At least then they would sleep secure in the fact that they wouldn't meet the fate Viktor had suffered – thrashing wildly, desperate to survive, desperate to break out of his tent, spluttering, suffocating and eventually succumbing to the cool asphyxia of drowning, trapped in his nylon tomb. And now at peace, forever, 1,000 feet below the ice, drifting with the Arctic currents. Viktor's death didn't bear thinking about. They had to move on, for their sanity if nothing else.

Jack took the first bearing south-south-east. After some discussion they agreed that the calculation for geographic offset was approximately 75 degrees, since the needle pointed southward toward the magnetic Pole some 500 miles to their south on Canada's Cornwallis Island. Jack concluded that information such as this is stored in the rear of our minds, the section of the brain reserved for specific facts and figures that one rarely needs. Jack was always amazed at how often he managed to forget the very things he had trained so hard to learn. Information such as this, although vital at the time, loses its relevance when spreadsheets, board meetings and late-night drinking sessions are the daily norm.

They had one insurmountable problem, however, that even a sound compass bearing couldn't solve; they were drifting, totally disconnected from the pack. The readings would be obsolete in a matter of minutes and then there was the ice. Jack and Jim decided to make safe all their kit and pack. The barometer remained strapped to Jim's makeshift sled. The weather was clear and calm and they sat, alert and quiet, in disbelief of their predicament. Viktor's disappearance hung over them like a dark foreboding cloud and as the hours passed a sense of hopelessness engulfed them.

★ ★ ★

It was then that Jack noticed the figure walking toward him on the water. He had been staring toward the south for over an hour, his snow goggles fixed on the horizon, when he noticed the man. Could it be Viktor? Jack's heart raced. But the man moved in a different manner and he was impossibly tall. As he approached Jack could see that he was wearing the telltale great coat and the felt trilby. It was Beuys.

Beuys stood now no more than twenty yards from him on the dark water, his body undulating with the rhythm of the current. As Jack craned forward for a closer look, his hand shielding his eyes from the harsh sun, he realized the water had come together and become something other than liquid. It was not altogether solid but a new amorphous substance, rubberized, glutinous, malleable. It was then that he remembered the Inuit and their thirty words for snow, the sixty variations of sea ice, and realized that this was shulia, rubber ice, an Arctic phenomenon, the result of the early refreezing and coming together of the pack after high temperatures. Beuys had known that the water had changed. He had proved that it was safe and could take the weight of a man. He turned his face, now masked in shadow, his greatcoat trailing in the wind, and he walked back into the snowscape until he was far from view, dissolving into the haze and mist of the southerly snowfields.

★ ★ ★

Jack snapped to, jolted by his apparition. He grabbed Jim and told him, dragging him to the barometer, laughing for joy. They hugged and sat quietly again, then they both stood up and Jack produced a ruble from his parka pocket. Jim watched the coin spin and looked up, thanking a higher power. Jack decided to attempt the crossing. He would do it on the long snowshoes and he would do it quickly.

Jim secured a length of rope around Jack's chest and locked it off with a bowline knot after tying it double at the waistline. The makeshift harness meant that if he did go in at least he had some chance. The sled and kit would come later; for now they would need to see whether Jack could make it without falling in. Then Jack made his move: holding on to Jim's outstretched ski pole for support, he stepped out, down on to the surreal surface of the shulai, and it held him. Letting go of Jim and balancing precariously, Jack took the next step and then the next, an unsteady water boatman moving diligently across the surface of the open sea.

The rubber ice held, Jack's weight displaced by the oversized snowshoes. He took yet more steps, then climbed up and fell face first on to the surface of the solid section of firm ice once more, elated and alive. Jim tied off the kit and Jack dragged the sled across the open lead; then he belayed Jim, slowly at first, but Jim was such a good dancer, lighter on his feet, cocky almost, his fear reserved for the bear as Jack's was for the water. Then they both stood firm and safe, their legs feeling the solidity of the three-foot-thick section, the whole of it now before them, the long route back to Sredny.

Four hours later, after crossing countless shallow overflows, they picked up their old tracks from the day before, still crisp and firm, despite the previous day's high temperatures. Together they moved at a painfully slow pace, tiny black ants crossing the endless whiteness of the Arctic Ocean. Thankfully, the open rubble-free sections of pack offered little resistance to their weighty, improvised pulks and their progress was constant, a good end to a very bad day.

There is a navigational mantra that says: "Just because you are lost it doesn't follow that your compass is broken." Jack and Jim were experienced enough to trust their compass, and as dusk fell and the pink half-light covered the horizon they came to a familiar, yellowish section of snow. In less than fifteen hours they had made it back to camp four, the dogs' night-time beds still indented into the snow and the odd wisp of dog hair snagged in the ice. They hugged each other tightly and cried together like children for the first time since their youth. In their hurry to retrace their tracks and make land they had hardly talked all day, stopping only to eat a brief lunch and take on fluid. Now alone but warm, they kept hold of each other. Jack fought hard to keep back the tears, but the sight of the dogs' beds was too much and their grief acted as a deep and painful release from the tensions of the past twenty-four hours. They had survived day one of the ordeal, survived the rubber ice, the open leads, the overflows, and tragically they had survived Viktor, the great Russian explorer lost to the open sea. Two kids from Minnesota had made it, this far at least, and Jack knew now that they had a chance, as long as the temperatures held low enough to keep the pack from breaking up, and as long as they held their nerve.

As the spring sun dipped low, never quite leaving the horizon, Jack cranked the stove and hauled all their kit into the tent, a final breathless effort at the end of a traumatic and grueling day. After a small silent dinner of pasta and beans, they lay back into their bags and fell fast asleep, a deep exhausted sleep one only experiences when one has simply nothing left to give. Outside the wind had died down and a frigid breeze gently caressed the walls of their tent. The temperature was dropping and with it, they prayed, lay a safe passage home.

★ ★ ★

Jack wasn't sure what first alerted him to the fact that they were not alone. Whether it was a primal sense of knowing or just a need to take a piss that woke him he could not be sure, but whatever the cause, he woke with a start at about 3am. The wind had picked up again, but as he lay alert and rigid in the dark tent he swore he could hear a faint shuffling in the snow outside. Jim lay oblivious to the presence of danger, snoring happily inside his bag. As Jack lay silent, his mind raced and he pinched himself hard on the arm to make sure he was awake and that this was not a dream.

Was it the wind or a nosy Arctic fox, or was it his worst fear, a polar bear? Then he heard it, a low, deep grunt. Jim turned in his sleep. For fuck's sake don't wake now, he thought. The bear was close, sniffing along the snow valance to Jack's left. He had sensed something. Was it the smell of last night's dinner or of something warm inside the alien form of the tent? Maybe the bear could taste Jack's fear, his sensitive nose deciphering the strange and subtle cocktails of toxins and pheromones exuded by the human body's various sweat glands in time of anxiety and stress. Jack watched transfixed as the side of their tent pushed inwards, morphing into the shape of the huge snout and head of a massive bear. The nylon-clad head froze and moved slowly to the right, then to the left, as if attempting to locate the object of its interest, its radar active, scanning for its target.

Jack carefully rolled over to Jim's side and, pinning him down, holding him firmly by the mouth, prodded his friend. Jim woke slowly, struggling under Jack's bulk. He whispered in Jim's ear, "Just don't say a word, not a fucking word."

Together they lay motionless, tracking the huge form with only their wide eyes, unable to speak, transfixed with the terror known only by hunted prey. They were now very much in the food chain and they knew it. Their only hope lay in the faint chance the bear would get bored and move on. After almost half an hour the animal withdrew his long neck and turned his attention to the makeshift sleds. They could hear him pounding the plastic trays and runners, repeatedly bouncing and jumping down on the sleds with his forepaws, a painful reminder of the uncontrollable rage he would inflict on them should he get hold of them. This was no place for a human to be. It was the bear's patch, it was his territory and he wanted them gone. He could smell humans and he knew that the smell meant danger. He just couldn't quite locate them. From a young age his mother would have taught him to avoid the noisy people with their skidoos, their guns and their unworldly flying machines. Now in his eighth year, these were his first humans and his naturally gregarious adolescent nature drove him to investigate further. But his intentions had not yielded the food he craved. In spite of his inquisitiveness, a stronger inbuilt intuition warned him to be careful. The bear didn't like the unfamiliar form of the tent – he had never seen anything like it before and it spooked him.

By morning he had moved on to hunt for unwitting seals, a more familiar quarry and a sport he knew well. Jack and Jim lay awake the rest of the night, unable to relax, unable to breathe fully. Cautiously emerging from the tent and their living nightmare at daybreak, they saw the bear's huge seventeen-inch tracks leading off to the north-east. For the time being at least he had disappeared from view, not so far as never to return or to give them any sense of security, but just far enough, they hoped, for them to get back on the trail, a task for which they now needed no prompting. They knew they needed to put as many miles between themselves and the bear as possible. They also knew that if he was not successful in his hunting by the next night he would return, hungrier and more stubborn in his efforts to feed.

The day remained cold. It was significantly colder than the previous day, ice crystals forming instantaneously on Jack's beard as he exhaled with each breath. By 2pm the temperature had hit minus 25. The wind picked up and with it came a new and silent enemy, exposure and frostbite. The never-ending problem with man hauling in the Arctic was trying to control overheating. The added stress of a bear close by had a natural effect of releasing more adrenaline and in so doing more heat. The bear was stamped into their conscience. Every pressure ridge and ice fissure concealed his bulk. The anxiety was dreadful, the pace fast going and hot. Jack just couldn't get his body temperature right. First he was too hot. Stripping down to thermals and then down again to his ventile wind suit, he found the wind cut into him. So he started to push the pace. Jim, always a racing snake, seemed stronger that day, probably on account of his large fluid intake the night before and his few more hours of precious sleep. But at full tilt, although his heart, lungs and legs were burning to overload, Jack managed to get warm and more importantly began to control his profuse sweating. Stopping every hour to take on board fluids, they finally hit their rhythm, the rhythm that Viktor a week earlier had been so intent that they should find. Feeling strong and walking on rubble-free, solid pack, they had decided to keep moving until they were too exhausted to move on further and then set camp. Mentally the bear was still with them, and although many miles away, he weighed heavily. In their collective imagination their fear of the polar bear drove them on and in so doing drove them ever closer to land.

★ ★ ★

By the time they had set camp on the evening of their seventh day, Ursula had not received a radio call from Viktor for over forty-eight hours. She was worried, extremely worried, and at 8pm decided enough was enough. At 8:10pm she called Major Alexi Aleievich at the airstrip. Alexi had been stationed with his search and rescue (S & R) crew on a two-year attachment to this, the highest and most remote Russian flight mission. Major Aleievich had been flying Mi8 choppers since his teens as a young lieutenant in Afghanistan in the mid '80s. He had requested the posting to escape from the bureaucracy and torpor that had infected the majority of once-promising airforce officers. Getting paid a regular bonus for his remote and some would say tedious mission, Alexi was happy to save the money and make plans for his retirement, which he planned to spend in the densely forested hillside town of Lavriki, a short drive outside St Petersburg. During his posting Alexi and Viktor had become close friends, flying countless sorties to the North Pole base camp of Borneo together and numerous S & R missions in the surrounding archipelago.

As he sat in his small office beside the icy airstrip listening to Ursula's controlled but wavering voice, he knew there was a problem. Talking calmly to Ursula, he assured her he would leave at first light. He had noted their proposed route and had all the GPS waypoints that Viktor had already detailed to Ursula. If there was anyone who could find Viktor it was going to be Alexi Aleievich. He would find her husband, his friend and the two Americans. He gave her his word and she was reassured.

That night the wind turned. Now a strong southerly howled and fought its way northwards through the gullies and channels of ice rubble. Inside their tent Jack and Jim were blissfully unaware of the fresh signals and smells that their evening meal was now transmitting across the pack. Jack had decided that due to the plummeting temperatures they would store their food in its sealed container inside the tent and not on the sled. The freshly finished bowls of tuna fish pasta could wait until morning; besides, they rationalized, they were too tired to clean up now. Better to get their heads down. It had been a terribly long day.

As Major Aleievich walked out to the hangar in the early hours to prepare the chopper with his three-man crew, the adolescent polar bear located a strange and curious array of smells on the fresh southerly wind. Following his nose, against his instincts to move further north, he about-turned and began to retrace his tracks toward the new inviting aromas. Just as he did when hunting seals or other prey, the bear lumbered southwards carefully, his nose held high into the oncoming wind, a silent predator shielded from his prey by the force and direction of the high wind. His great paw pads made easy going of the firm pack, displacing his 1,000-

pound mass evenly across the thick refrozen crust, which was now as tough as tarmac. After no more than two hours he had covered over ten miles and now he rested only 100 yards from the strange form he had inspected the night before, the source of the inviting smells. Finding a large indentation to the side of a small ice fissure, the bear lay down on his huge forepaws and watched his quarry with keen intensity. He was used to the waiting game, it was what he had been taught by his mother many winters ago. Lie and wait, the seals would come.

At around 6am Jim awoke. Jack for once was still fast asleep, deep in dreams, and deciding not to wake his friend Jim silently slipped on his down-filled camp boots and parka and headed out into the Arctic twilight to take his ritual dump. The light was fantastic, clean and new, raking silver rays across the horizon. The entire pack shone with a monochromatic lustre, betrayed only by a subtle pink hue that grew with every minute from the east. It was without doubt Jim's favorite time of day. He walked cautiously, stopping about twenty yards from the tent, aware of his vulnerability during his ensuing ablutions. Hunkering down next to a small ice block, he unzipped the trapdoor of his thermal sleepsuit and exhaled a long plume of frosted breath as he took his first crap of the day.

Barely yards away, the bear was watching. First he watched the clumsy human leave the strange form, then he slowly craned his great neck, following him to the ice block. As Jim crouched down, the bear, making not a single sound, stretched out and covering his large black nose with his paw began to inch toward the unsuspecting prey.

Jim had left the tent's zip undone in his rush, and Jack was awoken by the first rays of daylight dancing across his face. He rolled over to check on Jim and found he was gone. "Fucker," he muttered under his breath. He could at least have zipped up the tent, he thought. Rolling over to shout to his friend, Jack watched in horror as the now visible bear crawled slowly toward the ice block and the unsuspecting Jim. The situation was fast getting out of control. Jack quickly put on his boots and shouted in a low, strained, teeth-clenched voice to his friend.

"Jim, there's a bear, coming your way!"

Jim's head came up in a flash. Squatting rigid and alert in the half-light, he spotted the bear now only ten yards from him. Jack dived back inside the tent and fumbled in the hood of his daypack for the flare gun, which aside from his ice axe was the only weapon they had between them. Shouting at the now standing bear, he pointed the large-bored pistol, his hand wavering with fear. Jim by now had slowly managed to backtrack toward the tent, but as Jack fell back inside the opening the bear lowered his head and charged. Jim managed to control his desire to run long enough for Jack to take aim at the moving bear. Standing in the door of the tent he closed his left eye and nervously fingered the trigger while tracking the bear, which was now pacing to and fro in an irritable and confused manner. The bear turned its head toward the tent and stared for a split second at Jack. Now there were two humans.

Trying to take control of the desperate situation, Jack called over to his friend. "Jim, when I fire this pistol you get back to me, okay."

"Yeah, dude, whatever, just make sure you hit him."

Jack aimed the flare pistol carefully and squeezed the trigger. As the firing pin hit the small center-fire charge at the flare's base, the pistol jerked in his hand with a hollow pop and a bright orange trace of phosphor snaked toward the bear, arching over the animal's back close enough to singe the fur on his rump. The bear spun around and stared at Jack, lowering its head, its ears back, under threat – its black dead eyes sent a terrifying and piercing glare in his direction. As the bear turned back to look at the fizzing flare he angrily stamped it into the snow, only to recoil from the sharp burning sensation as the dying embers fused into the hard skin pad of his paw. The bear was incensed.

As Jack fell back into the entrance of the tent he quickly fumbled with the release lever on the side of the pistol, pulled out the spent flare and quickly loaded another twelve-gauge cartridge. Managing to muster the courage to stand once more, Jack looked over to Jim, who was crouched frozen with fear.

"Jack, for God's sake hit him . . . please, just do something . . . *please* do something . . ."

Jack knew time was running out. As he aimed for a second time the bear paced back and forth, now equidistant between the two of them. First the bear looked at Jim, then at Jack, sizing them up, deciding which one would make the easiest prey. Again Jack closed his eye, looking over to Jim for reassurance, but this time the bear fixed on him and Jack found himself unable to move, unable to summon the strength to pull the trigger, unable to act at all. As they stood there, the impossibility of the situation dawned on Jack. The fear of missing again began to eat away at him and he realized that if the bear charged he would need the last round to save himself.

As Jack hesitated and his mind raced through the options available to him, Jim made the biggest mistake of his life. He began to run. Jim had given the bear the focus he needed and in a split second the animal charged again, cutting off Jim's escape. Lunging forward, he swiped at Jim as he headed toward the tent. The blow hit him on the buttock with such force it literally picked him up and sent him sprawling into the snow. Jack was paralyzed with fear. Worse still, he found himself unable to move, frozen with dread, and watched, helpless and impotent to act, as the bear set about flailing his friend. Waving the loaded flare pistol above his head, Jack started to scream. "Stop, you cunt, stop!"

Jack sobbed but he couldn't muster the courage needed to fire another shot. Any interference on his part would surely result in the bear turning his terrible ferocity on him. And what if he missed again? The thought consumed him and he sat helpless, screaming as the bear tore into his friend. Jim attempted to roll into a ball, trying to contain his ripping pain and fear so as not to cry out, but soon it was too late. Jim was wilting under the rain of devastating, crushing blows that opened up his back and abdomen, cutting him with deeply lacerated, clawed gouges until the snow oozed pink with his thick arterial blood. Moments later, the bear, bloodied and exhausted, stopped and stood over Jim, panting huge clouds of steamy meaty breath over his victim. Jack lay cowering in the tent's entrance, sobbing until he had nothing else to cry. Then the bear did something unexpected. He turned his head toward the sky and, sensing something unfamiliar, began to lope off, his huge paws leaving a visible trail of blood across the pack. Once again he had been spooked. His highly tuned senses had stopped him eating his hard-won meal. There was something in the air, a sound he either didn't know or like, and all he knew was that he wanted to escape it. Soon he was gone.

★ ★ ★

Alexi spotted the bear first, running at full tilt across the frozen ocean. He swooped down low to get a closer look and watched the large animal crash through low ice walls and stagger powerfully across silvery sections of mirror-like refrozen overflow. There was something about the bear's movements that concerned him. The frantic, almost distressed nature of a disturbed bear or perhaps the dark black singe marks on the bear's right flank alerted him to the fact that something about this bear was wrong. Banking right, he flew back in the direction of the bear's flight. Within seconds Alexi spotted the small black domed tent and the pathetic, lifeless form lying in the adjacent bloodstained snow. Jack, now inconsolable with grief, managed to stagger to his friend, first kneeling and finally lying next to him as if to keep him warm. As the chopper came to rest on the pack, spindrift covered the two prone figures and for a brief moment covered any sign of the brutal attack.

The flight engineer was the first to reach Jack. Before the Mi8 could land, Boris Sergei Serov jumped the last five feet on to the hard snow below and raced across the pack with his medical kit. Kneeling down in the rotor wash of swirling snow, he tried to check Jim's vital signs but Jack pushed him aside, his face fixed with a terrible mask of red, incomprehensible anger and fear. Boris grabbed him and held him tight with his short powerful arms as Jack fought to stay with his friend, still gripping the flare pistol. Boris took it from his grasp and in a deft movement opened the chamber. To his surprise he found the pistol loaded. For a brief moment he caught Jack's eye until Jack, calmer now, looked away in shame.

"I am here to help. Please let me help him. We need to get you out of here now, okay," Boris pleaded with the distraught Jack, and as he stopped struggling he began to work on his friend.

First he checked Jim's vital signs. He had no respiration, a faint pulse. Boris started working on Jim's sternum, and with his large gloved hands placed over each other, fingers interlaced, he began massaging in a fast rhythm, trying to resuscitate Jim, trying to coerce his flagging motor centers back to life. Every fifteen compressions Boris went back to Jim's bloodied face and with a well practiced movement pinched the nose and extended the jaw. Being careful to protect his lower neck and cervical spine, he blew two deep breaths into Jim's mouth, watching intently, his ear close to Jim's chest, for a pronounced rise and fall, and then he checked the airway. He alternated his routine, back to the chest with fifteen more compressions, two respirations and then began the cycle again. Jack slumped back in the snow and stared on with blank, vacant eyes until in a blur of slow motion he felt strong arms lifting him higher and higher above the ground, the snow swirling, the wind soothing him, the rotors' dull rhythm numbing his torn senses.

Jack remembered closing his eyes and then nothing but a silent, surging, black, warm nothingness smothering him like a felt quilt. As the nausea took hold of him he rolled over and began to retch repeatedly until there was nothing left. He lay on the warm, foam floor of the chopper and slipped, unconscious with fatigue, into a deep stupor. He was going home and Jim was next to him, his friend, a lifeless, broken body wrapped in a survival blanket. Jack had survived and he was going home, only this time he was going alone. Boris' potentially lifesaving procedures had been in vain. Jim had hung on for over half an hour but as the massive wounds ebbed his life's blood into the cold snow his peripheries had shut down and when his core temperature dropped his body had gone into hypovolemic shock. There was nothing anyone could have done. No crash room, no ER in a modern hospital could have brought him back from the eternal journey he was going on. His injuries were too traumatic and he had passed away out there in the cold, on a beautiful spring morning in Siberia at the hands of a magnificent predator. The Dolgan people of the Siberian Arctic would say that it was a good death for a hunter, but for Jack and the crew of the Mi8 it was the most terrible thing any of them had ever seen, a pointless waste of a promising young life and the certain death of a bear that couldn't be allowed to kill again.

★ ★ ★

The news of Jim's and Viktor's deaths hit the tiny community on Sredny like a nuclear warhead. Russia had lost one of its great Arctic explorers, Ursula her beloved husband, Mikaela her dear brother and Jack his best friend. News of the tragedy had traveled far and wide and within twenty-four hours the ancient party-line phone system to the met station was jammed with incoming calls from Russia's press and media, clamoring for information on the double tragedy. As Jack lay unconscious from his ordeal in a fitful state of shock in the small medical room at the met station, with Mikaela by his side, Ursula had the impossible and unenviable job of organizing the search for Viktor's body and the repatriation of Jim's corpse to the USA.

Soon the US news networks – CNN, ABC, NBC – the BBC World Service radio and key elements of the European media had got wind of Jim's death, a westerner, one of their own. A fatal mauling by a large predator was high on their syndication sales tables. Government officials, the mayor of St Petersburg and the coroner's office in Norilsk had to be briefed and paperwork completed. Viktor and Mikaela's brother, Eugene, had flown in to help look after Ursula and Mikaela, who after two days were themselves in a total state of shock and exhaustion, inconsolable at the loss of their beloved Viktor. Only after Jack had been given sedatives on the day of his rescue did the awful news about Viktor's death emerge. Alexi for one had found it hard to imagine that a man as experienced in polar travel as Viktor could die in that way. However, when the full story was recounted everyone realized that out on the spring ice pack such open-water leads are a daily occurrence. To be camped on one as it opened during a storm at night was one of life's frequent injustices of time and place.

The shock of that fatal day had hit Jack so hard that within twelve hours of Jim's death his body had gone into a state of non-life-threatening shock, a common self-preserving physiological reaction to extreme trauma, both mental and physical. It was as if his body had shut down by command of a single switch, which in a way it had, his overly active brain overriding the basic function of his body's motor reflexes to allow him time to recuperate and take stock of the tragedy. Mikaela had tended to Jack throughout his recovery, a therapeutic and cathartic remedy to her own personal loss. She even felt somewhat responsible for the chain of events and in a perverse way, she had been. After all, she had set up the trip, made the introductions and got Viktor involved.

Jack for the most part lay still, his eyelids flickering, his breathing shallow. He had lost weight on the trip, maybe as much as fourteen pounds, and he looked pale, the color having faded from his normally ruddy cheeks. Mikaela sat patiently by him for many hours at a time. She held his hand, caressing his fingertips and talking to him constantly. For the most part her patter was mundane – what they had eaten that day, the changing weather, how Ursula and the team were bearing up. But she also talked about the two of them, the past few weeks, anything that would give him a connection, a reference to their time together and for her past affections, anything that could explain to Jack how she was feeling. Mikaela's time alone with Jack in the sick bay was very important for her. It helped her think her feelings through, devoid of pressure, and it made her sad that now with Viktor gone things would be different between them.

Until the tragedy, Jack and Mikaela had been in a familiar place, both of them, from a relationship perspective, at the beginning of a long road. The trip was meant to have been so wonderful, escaping from the big city together, allowing themselves the opportunity to really get to know each other. But now, with Viktor's death, things had changed significantly, despite Mikaela's previous passion. On reflection, she knew that the past few weeks had not been enough to cement what they had together, and instead of an affirmation of love, she was left only with doubt. What terrified her was the growing realization that the intensity of her feelings for Jack had died along with her brother. She had heard about Jack's episode in the chopper with Boris, the loaded flare gun, his inaction, him not being quite the man she thought he was, and that added to her confusion.

Mikaela studied Jack's fine features on his pale bearded face and she traced a line with her slender finger across his nose and chin, touching his lips, lips that only a few days before she had been kissing tenderly. Then she remembered their last night together before he left, his detachment, then not a single radio message, and the pain she had suffered and how used she had felt. Whatever the reasons, over the past few days she had had enough time to reflect, alone in her room in the met station, maybe too much time: New York, her career, meeting Jack, the heady rush of it all. And now, looking at her man, a man she had wanted so much to be with, his intoxicating energy, his passion, his love of art ... it all seemed to be fading away.

Her brother's death undeniably had a great deal to do with her change of heart, but there was a deeper realization that had begun to gnaw at her. It was the fact of their disparate lives, his in New York City, hers in Russia, which she had felt the minute the plane had touched down in her motherland. They were too different, worlds apart, and having spent this time away she knew she didn't want to return to a foreign city where she felt so lost, where life was such a struggle. In Moscow or St Petersburg it was easier, the movie work; she was quite well known, and there was always modeling if the film work dried up. The truth was that she had been missing home too much – the culture, the language, her family – and she needed to be with Ursula, the kids and Eugene now.

Mikaela had come to recognize what made her tick, her very life-blood ingrained in the soil of Russia. She needed to be here mourning for Viktor's soul, lost under the ice, forever floating in the frigid Siberian ocean currents. It was Viktor's icy tomb that obsessed her; she felt an ice-cold wall of resentment growing within her, a defensive barrier to her past affections, and she knew she could no longer continue her relationship with Jack.

Initially the two of them were after the same thing – it was all they had wanted at the time: the sex, the chase, a wild time, pure unadulterated mutual lust, no strings attached. Then something had changed in Jack, he softened, and she had liked that until she came home to Russia and saw that for her it couldn't work. He had it all and more – the money, the apartment, the successful career. He would not be able to leave his life behind him, why would he? Surely, she reasoned, Jack had too much to lose? Whether or not she was protecting herself from any future rejection she couldn't say, but she decided not to tell him what she had found out after visiting the drugstore at the airport. She had hidden the small indicator from him and planned to save it until just before dinner on the last night before his trip.

That last night she had wanted to tell him her news so much it hurt. But she understood that it wouldn't have been fair on him, his focus and energy would have been set off kilter by a simple plastic tube and its brilliant blue window. How a color could change a life. But it had, and she knew she would keep it, the new life growing inside her. Jack didn't need to know, not now, not in his present state, he was too vulnerable, and even Ursula agreed that he might do something rash, commit to something he couldn't make good on, persuade her to do something on his terms, something that in time they both would regret. Mikaela wasn't going back to his city, she would remain in Sredny with her family, have her child, replace a life lost, and only after their child was born would she tell him. She thought it was best, to make a clean break and go it alone.

★ ★ ★

As Jack emerged from his week-long sleep it was clear to everyone that he had far from recovered. He was understandably low, yet his distance and strangeness made it easier for Mikaela to do what she knew she must, undergo the process of removing Jack from her feelings. It would hurt as much as the burden of her secret, as if it was trying to rip her open, like a conscience, burning away at the heart and the logical part of her brain. But she could be so cold, as tough as they came. She was grieving for her brother and to some extent for Jim, and that pain tempered her resolve. Mikaela decided she would be there for Jack only until he was better, "up and at 'em" as he used to say. And she had to keep him away from her love; after all, she would need all of it, now welling up inside her, for her unborn child. That growing life would take all her energy and focus from now on.

On regaining consciousness Jack had clammed up, refusing to talk about the tragedy, answer questions or even defend himself. The reasons for his inability to discuss that day on the ice were both complex and, after analysis, strikingly simple. Ultimately he blamed himself, not just for Jim's death but for Viktor's too. From his somewhat paranoid perspective, he saw that he had organized the trip, planned the route, pushed the course and survived. The fact that he hadn't suffered so much as a scratch meant he was determined to pay emotionally and mentally, a self-imposed fine of guilt and culpability. The victims of post-traumatic stress disorder commonly feel a deep-seated anger, a hatred and contempt for those around them who have not shared in the experience and in turn a corrosive aversion toward themselves. Jack's insistence on self-blame was the key factor in his alienation of others and ultimately of those closest to him. He even managed to rationalize this behavior in a number of outbursts toward Mikaela.

"I don't like what I see, Mikaela, at night in my dreams, awake, looking in the mirror, right now. I don't like who I am. That's it, simple. I am a coward and I let my best friend die."

On two occasions Mikaela, her eyes full of tears, tried to intervene, begging Jack to share his fears and his sadness, to describe to her the scene of Viktor's drowning. He refused, and stormed out of the room in a violent outburst of frustration and anger. Later that night, after a pathetic attempt to apologize for his unreasonable behavior, he suggested he might leave on the next southbound flight. Mikaela, by now beyond caring, had the opportunity she needed and walked out, refusing to see him off. Turning to Jack in a fit of rage and sobbing bitterly, she shouted, "It's over, Jack! We're over. You ruined everything."

And then she said it, the thing she would later regret, a lie, and as the words slipped from her mouth she knew they weren't true. "Their blood is on your hands, Jack. Boris, flight engineer, he told us last night about flare. You right to blame yourself, you selfish bastard. You let friend die, you big man Jack, you tough guy. And Viktor my brother, only you know about that, eh Jack!"

Jack stood confronted by Mikaela, Ursula and Eugene, shocked by the vehemence of her outburst. After she fled the room the others tried to console him, to explain to him that she was not herself, she was delusional even, over-stressed and emotionally drained. But their words did nothing to help. Jack was broken by them, utterly destroyed and confused, and said nothing. He stayed standing as they all left the room, silent and in tears, and remained there for a while, alone, sadder than he had ever felt before. The room began to close around him, trapping him, leaving him with no way out except for a small door. Jack could tell it was far too small to fit through. Soon he was enveloped in the coffin, and all around him became dark. No space, no light, no one, just himself and a fear of being trapped inside for ever.

It was only after some time, standing there desperate and cold, that he felt the warmth of another. He opened his eyes and she was holding him, whispering in his ear and sobbing, pleading with him for forgiveness, not to hate her for her harsh words, begging him to understand. But she knew he could not, that whatever they had had was dead in her heart and in his mind. Mikaela had made that clear, and to Jack there could be no turning back. He could do nothing but hold her hand limply and look down, fresh tears landing on his boots, dripping on to the cold stone floor.

★ ★ ★

Jack left Sredny the next day on the weekly Antanov bound for Khatanga. Two days later he was in St Petersburg waiting for a flight home. He had checked into St Petersburg's Grand Hotel Europe and spent the afternoon in his top floor terrace room, lying on the huge Swedish duvet, feeling its luxuriance envelop him. His body ached and the cool cotton felt good against his skin. As he closed his eyes the vision came almost immediately and the moment was ruined. There was too much blood. Jim's body lay motionless on the floor of the chopper.

Jack walked toward the french windows and opened the doors on to the large classical balcony, a cold blast of fresh clean air hitting him full in the face. The smell reminded him of the icy blasts back home in Minnesota and the ozone calmed him, soothed his troubled mind. Below him was the famous Arts Square, offering views of the Church of the Spilt Blood, one of St Petersburg's most famous landmarks. Art and spilt blood, how relevant these symbols were now. There had been so much blood, and it had spread everywhere.

After confirming his outbound flight for noon the next day, Jack set about organizing his equipment, which had been hurriedly thrown into two large sled bags. Sitting naked on the parquet floor of his suite, the balcony doors swinging in the wind, he grabbed his fur-lined parka, slung it over his shoulders and proceeded to make a large pile of all his Arctic clothing that needed washing. At the bottom of his bag lay the blood-soaked windsuit he had been wearing on the day of Jim's death. As he laid it out on the floor he checked the inside pockets, only to discover the postcard Mikaela had given him the night before the fateful trip. The card, given to bring him good luck, a photograph of Beuys sitting shrouded, head bent into his fur coat, showed a man alone, a man looking inwards. Jack stared at the card for several minutes and then, looking up, caught sight of himself reflected in the balcony window. How had it happened, the transformation, so close to the image of Beuys deep in thought, shrouded in fur? As he stared at his image his mind began to race: KLS, Groub, his work, his passions, his friends, Microstem – and underpinning it all a deep-seated dissatisfaction with himself, his work, his life. This dissatisfaction had in turn driven him to make the fated expedition.

Jack thought back to the first time he had seen the original sled at Groub's gallery, only a few weeks previously. He had been struck by the power of the art but also by the power of the artist, a man who had been forged by his own painful and traumatic experiences during World War Two. Jack thought back to the inadequacy he had felt confronted by Beuys, and the irony of his current predicament was not lost on him. Something had changed in him, something irreversible, negative and self-destructive. The events of the past few days had resulted in an extreme experience, a love lost and a friendship gone for ever. Now Jack was standing on the edge looking over into the abyss, partly to the dark side, to some extent just as Beuys had done all those years earlier.

Jack picked up the windsuit covered in Jim's dried blood and held it close to his face. Closing his eyes he smelled the blood, the sweat, the traces of adrenaline, and soon he was back there, watching, a spectator at a deadly gladiatorial contest, a contest no man could win. He decided there and then that he would never let it happen again, the inaction, the waiting, the futile hoping for his life to improve. He realized that despite the loss of his dearest friend, he had gained a new dimension in understanding the dark forces of nature, together with a clearer understanding of his own shortcomings and fragility. Fate had granted him what he most wanted, a life-changing experience.

In his hotel suite in a bustling cosmopolitan city on the edge of Russia, Jack had found the honesty to acknowledge his true self. He was a man stripped bare, as fallible and weak as other men. A man who when it had mattered most had lost his nerve, and a man who had failed to save his friend. Jack remembered Groub's parting words of advice the night before he departed for Russia: "Be careful what you wish for, Jack, you may just get it!"

Jack stared out across the snow-covered rooftops far into the cold distance, over the milling traffic and the passers-by, the icy streets, church steeples and grand Tsarist Palaces, northwards toward the sea and the ice that lay many hundreds of miles away. As he craned forward to see that distant place, his face hardened. The spark in his eyes died and went a colder shade of blue, his breath causing the damp windowpane to mist over the grey urban landscape below.

Chapter 7

In Jack's absence KLS was in trouble. In the little under a month that Jack had been away, the senior analysts from Lou's research department had informed Lane by urgent memo to expect a radical slowdown in the technology and dotcom sector. Warnings of a downturn had been visible as early as October 1999, but by mid March 2000 the speed at which the internet stocks were falling had taken even the most cynical investors by storm. This was only the beginning, the tip of the iceberg.

Lane had kept his ear to the ground regularly enough to sense that times were about to change. He had seen the warning signs in late 1999. He had smelled it in the market. His nervousness had been evident in the combined pressure he and Lou had applied to the entire KLS Corporation to IPO and trade sale as much of their 2000 portfolio as possible pre-year-end, while keeping a lid, publicly at least, on the impending downturn. In this they had made a serious mistake. Lane of course had been there twice before, once in 1974 and again in 1987. He had been around long enough to read the signs and he wasn't going to be left holding equity in a pile of worthless businesses. Furthermore, he didn't plan on losing the banking business of some of his most valued clients. Lane needed to control the situation and challenge the existing obligations to those companies most likely to fail. By securing funding for the strongest performers in his technology portfolio, Lane planned to share the fiscal responsibilities for their continued survival with valued co-investors from the big five investment banks to keep up credibility and diffuse any signs of panic. Worst case he needed to wind in the reins to the substantial KLS exposure, write down KLS's most high risk pre-IPO propositions and batten down the hatches on all but the most resilient of blue chip "brick" stocks. After all, no one knew how long the storm would last.

But the ferocity of the crash had caught even Lane off guard. The speed at which the boom was turning to bust had meant the market was deteriorating so fast that panic was setting in, as warning lights flashed "sell" across the city's trading screens.

On the 15th of March, the day of the KLS board meeting, only five days after the NASDAQ had peaked, bears began their panzer-like stroll across the world's financial institutions and the dotcom markets went into freefall.

The first and most high-profile stocks to fall were the blue chip giants of technology; Cisco, Dell, Intel, Oracle and Microsoft, followed by Amazon, MusicJungle, E-bay and AOL as billions of dollars were wiped off their over-inflated share prices in a matter of days. The reasons for the crash were numerous but revolved around a simple premise; that the technology market had all along been a house of cards. Whereas companies used to gain a valuation based on turnover, technology stock had on average been able to attain valuations on future cash flows at multiples at high as 200 times projected turnover thanks to the research spin of the investment banks. The effect of this realization on the market was dramatic. The resulting reduced market demand for products and services would be the nail in the dotcom coffin as the growth curve of online buyers began to fall away. Within a matter of weeks Cisco had dived from being the most valuable company in the world with a share price of $68, to $23, two-thirds of its value lost in Wall Street terms overnight.

The market concern was that Cisco, Microsoft, Oracle and Dell were the big boys, blue chip in every sense of the word. If it could happen to them, the unbranded technology companies and dotcoms didn't stand a chance. It would be a bloodbath.

★ ★ ★

By the second week of March 2000, KLS had written off a number of key, cash-reliant businesses after their sales teams had reported a record number of recently failed IPOs.

The capitalizations and share prices of these businesses had dropped in more than two cases by over 99 percent. The new unquoted businesses were quite literally unable to attract even moderate interest in such an unstable market.

Unlike Jack's personal tragedy, the ramifications of the economic disaster that was bombarding technology stocks was about to influence the economy on a global scale. Few had seen it coming. But for those that did, selling in the pre-March 10th high, the rewards would be massive. Billionaires were being made as quickly as billions were being lost. The cycle of cause and effect that dictated the current flow from peak to trough in the now hostile Wall Street landscape was in full and unstoppable motion. Not since the Dutch tulip market frenzy of the seventeenth century had so many been duped by so few. Those that had set the market would be left holding the can: the banks, the VC houses and more specifically the analysts who had called the stocks and thus created the frenzy. Heads would roll and in time corporations would fall.

★ ★ ★

It was into this climate of corporate fear that Jack now returned, his plane touching down at JFK on a cold winter's day in mid March, Jack broken, exhausted, his defenses torn and his self-esteem battered. He had little idea of what awaited him. That he had been partly responsible for the current downturn was a matter for debate; the ones he had called to go north, their share prices rocketing, had done just that. That few businesses would be left standing was also part of Jack's investment mantra. But Jack knew the senior board at KLS would need answers and they would demand accountability.

Lane Connor, the KLS ship's captain, was only too aware that difficult questions would need to be answered and the external information flow controlled. If things got too heated he might need to exercise some surgical managerial clout. People would be fired, there would be a clean-out – in Wall Street there always was. To survive any "class action" reprisals from shareholders and formal investigation from the market's governing bodies, he might even be in need of a scapegoat down the line.

For the second time that month bears were roaming close by and Jack was unwittingly about to embark on the second front in the battle for his personal survival.

★ ★ ★

Back home and safe in his apartment, Jack slept for the first few days. He didn't bother to eat much and woke only to take on fluids. His stomach had shrunk on the trip and with it his normally voracious appetite. He left the phone off the hook, his cellphone switched off in his parka pocket, his laptop folded away. He had grabbed a copy of the *Wall Street Journal* on the flight and this constituted his only reading material. It was all so depressing and unreal, how everything could have folded at once. He began to worry about it all – KLS, his future responsibilities, especially Microstem.

From the confines of his bed Jack lay on his side staring at the sled. The huge plasma screen perched on its high wall bracket cast a surreal glow across the darkened apartment as Bloomberg's incessant pages scrolled a stream of brightly colored share statistics across the room. Initially Jack had been mesmerized by the unfolding drama as the markets dived into freefall, but now, after just a few nights at home, that didn't seem to matter at all, nothing mattered any more, and the neon colors dancing across the perspex box, wooden floor and stark white walls became a welcome distraction from the inevitability of sleep, a soothing interplay of light on tired, sad eyes.

For the most part bed seemed a good place to be. Jack had tried pacing, sit-ups – push-ups had worked for a while, the caged animal routine – but after a while and a few hundred reps and smashing his fist into two bathroom cabinets, the bed was definitely his safest option. And the artificial light – well, that had made it, in-room Aurora Borealis without the cold, without the fear, without his lover, without his friend.

One thing though hadn't changed. The sled still dominated the room. Jack had wondered if it would still captivate him, if its symbolism would now seem strangely muted, now he too had seen so much. But he was wrong. If anything it radiated an even greater power, while he watched it from his bed until he drifted off into fitful bouts of sleep. He had needed this time alone, back in his space, time to compose himself, to get things straight.

He had called Annie first. He had promised to see her, but three days on he just couldn't motivate himself to see anyone. Annie had been so worried, and had heard all the news from Jack's mother, Laura, and from Bob, who had been kind enough to take her for lunch. Annie had been so shocked and heartbroken by the events –the whole affair had made her cry. Jack was her boy and she was damned if anything or anyone was going to make his torment worse. She would see to it. She would look after him, protect him from the press, from KLS. Furthermore, if he wasn't going to invite her to his apartment, well, she would just have to take the initiative.

The loud buzzer startled Jack but he was more shocked at the sharp rapping on his apartment door. All guests had to be permitted entrance from the lobby videophone, but somehow an uninvited party had breeched the watchful eye of the concierge. Annie had worked that beautifully, slipping Jenson, the old lobby janitor, a subtle sexy wink. The kind-hearted cleaner had been only too pleased to allow Jack's two familiar friends access to the penthouse elevator.

Behind the safety of his oak door Jack froze – standing naked, a thickset figure now stripped of his excess pounds. As he turned to the door he had

147

caught a glimpse of his reflection in the hall mirror. His face looked leaner now, his eyes ringed with dark circles through lack of deep sleep, his hair wild and unkempt, his beard ragged and half-grown. Grabbing an old towel from the bathroom floor he slowly wrapped it around himself and, holding the two ends loosely together on his hip, peered into the deep spyhole in the door. Bob, anticipating Jack's response, peered back at him, and Jack stood back slightly spooked.

"Open it or I'll shoot," came Bob's feigned gangster reply, and Jack smiled briefly and opened the door on the chain.

"Not today, thank you," replied Jack, trying to muster some sense of humor.

"Are you decent, young man?" came Annie's shrill voice. "I mean, you don't want to make a girl blush now, do you, Jack?"

"Not much chance of that..." jibed Bob.

Laughing weakly, Jack slipped the chain and let the door swing open freely. Smiling warmly, Annie looked at him and pretended not to notice his unkempt half-naked state.

"You look, how shall I say, in need of a shave and a good shower."

"Guess that's about right, Annie – you been okay?"

"A fair sight better than you, my dear. Now how are you?"

Bob stood in the hall and watched as Annie gave Jack a tender hug. Jack caught his eye over her shoulder and smiled weakly, giving his friend a wink. But despite Jack's outward display, Bob sensed that his friend was far from okay. As Annie set about collecting Jack's clothes from the floor, Bob walked towards him and put his arms around his friend. Jack held Bob with one arm, his right hanging limply to his side. Leaning his head against his friend's shoulder, he closed his eyes and let out a sigh. Bob hugged him hard and felt Jack gently tremble as he began to cry.

"It's okay, bud, we'll work this out, I promise, it'll be okay, buddy, it'll be okay."

As Bob tenderly rocked his friend Annie watched, tears welling in her eyes.

"I'm sorry," whispered Jack.

Bob held him tighter. "You don't have to say that," he whispered.

"Oh, I do, Bob. Christ, I do."

Over the next few days Bob and Annie did what they could, taking turns to stock Jack's fridge, cook for him or just sit and listen. Bob had even offered to call Mikaela, bring her back if necessary. It just didn't make any sense to him – they had seemed so well matched. But Jack would have none of it. It wasn't that he blamed her, she had been right to be angry, she had lost her brother, after all, but he just couldn't understand the spite of her outburst. Even if she had been right, it hurt too much to bear.

It was on the second of these visits that both Annie and Bob noticed Jack's vacancy. He had been talking about the first days on the trail with Viktor and Jim, and he had just tailed off, and then nothing. Bob had known Jack to get distracted when confronted by art, but only for a few seconds at a time. At Aslop's he had been known for always being very switched on. Since their childhood Bob had witnessed him occasionally drifting off even in mid-conversation, but he was so visual and they were young and Bob had concluded that he was most probably thinking about girls.

On the whole they agreed that he was on the ball but also slightly eccentric, big ol' sensitive Jack. But now Bob began to worry as Jack stared out into space. Annie had seen it too, watching him from the corridor of the office as he looked out across the Hudson. But he only did so on the sunniest, clearest of days; after all, she had always rationalized, it was the most stunning view. But Jack seemed to be elsewhere; only when Bob brought up the subject did he seem to return, and with his new-found concentration came the questions and analyzing.

Soon Annie was delivering all the relevant files and spreadsheets to Jack's apartment, turning the corner of his large studio into a makeshift office. He seemed to be especially interested in the state of his finances, worried almost. Annie, armed with a letter giving power of attorney, spent the early part of Jack's second week in New York compiling a succinct statement of his affairs.

Groub had taken to coming round to Jack's loft at lunchtime, and Annie observed that in his presence and occasionally that of his old friend Ingvar, Jack seemed almost his old self. They talked for hours at a time, and during their meetings Jack made copious notes. De Blevis had spent time in the apartment too, shuffling in and out with great sheaves of documents and files. These three older men had such a way with Jack, and he with them, that Annie wondered on more than one occasion if their connection was not entirely unpaternal. It was as if he needed their support and they his, a symbiotic relationship if ever there was one.

As the days went by Annie watched Jack get stronger and come out of himself. Then one day he shaved and got dressed in his favorite Prada suit. Annie was quite taken aback by his transformation, the old Jack almost, but leaner and trimmer. And she knew he wanted to get back in there, back in touch with his former aggression.

The focus of his new interest in the market had been the crash of his infamous musicjungle.com stock, which was now teetering at $12 a share and falling. Jack knew this could mean trouble, even though it had been an accurate and straight call. Those who had heeded his research were now rich, and if people had been late to invest, well, that was the game, high risk, high reward. After all, he had not called it to keep going up, just to reach a pre-set high. In fact, most of the other predictions were also coming to pass. The sector growth he had had such concerns about only weeks ago had ended. He needed to protect himself from any repercussions and he needed to protect Microstem. He knew KLS would soon begin the cull of all but the most profitable propositions in their portfolio.

★ ★ ★

Before Jack could get back into it at KLS he needed to tend to a more personal matter. Early the next morning, with Lane breathing down her neck, Annie booked Jack a limo to take him upstate to Syracuse to visit Jim's parents. Since Jim's death, he had dreaded this day but there was no getting out of it, no email, telegram, flowers from Annie nor rearrangement in the diary. It was an unavoidable and most grave responsibility. He owed them that at least.

On the way out of the city Jack asked the driver to make a small detour to Bob's apartment. It was hard for him to begin to explain the responsibility he felt, the guilt that weighed on him. Bob, fighting back his tears, took his friend in his arms.

"I'm just glad you're out and about now, buddy. I'm so glad you're home safe. It will be okay, you know that, don't you Jack? It will get better every day, dude, just takes time."

Jack was too choked to reply. For the past days he had felt more emotional than he had ever done in his life. Whether he was watching a TV soap, reading an article in a magazine or watching people interacting in the park from his apartment window, Jack had caught himself over-whelmed by a compulsion to cry, a deep and irrational response to absurdly mundane occurrences that now struck a deep and often sentimental chord. Despite feeling foolish and almost menopausal, Jack could do nothing to counter his newfound feelings. Bob was touched by Jack's response. They arranged to meet up the next week but as Jack walked away down the street Bob was left with a nagging feeling. There was something in Jack's eyes and in his manner that worried him; he had seen it in his apartment, the alienation, the sense that he alone had to reconcile his loss as punishment for his proclaimed inaction. Whatever the reason, Bob felt frustrated by his inability to truly share the experience, because he hadn't been there. But what was he to do? He had to spend some time with Jack. He would make it happen, one way or another.

★ ★ ★

The journey upstate took a little under five hours. Jack had always hated the drive, ever since he had first taken the Greyhound to Syracuse as a teenager, visiting Jim's dad who had just received his first professorship at the university. The move had been quite traumatic for Jim, since he had decided to stay in St Paul and graduate high school there. At eighteen it had been no big deal, in fact having his own apartment had been a real plus with the chicks; it was just that now he had to do it all himself, study, wash, cook. Mr and Mrs Williamson had little choice but to let their only son graduate on his own. The professorship was too good to turn down and in light of their financial situation they had agreed as a family that it was the right thing to do. To take Jim out of high school would have been a disaster for a boy who already had enough distractions in his life. Although they had been good friends for many years, it was at this juncture that Jack, Jim and Bob had formed their close bond. In fact, Jack's family became a surrogate one for Jim, who spent nearly every weekend with the Wylers in Ely. It had been in these formative years that Jack and Jim had made the bulk of their trips together and had formed their bond with the wild – a bond nurtured by Jack's father.

Soon after Joe Wyler's passing, the three friends had felt it, a piece of their past lost, a tremendous void. The element of strength, certainty and security that Joe had so embodied in their younger years was gone for ever.

Bob and Jim had driven straight to Jack's place the minute he had landed back from Alaska. That first weekend, before the funeral, they had grabbed their kit and headed out into the woods. After some hours of gentle walking they had come to a familiar clearing in the trees. The forest was silent, and as they shuffled through the fallen pine needles and crisp-frosted earth the ravens could be heard cackling in the bare birch branches. Brushing the light dusting of snow from some small boulders, the three arranged the lichen-dappled rocks into a circle. Bob and Jim dragged a dry deadfall to the firestones and set to work with the flint and bark tinder. The lichen and twigs soon began to take, the dry log spewing aromatic clouds of green moss smoke upwards until enough water had evaporated from the wood and the fire took hold of the wood's sinuous fibers and crackled fiercely into life.

As the three settled down on their well-worn ground mats, shoulder to shoulder, zipping up their old down-filled parkas and rubbing their gloved hands in front of the flames, Jim produced the Jack Daniels and passed the bottle to his friends. Without speaking they each in turn took long swigs, gazing into the fire, and gradually they began to relax. So the childhood stories began, Bob recounting his favorite anecdotes: their first encounter with a wolf pack, the day Jim had fallen into the creek, how hard they had laughed when they had had to langlauf home naked and wet after skiing into an overflow. Jack sat and listened, choked with emotion, his eyes full of tears, but smiling, trying in true fashion to keep control.

In the end, their friendship came down to one thing – the thing that made each of them tick; a mutual love for the wilderness, a love fostered by Joe. They promised Jack, and they promised each other, that they would always be there for one another. Whatever happened in their lives, however rich or poor they became, they promised each other that at least once a year they would always get back to basics, get back to the woods, ice and snow – in memory of Joe, the old days, the best years of their lives.

And now Jim was gone too and a promise had been broken. He hadn't been there for his friend and there would be no more trips together. That much he knew.

Jack wiped tears from his cheek with his sleeve and stared out of the window of the Mercedes as it powered its way north. The whole route had never seemed so depressingly grey, the dull, flat fields, the gnarled, sparsely foliaged trees helping to coat the surrounding countryside in the dry, dirty brown malaise of a late snowless winter. Only on leaving the confines of the urban landscape did Jack fully appreciate the drabness of the surrounding countryside, no snow, no vistas, no big sky, no wildness, and certainly no inherent beauty. Even in contrast to the bright, vibrant neon excesses of the city, the route north disgusted him. He loathed it because there were no extremes here, no peaks on which to focus, no altitude, no aspect, nothing to help distract his mood. Just mediocrity, planned, farmed, built and tendered; the land here lacked the commitment of the wild of true nature. For the most part it really didn't know what it was, part commuter-belt, part farmland; even the few wooded areas lacked the commitment to call themselves a forest. The hours dragged by.

By late afternoon the limo had pulled into downtown Syracuse. Jack directed the driver east along Erie Boulevard, past the Niagara Mohawk electricity building to the corner of First Street, and then up the hill to Campus Lower Road, past Manley Field House and cemetery to the wooded cul-de-sac of St Stephen's Place. The Williamsons' house faced him just twenty yards away on the left-hand side, and Jack, focused on the large house, barely acknowledged the driver as he climbed out of the limo. He stood on the broadwalk and swallowed hard, never taking his eyes away from the ominous old white and weathered clapboard house that now represented the greatest challenge he had ever faced. Taking a deep breath, he walked purposefully across the road and pressed the tarnished, porcelain buzzer. There was silence. He pressed the bell one more time.

The wait was murderous. After a short while Jack heard the sound of footsteps as June Williamson, Jim's mother, shuffled toward the door.

"Jack?" came a quiet, kind voice. "Jack, is that you? How are you? How are you, my dear?" she said as she opened the door. June had obviously been crying, her eyes red and swollen as, arms outstretched, she gave Jack a warm hug, her feather-light and fragile frame cradling Jack's large torso. She kissed both his cheeks tenderly.

"It's been such a while, Jack. It's so nice of you to come."

June, now in her late sixties, looked so much older, so much frailer than Jack had remembered.

"How was the trip up, Jack? You seem to have made good time. Just under five hours, was it?"

The relaxed informality of her tone was somewhat disconcerting, as if Jack had dropped round to call Jim out for a few hoops. "Yes, we made good time. Is Peter in too?" he added nervously.

Without answering, June led Jack into a large, open sitting room. Peter Williamson, Jim's father, sat sprawled in the easy-boy, fast asleep.

"He's having a bit of a rest, Jack, but we can talk. Can I get you a drink? A nice cup of tea?"

"Yes, June, that would be good, thank you."

The offer of tea allowed Jack another legitimate obstacle, another reason to delay his confession. June went to the kitchen and returned two minutes later with a large pot of chamomile tea and some homemade cookies. In the most casual way, June turned to Jack. "How are you coping, Jack? It must have been so terrible for you."

153

"Oh, I'm okay, I guess, June, but how I am is not why I'm here. I've come to see how you are coping and to apologize. I've come to ask for your forgiveness."

June sat back in her chair and Jack could sense she wouldn't be able to keep it together much longer. No mother should outlive her son. "Jack, please don't do this to yourself. Jim knew the risks, you both did. You can't blame yourself."

"She's right, Jack, you can't beat yourself up like that," added Peter, who had just woken up. He pushed the large wooden lever to the left-hand side of the easy-boy and rocked slowly into an upright position. He smiled a kind, warm smile at Jack. "Come here, son, I've got this problem with my back. Give your uncle Peter a hug."

Jack bent over Peter and held him. He had been totally unprepared for their response.

"Jack, you see, if Jim was to have had a choice of where he would have liked to die, and I truly believe this ... well, he would have wanted to go out there with you, doing what he loved. Out in the wild. He lived for those trips Jack, absolutely lived for them. I suppose it would be true to say they gave his life a certain purpose."

"But the films, his work, he was so engaged with it all," protested Jack. "He didn't want that ..."

"No, Jack, no, he wasn't. He hadn't made a film in over three years. We know this because of his debts. I'm afraid he wasn't completely straight with you about all of that, or with us for that matter."

"I guess he didn't want to ask for anything and he was also conscious of being a bit of a failure compared to you ..." added June.

"Well, you can see his point. He was always a bit unemployable. Liked to keep his own hours I guess is a polite way of putting it," added Peter.

They all laughed and in doing so broke the ice. June and Peter looked fondly at each other as June went to sit on the arm of her husband's chair.

"The morning of Jim's death, I knew something terrible had happened, I could just feel it ... I guess we did our grieving then, Jack. It was strange. We both knew. Guess Jim's spirit came to us and warned us, something like that. But in a sense we are relieved he is at rest now. We really sincerely mean it, Jack, and we want you to know we harbor no bad feeling toward you. Jesus, you are practically family. You did everything you could have for him. We also know that you have taken it rather hard."

Jack swallowed. "He was the brother I never had, you see. Ironically, I was just as envious of his lifestyle as he may have been of mine. Yeah, I can see that now – how weird," mused Jack. "But I really wanted to tell you both something, I mean as a form of confession. I wouldn't be able to live with myself if I didn't get this off my chest, you see. I let Jim die, it was entirely my fault. After the first shot, I reloaded. I had four spare flares. I had a loaded flare pistol, you see, and well, I was too scared. I thought the bear might come for me . . . I just didn't use it."

Peter and June tensed and studied Jack closely, "You had a loaded flare pistol?" asked June, the surprise evident in her voice.

"Yes, a fully operational flare gun. Viktor had left us with it the night he drowned and as the bear was attacking Jim I pulled it out, but because of the distance, I mean, it was so close, maybe only fifteen yards, I was terrified the bear would attack me if I missed. I froze, I . . . "

Peter slowly stood up. Jack looked up at his friend's father as he walked across the room toward the window.

"Jack, fifty years ago I got myself shot in Korea. Stupid really, but I was in the wrong place at the wrong time. Now some might say I got shot because I didn't act. I was also scared Jack, shitting myself. Too scared to move in a firefight because my friend had been blown away next to me. Now, was I a coward? Did I kill my friend? The answer's no, Jack. Some nasty little yellow fella killed my buddy and a polar bear killed my son, not you, Jack, not you. You see, Jack, this is what we do, we try to find a reason for it all, but in times of danger things often follow a predetermined course. It's the law of chaos. You didn't make that bear kill Jim and if you had fired and missed, with what – a puny flare? – well, the bear would have probably killed you too. People die, Jack, they die for a range of reasons and in Jim's case it was just a terrible coincidence that he happened to run into that bear. In a sense, you could even say it was his turn. I just won't have you beating yourself up over that, Jack. Life's too short, trust me, I know. Last month we lost our son and that's a hard space to fill, but that had nothing to do with you, Jack. It had nothing to do with you."

Jack began to cry, cradling his head in his hands he wept while June and Peter Williamson sat next to him, holding him, their last connection to their only son.

★ ★ ★

As the days went by Jack couldn't get the Williamsons out of his mind. In his professional life at KLS someone was always accountable, someone always won and someone always lost. You either did the deal, won the

155

business, processed the transactions or called the shots. It was that simple. Since meeting Groub in January, that whole value structure was being challenged. On the one hand Groub had displayed an illogical and surprising generosity; the trip had resulted in unexpected tragedy and now he had experienced unexpected forgiveness from those most likely to demand accountability and answers. But in spite of the Williamsons' kind words and support, Jack had been unable to face his own mother. He had spoken to her on the phone and no doubt he would see her at Jim's funeral, but he couldn't face the trip home, not now at least, there was too much to do. He wasn't ready for that journey. As the days went by Annie witnessed that rather than withdrawing further into himself Jack was getting stronger and more focused. Something was driving him.

One evening in late March Jack received a message by courier. Hans Groub wanted to visit him again. He had something to discuss. He was concerned about his good friend; he had something important for Jack and whatever it was it couldn't wait. As always, Jack was glad to meet with Groub. They talked together for hours, and in Groub's relaxed company Jack found himself able to recount the entire story of Jim's death for the first time. Groub was excellent at listening and was eager to share advice and empathy in even order with his friend. He had brought with him a small envelope, and inside it was a handwritten note.

> The coyote and the crow were fools
> Yes
> But when you listen carefully and you look closely
> They teach you more than the cleverest
> They listen and see.

Groub's first wife had died of cancer in the summer of 1978 and Joseph Beuys had visited Hans on the eve of the funeral. Beuys had given him this note as a tribute to friendship, to Nature and to the power of art. Now Groub wanted Jack to have it. Jack was so touched he was speechless. For the first time Groub spoke of the "rebirth" of Beuys, a man recreated at the center of a legend. A legend Beuys had created himself, not fiction, not wholly fact. The concept of Beuys' rebirth was a hard one to grasp, but as Groub explained his transcendence from German soil to Asian soil, from western practicality to eastern mystic, the relevance of his story became clear. As far as Beuys was concerned he had been reborn in the fuselage of his burning Stuka plane, in Asiatic Russia. He had been reborn "to seek nothing less than to heal souls".

Groub explained how Beuys saw himself not just as an instigator or a catalyst but as the very vessel for society's change, "the savior of our ecological and spiritual ills, not in a religious sense but in a metaphysical way".

"You see Jack, you know now, probably as well as anyone, what he was saying. He was offering us a way out, away from logical action and thought, a way to instinctive action, spiritual enlightenment. He was offering us quite simply 'the way'."

Jack told Hans about his experience in the elevator, about Mikaela's good luck postcard, of his desperation and fear at losing Jim and the unnerving feeling he had of being watched, shadowed by something intangible. And then he described his nightly dreams, his "moments", the sense of premonition he had felt on the pack, the icy black water, the huge polar bear and his inaction when it had mattered most, and finally his hatred of himself.

"You see, Hans, if I tell anyone else this I'm convinced people will begin to say I've lost it, but I can feel something now. Not out there on the pack when I most needed it, but now, since Jim's death. I can't explain exactly – it's as though the experience has jolted me awake subconsciously, dislodged something that was blocking my thought processes...I can't quite explain how it feels. It's as if I can see a way through it all now. Like I've solved the riddle and found the missing piece of the puzzle."

"That riddle, Jack, I bet it goes something like this..." added Groub. "And yet his soul is still among us and he is showing us the way with his works which are like so many beacons in the night."

"That's it exactly, Hans, that's exactly what I mean! Where did you get that from?" asked Jack, amazed by the lucidity of the quote.

"From the book *The Essential Beuys* by Alain Borer. You are not the only one but I feel you understand it better now, since the tragedy, no?"

"But what do I do now, Hans? What will I do now?"

"You will have to dig deep for that answer, Jack. Look into your true nature...I am afraid, beyond that, I can't be of much help. It lies within you. Just remember what Beuys believed: 'Kunst is Kapital.' Everyone can be an artist, Jack, invest in your passions. Don't be afraid to take up that challenge, to take that leap of faith. After all, with the markets and KLS in their present state, what have you got to lose?"

★ ★ ★

Jack couldn't sleep that night. Groub had got to him, as he always did, where it counted, in his heart, and Jack knew he was right about the passion thing, making a change, making a difference. When sleep did come he slipped in deep, and through that vessel back into his old room, back home in Ely.

Joe was there for a short time and then he was gone and Jack was alone, a teenager, frightened and scared. He remembered that feeling of loneliness above all else, that and the helplessness at not being able to do anything for his dad, who had just passed away. Joe had fought for a while and then the pain must have been too much; Jack had just to sit by, like he had done with Jim, and do nothing. It wasn't quite the same feeling but it sickened him nonetheless. Groub's advice was fatherly, without agenda, for his benefit and for him alone. Groub was right, this old, immaculately dressed father figure who had been so generous and now had his attention. He had got right under Jack's skin, in reality and in his dreams, and now Jack listened to him.

Groub didn't give advice like most people Jack had known. He didn't give any answers, and certainly didn't *tell* him to do anything. He just offered it up, put it out there, the idea, a seed to be sown, chucked around, thrown into the high winds to see where it would settle. Joe had been the same with his advice about the woods, the back country. They were similar, his father and Groub, and the connection comforted Jack. It is a well-known fact that adolescent boys need an external role model, someone to complement the skills and teachings of their parents. Over the past few months Groub had assumed that role; better late than never. Jack knew his father would have approved. Joe was an expert skilled in the ways of the boundary waters, hunting, canoeing, navigation, survival and tracking. Thirty-five years a park ranger, Alaska to the lower 48, he had seen some country, landscapes to die for. The beauty of the wilderness had offset the hardships of having little money, raising his family, the hard winters, his pick-up always being in the shop.

Now Jack came to think of it, Groub was the same; a man of refined skills and an expert with a classical eye, a renaissance understanding of beauty, fine things, the importance of art. And then there was his business acumen, his innate feeling for the deal. The wild and art, Joe and Groub, they were the ultimate old men. Laura could take the credit for Jack's early interests, since she had fostered his passion for paintings. But it wasn't until he had recently earned the money that Jack had really become involved, investing himself in art, so to speak. Now it wasn't enough just to look. Even seeing the galleries back home in Minneapolis and St Paul wasn't the same as living with the works, actually owning them, feeling them, letting them communicate. Groub had been instrumental in that recently, in the auction, competing over the haunting Basquiat, driving Jack to buy it, to win.

Joe would have been proud that Jack had got what he wanted through his drive and aggression. He had taught him never to settle for second best, but Joe would not have liked the painting. It would have given him the creeps, all modern art did. Jack smiled at that last thought. Christ, his dad was so stubborn about art and religion. But Laura loved Joe for everything he was and not for what he wasn't. He was her Grizzly Adams, her rock, her bit of rough. God, how they missed him.

Joe had once said matter-of-factly to Jack before a weekend in the bush and without a hint of passion, "Son, I'm your father, not your friend, so if I come down on you, you will know why." Jack had been so hurt at the time but now he understood. As he lay alone in his mother's room in his dream, he could hear his old man whimpering, suffering from the drugs and so frail and helpless. Jack, beside himself with grief and looking his father in the eye, promised he would make it all right. But he could not make it all right and he had gone to Alaska on another trip. When Joe died later that year he had realized he had failed, failed his father who had always been there for him, who kept him safe in the bush, out hunting on the trail.

Earlier during the illness Jack had taken to waking in the small hours and had stood by his old man's bed, keeping him cool, wiping his brow. Now in the dream he stood above Joe, who was smiling weakly. Groub was there too, and they had met, his father and his new mentor. And when Jack awoke, the first rays of sunlight dancing on his eyelids and coaxing him into his new reality, he had known what he must do. Groub had made it so clear that night and his dad was pleased. He would do it for his old man. Groub had meant for him to do it. He had to save Microstem. De Blevis needed to succeed. For his father he had to make it happen, he had to make Microstem a winner.

159

Chapter 8

As Jack was beginning to pick himself up, things at KLS were steadily falling apart. Annie, due to her attempts at keeping Lane and Lou off Jack's back, had been given an official ultimatum in the form of a written warning. Lane wasn't going to be fobbed off any longer. If Annie and her significant arsenal of resources could not procure Jack first thing on Monday morning, she could pack her bags. After all, what use was she?

Jack only needed one distraught phone call from Annie and he went ballistic. If they wanted a war, they could have one. No one was going to threaten Annie. If Ben was behind this he was going to pay; besides, Jack smiled as he took the elevator to the tenth floor, Groub was right, what had he got to lose? Hell, Lane could even have a piece if he wanted some. He deserved it as much, if not more than anyone. How sweet would that be?

Lane had seen Jack coming, literally. Managing and manipulating senior management for the past thirty years had given him the ability to turn most of his directors hot and cold in a single sentence. Jack, as hot-blooded and passionate as ever, was no exception. Jack had let him down, they had had a deal, and now with the no-show Lane needed a profound excuse to burn Jack. If Lane were going to save KLS a substantial termination package, Jack would need to be exposed for being unprofessional, guilty of misconduct, shown to have displayed poor management skills befitting a managing director and for conducting bad business practice and execution.

Since Jack's memo, Lane had realized that having an ethical trooper in the stable was going to be awkward, especially in light of Lou's somewhat blasé attitude to internal emails. The downturn in mid-March had meant that Microstem was now at the top of his list of ongoing businesses that were to be written off, and Lane was extremely confident that Jack would walk. The note to Annie had been just a sweetener, the cherry on the cake, the deciding factor. He hoped Jack would bite and make his job easier. Two birds with one stone was the name of the game, and Lane knew how predictable Jack could be.

★ ★ ★

Jack's first day back at KLS hung over him, a dark cloud of regret and foreboding spiced with anger. On reflection, KLS posed the least threat; after all, it was just business. After what he had just experienced in the Arctic, work seemed almost a trivial irrelevance. But he had one problem: he had let Microstem get personal, broken the golden rule. He knew he would have his back against the wall. To save it he would have to fight for it like a lion. He owed it to De Blevis, to do it by the numbers and then, well, he would see what then.

Annie had been a star keeping Lane, Lou and Peter away; they were like vultures soaring above a kill. Jack knew he was vulnerable. He knew he would have to watch himself at work; he didn't want them to know, indeed anyone to know, what he had been through. The sympathy, the chink in his armor, it would be the end. "Take some time, Jack, we had no idea ... How terrible for you ..." And all the time he would be thinking, "You're loving this." He knew they would be lapping it up, Jack Wyler being shown for what he was, a coward. There was also the Mikaela issue – the traders would have a field day, ditched, and why? Because he had hesitated, because he had gone for himself rather than saving his friend, the rich kid trying to buy his way to adventure like the Wall Street Everesters, the seven-summit crew, getting carried off the mountain by their sherpas when the going got a bit tough ... It always came back to that, the fact that he had planned the whole thing and then frozen in fear and failed his buddy. What did he have now? His job, maybe, but Microstem, that was still his and he was going to be fucked if they were going to use all the rest of it, the memo, returning late, his attitude, as leverage. There was no way he was going to take it lying down. If it was a fight Lane wanted, he had picked the wrong guy, today, at least; he wasn't in the mood.

Annie sat nervously at her desk, eyeing the digital wall clock, fidgeting. She knew Jack was coming in, she had pleaded with him to do so for her sake. But she also knew that something about him was not quite the same and that worried her. Before, when he had looked like losing it, there was always a level of restraint, a sense of proportion. But now, after the last ten days tending to him, answering all his questions, organizing his affairs, talking with Bob, locating his funds, it was as if he were planning something, something illogical. Bob had felt it too. That confirmed her suspicions; they knew each other so well, and if Bob was worried, what could she do?

As to the trip, that had come out easy enough. There had been a lot of silences but he had wanted to share that, Jim's death. Annie had tried to reassure him, as had Bob, that it was madness to beat himself up over it. Peter Williamson had put it the best way; it had been "Jim's time", his decision. He was a grown man; he knew the risks. A series of circumstances had led tragically and unavoidably to his death. It was a mutual decision to go on the trip, a 50–50 split, no one was to blame. But Jack had not bought into that one, the fate thing, it was as if he wanted to carry the responsibility to put the whole terrible affair into some form of order, cause and effect, a reason ...

And now it had come to this, the big showdown, Jack on the warpath. Annie knew the Mikaela issue was also to blame; after all, he had let her into his heart, not totally, but a lot more than most. Bob had noticed it the week before at Café Noir, the look in his eyes. He had seen the body language before but not that look, misty-eyed and smitten. Jack was falling for her, and then for it to have ended as it did – he was hurting badly, Annie could tell, and Mikaela had seen to that.

The elevator came to rest on the ninth floor and Annie knew it was him, 9am on the button, and as he walked toward her he smiled a knowing smile, and then it vanished and his face was hard again, as she had seen this past week; the joy had gone, his eyes grey and cold. He was dressed down, a polo shirt, chinos and a well- worn pair of Tods, but he looked smart and he had cleaned up well, got rid of the beard and even looked younger. And then he stopped, standing still. Annie could see him through her glass partition, alone in the entrance of his office staring out across the Hudson, not for long, but long enough for her to think it strange. Then he sat down, looking for something under the desk.

Annie got up and walked briskly to the entrance of his office and saw him, sitting on the floor, a smile on his face again, staring at the large Basquiat as if he was looking for something hidden in the work, a meaning almost. He stretched, bending his back from left to right, taking the sole of each shoe in his hand and remaining still for a time and then switching sides. Annie had never seen Jack train before, and as she watched him limbering up she noted how supple he was despite his muscular build. He turned to her, a half smile breaking across his face. "Hey Annie, don't worry, I'm fine. I could file letters in your frown. Lighten up."

Annie went a shade of crimson and smiled back at Jack. "Well, you are terribly odd, Jack, I just wondered what you were up to on the floor."

"Just trying to relax the old back – since the trip it's been acting up a bit, that's all. Anyhow, I could do with a bit of a warm-up for this one, Annie. I think I'm going to need it."

Annie knew not to pry further. "Well, you stand up for yourself, young man; they don't own you, Jack, remember that."

"Don't worry, Annie, I will, but you are wrong about that last point, you know that, don't you? You don't get paid what I've been paid for the past few years and have it your own way all the time, Annie. Just don't worry, okay, trust me. But shit is going to change around here, Annie, make no bones about that. It's just that you'll be fine. You do trust me, don't you?"

Annie looked Jack straight in the eyes, her kind face looking up at him. "Jack, you know better than to ask. With my life, Jack, with my life . . ."

Jack looked down, ashamed of himself, and Annie took him by the hand and squeezed it.

"I'll tell you something, young man. You're the best, Jack; I mean it, better than they are, by a million miles. Your new friend Groub is right about you, Jack, to trust you like he does with all that new art, he's a good judge and so am I. Now you go in there and stick it to that bastard and we'll deal with it, come what may, Jack. I mean it. Give it to him . . . okay?"

★ ★ ★

As Lane sat alone in his office he was caught somewhat unawares when Jack burst in without knocking. Penelope, Lane's buxom PA, rushed in after him, in hot pursuit.

Lane spun round in his chair as Jack, oblivious to the trap, launched into a volley of abuse.

"Don't ever threaten my staff, Lane, not fucking ever, okay? You want to threaten someone, well, take a pop at me!"

"Jack, Jack, calm down," cooed Lane, provocatively. "It's just we had a deal, middle of March, remember? It's now the twenty-ninth, that's two weeks late. I was worried, that's all, Jack, and I felt it was important for Annie to be transparent with me. I mean, she works for KLS; she's not your personal servant, you know, Jack. I just wanted to remind her of that and get her back in her box, that's all."

"Whatever, Lane, just leave her out of it. I've had something to attend to since coming home. Personal matters."

"Oh, personal, eh, Jack? Go on, what's her name? I mean, you are a director, Jack, you really mustn't let a little bit of tail get in the . . ."

"I'll stop you there, Lane. It's personal, so I would appreciate it if we left it at that."

163

"Okay, Jack, whatever you say." Lane could sense he had touched a raw nerve and he was intrigued. "Now let's sit down and talk all this through. As you have probably seen on just about every news program since March the tenth, we have suffered quite a radical slow-down in the tech sector, Jack. But I guess you know that or should I say, knew that..." teased Lane, a twinkle in his eyes.

"Yes, Lane, I've seen the news. Looking pretty shitty, isn't it? Well, I can't say it surprises me. You know how I've felt about the sector of late. I guess that's why I drafted you the memo..."

"Oh, yes, the memo, Jack. I suppose I don't have to remind you how sensitive all this is at the moment. I mean, a director publicly calling bullish positions on the sector while privately drafting those concerns, that could cause all kinds of waves."

"Yes, Lane. Oh, I see; well, I would have to agree, considering the content of the memo, the date it was written and the fact that all my recent work has been in administration within the department. Then yes, I can see that you would want to keep that a bit hush-hush."

Lane fixed on Jack. He was not about to lose this exchange. "Well, Jack, that's as maybe, but of course what is of no debate is that your most famous call has proved to be a disaster. Did you know musicjungle.com hit ten dollars earlier today?"

"A disaster, Lane, for who exactly? Surely not for KLS and its shareholders and the nicely selected hand-picked bunch of cronies who fully capitalized on the call. No, it certainly wasn't a disaster for them. If my memory serves me, they all got out around the $299/$300 mark, what, in some cases after eight hours? And you know what, in the current climate it was an accurate call. In fact, if it was supported by a market of like-minded moneymaking businesses instead of the shit stocks Lou has been calling, then I'm sure everything would be just fine. Because it will survive, somewhat scaled down, sure, but it will survive."

"Well, Jack," said Lane, matter-of-factly. "Who knows what the future holds? But for the present I guess I must warn you that KLS is going to have to make some tough calls on our portfolio moving forward. And in light of the market, I really don't think we will be able to keep supporting Microstem. In fact, Jack, bar a small life raft, for the insurance of our substantial stake, and for how shall I call it... good faith, well, we will have to let it go. I really am sorry."

"Let it go?" Jack had been anticipating this, but it still hit him hard to hear it, and with no build-up, no proposed action plan, no compromise. Lane had hit his mark.

"Lane, are you fucking crazy? KLS have what? Up to twenty percent of that business. And I tell you now, Lane, it's potentially huge. Jesus, if you want my head, Lane, fine, let's talk about it. But don't do this to De Blevis, not now. Do you know what signals that will send to the shareholders? Five million down and very little to show for it..."

"Very little, Jack? I wouldn't call twenty percent very little. That's a considerable holding and I am sure it will be snapped up. Come to think of it, I'm sure we have a claw-back clause, and since they under-performed on their milestones we will have control regardless...by my calculation, what, 36.5 percent?" Lane was probing, wanting to hit a nerve.

Jack turned his back on Lane, catching a glint of light off the water. He was smiling now and gritted his teeth for a second. Yes, you fucker, he thought, I've got you. He calmed himself and turned back to Lane, unruffled. "Control, Lane, you're kidding. Is that what you want? Why? Sorry to put a dampener on it for you, but I'm not sure you fully understand your contractual obligations to Microstem. I guess Ben hasn't given you an accurate picture. We haven't got anything like twenty percent. The contract that you signed clearly states *up to* twenty percent for *up to* ten million. That means that even with all the pre-contract life raft, you currently hold around five percent. Fuck, Lane, the shareholders are going to love that shit. Talk about a bad deal!"

Lane sat down, the color draining from his cheeks. "Up to..." he muttered. "I mean, what the fuck was that bastard Small doing? Are you sure?"

"Oh yes, Lane, completely. I guess you'd better have a look at what you signed. Very messy, all this, don't you think?" The sarcasm was clear in Jack's voice. Lane sat in silence.

"Okay Jack, how do you explain Ben's assessment of the business as a cash hole? I mean, he doesn't understand where all the funds have gone. Our last report told us they were 350K over their last tranche. How do you explain that?"

"350K over? How is that possible? Who told you that, their CFO?"

"No, Peter's new hot-shot accountant in corporate. I saw the figure only last week."

"Has Ben signed off on that too, Lane? I mean, if he is good for anything, it is looking at spend."

"No, Jack, he hasn't. I asked for their cash position independently. But why should he – you always tell me he isn't an accountant anyhow."

"No, Lane, but he is an eager little fucker and I'm sure it's worth checking them. Especially since that seems to be your main reason for writing them off."

"That's where you are wrong, Jack. It's not for that reason at all, that's just one in a long line of concerns. Benjamin has highlighted the biggest concern, that in the current market we will never sell a business whose product is at least two years from completion. People don't want jam tomorrow any more."

"Is that it, Lane? Is that your rationale? Forget value, it's cash now that counts? What's happened to you, Lane? Where's your vision? Your media boy has told you the obvious and that's why you're dropping them. Well, I'll tell you what, Lane, for once I agree with the little shit, he's right. Not a year ago, not even six months ago, but today, the twenty-ninth of March, he may well be right. I don't think we would have a chance in the current climate. I think we need to support Microstem for at least another twelve to eighteen months from our own balance sheet, without bringing on another dilutive investor. Yes, that's what Microstem needs."

"Well, Jack, here's the wake-up call. It isn't going to happen. Small also informs me he feels as an executive director you have lost your objectivity and should be more concerned with the current downturn and investing some time in landscaping us out of it, creatively so to speak."

"Oh he does, does he? Well you know what, Lane ... fuck him and fuck you! I'm not going to be able to spin us out of it and I won't go Lou's way either."

Lane's face reddened. "Jack, I will not be talked to like that. I advise you to withdraw that."

Jack was just getting warmed up. Whereas in the past he had listened to his inner voice, checked himself, breathed in and walked out, he could feel that he was losing his mechanism of control. He wanted to bring it to something, to get it off his chest, and he could tell Lane wanted it too. Christ, it felt good.

"Apology, Lane? No. Never. Creatively get you out of this? You're running a dirty business, Lane, and I've had enough. You see, Lane, I can see it so much clearer now, the whole deal, you, Lou playing it all into your own court, your back pockets! Come to think of it, I don't advise you letting other directors take another day's leave, not ever, because if they do

166

you might find they'll enjoy being free of that terrible smell of bullshit coming out of your mouth. I know for sure I did."

Lane was at cracking point. In all his years as CEO no one had ever talked to him in such a way, but true to form he kept a lid on it and with his self-control he felt a tingling of pleasure. After all, Jack had bitten. Now he would deliver the coup de grâce.

"Microstem, Jack, it's finished here at KLS as of now. You've lost the business. It's over, and I must inform you, Jack, you either grow up and focus on the market or you're finished too."

"Shut it, Lane," snapped Jack. "Do whatever you have got to do. Actually, come to think of it, why don't you go fuck yourself?"

Jack turned and walked down the hallway, winking subtly at Annie. The whole of the ninth floor sat in a state of shock at his outburst. Taking the elevator to the fourth floor, Jack walked briskly down the narrow corridor and kicked open the door to the men's room. Benjamin Small stood in front of the mirror flossing his teeth, a paper towel in his hand. Jack, without saying a word, hit him full in the mouth, sending him crashing to the floor. Blood poured from Ben's lip as Jack stood menacingly over him. Ben thrust his bloodied hands toward his attacker.

"Jack, no, please don't . . . "

Jack stumbled back against the hand drier, which began to whir loudly in the corner. "You little cunt, Ben. You fag. You stabbed me in the back this time. Do you know how much work had gone into that business?"

"What are you talking about, Jack? Please, I just don't understand."

"Yes you do, you snivelling little shit . . . you told Lane I had lost it, got too personal. That I was out of control."

"No, Jack, I said that as a director you needed to attend to the broad sector to help it attain some objectivity, that's all."

"And what about your constant sniping at De Blevis on the board minutes?"

"Well, I still stand by that, Jack. Ethical business needs ethical practice. I was concerned they didn't have the skill sets to run the business to our aggressive timelines. I still am."

"Well, you have gone and fucked it, Ben. Lane is going to write it off and you are most probably history too, since Lane was in the dark about the 'up to' clause in the contract."

"Oh, yes, I must say I was wondering if that would ever come to light. Their legal team got one over on me, I must confess. In light of Lane's aggressive deal I had to give on that one or I'm sure they would have been advised to walk. But Jack, please understand this. I never questioned the potential of Microstem. It's just that in our current framework I struggle to understand how it could be rolled out."

Jack dropped his head and let out a sigh. He suddenly felt terrible about his vicious attack on Ben. Taking a handful of towels from the dispenser, he ran them under the faucet. "Shit, Ben, I'm sorry, man. I guess you've got every right to sue me for that, man. I won't contest it." Bending over, he offered Ben the wet towels and a hand up. Ben, still shaken, took his hand and slowly stood up, holding his back.

"It's okay, Jack. I guess I have a bit of a habit of winding people up. I just have to call these businesses as I see them. That's my job, to look beyond the hype and predictions and see if there's any value. I guess we're similar in that. To be honest I think De Blevis is the most outstanding scientist, the best I have ever met. I was just convinced the business would fail in the current landscape of KLS IPO investments. Like a lot of brilliant ideas and propositions, I felt Microstem had always gone the wrong way to funding. You see, I feel it needs time and plenty of it, but what money comes without an aggressive timeline? Even philanthropic investors strike a seriously onerous bargain nowadays."

Jack couldn't believe his ears. How could he have been so wrong about a fellow colleague? After nearly four years of conflict, Ben was talking his language and he probably had been the whole time. Jack, being so quick to judge, had just never seen it before.

"You know what, Ben?" said Jack, dusting off Ben's back with his hand. "I think I know just the type of funding De Blevis is going to need. He's going to need an angel investor, and in light of what has happened today, I think I know just the guy. How much do they need on their current burn?"

Ben was taken aback. For the first time he liked the way their conversation was going.

"On my last predictions four million for the next twelve months, but I'm sure with a little juggling I could get their burn down. Yes, definitely, I think we could have our final trials completed within that time frame and under budget. Yes, definitely . . . but Jack, the markets, no one is going to invest now, surely . . . "

"Market smarket, my friend. Who said anything about raising capital from the markets?" Jack smiled.

Putting his arm around Ben, he led him toward the door. "I guess I owe you a beer, or is it a nose job? There's someone I want you to meet. I really am so sorry about all that, Ben . . . "

Ben laughed nervously, holding a hand towel to his bloodied nose, and together they headed toward the exit.

★ ★ ★

Jack knew he would have to act fast to save Microstem. Within twenty-four hours of his showdown with Lane, KLS had made official their decision to write off the business. The message would send a stark warning to the markets and help to convince skeptical shareholders that they were quick to respond to the crisis. In addition to the potential money saved, there were three more internal announcements. Benjamin Small, Annie Harper and Jack Wyler would be leaving KLS. No reason was given but the decision was effective immediate. The cull had begun.

Jack took the news well. After all, he had gone toe to toe with Lane. He had really let him have it, and no one ever survived that kind of exchange. But for Annie and Ben the news had been more of a shock. From Jack's perspective it was the responsibility of losing Annie and Ben their jobs that weighed on him.

Through the turmoil of Jim's death, Jack had begun to feel an inner calm. His entire value structure had been challenged to such an extent that any pain he now felt was matched in equal measure by a new and vigorous purpose. Life was just too damned short. The tragedy had proven that. But Jack's new found purpose wasn't to be confused with personal happiness, far from it. He had never been so sad. Within a month he had lost the four main structural pillars that had formed the backbone of his life: his best friend, his lover, his job and a sizeable amount of his capital. He needed to deal with it alone, in his own time, and the best way to keep it out of his mind was to keep himself busy. Deep inside Jack there was a plan brewing, a long- and short-term focus for his mind. Saving Microstem was a good starting point, and like all good plans, the concept was simple. As Groub had said about his passion, "Invest in something of value, invest in his future."

★ ★ ★

Jack needed a private table for a most private meal, and remembering his lunch with Groub, he called Lola's. Dinner was booked for Friday at eight. Over the following days he turned his attention to his finances. In total, he had managed to put away a little under 10 million dollars, including all his stocks and shares, which accounted for around 50 percent of his gross wealth. His considerable holding of KLS options would now be a matter of contention, and in the current time frame Jack had decided to write the whole issue off. Although the KLS options amounted to a considerable amount of capital, constituting half of his paper wealth, Jack knew he had no choice but to deal with that can of worms at a later date; in fact his lawyers could deal with it. Jamie Lovett, Jack's broker, had been a little surprised when Jack had asked him to sell the entire portfolio. Despite the falling markets, Jamie knew that with Jack's considerable cash wealth he could afford to sit tight and take a long-term view, so why the need to cash out? Jack, never very forthcoming about his affairs, chose to swerve away from the question. Jamie knew better than to push the point; after all, Jack knew the game and hopefully what he was doing.

De Blevis and his team had been devastated by the news. With their cashflow severed, De Blevis knew that as a company director, unless they could come up with immediate funding, he would have to cease any transactions with his creditors and file for voluntary liquidation. His invitation to dinner with Jack had seemed a little strange in light of the urgent matter of the company's cashflow. Surely a board meeting with KLS was more in order. Jack assured De Blevis it was best to wait a few days. He was watching their backs and they should sit tight.

Throughout the week Annie spoke regularly with Jack. She had to clear her desk and files by end of the day on Friday, and had to arrange for the removal of Jack's art collection. Jack had been so supportive, and now, in light of his invitation to dinner, it was hard to harbor any hard feelings there. After all, she had told him to give it some – and he had done just that.

Annie had been here before. In '87 she had lost her job along with 15,000 other Wall Street employees, but she had learned one thing. When you leave, it is best to do so with all the facts and files. Read between the lines, that was her motto, since one never knew when they might come in handy. The techies on the third floor had always supported Annie and now the recent installation of a zip disk proved invaluable. Immediately after her brief meeting with Lane, Annie carefully downloaded all archived emails, saved files to her 100mb disk and popped it into her handbag. Jack had been so good to her, and knowing him as she did, well, someone had to watch his back. She had heard the rumors and she didn't like what she heard. Lou's PA had such a big mouth, and if they were trying to pin their problems on Jack, he just might be in need of her help.

Ben had taken the news of his firing the hardest. Shortly after his episode with Jack in the men's room, he had been overcome by a feeling of helplessness he had not felt since falling foul of the constant taunting and bullying of his early high school years. Surviving the torment of grade school, Ben had sought refuge in the world of academia and had immersed himself in scholastic pursuits. A talented long-distance runner, he had managed to avoid the mandatory training sessions for football and wrestling at high school, preferring the solace of the track and the refuge of the library and computer room.

College had followed the same uneventful path until he met Jenny, his future wife, at a regional track meet. But it wasn't his athletic prowess that had brought Ben to her attention; it was his altogether unsuppressable habit of speaking his mind that she had found attractive. Here was a man quite clearly incapable of deceit, a rather quirky, awkward guy who, in a somewhat vulnerable way, was not unattractive. After his initial failure to ask her out, Jenny had taken the initiative and made the first move. With the threat of rejection removed, Ben felt his confidence grow and they soon began dating. By the time Ben had gained his first media-related internship they were married, college sweethearts set to take on the world.

But the dream had faded fast. His first firing from Fox Media had led to serious financial pressures that lasted over a year. Now ten years on and four jobs later, Ben began to wonder if he had progressed at all. Despite the often fraught nature of his contracting obligations, he had always shied away from direct confrontation. It was one thing to oppose board rulings, to delve into the fine print of the deal, to grapple with projected assumptions and raise rafts of official objections. It was quite another to stand toe to toe with another human, to be beaten, abused and ridiculed, to feel fear, terror in the face of an uncontrollable situation. Ben, in his wildest dreams, would never have thought he would have to suffer the humiliation of that kind of assault, not at his place of work, not in a million years. But his run-in with Jack had, if anything, acted as the catalyst, the deciding factor in a stark realization. He was scared, perpetually intimidated and in fear of others, and moreover he was frightened of being scared.

In Franklin D. Roosevelt's inaugural address as President in March 1933, during the Great Depression, he said, "The only thing we have to fear is fear itself." It was a fear that was rooted in a strong mistrust of the markets and institutions in which they had once believed. This much-used phrase had never been more relevant than in summing up Ben's ongoing concerns about the markets and his official responsibilities at KLS. After his one-sided dismissal by Lane, Ben had to spend a long and uncomfortable journey home to his house in Connecticut, once again terrified of delivering the news of his firing to his wife. Things had not been going well for the Smalls for over a year now. Ben's long hours had left his wife bored and restless, and Ben sensed that a second confrontation was now looming. The facts were plain to see to everyone but Ben, who although a dedicated, faithful and loving husband had missed his wife's frequent cries for help. He was too wrapped up in his job to see that all she wanted now was a baby and the emotional security of a doting, financially secure husband. The baby issue was probably the most contentious and tender, since Jenny had already suffered a miscarriage at five months, over eighteen months ago. Ben had felt somehow impotent and powerless to console his wife, who in turn blamed herself, their marriage, her time alone, her unhappiness during his long working hours and ultimately Ben. As he parked his VW Rabbit in the driveway of his cottage, Jenny Small looked out of the drawing room window, her hand shading her eyes from the glare of the car headlamps. Ben sat in the car for a while and watched as Jenny, in her dressing-gown and slippers, opened the door then turned and walked back inside the house. Ben felt as low and unhappy as he had ever felt. Looking in the rear view mirror, he touched his swollen top lip and parted his hair nervously with cold clammy fingers. Summoning up the energy, he turned off the ignition and walked slowly across the small cinder driveway to the warm light of the doorway.

"Hey, honey, how have you been?" he called to his wife.

"Not bad. There's a letter for you by the door, Ben. Close the door quickly, darling, I'm freezing."

Ben recognized the writing on the envelope. It seemed familiar to him.

"Dear Ben, I would like to invite you to a special dinner ..." it began. Ben's face lit up. Who would have thought it, he beamed.

"Darling, we've been invited to Lola's this Friday, and um, darling, we had better have a chat. I've got some news I think we should discuss."

★ ★ ★

Groub had been right, Jack was convinced about it, about the passion thing. The dream, Groub and his dad, had convinced Jack about that, and true to form Hans had sowed the right seed in his mind. Now it was time to do something about it, to act.

Groub was sitting with Ingvar in his drawing room when the phone rang. He knew it would not have taken Jack long to see the logic, the anti-logic even. But he had surprised him with his offer. Anyone else might have thought Jack mad, questioned his sanity, especially after such a rough ride, but Groub could see the brilliance in it. Very Beuys, they concluded, very artistic.

Ingvar was intrigued by Jack's plan. It was bold, and fiscally highly irresponsible, but it could work. Eight million dollars would be an adequate amount, and he had been impressed with the reports on the business plan, the credibility of Microstem's management and the projections, an eye-watering bottom line.

Ingvar had always had a thing for the biotech sector, ever since his stewardship of KLS in the early '60s and then, with thalidomide, he had gone short on the sector and stayed there, until now. Microstem appealed to his philanthropic sentiments. With a new way to treat Alzheimer's, Parkinson's, it was an investment in his future; what with the one-in-three projections of cancer these days it seemed nearly too good to be true. Jack's plan was a serious opportunity and between them worth the sweat equity.

For Groub it was intoxicating watching Jack respond to his predicament in a truly creative way, even if divesting himself of so much of his wealth at this early stage seemed crazy. The solution was brilliant, though, to combine a scenario that would cut him free, free from choice, free from Wall Street. How could he advise to the contrary, since Jack was proposing to do exactly what he had advised him to do, invest in his passions?

But there was a risk, and Ingvar wanted to make sure Jack knew it, a risk that he could lose it all, everything he had worked so hard for. To put it all into De Blevis, his team and the board, to trust Groub and Ingvar and the others. He had a good eye for management, people he could trust, but for only 3 percent of something that may very well fail – it was bold, Groub and Ingvar had to give him that.

For much of the day together they had thrown it around, tested Jack's resolve, pressed deep into his reasoning and he had come up trumps. Ingvar had kicked Jack's tires all around Wall Street since they had first met, and the word kept coming back the same: he had the eye, he had proved it by picking the winners. The death of his father, it all fitted together, and that was good enough for them, the old guard. They had lost so many friends, fathers, mothers. After all, it wasn't their capital, their entire life's fortune they were gambling.

The sled, Groub had concluded, should be blamed. Jack had found that one funny but in a way Groub was right. The journey had begun with a work of art and Jack was about to seize his chance to go and explore, to cut free.

★ ★ ★

By midday Friday all Jack's dinner plans had been finalized. As he stepped from his car outside Lola's he felt the familiar sensation of butterflies in his stomach. It was going to be a big night. Jack waited with Hans at the entrance of the private dining room to welcome his guests. Ben and Jenny were first to arrive, followed by Johan De Blevis and his long-term partner, Bob, Teresa and Annie. Last to arrive were Ingvar and Nelly Soderstrom. The table was lit beautifully by long, cream, beeswax candles and laid with fine silver and starched linen. Each place had been carefully assigned with a hand-engraved name card. Waiters stood around the table with a selection of champagne cocktails. The tone was set.

After a few minutes of informal introductions and small talk, Groub, on Jack's insistence, introduced himself and asked the company to be seated. Jack sat in the center seat at the large, round, oak dining table as a fine bead of sweat dripped down the right-hand side of his face. He hadn't felt this nervous in years. Taking a deep breath, he took his table knife and lightly tapped the crystal wineglass to his left. The table fell silent as, smiling, he slowly stood up.

"Thank you all so much for making it here tonight. I hope you have all had a drink. I really wanted to get you all together as close friends and work associates to share with you an idea I have been mulling over. I'll try to keep it as brief and to the point as I can, since I also wanted to use this evening as an informal 'thank you' to all of you who have been so involved with my life of late. Some of you have known me for years – Bob, Annie, mentioning no names. And others I feel I have only just begun to know." Jack smiled, winking at a slightly embarrassed Ben. "As some of you will by now know, two rather large events have occurred recently that have made me do a lot of thinking. Both I feel responsible for and only one of them was avoidable. The unifying factor in both events has been that I have had time to step back and assess my life and my work. What I have found has led me to a simple conclusion and moreover a need to keep you all, my dear friends, close. So, enough of the preamble . . .

"This month I lost my best friend, Jim Williamson. I really don't want to go into the circumstances of his tragic death now, but it has acted as a catalyst for me and for that I must thank you, Jim." Bob Anders caught

Jack's eye and gave Jack a kind smile. "The second event was not entirely unconnected to the first and has resulted in my immediate departure from KLS and somewhat more regrettably the firing of you, Annie, and you, Ben. I am so sorry for that, as I know how much you both enjoyed our work there.

"There is rarely an event without a repercussion. Life seems written that way. So my last apology goes to you, Johan, since my departure from KLS would appear to have affected you and your wonderful business too. They say good investment bankers never let it get personal. Well, to be transparent, I'm not and it just did, but more on that in a moment. Lastly, I would like to introduce to you a very dear friend and recent mentor, the revered art dealer Hans Groub. Some of you have suffered because of my passion for contemporary art. Hans has helped me focus on this area of my life and a lot more besides. But my art collection is not the subject of tonight's dinner. Friendship and business are. I count all of you my friends and I have a proposition for you all.

"Two years ago I stumbled across a very wonderful man, a man with the vision to help cure a debilitating disease. The same disease that killed my father and that I'm sure has affected the lives of some of you as well. Johan De Blevis and his team at Microstem, I believe, have the potential to take Parkinson's head on and pioneer stem-cell patents that will change our world. This week Lane Connor and the KLS investment bank have tried to scupper that dream. By Ben's figures, it would appear that Microstem are no more than twenty-four months and eight million US dollars away from that dream. With your help, I believe we can make his research projections a reality.

"Now, I want to make something clear. I haven't gathered you here tonight to discuss funding, as I will show that that is attainable. I have asked you here tonight to consider a proposal, a business proposition I guess you may call it. Johan, please forgive me if this is all a bit of a surprise, but bear with me. I need to lay out my plan. Bob Anders, everyone, is the man who gave me my first break in investment banking. We've been friends for longer than I can remember and I want you to trust me, Bob, when I say this. Of all the financiers I have ever met, you have the track record and focus to add significant value. Here follows what I propose . . .

"I will take the lead on attaining funding for Microstem for the next twenty-four months. I would like to ask you, Bob, and you, Ben, with your respective experience in investment banking and corporate finance, to sit to the left and right of De Blevis over the period. Annie, I want you to head

175

up the coordination team and to help liaise between Johan's scientists and the business and financial management. You have been a most wonderful PA over the past few years and I know you are capable of handling the responsibility. I would also like to introduce you all to Ingvar Soderstrom, futures billionaire, art collector extraordinaire and ex-CEO of KLS. I have already talked with Ingvar and he is excited enough about the proposition that he has agreed to be chairman. Hans Groub, with his not insubstantial understanding of value and brand building, will also be a non-exec. So that's it for starters. I would now like Johan De Blevis to say a few words to you about his work."

★ ★ ★

De Blevis had been asked by Jack earlier in the week to prepare a short introductory talk for the dinner. He was thrilled that Jack, now unemployed himself, had seen fit to network for him with such a prestigious team. Since hearing the news from KLS Johan had been in a daze, his life work up in smoke for the second time in three years. But he was determined to put a brave face on the grim reality. Unless Jack's efforts were successful, Microstem would be in liquidation within the month.

Johan talked for around fifteen minutes, summarizing the opportunities and threats surrounding the success of Microstem. To conclude, he emphasized the need for strong financial management aligned to the success of the business. Using the KLS monthly board hurdles as a "sword of Damocles" analogy was a poignant metaphor for how best to suffocate creativity in biotechnology research. Once again, Jack stood to summarize and take questions.

"So there we have it. What I am proposing is a partnership between our respective skills, the foundation of a good business and an evangelical, equity-incentivized management team with no out-of-house dependency. Money in the bank day one, pedal to the metal. I hope this makes sense. I imagine you may all have some questions."

The table was silent. Ben and Jenny looked at each other in disbelief, and Bob looked equally surprised. Annie sat glowing, her pride at being asked to become involved evident. Bob was the first to come forward.

"Okay, Jack, here goes. I buy into high risk, high reward, but friendship aside and of course the honor of being asked, who will fund Microstem? And with regard to our salaries, I mean, as you know, I've got a family, man. I'm sure I speak for most of us here in that we would need some form of security over the period. We have all witnessed how capital is apportioned to these types of businesses. It's dripped in. Jesus, Jack, that's what I do on a day-to-day basis. In this climate, how can we be sure, even if we bought into the whole concept, that the funding will not stop, like it clearly just has?"

"Yes," added Ben. "I'm sorry to put a downer on all this, Jack, Johan, but the alteration that is brutalizing the tech sector will mean the clever money will be even harder to attain. They will want their pound of flesh, Jack. Eight million is a lot right now for a business with few concrete assets and a two-year road to profitability."

"No, good solid points, gentlemen. All noted. Well, I might as well come clean. There will be no contracts in this fundraising since the money is guaranteed, eight million dollars day one, wages underwritten for the next two years, absolutely watertight. Beyond twenty-four months, well, we are planning for success, but if we fail, then yes, I guess the risk lies two years from now."

"Guaranteed? You mean it's already been arranged? I just find it hard to believe that even philanthropic money comes that easy, Jack. I mean, the Finkel Foundation, as just one example, is infamous for its onerous contracts," replied Ben. "How can you be so sure until the deal is done?"

De Blevis turned to Jack. "Yes, Jack," he agreed, "even the government grant route would mean a total sell-out. We would come away holding very little, even with the scientific foundation scenario. I know about it, I've been there with the University of Pietermaritzburg."

Jack remained seated. He felt composed and cool, relieved even that the group's focus and objections were not directed toward De Blevis' credibility and the viability of the proposition but on the detail of the funding. "Well, guys. There will be no philanthropic funds or government money, not even scientific grants. I will fund the project personally."

There was silence. The table was stunned. Only Hans Groub and Ingvar remained composed.

"Jesus, Jack! How much have they been paying you?" added Bob, the sudden shock visible on his face.

"Obviously too much, Bob, so I guess it's time I put my money where my heart is."

Annie, Ben and Johan sat speechless.

"So ladies, gentlemen, what do you say? I'm not letting you start your meal without a yes, by the way . . ."

177

Jack sat back down and surveyed the table. Annie, the nervousness evident in her voice, was next to speak.

"Jack, I've got to say you've blown me away. I'm probably speaking for everyone here when I say how honored I feel to be offered this opportunity, especially in light of some of our current employment status. But where do you fit into Microstem? Will you be CEO? I mean, eight million, that's a giant stake in the business, Jack. Will I be reporting to you?"

Again there was silence. All their eyes were fixed on Jack.

"Maybe I should answer this one, Jack," cut in Hans Groub. He stood up and, gently resting his hands on Jack's shoulders, addressed the table.

"Since I met Jack in my gallery a few months ago, I have come to know a most remarkable man I can now safely call my friend. I have seen him in that short time rise to some very difficult challenges and display quite unreasonable generosity with both his time and his personal wealth. I think I am correct in saying this generous investment in Microstem, a business Jack is absolutely passionate about, quite literally comes with only one string attached. This I have had to insist on for fear of my friend taking almost nothing, a mere three percent holding, fully dilutable on any further fundraising. After all, everyone present is being asked to take a risk too, and with this meager equity allocation, there will be plenty to go round, I'm sure you will agree. For your information, Jack has a belief in the equity value of this business; after a further three tranches of funding with approximated dilutions of thirty percent, he believes one percent in the business will be worth over ten times his initial investment. So look after your stakes. Jack sees it as a bet more than anything else, and if he is right, there will be something for him and his family in his dotage. If he is wrong, a higher percentage would be, how shall I say, irrelevant.

"Since Jack returned from his Arctic trip last month I have, to be quite frank, advised him against such a radical gesture, but in this he is quite resolved. His feelings are quite simply of a most genuine and, if you may permit me, Jack, artistic nature. Jack has come to recognize money as a tool, an asset but also somewhat of a burden. To relieve himself of his burden and of a predicament to which he could see no end, that of a Wall Street gun for hire, so to speak, he has recognized what few of us have had the vision to realize. That only when we are truly without possessions and wealth can we find our true self. For those of you wondering about his guaranteed financial security, his day-to-day money, he will quite simply have none. This is the way Jack wants it. Obviously he has set aside a contingency for any tax obligations and for his family, as well as that of Jim Williamson. To the rest of us he has offered us inclusion in the Microstem project and a shareholding thereof. Aside from this, I guess you could say he will be cleaned out. I must say, I've never heard of anything like it, but Jack, as I am sure you all agree, is no ordinary man."

Bob couldn't control himself. "But Jack, Hans, this is madness, guys. I mean you can't give it all up. Surely you are going to get involved with the project yourself, run the ship or at least take a view and guide De Blevis."

"No, Bob," replied Jack. "I'm afraid that's the catch. After today, you'll all be on your own. That's why I've picked you guys. Ben, I'm counting on you to be as diligent and honest as I know you can be. Bob, you've got the skills. This one could, if you play it right, make you all very rich. De Blevis and his team need you, that's why I've done this thing and you are the only ones I can trust. Ingvar here will be on the phone. Aside from Bill Gates, there's no one else I know who can pick up the phone to Warren Buffet 24/7, and he hasn't lost to the old man at bridge now for over a year either, so you will be in good hands. He has been around, guys, and is committed to getting Microstem public. There is nothing I could possibly add that you cannot do. Trust me."

"So, if you are not going to be working with us, Jack, what are you going to be doing? Don't tell me you are going back to school. Jesus, you're not going to join some sect or the church or something?"

Jack laughed out loud, "No, Annie, nothing like that. I'm going to do something for me, guys. I'm going home, back to Minnesota. I need to get back to some fundamentals, that's all, then we'll see. I've realized I need to be away from the city for a while, have a bit of a change of scenery. So, team, enough about me. Decision time . . . is it a yes or what?"

Chapter 9

Laura Wyler was out in the garden when the telephone rang. She spent the best part of every day outside, pruning, digging and tending to her plants and trees. The exercise and wellbeing of working in the elements had kept her lean and fit, in fine fettle for her fifty-seven years. Although she had turned grey shortly after Joe's untimely death, she had been careful with her appearance, a confidence thing more than vanity. She had looked after herself, eating well, exercising daily with long walks, having to keep it together for Jack and her daughter Holly. As the years passed so had her grief, and in time her smile had returned and laughter too. Laura was still pretty, her high cheekbones, clear skin and dark eyes giving the impression of a woman at least ten years younger. Ask Laura her secret and she would have told you it was thanks to her love of the Lord, but her friends knew differently. Laura loved her plants and the work kept her young, as did her kids. Although she didn't see enough of Jack, when she did he reminded her so much of Joe it sometimes took her breath away.

Since Joe's death, the garden had become her major focus, apart from looking after Jack's teenage sister, who, typical for her age, spent more time out than in. Holly had matured early and without the guidance of a strong father figure. Laura had been beside herself when she had caught her daughter in bed with a boy the wrong side of her sixteenth birthday. Laura had no choice but to turn to her son. Jack was calm, even if she sensed his amusement at his mother's embarrassment. Jack had told her to let it go, despite all her religious beliefs and her feelings about sex and marriage. Laura had listened to her son. After that Holly had seemed to calm down a bit, sensing the pain the episode had put her mother through. Now eighteen, Holly was entering her last semester at high school, a beautiful, athletic raven-haired beauty with her whole life ahead of her. It made Laura so proud, but sad that Joe hadn't seen his daughter grow into such a stunning, if free-spirited young lady.

If Jack was right and her daughter's fun-loving nature could not be tamed, Laura decided her garden could be. The lawns, various greenhouses and covered yearling patches were, however, more than a passing release from her maternal frustrations. The garden presented Laura with a monumental challenge, an ecological triumph of womankind over nature. The plants and trees provided Laura with a focal point to her day, a passion so pure and relentless that she was often to be found into the early evening pruning, planting and planning for the next installation to be carefully nurtured in her oversized, temperature-controlled arboretum. Northern Minnesota is not the ideal environment to grow exotic hardwoods or any non-resident flora. The winters are known to be some of the coldest in the northern hemisphere, perfectly described by native Minnesotans as "Siberia with drive-ins".

Since Joe's death, Jack had been more than willing to foster his mother's green-fingered passion. If he was brutally honest, he had been glad to provide the distraction from the trauma of losing a husband that gardening had offered her. Jack had generously funded Laura's various non-indigenous acquisitions and all the technical humidification and tempera-ture-control housings. If Minnesota was Siberia in the winter, it was closer to London, England, in its short and wet summer. With the last snows and ground frosts disappearing from the lakes and muskeg in late May and early June, Laura had just two months to work outside before the mists and cold rains of the northern fall dragged Minnesota swiftly back into the icy grip of a mid-October winter.

If the atmospheric and climatic propensity for harsh weather proved a testing challenge for Laura, Minnesota offered Jack a viable absolution from urban mediocrity, an all-over cleansing of body and spirit from the controlled, air-conditioned city environment. It was this wild and extreme place that Jack loved so much, and now he planned to return, but not for his usual fleeting weekend visit intercut with frantic emails and long-distance business calls. Jack was coming home now, not only to Ely the town, his mother and his sister, but also to the land itself, the soil, the trees and the air. He was coming back home to rest, for a while at least. He yearned for the space, the smell of the woods, the silence. He could taste it, and now more than ever the promise of the backwoods reassured him. Ely would be an affirmation that what he had proposed was justified and right, that he hadn't lost it, that it was a good choice, the right choice. Here he would begin his journey and kick-start his life.

Jack replaced the receiver on his Bang & Olufsen brushed steel wall bracket. "Typical," he mused. "I fund her greenhouses and now I can never speak to her." He smiled to himself and carefully closed the door to his apartment, pausing momentarily to survey its bare wooden floor, empty shelves and bespoke wall cabinets. A large shipping crate sat solitary

181

in the middle of the room, with instructions attached with gaffer tape to the large facing panel.

"Good old Groub," muttered Jack as he turned the key in the lock and, turning away from the large, oak door, kicked his huge sled bag along the newly waxed hallway toward the service elevator.

★ ★ ★

Jack arrived early at Duluth airport. He always hated the balls-ache of the change in the Twin Cities, but he made the connection and sat calm and composed on the forecourt of the small, domestic terminal, glad to be out of the bustle of New York. Normally he had a car waiting or, if he ever got through, his mother would make the three-hour backroads trip via Aurora to pick him up. But today of all days Jack wanted to make the journey on his own. The Hertz office was the only office manned at the time, and Jack decided he would rent an SUV for a couple of weeks until he had sorted out his movements. His mom only had the one car; a clapped-out Ford pick-up, and the last thing Jack wanted was to be stuck out in Ely without a ride.

There was still a good amount of snow on the ground, and certainly for the uninitiated the winter commute could be slow-going and in parts treacherous. The Dodge had new snow tires that made the ride slightly less lethal but not enough to make it safe. Modern four-wheel drive and ABS was harder to manhandle round corners, especially if, like Jack, you liked to throw the car around, over-steer and slide it round so as to scare the shit out of yourself. It had been a while since Jack had been able to let rip on a good piece of road, and to its credit the Durango and Jack did well not to end up in a ditch on more than one occasion. He opened all the windows, cranked up the CD and gave it plenty of juice as he powered his way north. It was a clear day, fresh and new, and with the wind in his head Jack lost himself in the driving. It felt good.

In a little under two hours the Dodge sat simmering in the driveway of his mother's house, a fine and audible metallic tinkling coming from the V8 as it sat cooling off in the late morning spring sun. Laura, still unaware of Jack's arrival, was crouched in the farthest corner of the greenhouse, pruning a young rhododendron recently arrived from Nepal. Deep in thought, she leaped halfway out of her skin as Jack crept stealthily along the greenhouse wall and up on her from behind, silent and deadly, especially so for a man his size.

"Jesus, Jack! You'll kill me one of these days, darling! What are you doing here? You could have at least phoned. I don't know what we've got in the fridge but I know for sure you won't want it for dinner!"

"Mom, Mom, calm down. I did try to phone but I guess you were either in here or out. Re the food, don't sweat it; we'll get a pizza. It's great to see you, Mom, it really is."

Laura looked closely at Jack. He had changed, and she could sense it, something in his tone, his eyes and his manner. The sense only a mother has when one of her own isn't quite the same... "So, Jack," she responded, careful not to give her thoughts away, "to what do we owe this unexpected pleasure?"

"I was missing this place, that's all, Mom. I was missing being home, have been for a while I guess, so I decided to take a bit of time off, you know, to kick back..." Jack stared at the floor. All of a sudden his throat filled with emotion and hit him hard, a wall of pain, guilt, shame and deep sadness. Here he was in the process of bullshitting his mother. Fuck that. He needed to get this out.

Jack looked at Laura and she knew, deep in his eyes, deep inside, he was certainly not okay. He needed her and in her heart she needed him to need that kind of love. God, how she had it to give, and anyhow her plants could wait. However much love she had given them, they had never reciprocated the compliment, not physically anyhow. Jack needed her, her son was home and that was enough.

Gently she stood up and took Jack's massive frame in her arms. And as she did so he began to cry, slowly and silently at first, as she rocked him from side to side. As she rocked him it began to come out, all of it, the kind of emotions a man doesn't feel right expressing but needs to. With words came the tears, the pain and wailing like she had never heard, crying like a wounded animal alone in the forest, earthy and primordial. How it hurt her, but she held on and on until Jack had nothing left. She had heard about Jim briefly from Jack himself, then from June Williamson and Bob Anders, both of whom had felt he had been bottling it all up. So his visit was if anything a little overdue. But that had not bothered her. Jack had always kept his shit pretty tight and no son wants to dump that kind of emotional baggage on his ageing mother. It was just that with Joe gone there had been a huge emotional hole left to fill, and Holly's daily escapades skipping school and fooling around with boys had only half-filled her emotional and motherly whole. Now though she was complete, a mother once more, needed, legitimate, justified, in demand and, if she was honest, not a little scared.

Later that night they sat together watching TV, a fire lit, full stomachs, and Jack knew then that there would be no turning back. He had done the right thing. He had no choice. Hauling his sled bag the two flights up the broad wooden stairs to his attic bedroom, Jack collapsed exhausted on his old bed. High school football photos, college flags and pictures of old friends adorned the walls. It was as if in coming home he had walked back in time to his roots, his genesis. He was a kid again, a whole life unpolluted by loss, failure and success. In his room his father was still alive with the hunting mementos, his first whitetail buck skull mounted for him by his dad, his knife collection sitting as it always did in an old shirt box beside his dresser and his art books, his beloved art books, neatly ordered and stacked on the shelf.

If Jack were to analyze his collection of childhood belongings, passions and interests, very little in him had changed. His passions had remained the same: the wild, art, hunting, knives. However, the innocence and uncomplicated simplicity of his childhood was missing, not in the physical make-up of the room and house, but within him, where the flame was dead, as dead as it ever could be. As Jack lay alone in his room that night and drifted off into a fitful sleep, he was as convinced as he could ever be that his joy would never return.

★ ★ ★

The next morning after breakfast, Jack joined his mother in the gardens and greenhouses. She had never had his attention before, and now he seemed as interested in her passion as he would ever be. For Jack it was the very concept of artificially growing and cultivating a garden that put him off, since he couldn't see the point of the whole process in the first place. Cultivation meant civilization, and civilization to Jack, as it had to some extent to his father, meant exploitation of a natural resource. Sure, a privately owned garden on the outskirts of a small, northern town was fine, but huge tracts of land laid out for theme parks, farmland, roads and leisure ways were wrong. Laura knew how he felt, but despite his hard-line views on what constituted ethical conservation, and to some extent in spite of himself, he was not unimpressed by what she had achieved. It was beautiful, a true labor of love, and Jack felt a tingling of pride in his mother's new-found professionalism. After retiring from her part-time position as an art lecturer at the University of Minnesota, Laura had yet again excelled at what she loved doing. In part, Jack had helped that transformation from academic to gardener extraordinaire to become a reality.

The area of his mother's new expertise that interested him most was the organic growing of vegetables and her herb garden. Sage, coriander, thyme, lavender, cumin and wild rosehip all grew within the confines of her modest acre. Cloudberries, wild elderflower, raspberries, bearberries, wolf's tooth, bear claw, all grew with such abundance that despite his recent rejection of the business world, Jack couldn't help thinking Laura was sitting on an organic and natural medicinal goldmine. He told her so, and they laughed together. When would he just enjoy the garden? With Jack there was always an angle – Laura loved him for that and at least he still had his sense of humor.

After a light lunch of home-baked bread, tomatoes and English Cheddar, Jack excused himself and returned to his attic room. Sitting on the floor, he began to go through the many boxes of old books and photographs that his mother had lovingly stored, awaiting the rare occasion when he might actually throw something away. Each book, each photo, injected a memory and a smell, a feeling Jack hadn't had in years. Deep at the bottom of the last box in the row, he pulled out a copy of a book he hadn't seen since his early teens, *An American Alone*. He had begun but not actually finished the book years ago when his old man had given it to him. How odd, he thought, Dad never gave me books to read, always too busy teaching me himself, but as Jack turned the page the inscription was clear.

> To my dear Jack,
> This guy was a one of a kind but don't believe the hype, he's still out there!
> My love,
> Daddy XXX

"Love, daddy. For fuck's sake, why, Dad?" Jack sat silent. Composing himself, he grabbed a cushion and began to read . . .

Everett Reuss had disappeared in Utah's south-eastern canyon lands in 1934. He had last been spotted by a shepherd near Davis Canyon and had never been seen or heard of again. An avid explorer, adventurer, dreamer, poet and not to mention hopeless romantic, Reuss had traveled much of the American south-west, staying on reservations and alone, sometimes for months at a time, living off the land. An accomplished trapper, woodsman and hunter, Reuss had in his short life become somewhat of a legend with the local Navajo people, as well as the darling of the east-coast literati. His stories, syndicated with both *Esquire* and *American Today* magazines, had generated a veritable cult following among idealistic Europeans, east-coast hopefuls and drifters wanting to pitch their wits and bet their lives on a new life west of the badlands. Often referred to as "the Kerouac of the canyon lands", Reuss came to embody the romantic ideal of beauty and freedom in nature. At the time of his disappearance he was twenty years old.

For generations, Americans had survived the trials of living off the land. From Alaska and the Yukon as far south as the Mexican borderlands, the American dream had held on to its piece of the pie against all odds, elements, wildlife and aggressive locals, but never before had one American typified the seal of this quest as much as Reuss. His was a quest for self-truth in the wilderness, and for the answers to the age-old question of what it is to be American. Reports of Reuss had been forthcoming from travellers who swore they had made a sighting as recently as the mid '70s. So pure was Reuss in his pursuit of his personal nirvana that he left all his belongings at the trailhead and even changed his identity to suit his new incarnation as a wild man seeking enlightenment in the desert. From time to time at various trailheads and campsites along his recorded and known route, carvings had been found confirming his new identity and time of passing. "Nemo" was his newly acquired name – "no one" in Latin, the irony of which made Jack smile.

"Nemo, I like that, I really do," he muttered to himself.

★ ★ ★

Laura had to call twice to get Jack down for dinner. He had finished the book in a little under two hours.

"How are you getting along up there?" asked Laura.

"Good, Mom. Good," replied Jack. "It's crazy how I've forgotten so much of what was up there. Literally a lifetime ago, I guess, since any of that stuff has seen the light of day."

"Well, actually Jack, that's not quite true. I read up there all the time. You've got one of the best collections of post-modernist reference material this side of Duluth County. To be honest I think most of it used to belong to Duluth County, but then that's another story." Laura smiled naughtily.

"No, all my art books are from the university library. That's stealing, Mom."

"Not really, Jack. I intend to return them one day. Look on them as a long-term loan..."

"I suppose you've been deep in your books on Beuys. Birdy told me some time back you blew more money than our house is worth on a sled, or should I say *the* sled."

"Well, Mom, for once you will be relieved. I was actually given it... Then again, I guess you are going to struggle to believe that one, right?"

"No, no, darling. If you say that is how you came by owning one of the most seminal of Germany's post-war sculptural icons, I will believe you, honest... cross my heart."

"Well, Mom, that's by the by... but I was reading a book Dad gave me about that guy Reuss."

Laura went silent. Putting down her fork and knife, she looked slowly up at Jack. "Now darling, I really don't think you should be wasting time reading about that loser. Jesus, your father was obsessed with the man, to the extent our honeymoon in '61 was spent following his idiotic rambling around Arizona."

Jack looked shocked.

"Oh, no baby, I don't mean it like that. We had a wonderful time. It's just Joe had a thing about losing himself in the wild. Guess that's why he ended up a park ranger. But so much of it, all that romantic stuff, was such a crock. I mean, living on your own, who would want to do such a thing?"

Jack began to feel a little uncomfortable. "Hey, Mom, look, I was just reading the book, okay. Let's leave it. Beuys, that's safer ground, I guess. Tell me, did he ever get out there again after the war? I mean like, out there. You know, revisit the Crimea, search in the trees for what he found there originally?"

"Not that I know of. You see, after the war Beuys had some serious issues. I think he was sectioned before he got back his faculties, so to speak. But he made quite a few trips to Ireland and Europe during what he referred to as his 'traveling years', his years on the road. I seem to remember it was after he finished up his professorship in Düsseldorf, or should I say, after his professorship finished him... he was never the same again. I, for one, feel he had always been a bit touched, Jack ... quite crazy actually, mad as a hatter!"

★ ★ ★

A huge whiteness lay before him, seductive, crisp, new as if beckoning him into itself, luring him before finally cloaking him in its beauty. Beuys stood on the snow, barefoot but wrapped in his great coat with his favorite fur collar. Jack turned away, sensing that this was somehow unreal and impossible, but just visible to his left, maybe twenty yards away, sat Jim, warm, relaxed and getting the stove going, just like he always did after a hard day breaking trail. Jack knew then that it was all okay, everything was just fine. That and the feeling of strength he had in his body, his legs, was a reassuring feeling and the security he felt was not unfounded. His friend had come back. So long as Jim was there all the other things that had been troubling him didn't matter any more. Not now, not ever.

Jack walked toward Jim, but as he approached his friend seemed to move away, beyond his reach. Jack stopped. The snow was wet and deep and as he stood only yards away now, he realized he would have to try something else. The frustration was maddening.

"Jim, Jim, it's me, Jack . . . Where have you been?" he called, desperate for a reply.

Jim looked up away from the fire and looked straight at Jack, then through him, and smiled the kind of smile that said more than it meant to, more than a smile should. Jack knew the smile belied fear, a fear of something deeper, of the unknown. Jack shouted again, louder this time, but the more he shouted the more mute he became until no sound at all came from his lips, his throat a redundant organ, powerless and without audible function. Then Jim was gone and a wet patch of snow was all that remained, a pool of meltwater stained a faint pink, a light smear of blood barely visible but there none the less.

Jack was sinking into the snow at a pace beyond his control. Down and down he went until panic was overcome by resignation. "Help me!" he shouted up at the figure of Beuys. "Jesus," he pleaded, "help me . . ."

Beuys turned away, his long coat flowing in the wind, parting to reveal his legs beneath. He was thin, painfully so, but despite his frailty he loomed large, larger than a man of his build. He had an almost majestic presence, an austere aura, and Jack felt dwarfed by him, insignificant and small, like a child. For what seemed an eternity, Beuys stood there with his back turned and his head shrouded beneath his grey trilby with its black linen band. Jack stopped sinking and stood too, waiting for the great man to make the next move, grandmother's footsteps on the ice.

Then Beuys let out a faint sigh and in a low broken English he muttered a sound, then a sentence. "We go . . . this way, Jack. This way."

Jack was now free, and as quickly as he could he walked toward Beuys, the snow now holding under him like tarmac. Beuys raised a long thin arm and pointed. As Jack followed his line he saw it, in the distance, looming large, a faint ridgeline, a range of mountains thrusting skywards out of the pack. Jack began to feel faint; this was just too much, too much for a mind to compute and connect with. His reasoning challenged, his balance gone, and the feeling he had in his legs, that knowing, the security of his friend gone once again, it not having been real.

There were too many questions but now he needed answers. The message in the elevator, Jim's death . . . As he turned, his legs held strong again. He felt they were going to hold better than ever now. They would take him where he needed to go, after all, that was what they were there for. He sensed that he already knew everything; Beuys was gone, a faint shadow on the horizon, and in his place sat the sled, its well-oiled wooden slats resting on the forged, slightly rusted runners. His vehicle had arrived, the only primitive transport he would need was safe and beside him. Now all he had to do was slip on the harness and pull the sled for all he was worth. His legs, his heart and his lungs could do it well. His legs and his sled would take him and all the kit he needed toward those mountains. He would go toward a place where he had never been but that he somehow knew. Somewhere deep inside of him he knew that place. He could feel it.

★ ★ ★

Laura had been calling Jack for a few minutes. Jack, still half asleep, slipped into the bathroom and splashed cold water on to his warm, sheet-creased face. Focusing in the mirror, he studied each side of his face for stubble and decided he would not have a shave today. Maybe, he thought, he would leave it to grow for a while. The dream stayed with him, and instead of fading, as dreams so often do, it got clearer and more lucid. It was a time release of emotions and imagery that dripped through his subconscious and began, slowly at first, to inform his actions. This was Jack's dream and for Jack alone. After all, he reasoned, what kind of a man follows his dreams?

His mom's cooking tasted good. Home-baked muffins, eggs, bacon, wild mushrooms, tomatoes, even the juice tasted different. After breakfast he went back to his room. There were so many things he needed up there, things he didn't even know he needed, things lost, forgotten, boxes upon boxes of memories, memories he would be needing now. He was hungry for it; greedy for all that stored information from the past. He began to make a list, checking off and annotating reference material that now seemed so essential. Soon the pile grew to include atlases, maps, his hunting logs, postcards, photo albums from his Alaska hunts with his dad, family holidays in the boundary waters, his college books, *The History of Man* by Redfern, Leakey's journals in the Great Escarpment, Shackleton's *Endurance*, Messner's *Free Spirit*. It was all here, carefully shelved, ordered and boxed thoughtfully by his mother, the books that had first inspired him and fueled his teenage dreams. For hours Jack read, marked off chapters, scribbled down notes. As night fell, he was done. A month of reading was a month of preparation waiting to be absorbed, downloaded and rekindled. It was tinder for his mental fire.

Jack laid out a large 1:250,000 map of western Alaska. There was something about that ridgeline, something familiar to him. Jack had to find out, search for all the clues and solve the problem. Joe had been a meticulous planner. He had lived by the motto of the seven Ps: "Prior planning and preparation prevents piss poor performance." The margins to the side of the map were referenced with detailed timings, coordinates, names and addresses in his father's unmistakable scrawl. Three years before his father's death in the fall of '91, Jack and his old man had made their last trip together hunting bull moose just north of Lake Iliamna in western Alaska. After three wet and eventful weeks fly camping they had had to make a detour to pick up a sick Indian woman from a village at Lake Clark. The weather began to come in but the pilot had made a good choice of refuge. Resting beneath the rolling peaks of the Kuskokwim mountains they had spent a freezing night huddled together in the small plane, cutting free at first light after a break in the weather. Jack had been sitting in the rear of the Beaver and as they had risen above the mists of the muskeg floor, Jack had marveled at the beauty of the range. Taking a series of snaps out over the wing, Jack remembered the words of the bush pilot: "There are a million square miles out there, son, and not one road. Damned if that's not a bitch of a wilderness, finest piece of bush this side of the Bering Sea."

It had all come flooding back. Jack had been given a new German Sauer 30–06 by his old man for the trip, a caliber his father believed to be the most versatile big game rifle cartridge ever put through a weapon. He quickly stood up and walked briskly toward the other side of the attic. There in a bookshelf sat his old music box. He gently lifted the lid and was amazed to hear the minute clockwork cogs roll into action, as gentle high-pitched notes fused together to create a beautiful Russian melody. Jack opened the lid wide, eyes closed, until the key made its last turn and the tune stopped. Carefully removing the wooden compartment that covered the calibrated wheel housing, Jack peered into the belly of the box. To his relief it was still there, the key to his gun safe.

Opening the small wooden wall cupboard to his left, he got down on one knee and fitted the seven-lever mortise key into the lock. One strong movement heard all the levers swing out of position and the door swung open. Jack's rifle leaned against his father's pump gun, still wrapped in a silicon cloth. He took the rifle out and racked the bolt. The action was perfect, and flicking the release switch to the left of the receiver he removed the bolt and held the chamber close to his eye. He peered at the bedside light down the 11-twist free-floating barrel. Not a speck, clear as a die. Removing the three-shot magazine, Jack swung the lever on the scope mount downwards and in a well-practiced movement removed the Schmidt and Bender 6*42 telescopic sight. The gun was now fully stripped down and Jack held it to his shoulder. Hunting rifles of this grade are never normally supplied with iron sights but Joe had made a special request to his importer that they be fitted. Hunting in the freezing mists of the Alaskan range can render even the most expensive scopes useless. Joe, always aware that the Alaskan hunter is only marginally removed from the food chain, made a point of having all his rifles fitted with this back-up.

Despite it being spring, the attic was warm and Jack had begun to sweat. Removing his shirt, he laid the rifle on his bed and turned to get the ammo pouch from within the cabinet. Squatting down, he felt inside the floor of the metal box and then, relief evident on his face, pulled the thick, tooled leather wallet free from under the butt of the remaining shotgun. Pushing the brass-fixing stud through the leather hole, Jack lifted the top face of the wallet upwards to reveal a neat row of five rounds of 30-06. Stuck to the underside of the cover was what Jack had been looking for. A photograph taken from a plane window of a distant mountain range, the Kuskokwim range of western Alaska. His prize in hand, Jack walked back to the bed and sat down. That was it; he knew it, the range that stood as the gateway to more than a million square miles of wilderness. Even Everett Reuss would have marveled at that, Jack thought. "How would you have coped out there, hey, Reuss?" Jack mused. "Beats the shit out of the desert. Jesus, does it. That's real country. That's the bush all right."

191

Jack had been up in his room for two whole days and Laura was getting worried. Aside from the missed meals, it was as if he had shut her out and Laura wasn't going to take that lying down. She would work this out with him. What Jack needed was to get outside and take the air. As he stumbled down the stairs for dinner, she noticed that he was carrying some excess weight. It wasn't that he had got fat, he wasn't fat by a long stretch, his frame was massive, always had been, it was just that he seemed to have lost his definition and where his stomach had once been lean and tight, there was now a noticeable paunch.

"Oh, how kind of you to join us," teased Laura in her best southern accent, "Well boss, food's a ready. If, that is, you is, sire!"

Holly laughed aloud.

"Hey, you can shut it for one, sis," replied Jack. "Little girls should be seen and not heard."

"Oh really, well, big boys should not have such big bellies, Jack. It's just sooo not sexy! Where's your six-pack gone, Jack? All that desk work, eh!"

Laura and Holly looked at each other and all three laughed.

"Yeah, yeah," conceded Jack, "I haven't been getting in the training recently. It's been a bit . . . "

"She's only pulling your leg, Jack. But darling, you have such a great physique; it's what you put in your mouth that worries me. I think I need to sort out your diet, get you back on the straight and narrow. Good organic, home-grown home cooking, without the cookies and ice cream, okay!"

"Yeah, whatever you say, Mom, but you're right. I've been piling it on a bit at the moment, what with the situation at KLS and since Jim's . . . well, I haven't been motivated to get back into it."

His mother's jibes had struck a nerve. Jack wasn't in his twenties any more. He was thirty-five years old and big. For a while now, since before the trip, since his promotion to MD, he had felt it slipping. What better place to get back in shape? After all, he was going to need to be in the best shape of his life for his next journey, his life might depend on it.

For the next few weeks Jack slipped into a new routine. He would train, run and work out in the hills around Ely in the mornings, have lunch with his mother and spend most afternoons reading in his room. He cut a deal with Laura that he would take the family out to eat at the weekends if she cooked for him all week. Laura was thrilled to be needed, and as the days went by she noticed a marked change in Jack. He slept well, ate well and was soon back to his old self, running everywhere. Relaxed and seemingly carefree, he had also dropped a few pounds. She also noticed that he had a renewed purpose.

On Jack's last weekend at home he made an announcement that he would be going on an expedition with some friends. That was what he needed. He was rested, and even after close examination by his mother's knowing eye, he seemed a different person from the Jack who had arrived home, broken and drained, not a month before. The one question Laura had struggled to get out of him was what he planned to do now. Sure, she knew he had money put away, although he had omitted to tell her about his dealings with Microstem. But at no time did Jack give her any indication as to what his career move might be. It was as if he hadn't got that far, that he was still mending, and she had not pushed the point. He had in his short life earned more money than practically the whole of Ely combined. It was just that it was unlike Jack. He was always discussing his plans, business concepts, the future. But now it was just this trip. Laura had seen all the books, the maps, the kit – but all this for just one trip?

In one sense she was glad of his attention to detail. Joe had always tried to drum into Jack and his pals the necessity of planning for every eventuality, but all this for a trip away with Bob and the others...? Still, she rationalized that boys will be boys and Jack was a big boy now, he was a man, independent and of his own mind. But he was still her boy, her little Jack, and to see him so down just days ago, and the loss of his friend...There was something not quite right – she couldn't put her finger on it, but this trip gave her the fear, the feeling a mother gets, a sixth sense something might go wrong. Or maybe she was just clinging to him too tightly. She really loved having a man in the house again; it was like a piece of Joe had returned. God, he was like his father. And as for that dreamer Reuss, well, talk about DNA...that was just plain spooky.

★ ★ ★

It was now late May and the summer would soon be upon them. Jack was as ready as he was going to be. After a weekend of packing his sled bag and rucksack and organizing all his travel documents and tickets, he was finally set. Although it was late spring in Alaska, he knew that the short season would not last long and he would need new mukluks for the colder months. Stopping in at Steger Mukluks downtown, he bumped into Ollie

Henson, his father's boss in the park service. They chatted for a while and as they parted Jack said something strange, something that reminded Ollie of Joe. Discussing Alaska and the far west, Ollie had asked Jack how he planned to get his pick-up after the team had finished the trip.

"Oh, by radio," replied Jack.

"Well, how long you going to be there, Jack?" pressed Ollie.

"Oh, just a month or two."

"So why the mukluks, Jack? You won't need them up there. Too wet, far too wet. Best get them in the fall, good sale prices then."

"No, Ollie, you never know, I might stay on for a bit, you know. Could come in handy, mukluks, especially in the winter."

"Jesus, Jack. I don't advise you staying up there for the winter. Where did you say you were going to be?"

"I didn't, Ollie, I didn't say. Sorry, but you know what it's like in the town, gossip and all. It's just that we're planning a first and I'd prefer to keep it a secret, just in case I fail and all..."

"But I thought there was a team of you up there? Or is it a solo?"

"Hey, Ollie, what's with all the questions?" Jack was visibly annoyed. "I'm heading off to Alaska with the guys on a trip, that's it, okay?"

"Well, you take care, Jack. You take care. Last time I was up in the west we had a bitch, your father and me."

Jack turned to Ollie, "You were up there with Dad? I thought you guys met in the boundary waters."

"No, Jack, we met in the Togiak wildlife reserve in the sixties, just at the end of the Kuskokwim range. You heard of it, right? Just about the most remote area in those parts, shedloads of bears up there, no roads..."

As Ollie turned to shake hands with Jack, he had already turned and walked away. "Christ, he's like his old man," muttered Ollie. "So goddamn secretive, never makes any sense either. Radio, up there? Damned if you can get a signal over those mountains. Not in a million years."

★ ★ ★

The one thing Jack hated about Ely was the gossip. Everyone knew everyone else's business and he was damned if anyone was going to know where he was going. Ollie had come close enough, and the whole town would know before long. It was time to leave. Jack kept his departure low-key. Laura was sad to see him go, but despite her concern over his long-term plans she was thrilled to see him looking so relaxed, rested and fit.

194

That and the food was her doing. When it came to nutrition she knew her stuff. "Eat like a hunter-gatherer," she told him for the umpteenth time. Fresh meats, vegetables and fruits were all he needed. She knew that well, just like she knew her boy.

Jack sped south to Duluth and made his connection to St Paul in record time. The snows had by now completely gone, aside from dirty grey patches lying in the shaded roadside ditches and under the bellies of the most sheltered pines. Spring in Minnesota had truly arrived. With a few minutes to spare, Jack called Groub from the terminal payphone.

"Hey, Hans, Jack here. How's it going?" They talked for a few minutes, then, realizing the time, Jack got to the point. "Hans, listen, I've got to keep it brief. The package, yes, I have an address for you. Please have it shipped by Fedex to unit 514, the clearance depot. Yes. Where? Oh yes, Anchorage airport. Yes, Hans, Anchorage. Anchorage, Alaska."

★ ★ ★

Laura sat alone in the house once more, the envelope in front of her. God, how she hated unannounced letters. They always brought bad news or bills. Why couldn't people just talk? Now she was annoyed with Jack. Somehow he had cheated her, smiles and kisses and then this. She just knew from the moment she saw it sitting on her bedroom dresser. Sliding her silver paper knife under the gum line, she pulled out the handwritten note. Attached was a check. No, it wasn't a check, it was a seven-figure endowment!

Dear Mom and Holly,

I've gone away for a while. I guess I wasn't completely straight with you when I said I would be away on an expedition. I guess it is going to be a bit more than that. But Mom, you have to trust me. I need to do this for me. Please don't worry. I will be fine.
This is for you both. Hope it helps, living, the garden, a trip somewhere nice...

My love, always and forever,
Jack

Laura dropped the note and held her hands to her mouth. She hurriedly made her way upstairs to the attic bedroom and sat on the bed. She could feel him, the bed still warm and indented from where he had been sitting. The books were stacked neatly in a pile. She knew what she was looking for. The book on Reuss. Frantically she scanned the titles on their spines. But already she knew it wasn't there. She knew, as well as she knew the pain of giving birth to Jack, as any mother in connection with her kids knew. He had gone, with that book filling his mind with madness and the book on Beuys and the maps. Why hadn't she thrown them away when Joe died? Why were they so alike?

"Damn you, Joe," she cursed. "Damn you for encouraging him, making him so self-reliant, and damn you for dying and leaving me alone." Sobbing now, Laura slipped to the floor, weeping loudly. "Why Jack, why? Why weren't we enough for you, why?"

Part 2

Nemo

Chapter 1

North-western Alaska is not a kind place. People can really suffer there and the romance of the place doesn't last long, the Interior sees to that. The terrible record-busting cold, the long winter months, the endless darkness . . . it's known by locals as "the bitch". You either love her or you hate her, but she never ever lets you forget that she's there, gnawing at you, eating you away, until one day you crack. Minus 60 does that. Engine oil freezes at minus 40, and dogs will not run in much over that. The moose and the barren ground caribou (the food source), they bed down, melt into the landscape. The wolves, the hunters, they either find a den site and curl up together, forgetting their differences, or they die and leave contorted, gnarled corpses covered by drifting snow. The sleepers – the beavers, grizzlies, marmots, ground squirrels, muskrats and snow voles – are deep in their respective homes, their metabolisms shut down, their core slowly pumping life-giving blood around their vital organs, drip-feeding their peripheries so as to avoid infection. Even the snow hares take refuge on the coldest days, as does their deadly adversary, the solitary Alaskan lynx. All life stops at those temperatures and in the Alaskan Interior it gets even colder. Whip up a bit of mid-February wind chill blowing off the Brooks Range and you can imagine minus 175 at Fort Yukon. It's as cold as it gets anywhere on the planet, period.

Surviving off the land, or "living subsistence" as Alaskans call it, takes a special kind of man and it takes a special type of preparation, months and years of it. The shelter or cabin must be built and weatherized by mid-September and the first snows, and seven months of firewood must be cut, chopped and stored. Dry and canned supplies must be flown in, dried meat hung, fish weathered, kerosene filtered and spare lamp filaments purchased. The rifles need a winter silicon greasing, sights tested, ammunition stored. Then there comes the transport. For the bush Alaskan, the plane is more common than the car. The fuel drops must be made and the caches marked with GPS, near enough to the rough lake or river landing strips and well visible with snow wands. All spares must be flown in and cached. The radio and the spare must be charged and a small portable generator close to hand. The spare skids need to be tested and ready for changeover. Floats for summer use are swapped with hand pump inflatable skis for all winter landings. Skidoos in the bush are still taboo. Too heavy to fly in and too temperamental for remote travel for all but the greenest of Alaskans to rely on them.

Much more preferential is the dog team, and with the teams a minimum of twenty-four good running dogs is required, to run a trap line, in any case. Where there are dogs there is work: food must be prepared daily, soups boiled, essential supplements added. Harnesses need testing and spares need to be packed, booties for frostbitten feet prepared and plenty of moose hide brought in for patches. The dogs are the lifelines. But they themselves are constantly in danger, for where there are dogs there are wolves. There's nothing a timber wolf likes more than a husky, hence the numbers a trapper will lose. Close to a quarter of his dogs in a season; in-fighting, hypothermia and the wildlife see to that. But to a solitary trapper the dogs provide the only surefire way of running the trap line and if need be, getting out. They also provide a distraction from the monotony of the dark winter months and essential loving and unconditional companionship.

Skis, snowshoes, mukluks, bunny boots, hip boots (for overflow travel) are also needed, but with the average trapper living over 300 miles from the nearest town, a walk out is often fatal. Then there is the personal kit. On average a trapper will need two sets of thermals (trappers tend not to wash that much), three pairs of gloves and a spare set consisting of thermal fleece and leather / GoreTex outer with down inserts for cold days, two fleece suits, one down suit, one windproof and fur-trimmed parka, goggles, balaclavas and various fur hoods and wolverine hats. All this is just for starters, because on paper at least it looks attainable, logical even, shelter, food, transport, warmth . . . But the reality is the killer, seven months, nearly 200 days or 4,800 hours of darkness, sub-zero temperatures and mind-numbing solitude. It is the solitude that gets to you, the cabin fever. Even the most experienced Alaskans sometimes succumb, lose it, shoot their dogs, their wife, their kids and then themselves.

Every winter paves the way for a series of spring police reports, including homicides, natural deaths and disappearances, all centralized at the Federal building in downtown Anchorage. But Federal manpower, local sheriffs, police departments, Bureau of Land Management and even the Department of Fish and Game have no real way of dealing with all the disappearances, not unless they have clues, tangible evidence to connect loss to time and place, a name, even a sighting. So for those who fail to turn up, whether ill, injured, dead or just missing, their fate is often sealed. It is in the spring that the cost is counted, along with the fur pelts and skinned meat. And it is in the spring that the cycle begins again and the lists are updated, the lists of those that have been beaten by "the bitch".

★ ★ ★

It was December 2000 and all Palmer's sheriff Pete Stetson had was a name; a name, a wallet and some clothes, to be more precise. US Customs at Anchorage also confirmed the arrival of a large crate containing an artwork, shipped by Fedex up from New York and signed for by a Mr Jack Wyler in late May. It was the same guy all right, the names and the driver's license ID matched right up. The artwork, well, that was just a total mystery. Other than that Stetson didn't have much to go on, since the FBI had confirmed that none of the cards had been used since his disappearance. Seems like this Wyler fellow had been on some kind of expedition. The till receipts in his wallet confirmed that he had bought enough rice and pasta to feed an army. He had also bought a saw and a large camp axe, enough 30–06 ammunition to shoot every day of the moose-hunting season and a large tarpaulin from Traders PX store downtown. In total, Jack Wyler had spent five days in Anchorage before taking the train north to Fairbanks. By all accounts, though, he never arrived, or at least the two train guards and station staff never saw anyone of that description pass the ticket gate.

A small duffel bag with all his personal effects, travel clothes, old sneakers and credit cards had been found by a hiker about thirty clicks south of Talkeetna in mid-June. A local police search of the surrounding area had come up with a blank, not so much as a sniff of this guy. There really was nothing else to go on. In fact, over the summer and fall Stetson had processed virtually nothing untoward. In early November there had been an unconfirmed report by a big game trophy hunter from Wyoming. Unregistered cabin, a stolen moose trophy or something ... Stetson had figured it was a bit of antisocial backwoods behavior from some solitary Nam-Vet out near Bear Lake. But this guy Wyler, he was a city gent, an investment banker, real swanky by all accounts, couldn't be a relationship there, no way. It was as if he had just disappeared, vanished from the face of the earth into thin air.

Wyler's mother, Mrs Laura Wyler of Ely, Minnesota, had first filed the missing persons form in September. A local park ranger from the Quetico boundary waters area in Minnesota, Ollie Henson, had advised her to report her son missing. Ollie had by all accounts quizzed Jack Wyler shortly before his departure and had been concerned by Jack's evasiveness. Laura had resisted Ollie's meddling in her son's affairs, convinced that he would contact her when he was ready. However, four months and no word after he had left for an expedition to Alaska "with some friends", she had decided to alert the authorities. Sheriff Stetson had feared the worst. The time issue was a problem. The longer they are missing, the worse the news. From the outset he suspected, as he had rightly done many times before in so many of the missing persons cases he had to process every year, that it was far from certain this guy would show up, ever. Unless, of course, they were lucky. Lucky from a processing perspective, that is. With the discovery of his personal effects and the fact that he seemed to have disembarked the train at one of the many unscheduled stops, alone and in the wilderness, the odds of Mr Wyler being found alive, over eight months on, were not good at all.

If Jack Wyler ever did show up, Sheriff Stetson knew the form. He would be in a lake, an overflow or wedged between rocks in the Chatnika river, or be found by a backpacker where he had fallen, now frozen after the long winter, white and gnarled, like they always looked, and the teeth, the gums peeled back, withdrawn, freeze-dried. No, if this Wyler guy had got lost out there in the bush he must be dead, reasoned the sheriff. If he wasn't, surely he would have contacted his mom, canceled his missing cards, tried to get money . . . tell somebody.

But there was one problem with the whole Wyler business that kept it from being a closed case. There was a clue on a scrap of paper, a question that niggled him. Whatever the motivation, whatever the reason for Wyler keeping it in a wallet he had quite obviously discarded, it was all Stetson had to go on. A folded piece of copy paper found in Wyler's wallet, slipped in behind his credit cards. On it was printed an extract from the journal of a man called Everett Reuss, whoever he might be, dated 1934:

I shall go on some last wilderness trip to a place I have known and loved. I shall not return. When I go, I leave no trace.

It was the last line that bothered Stetson. "I leave no trace." Maybe it was a coincidence, but Sheriff Stetson didn't believe in coincidences. Leaving no trace bar the duffel bag was exactly what Jack Wyler had done. He had left no physical trace at all. He had vanished.

Stetson was annoyed with the whole affair, like a stone in his shoe that wouldn't budge.

"Shitty business really, a missing persons, missing, presumed dead," he scowled to himself. It was an open case, open to discussion, rumor, falsehoods and gossip. Stetson concluded his report, not in those exact words, but the conclusion was the same and that was what he felt with his logical head on anyway. That was the job. In his role as Sheriff he took it all on, that and the mundane: rescuing a neighbor's cat or breaking up a mid-winter domestic, the odd speeding ticket, drunk and disorderly Indians on pay day. Diffusing emotional bombs summed up most of his workload as counsellor, negotiator, conflict manager, all for 50,000 dollars a year, a house and a state pension. But there were worse deals, worse careers and certainly worse locations. He could be back putting his neck on the line in Detroit. Besides, Pete Stetson was a lawman, the only lawman in this neck of the woods, and upholding the law was what he knew best.

Generally his logic and a cool head got him through his twenty-five years of working some of the roughest neighborhoods in America. Palmer had been a once in a lifetime opportunity, a chance to start over at forty-eight years old, finishing his days on the force running a small town Sheriff's department. Stetson liked Alaska. The people had an identity he could relate to. They weren't American, not in their eyes anyhow, they were Alaskans, and not a single one of them had ended up in America's last frontier without meaning to. You don't just turn up one day and say, "Hell, I'm going to live in Alaska." Those that do last half a season and certainly never make it through their first winter. To live in Alaska, in the bush at least, you really had to mean it, you had to want it deep inside. It struck a chord with Sheriff Stetson the moment he walked out the back door of the police station and took a look around. It might be a sleepy town, he might even get soft working there, but the views, the air ... Detroit, well, it wasn't even worth comparing.

Stetson was a fact man. In the force, more accurately in the detective department, there were only two types of cops, fact men and gut men. The truth was that all the best detectives in downtown Detroit's 9th precinct had a good smattering of both these essential qualities. But Stetson believed that the facts were not fallible while his emotional and instinctive intuition was. The facts, piecing together tangible evidence methodically, that was the way he did it. But this case, so easy to write off now, too easy really ... in his heart, in his gut, that was another matter. Something kept him intrigued, his gut instinct for once overriding his logical mind. He couldn't quite put his finger on it. It was as if this Wyler had planned his disappearance with almost military precision. It was as if he had been controlling the affair somehow either from beyond the grave, or predicting Stetson's mindset even, playing the old "dog with the bone" as if he wanted to be found, dead or alive. Stetson wasn't sure but he knew one thing, this Wyler business wasn't over. Hell, he hadn't even committed a crime; it was just that the paperwork needed to be signed off. Whatever the report might say, it wasn't a closed case, not for Sheriff Stetson anyhow. Not until he had more evidence, not until he had the facts, that and Wyler's corpse in his hands, could he let this one lie.

Chapter 2

Jack was annoyed with himself. He had been careless. He lay prone, low, a faint blur in the tree line, his huge frame hugging the contour of the gradient, holding his breath, squeezing shut his eyes so they hurt, making himself disappear. The hunter, reaching the top of the snowfield, took one last look behind him and, seeing only fir trees, pushed on up the trail toward safety, toward his plane, his wife, his kids. Jack could tell he was really rattled, and seeing him take off like that, he would have been lying if it hadn't made him smile, just a bit. Jack had really freaked him out, but then again, imagine leaving the choice cuts, the thigh, the saddle. Jesus, what an amateur. As he watched the hunter leave the kill and move down the slope, he was lucky a late winter grizzly had not come out for it. Leaving it there in the fresh snow, leaving it out there as an offering, a tribute, even a tribute to Nemo. Yes, that was what it was, a tribute to the infamous Nemo, a tribute to "no one".

★ ★ ★

Beuys had led to Reuss, it even sounded right, and now Reuss had led Jack to this wilderness, a million square miles of it, a wilderness without boundaries, the last frontier. The past seven months had been the hardest Jack had known. Withdrawing himself physically from the civilized world had needed luck, but in retrospect had been the easy bit. It was essentially a liberating experience. Jack's rationale was simple. If he lost his physical identity and ability to support himself in the material world, he would have no choice but to embrace the wild. His supplies of sustainable non-perishable foodstuffs had been calculated to the last day. He had it all worked out. He had given himself just over a year, a spring, a summer, a fall, a winter and a second spring, to see if he could do it. He would lose himself in the struggle, pit himself against nature and work out his demons. Beyond that he couldn't say, but he knew the first months would be the most critical since he needed the short summer to establish his base, build his cabin, hunt, fish, dry meat, cure pelts, store wood, lay his trap line . . .

Boarding the train to Fairbanks had been his ace card, his textbook scenario straight out of a movie. Get on a train as Jack Wyler, jump off when no one was looking and disrobe. Bye bye Jack, hello Nemo. It was as simple as that – any attempt by his past life to find him now would have to solve that one first, and Jack didn't give that much chance. Since he wasn't planning on taking any out-of-state transport or using his credit cards, he had no further need of them. As the train slowly meandered north just outside of Denali National Park in the shadow of the great Mount McKinley, Jack carefully slid the large cargo doors to one side and slipped on to the snowy bank. He stripped totally, changed into a fresh set of clothes, and running deep into the woods threw his grip and old clothes by the tracks. Jack knew it was just a matter of time before the grip would be found. Meanwhile he cut back to the main road, a fitness fanatic in sweatsuit and windbreaker, and with his pockets full of cash hitched back to Anchorage. Jack had hired a small lock-up in the city outskirts and bought an old Ford pick-up for dollars. Filling up the old jalopy with fuel and all his supplies and the still boxed sled, Jack drove the old V8 south to Homer, where he spent a day feeding the eagles on the spit. It was perfect. For the first time since joining KLS he was a nobody, a free man.

Jack drove to the Homer airstrip and chartered a K2 aviation Cessna 206 for a short one-way fishing trip to Great Bear Lake, just south-west of the Kuskokwim range. The pilot didn't blink an eye at the sizable amount of supplies or the one-way request. There were over ten other operators flying the Kuskokwim and besides, Jack had a high-frequency radio. Jack talked the trip up, stressing that he needed to set up camp to await the arrival of his buddies the next week. How long would he be out there? Hell, till the beer ran out. The sled he kept boxed became eight crates of Buds, a surprise for the boys. It was going to be one hell of a fishing trip.

As the plane took off, banked and flew back south-west to Homer, Jack felt the fear rise in his belly. He knew now he had done it for real this time, not just a quick weekend away, an extreme vacation. Now he had severed his physical links with the civilized world, his family and friends. Watching the plane disappear across the treetops of the endless carpet of pine forest, Jack felt his first pangs of regret. His mother, Bob, Annie, the Microstem project, he had it all back home, and yet unless he had made this journey he would have cracked. He knew that. Closing his eyes, he was back at college, in the dorm, his first year away from his mom and dad, and he felt so alone, strange new people, faces, sounds. The sight of the plane fading into the void of the landscape had also reminded him of his first days at college, watching his old man driving away in the pick-up at the start of another semester.

Now that the plane had gone Jack surveyed the beauty of the place, each yard of virgin earth untrodden by humans before him. It was so strange being alone in the muffled silence, taking in the smells of the forest, the fresh pine needles, the earthy pungent aroma of life and decaying vegetation, the verdant canopy of green, the mild summer temperature. The nuances of his new and adopted home swept over him and somehow eased his anxiety and soothed his senses.

Jack had made his decision and there was no going back. He knew the dreams would take him there soon enough; to Sredny, Jim, Mikaela, his mom and all the pain he so wanted to rid himself of in the mountains. But for now he could feel his fear subsiding and with it came a feeling of resolve. He knew he would have plenty of time to stop and take stock, but now he needed to act before any other planes passed overhead, before he was spotted and before he changed his mind.

★ ★ ★

Jack raced into action. Quickly he broke down the supplies in order of priority: foodstuffs, camping gear, survival equipment and fuel, and began the grueling load carry through the Itulilik Pass. Bivouacking each night in his GoreTex liner to save on weight, he humped over 800 pounds of equipment over the pass during the next three weeks and by mid-June made his final trip into the valley beyond.

Standing on the ridge, Jack caught his breath as he looked out across the forest. The valley below stretched out before him, an emerald patchwork of summer colors. The view was so spectacular that for a while he stood transfixed, mesmerized. It was all here, in this one valley, his chosen valley, the river, protective mountain peaks to the north and no lakes. With no possibility of planes landing that meant solitude. The salmon needed a good fresh run and he could see that the fishing would be good. But the threat of winter haunted him, a distant cloud on the horizon, a sand clock set in unstoppable motion.

Jack located a dense patch of forest not three miles from the trailhead of the pass and over the next few weeks he cut into its impenetrable darkness. Felling by hand axe, he sawed down as many as ten trees a day. He had studied his books well. He would need over sixty-five pine trees for the build, and these would have to be pared down, stripped and cut into loose joins. Since he had no adze to make the classic Swedish joins, Jack decided to make his house as solid as possible, logpole style, insulating the gaps with tundra tussocks and dried muskeg moss, filling all the warp holes with damp masticated soil.

That first night Jack made a large lean-to, cutting young pines to form a raised base off the damp tundra on which he could sleep. The roof gave partial cover overhead, with steeply sloping limbs thickly covered with pine branches and roughly cut clods of tundra. Positioning the back of the lean-to toward the direction of the north wind, he cut a deep fire pit a yard in front of the shelter which he filled with dried lichen and tinder for his night-time fires. Toward the end of each day he collected a selection of dead spruce logs, branches and dried foliage and laid the longest of the branches in the pit. Carefully feathering his fire sticks, Jack used the angular spine of the blade of his pocket knife to strike the flint, igniting the carefully amassed dried tinder with shower upon shower of glowing hot sparks. Within a few minutes the largest logs had taken, the oil-rich bark curling and crackling in the blue flames. Soon the entire fire trench was ablaze and Jack lay content and exhausted in his new open-ended shelter, with no need of a sleeping bag, resting on a bed of dried leaves, pine needles and his pack, drifting in and out of consciousness, in and out of reality.

The hard work of building the cabin had proved most therapeutic and in a little under three weeks the basic structure was nearing completion. Jack had worried for the first few nights that he would need more stimulus to keep his mind busy, and for a time he deeply regretted not bringing a good quantity of books. But as the days wore on the very effort required to make a simple cup of tea or a light meal meant he need not have worried. By the end of each day he was totally exhausted and wanted nothing more than to lie back in his lean-to to think and relax alone in the wilderness by his warm fire.

The roof of the cabin had proved the most problematic part to erect and Jack was conscious of how important it would be to make it as weatherproof and insulated as possible for the long winter ahead. In the end he decided to let his creativity get the better of him and improvise the roof's structure. The early fall rains would allow him the time to fine-tune his creation before the ice and snow arrived. In the end the roof was laid around a half-tepee-shaped structure of split pines forming a tight grid and covered with thick sods and earth. After a week Jack reapplied the grass and a second layer of smaller sticks to increase the roof's resistance to wind, creating a green, muddy weave of branches and soil that he packed down hard.

The result was not pretty but Jack was as proud as a peacock. It was the first home he had ever built, and the thought of his spacious loft in New York City left him cold. Within his first month Jack had finished his winter home, chopped all the surrounding stumps in the clearing into usable fire logs and made a primitive stone hearth with an open chimney in the corner of the cabin. To guide the smoke from the cabin, Jack's improvised pitched roof acted as a funnel and did the job, although the cabin looked somewhat peculiar, resembling a squat, rectangular tepee. But it worked. The smoke sat at the angle of the roof as it climbed toward its apex and allowed for almost seven feet of smoke-free living space.

Jack had decided to focus on his shelter and in so doing live on a strict and regimented diet of wild rice, beans and pulses which he had brought up from Ely, courtesy of his mom's underground store. Soaking the beans in water gathered from a nearby stream, the seeds and pulses provided Jack with the essential carbohydrates and proteins needed to maintain his strength and muscle mass. His fitness had improved to such an extent that he no longer felt lethargic and tired, even after grueling days of humping loads. His body had become taut again, the type of tone that can only come from extreme aerobic exercise. Although he had lost some of his bulk, the effect was to make him look even larger; such was the density of his muscular physique. He knew that he was going to need all his strength, stamina and reserves for the hunting that had gradually started to become a somewhat frustrating obsession.

Traditionally the Kuskokwim range was one of the great hunting blocks in Alaska. The only problem was that it was so vast and the game sometimes transient. The *Alaskan Atlas and Gazetteer*, the bible of all Alaskan cartography, allocates the entire Kuskokwim range to page 131. The similar-sized block to the east is denoted across twenty-nine pages, the truth being that the Kuskokwim is largely uncharted and virtually unpopulated, bar the village of Aniak and the costal village of Unalakleet to the north-west. The caribou had moved to a more northerly latitude, cutting through hundreds of miles of low-lying impenetrable muskeg toward the Brooks Range and their summer pastures. So Jack pursued the relatively static population of localized moose that fed on sedges and young willows on the near slopes and the valley floor. But the moose had stayed high that summer because it had been so warm, and Jack didn't sight the massive ungulates until late August. Time was now against him.

After a further ten desperate days hiking out blind into the bush, hoping to cross-grid on fresh spoor and signs, Jack successfully tracked, stalked and killed his first bull, a magnificent twenty-four-pointer. It had taken Jack almost twenty-four hours to carry and dress out the moose, since he knew he would need to use everything. After having sawed through the rib cage, cleaning the hide with his small pocket-knife had presented the biggest problem for Jack. But with little else to do in the long summer evenings he managed to rub enough brine, and over a quarter of his precious salt supplies, into the pinned hide to make it malleable. At last he had an insulating surface for his cabin floor, an oily, smooth, waxy-bottomed, warm, comforting hide. Now he could stretch out his tired limbs at night as he lay next to the fire, exhausted but complete, a hunter alone in the wilderness.

The bull moose had broken his hunting cherry. With the kill his bad luck spell had been lifted. As his mountain fitness grew, so did his alertness. After almost two months, Jack had begun to "tune in" and instead of fighting the bush he began to understand it. Rather than hunting all day, he rose early and headed high on to the northern slopes of the Kuskokwim. Then he lay up close to the tree line, hidden and calm, and waited. The moose liked to graze the plentiful summer crop of black spruce, fiddle fern thickets, creek bed weeds and low Arctic willow fields. For hours the moose would gorge on rock tripe, lichen, reindeer moss, bearberry, crowberry, yellow sedge, milkwort, tundra tussocks and lush summer tundra clumps as Jack watched and waited. Jack rarely saw the moose break cover and venture into the lush and open pastures, so tuned were its survival instincts. While the wary moose fed, Jack slowly moved into position; when he was within a 100-yard range he took his carefully placed heart-lung shot, smashing through hair, skin, blood vessels, sinew and vital organs. The 180-grain hollow-point bullet finally lodged in the opposite femur, splintering the bone so completely that the leg quite often broke off at the joint upon impact. The combination of well-placed shot and devastating velocity meant Jack rarely needed to take a second shot. Sometimes the moose would run, literally dead on its feet, heart obliterated, lungs perforated, his massive muscle memory driven by adrenaline and flight reflex, only to crash down, stone dead, not fifty yards from where he had first been killed. This phenomenon fascinated Jack, who after killing his first moose as a teenager, all those years ago, had been horrified to see his trophy run, pink, frothy, oxygenated blood pumping and gushing out across the willows and stunted alders.

On most days throughout late August and September, as the sun got high in the early autumn sky, Jack would make a small fire with feather sticks, birch and pine needles for tinder, the sweet-smelling birch limbs crackling and smouldering as he lay back to enjoy the view. The light breeze kept the dying blackfly and mosquitoes at bay and kept him cool in the warm midday sun. He would cut some of his first dried moose and, using a sharpened stick, would sit back and cook the lean meat, curing it with the fragrant wood smoke which flew in graceful eddies skyward, taking the delicate aroma of roasted meat high on the wind. Jack was in his element. As the afternoons began to cool down and September grew old, Jack would scan the valley beneath him and then descend to a lower hide and wait for dusk.

As the light began to fade, moose and even the occasional grizzly could be seen breaking cover and taking a welcome drink in the vast bend of Crooked Creek on the mighty Kuskokwim River. But Jack never shot the bears; on the contrary, he paid them the greatest respect and tried to keep his distance at all times. There was something about the bear, the bear that had killed Jim, that was somehow sacrosanct. The Alaskan brown bear stood for too much, it didn't represent the Alaskan wild, it was the wild, the beauty, the danger, the grace and the majesty . . . A couple of times a grizzly had passed near to his camp but Jack had managed to frighten it away from his makeshift smoke store with an overhead volley from the 30–06. The way he saw it, they need not bother each other – there was after all enough room in the Kuskokwim for both of them, even if Jack was outnumbered 25,000 to one!

Throughout the early fall Jack followed this same regime, taking seven moose in a little over three weeks. Jack would cut the meat, starting with the tender saddle and moving on to the juicy rump. Rendering it into lean strips and keeping the fat attached for nourishment, he hung them in rows in his makeshift wind-assisted "smoker", using a small roll of muslin to keep the blackflies and mosquitoes at bay. As the mosquitoes disappeared and the dry wind penetrated the thin strips of moose, the meat began to cure well and tasted not unlike rare venison steak. Jack let it hang until the meat took on a rich brown patina. The moose meat would be his protein staple, the muscle-maintaining ingredient that would keep him strong and healthy throughout the long winter.

Inside the small cabin the sled took pride of place. Until now Jack had taken the trouble to keep the felt blanket, pressed metal flashlight and tin of fat with the razor firmly strapped to the well-oiled pine seat panels. He had added the Samurai knife to the installation after the cabin had been completed and had enjoyed rearranging the objects, giving them a sense of order; indeed they were all familiar and quite useful. Jack had even filled the flashlight with new long-life batteries and a powerful halogen bulb. The only unusable object was ironically the knife, since the long tanto blade was without a handle, the rusted tang protruding from its felt sheath. Cleaning out the moose pelts had been a real chore with the pocket knife, as had many of the bush tasks that he had to perform. He had until now overcome the problem by traveling everywhere with his camp axe, but the edge had become dull and anyhow he preferred using a large knife for all but the toughest tasks and wood-splitting duties. A large blade was so much more versatile and he preferred the feel of the knife.

Carefully unraveling the felt roll, Jack studied the blade for the second time on close inspection and was surprised to see the faint indentations of a signature, a Japanese character, subtly engraved into the hilt of the blade. He had expected the steel of the non-tempered variety, a raw stock used for sculptural work and easily malleable. At best he had hoped it would be German, like the runners on the antique sled, Solingen steel, since the Samurai edition was an artwork, a metaphor more than anything else, and certainly had never been designed for practical use. This blade, Groub's last present before his journey, was not of low-grade stock. This blade was special.

Jack held the knife by the raw steel hilt and extended it out in front of him. He looked along the spine of the blade with one eye closed. It was straight as a die and extremely thick, over a quarter of an inch. The back of the knife was rusted but Jack could tell that this was no more than contact erosion recently formed by the damp environment of the forest. Sitting cross-legged on the floor, he pulled a large log from his fire pile and placed it between his feet. Digging the tip of the blade into the soft wood to hold it firm, Jack gently ran his finger down the blade. At first he couldn't detect a good edge and tried again, pushing harder. Suddenly he winced and held his finger to the light. The blade had cut deep into his thumb, and dark red blood oozed from the clean cut, as fine as a razor's edge. The edge was pretty clean and Jack sucked his bleeding thumb for a moment before wrapping a cloth around the wound. Excited now, he rubbed at the rusted side of the blade. To his delight the rust and grey oxide wiped clean away. With continual rubbing the blade was soon gleaming in the light of the fire, showing only minor pitting on the hilt.

Jack held the blade once again to the light of the fire, letting his eye contour its whole length, and smiled to himself as he noted the tell-tale waterline running an inch from the cutting edge. He studied the body of the blade and noticed the matt grey patina. On closer inspection he could see hundreds of intricate fine-fold lines. This was no ordinary blade. Jack knew that only the finest swordmakers in Japan had refined the folding damask blade and water-cooling techniques of the Samurai masters. "Good old Groub," he muttered under his breath, "only the best for him ..."

The Samurai knife was an original, a beautifully executed "Mark 1", the blade having been commissioned specifically for the artwork, and like Jack's sled it was unique, superior in quality and conception to the series of editioned multiples. Groub had been so wise to give him this knife, the perfect tool for survival in the wilderness. Its massive sweeping ten-inch blade was the perfect dimensions for a survival knife, for cutting through deep brush, paring and skinning large game, strong enough for chopping wood for shelter, manageable and ergonomic enough even for delicate tasks and the preparation of small fires and food. The steel was the best, possibly the best money could buy, water quenched and tempered to endure extreme heat and cold yet extremely flexible. It had a diamond-hard edge supported by a softer flexible spine, virtually unbreakable. But in its present state it was virtually useless because it was without a handle, unable to be gripped and utilized.

Jack held the knife in his hand. The skeletal handle was over six inches long and he considered wrapping cord around the tang for a good grip. But he had used cord grips before and with heavy chopping they could chafe. Then it hit him, the moose rack in the corner of the cabin, and he knew what he must do. Joe had showed him how with a small blade he had found in a car boot sale back in Ely. He had rehandled a blade with antler for Laura, into a butter knife or something.

Jack set a large pot over the hearth and brought it to the boil. Feeling the antler points for suitable girth, he deftly sawed the point from the antler rack with the hacksaw on his Leatherman tool and rubbed the rough edges away with the nail file. The antler was beautifully veined, stout and well curved at just under six inches long, and fitted his hand perfectly with room to spare. Jack was glad to see that the circular core of the bone was a creamy yellow, slightly honeycombed but well structured, since the metal tang would need enough bone marrow to be set into. Dropping the sawn antler into the boiling water, Jack placed a lid on the pot and let it boil. The strong aroma of boiled bone, bone glue, filled the cabin and reminded Jack of the rabbit-skin glue canvas primer his mother had used before she started work in her painting classes. It was a familiar smell and reminded him of home.

After a couple of hours, Jack took a wooden spoon from the fireside and reached into the pot, holding the steaming antler in a thick towel. Joe had taught him well. He took the hilt of the Samurai knife and, holding the blade by the rear, thrust the antler down and on to the hilt. The carbon steel cut cleanly into the soft gelatinous core of the antler until the handle came to rest on the spur of the hilt. Jack wrapped the cloth tightly against the handle and, ripping the ends into two halves, tied the handle to the blade. Then he up-ended the knife and rested the blade in a safe corner of the cabin to settle. As the temperature dropped in the cabin, the warm soft marrow in the handle began to dry and contract around the blade until it held fast around the tang of the knife.

By morning the handle and knife were as one, a strong, beautiful melding of carbon steel and bone, ready for use in the wild for the very first time. Jack rolled the knife back into the safety of the felt material, smearing a layer of fat from the tin along the blade to prevent further rusting, and fastened it together with a thin strip of hide. He placed the knife back on the sled next to the other things ready for use. Now the sled was as ready as it should be, as ready as Beuys would have wanted it but would never have believed it would be.

Even with his not insubstantial capacity for creative thought, for all his "out of the box" artistic conceptualization, would Beuys have dreamed that his knife and sled would end up being used in this way? The first of so many multiples, designed to democratize the ownership of art and relate something of his own personal trauma to a removed and uncomprehending audience. It was a huge step for his infamous creation, for his "vehicle of the tribe", the very metaphor for Beuys' war experiences on the Steppes of the Crimea, now not a million miles away and a not dissimilar environment. The knife would be used for its original purpose as man's first tool, Jack's first tool for his survival and protection, and the sled would again be used in the transport of essential goods, meat, matter. It was as it had been meant to be, at least, that was the way Jack saw it. Groub, for one, would have been proud!

★ ★ ★

As the days grew shorter and the night-time temperature dropped, Jack spent hours staring at the fire, lost in thought. Occasionally he would work on the skins but in general he preferred to sit and think, to meditate and watch the bright flames dancing on the stone hearth. The sled's time was coming, as the snows were coming. As Jack watched the shadows retreating and the sun rising to the east, he wondered at the rhythm of the seasons: the rising of the sun like the coming of the winter was inevitable, unstoppable, a reality that he had no control over.

Then, on a black night in late October, it began slowly, like a mist descending on the valley. The temperature dropped and the icy fingers of frost began to spread claw-like across the Boreal forest. First to freeze was the muskeg, bound together into a solid grid of ice, the small waterways interlacing the seascape of tundra tussocks into an almost brittle and solid surface. The wind whipped up and with it dark clouds formed in the pitch sky to the west. By first light the air was muffled as watery snowflakes began to fall. But these early snows did not melt in the midday sun as they had done the week before, since the sun had not risen much above the horizon that day. Overnight the glory of the fall had given way to a stronger, less transient season. Winter had come early to the Kuskokwim. The orange and red leaves lay on the hard ground and within no time at all they were completely covered with a thick blanket of fresh snow.

Jack shivered and prodded the small smouldering log. A small flame appeared, danced and then died. He opened the door to the cabin and was taken aback by the change. There was whiteness everywhere. Slipping into his felt-lined snow boots, he headed to the wood store and carried a few short logs into the cabin. It was cold now, frigid, and he quickly shut the loose-fitting door as the fresh icy morning temperature crept in behind him and filled the cabin with its chill. Jack knelt by the logs and with his hand swept the floor for dry tinder. Using his flint stick he began his twice-daily fire-building ritual, carefully striking the rod hard a couple of times at just the right angle, using the spine of his pocket knife, as large sparks flew on to the dry birch bark. Cradling the smoking tinder by his mouth, he blew, gently nurturing the flames, coaxing them into life. The silver bark began to smoke and curl as the flame took. Soon the fire was raging and Jack laid down the dry logs in a perfect pyramid. As the stones began to take on the new heat and radiate warmth around the cabin, Jack turned his attention once again to the sled. Now it would come into its own, he thought. Now it was going to be used for real, walking the trap line, carrying out the skins.

The glow of the fire soothed him; it was so familiar, the activity of staring into the flames, watching "bush TV", as Joe had called it. Flames of a thousand fires he had made over the years, the flames of so many memories. Jack began to doze off; he could feel his eyelids getting heavy and he closed his tired eyes, letting the moose hide take his weight, the luxuriance of the pelt supporting his body as he stretched out ready for sleep.

The dreams came clearer than before, now he was away from human stimulus. Mikaela was there at the met station waiting for him to return. She looked so vulnerable somehow, in the cold kitchen among those old Russian pots and pans, waiting for him, as he stood in the hallway hidden from her. Jack could sense her fear and in turn he felt it too, the fear of being alone.

At the time it had not been too hard to walk away and fly south to St Petersburg, numb to it all. Back then he had been ravaged by too much pain, too much anger at Jim's death and at Mikaela misunderstanding him, not waiting for him to recover. In a way she had made it easy. She cut their relationship off dead, hard as nails; it was something he hadn't experienced before, being dumped. Because back in the city that was how he did it. Christ, how it hurt. And now in his dream he could do nothing but watch her, alone in Siberia, in the small room, the pale yellow steam-stained kitchen walls moving inwards. Jack felt the pangs of regret for another failed relationship that could never be as it had been before.

He had opted out. Maybe her rejection had helped, but it hadn't been the main reason for him coming out here, to his valley, his cabin. After he had watched her for long enough he followed Mikaela as she got up from the kitchen stool and walked down the hall to her bedroom, the same room in which they had spent their last night together before the trip and before Jim and Viktor's death. If only he could have frozen that moment; everything had been going so well. If only he had made love to her the night before, even if it was for one last time. It was that moment he now regretted, a lost moment, a wasted chance to get closer and commit to her. In retrospect that night was the quiet before the storm. And Jack now stood helpless, unable to act once again, motionless and ashamed. Mikaela slammed the door in his face without turning round, hard with the back of her heel so as to make him jump.

★ ★ ★

The staccato report of the hunter's rifle shot jolted Jack from his dream, hitting him like a sledgehammer, his hair standing up cold on the back of his neck; the terrible fear of another human close by. For a millisecond he mourned his peace, lost now before he had achieved everything. For a moment he couldn't move. He strained to hear, and deep in the pit of his stomach he ached for the shot to be in his imagination, his dreams, but he knew he was no longer alone in his valley.

Collecting his thoughts, Jack now moved quickly and with purpose. He took his daypack from behind the door and filled it with some dried meat, his flint stick, a water bottle, the newly handled Samurai knife that was resting in the corner, and threw on his fur-trimmed parka. Once on the cabin stoop he slipped around to the rear. Being careful to keep a low profile, he ran from the clearing and rested in the dense foliage fifty yards from the back of the cabin. He hurriedly tied his snowshoes on to his bunny boots and, checking the chamber on his rifle in an instinctive action, sped to the safety of the far tree line. He made it to cover just in time. As the hunter moved down the slope toward the cabin, Jack shrank into the shadows and waited. Slowly and with great stealth he moved clockwise, like a magnet to an opposing force, through the trees, keeping his eye on the intruder. As the hunter found the passage through the dense wall of red spruce, Jack cut north out of the tree line and over the snow-covered ridge.

The dead moose lay in the snow, headless, its great cape shaved crudely away from its shoulders. Jack immediately set to work. He needed to repel the hunter, teach him a lesson and spook him, and what better way than to play the wild man, irrational, primordial even. Taking the newly-handled Samurai knife in his right hand, he pressed the blade deep into the thigh meat and cut upwards, dividing the ruby flesh until the thighs were pared in half. Then he grabbed the meat and strapped it under the top of his rucksack. He didn't really need the venison – his past months of hunting should last him through the spring – but at that moment he wasn't even sure he would or should go back. Besides, this hunter was both sloppy and noisy, and Jack decided to confiscate the quarry. Anyhow, it was rightfully his moose, his bounty, his valley and his range.

It was at that moment, kneeling in the pink bloodstained snow, his hands covered in fresh blood, his eyes wild, his body wired with adrenaline, that Jack realized he had changed. Enough time had passed since Sredny, enough time at least to act as an anesthetic to numb his pain and guilt. The dream of his feelings for Mikaela had been a turning point; any last tenderness he had felt for her had now been quashed, any weakness eradicated, and the regret he had felt at being all alone had been replaced by a primitive resolve. It was as if the past months in the valley had been

217

preparation for this gigantic step, preparing himself mentally, physically toughening him for whatever lay ahead. Until the gunshot and the sight of another human Jack hadn't really known if he had done the right thing, or whether he would lose his nerve and want to make contact with the hunter and his old world, his past life in the city. But he knew instinctively that a year in the wild wasn't enough; worst case he would need more time.

Jack Wyler was gone and his new identity was strategically marked out. This was Nemo's place now. Not just this patch of wilderness but the whole range, beyond the range, it didn't really matter, Alaska, the entire north, was his. What did matter to him now was that he could continue living alone, working it all out, rebuilding himself day by day, week by week, month by month, and if need be year by year. He would set himself no time limits.

Jack moved with ease over the snow, his over-sized Cree snowshoes displacing the weight of his powerful frame perfectly, walking on water. He headed north, over the next rise, and laid up in the far tree line. He saw the insignificant form of the hunter, breathless, out of condition, panting his way back to the kill, and he saw him stand motionless in disbelief, dwarfed by the forest, the mountains, the entire rugged landscape. He saw him move as fast as his legs would let him back to the east, to the pass and his plane, back to the world, a world Nemo felt no need for.

Although he suspected that for the time being his identity would be safe, since he hadn't been seen, Jack knew it would only be a matter of time before the hunter would report the alarming, mysterious loss of his meat. He knew the intruder would have connected the cabin to the man. After all, the hearth was still warm, but what type of man exactly – an antisocial loner, an alcoholic trapper, or a psycho, a real wild man? That could be the key, the cover he might need down the line to keep others away, the smokescreen that could keep his true identity hidden. If Jack Wyler played it right, Nemo would become a local myth, a legend, something altogether larger than the reality. But for that to happen, Jack knew, deep inside, he would have to leave his valley. Like the wind, the running water and the caribou, he would have to keep moving. The thought, of course, was pure madness; winter was closing in, soon it would be dark, no cabin, limited food, but since when did Jack, since when did Nemo listen to logic? Nemo listened to the seasons, to his wild instincts, and like the prey he had been hunting day after day, his instincts told him to be careful of men. His instincts told him to move on.

Chapter 3

Sheriff Stetson was glad the Christmas season was over. But the feeling of relief hadn't lasted for long. Now in mid-January he began to feel claustrophobic; the intense cold, the dark afternoons, insufficient sunlight, the Alaskan winter, took some getting used to. He had thought it was cold in Detroit, but now he knew that was nothing. At least the days there went on longer than a few miserable hours! Spending most of each afternoon in the office, traveling everywhere by car, walking less and generally getting cooped up inside had meant Stetson wasn't getting enough exercise and this had made sleeping difficult.

In the old days a few pages of a bad novel had set his eyelids closing, but now Stetson was having trouble switching his brain off. Before, in the city, that had been a problem too, but for different reasons. The trauma of the job, the daily nature of homicide division, had been awful, but years of it had numbed him, made him cynical and helped him deal with all the dead bodies. The Alaska job had come up at just the right time and had helped him push it all aside, clear the pipes of all those memories, all those crime scenes, broken faces and wasted lives.

Sheriff Stetson was now haunted by a new feeling, not trauma-filled but empty, a feeling devoid of risk, of living stress-free and with little purpose. Moreover, he was becoming ever more aware of a deep feeling of uselessness. He was uninspired, unchallenged and, worse, he was bored. Over the Christmas holidays he had begun to wonder if he had made a terrible mistake, coming up here to a foreign place so late in his career. He had wanted to broach the issue with his wife but that would have been a wasted exercise. She loved it, relished the lack of crime and violence, the clean air and a spacious house. Alaska to Mrs Stetson meant safety and security. Now she could keep track of her man, prepare a good meal every night, make him breakfast, look after him.

From Stetson's perspective he had too much time on his hands, and lying awake as his wife slept contented next to him, his brain raced. After a while his mind turned to his one "missing person", the one piece of intrigue in his otherwise uneventful and mundane life. It was the quote, the quote in the wallet, the words of Reuss, that wouldn't go away. If he had

219

been back in Detroit, it wouldn't have stayed with him because downtown he never had time for anything, certainly no time to ponder a "missing person", too many homicides-a-week piled high on his work roster for that.

Stetson quietly slipped out of bed, careful not to disturb his sleeping wife. Taking hold of the wooden banister, he walked carefully over the creaking third step and down the stairs toward his study. When he had first arrived in Palmer, three years earlier, he had slept better than he had ever done in all his years in Detroit. It was just so silent, so calm and so safe. But with the winter months this had changed and he had begun to get that feeling again, a feeling he hadn't felt since leaving the 9th precinct. This Wyler guy had got under his skin, or maybe it was Wyler's mother. She just didn't want to give it up. It was as if the entire "missing persons" findings were an irrelevant technicality and it would just be a matter of time before her son showed up. Stetson had put his finger on it, it was her faith, her blind belief that her son was alive, that ate away at him. That and the offer of the reward was enough to keep him on it; not that he was mercenary, it just would help, that kind of money always did.

At fifty Stetson had little else, mentally that is, to challenge him. Wyatt Earp had planned to lay down his gun belt in Tombstone but the peace had not lasted long. Stetson needed this Wyler thing, if nothing more than to prove to himself that he still had it, the nose and the ability to deliver. If he was honest he needed a dose of Laura Wyler's faith; Detroit had made him so hard and cynical. He needed to believe again, that Jack was still alive, that surviving out there was at least possible.

Stetson pressed the "on" button on his Think Pad and typed in his password. Opening the file on his desk he read the note again: "Everett Reuss 1934". As the computer booted up, he took a copy of Wyler's profile and the FBI interview with his mother. It seemed like the mom had a thing about this Reuss guy too. It was in the family by all accounts, drove her up the wall. The kid was impressive, a serious athlete, all-state, nearly made the NFL draft, but there it was again, first high school, then college, then work. He had taken it all to a certain level and then ... It was as if he had had it all and at the last moment he had sensed the destiny and security and become scared. The same with his work: cannery manager in Alaska, long-term girlfriend, dad dies, moves on. Aslop's in Minnesota, just before the promotion, moves on ... KLS managing partner ... makes some serious bread, then ... What had happened there? This really didn't make any sense. Stetson read the file and on the last page ... Siberia; losing his friend, tragedy number two. An interview with Jim Williamson's parents and then his resignation from KLS ... the kid had had some tough breaks. He was a searcher, a true free spirit, that was for sure.

Stetson went back to the high-school profile: 1986, selection for all-state championship bowl, absent. Absent? That was like an invitation inside the panties of any girl in high school. All-state football championship – the ring alone meant that in high school you were a god. Out hunting, Alaska, with his old man... "Due to bad weather diverted to the Kuskokwim range for emergency pick-up of pregnant Indian girl" ... Stetson had missed this, and in his books there were no such things as coincidences. Turning to his laptop he clicked online and brought up Google's homepage. If only Google had existed when he was working homicide in the 9th. Jesus, it beat the crap out of the Federal network files ... "E.v.e.r.e.t.t. R.e.u.s.s." Stetson read and printed and read some more. There was tons of info on this guy, literally mountains of documents, essays, critiques on the man. "1.9.3.4." He typed speedily: refine search, enter. He read on. The last sighting was by a shepherd. And an inscription in a cave, on a tree. Jesus, the guy had really lost it. Nemo, like the movie, this Reuss fellow, the guy who wrote the quote, the guy Wyler's dad had banged on about all his life, had changed his name just like the captain in... what was it? *Twenty Thousand Leagues Under the Sea*. His mind was racing. There it was again. Nemo, he had changed his name to Nemo. Translation from Latin ...

"No one. Fucking no one! Well, I'll be ..."

Stetson spun in his chair; that was it, the facts. Pulling the reports file from under the desk, he scanned the recent entries and indexed them with the relevant report. There it was, the hunter out in the Kuskokwim, spooked by the loss of his moose meat, blah, blah, blah, rests by a tree, scared shitless. Blah, blah...looks down behind trunk and "NEMO" carved into the bark. Bingo! Leaning back in his chair, Stetson pumped his fist in the air. God, it felt good, he hadn't had cause to do that for a while. Placing his hands behind his head, he exhaled. He was content and alive again.

"So, Mr Wyler, either Everett Reuss is alive and kicking at almost a hundred years old, scaring law-abiding hunters in the most remote area of western Alaska, or you've been made. Who would have guessed it...from city slicker to backwoods loner. I don't know if your mom's going to like this, Jack, but then again, each to their own. I think maybe we should meet. How about lunch on Palmer's Sheriff's department, how 'bout it, Jack ... how 'bout it?"

★ ★ ★

Jack didn't wait long before he began to move back down the slope toward his cabin. He knew he didn't have to – the hunter was long gone by now. Besides, as far as he was concerned his secret was out. It was time to move and move quickly, not for fear of the hunter but of what his report might bring. That and the weather were bothering him now. Winter was coming in, not deep winter but that was only a few weeks away. There was still a good amount of daylight and a thaw was always possible too. He would move north, skirting the mountains to the east and then into the valley and the low country beyond. If he could get to the valley of the Reindeer River flood plain at the foot of Mosquito Mountain by the end of November, he would have time to make a camp near the old summer mine head at Decourcy trail. Jack had heard about the old miners' camp, long since vacated by the summer workers. When the spring came he would be well positioned to move up following the ridgeline north to Cripple Landing and up into the Brooks Range. As he saw it there was only one problem. To get to Reindeer River and the passage north, he would have to cross the trail system used by the famous Iditarod dog-sled race. The race was held in February each year, so Jack decided he would sit tight at the DeCourcy mine until April. The journey to his new camp would take no more than a week, averaging on Jack's current fitness and substantial load, approximately eight to ten miles a day. Like all good emergency plans he decided to keep it simple. On the sled he could carry only his essentials: the bulk of his dried moose meat, the large fur pelt, his ammunition, sleeping bag and bivi bag, rice, pulses and cooking supplies. Finally, the sled was going to be used.

The next morning was fresh and clear and warmer than the week before. Jack, however, was not taken in by the temperature rise. In November, before the big freeze, the cycle of both frigid and temperate days allowed the ice to penetrate deep into the soil so all roots and plant shoots would be trapped, the normally pliable top crust bonding once more with the permafrost. By early January the ground would be like concrete, all life held in a crystal suspension, preserved and rigid. In this climate very little could survive, all mammalian nest building, foraging and burrowing having been conducted months before. Only the smallest of creatures could navigate the hidden undulations of the Arctic tundra. One such animal, the Alaskan dusky shrew, would burrow and build networks of tunnels between the frozen ground and the snow crust above, scurrying frantically back and forth, leaving its tell-tale dragline as it gathered the winter berries and other edible shrubs that constituted its winter diet. Moving constantly, on and on again, an inbuilt primal force ensuring constant movement, the shrew remained blissfully unaware of the predatory eagles and owls that would periodically dive, talons bared, searching tactically and without mercy for their warm-blooded, protein-rich quarry. Jack knew how tough the winter would be, he himself being humbly equipped to survive the gnawing predation of the Alaskan winter. But somehow, he knew, like the frenetic shrew, that he was doing the right thing; after all, it was in his nature, a precaution just in case. It was now or never.

★ ★ ★

The sled looked strange. Fully loaded it was precarious, to say the least. But it had been built well and originally designed to carry a cargo of two persons at speed down the slopes of the Bavarian Alps. It was adequate for the job in hand. Jack had lashed two waterproof sled bags either side of the seat slats, giving the sled a grounded, weighty gait. On top he had strapped the bulk of the meat, fuel and ammunition, lashed over with the large moose pelt for weather protection. Keeping his pack as light as possible, he carried his Samurai knife in its felt roll, a day's food, thermos, med kit and heavy parka. To the front-runners he tied two loops of 8mm rope with bowline knots and laid the two ends in six-foot lengths in front of the sled. He took a final look around the cabin and carefully closed the door. It was out of respect for all the hard work and for the protection the cabin had provided during his stay, more than anything else. He doubted his creation would be used again for many years.

Jack faced the line of trees before him and, without looking round, crouched down and tied the two ends to the rear ice-axe loops of his Bergen. He hopped up and down a couple of times to ensure all was safe and secure, then took the strain, leaning forward to almost a 45 degree angle to take the 250 pounds of weight. At first nothing moved. He leaned in again, gritting his teeth, his face contorting with the effort. This time the runners cut deep into the snow and edged forward. He adjusted the ski poles and leaned on each one in turn. Again he pulled, this time placing a foot forward, the relief evident on his face. The sled came now with ease. He was set. Slowly Jack walked forward, lifting his snowshoes high in a well-practiced rhythm. Step by step, he told himself. "Step by step," he repeated, "that's how we get there." In the back of his mind came a niggling voice. "Wherever *there* may be, Jack," the voice chided and repeated. "Wherever there may be."

★ ★ ★

The walk out to the DeCourcy mine had taken Jack a little under five days. It had been a tough trek, but he had kept to his disciplined routine of walking for eight hours a day with hourly rests and had followed his northerly compass bearing true, with very little variation. Deciding to keep to a direct line on his map had been a wise move, since the gradients hadn't been too bad and there had been no major river crossings. Since the route mostly followed high ground, he had had excellent continual high points that he had been able to cross-reference with his map. It was good to be above the tree line, looking out across the reindeer flood plain to the west and the spreading fingers of the tributaries.

For a good part of the way Jack had followed an old Indian trail. The wildlife had helped too, indirectly keeping the lower sections of the trail open enough for the sled to pass without too much snagging and hindrance from foliage. The sled had fared well, considering its ungainly, unaerodynamic shape, and had only toppled over a couple of times at the bottom of a steep slope. The hardest section of the trail had come toward the end, a 45 degree scree slope leading to the final ridge. After that it was smooth sailing to the tree line below, and Jack had sat on top of his sled and ridden it in for the last 100 yards of decline.

On nearing the ramshackle congregation of cabins, Jack used the available cover of the dense forest to his advantage, concealing his approach. Descending stealthily from the high forest ridgeline, he dropped to one knee and undid his improvised harness. Watching from the trees, he silently laid out his wax-bottomed moose pelt on the frozen ground. Lying patient and still he watched the huts for movement, for any sign of life. He watched and waited for most of the morning and at midday concluded that the coast was clear. Anyhow, he reasoned, he was beginning to get cold.

Leaving the sled under a large spruce, he ran as fast as he could to the closest of the cabins and pressed his ear against the wall to listen for noise. All was silent. To his left he noticed a small broken window pane. Peering through into the deserted room, Jack caught a glimpse of his own reflection. He studied his face. A luxuriant thick dark beard covered his face and neckline, and his hair was much longer now. He could also tell, in spite

224

of the beard, that he had lost considerable weight, his cheekbones giving his matted face a drawn, angular appearance.

He had known that face, that familiar look, before, and staring into his reflection he remembered the Basquiat door panel in his office. There was a sense of that primal look in his own eyes, but they lacked the darkness of the painting. There was more joy and fire in Jack's eyes. Then he remembered where he had seen the exact same look, that look of purpose, of being completely alive: in Viktor's journal, the faded photograph taken during his epic journey across the Arctic Ocean.

It had been almost nine months since Jack had last looked in a mirror, groomed himself or shaved, even studied his face. He looked so different now, almost unrecognizable even to himself, not the same vision that he held photographically in his mind. He had changed: any surplus body fat was gone and his muscles were leaner, longer and more vascular than ever before. Nemo had taken over more than Jack's mind. Being Nemo, living the existence day in day out, had transformed his body. Jack Wyler had quite literally metamorphosed, becoming at one with his new incarnation, his new identity.

★ ★ ★

The camp had been deserted for some time, judging from the rusted state of the various empty cartons and provisions that littered the inside of the huts and storerooms. Jack concluded that no one had been around for over two summers. The weather had been mild for an Alaskan fall, and by mid-December he had managed to patch up the sturdiest of the old miners' huts to make it fit for the bitter winter ahead. He knew he had done the right thing to move on. It had been a bold move, but as the fresh driving mid-December snows began their incessant onslaught, day after day he felt secure in the knowledge that his tracks would be long gone. Until the spring he would be safe and, more importantly, alone.

Jack's new home was larger than the one he had been used to, but this meant it was colder and took a lot more wood to burn to maintain a comfortable temperature. The moose hide made all the difference, laid out as a bed in front of the old wrought-iron pot-bellied stove. He barricaded the stove with smooth soapstones and dried, uncut logs that helped retain the valuable heat through most of the night. The cold weather meant that the moose meat had kept well, and although somewhat monotonous as a protein source, it did the job. In fact Jack was as comfortable in his new home as he could hope to have been. It was just that now he knew he would have to move on again in the spring or, better still, well before the winter gave way to the warmer months. If indeed someone wanted to find him and had bothered to listen to the hunter, the mine camp would make a logical place to look. This fact meant Jack couldn't totally relax and let his guard down. With the Iditarod trail only thirty miles to his north at the Flat Landing airstrip, Jack knew that during February he would have to spend much of his time either around the camp or hunting in the barren lands to the south, just in case.

There was, however, one major bonus about the rundown camp. There were books, mildewy, old and with pages missing but books nonetheless. In the milder summer months Jack had been surprised how little he had missed the comfort of a good book, probably because of all the physical work involved with the moose-hunting. But now, with the darkness coming so early and the long cold nights spent inside the cabin, a book was just what Jack needed.

One of the books was a small volume of poetry entitled *The Best of Robert Service*. Service, an Englishman by birth, had emigrated to Canada in the early 1900s and spent eight years in the Yukon, working the mining circuit in search of gold, fame and fortune. Ironically he had received his notoriety in pen and ink, not gold, his poems and ballads making him world-famous as chronicler of the working man's sentiments in torment and struggle, set against the backdrop of the barren Alaskan and Canadian landscape. One poem caught Jack's eye: "Men of the High North". Of the six verses, it was the fifth one that interested him the most.

You who this faint day the High North is luring
Unto her vastness, taintlessly sweet;
You who are steel-braced, straight-lipped, enduring,
Dreadless in danger and dire in defeat:
Honor the High North ever and ever,
Whether she crown you, or whether she slay;
Suffer her fury, cherish and love her –
He who would rule he must learn to obey.

Jack was touched by the poem and concluded that despite the tremendously romantic notion of life on the frontier, Service had hit on the thing that had brought him here, not something learned or academic but a heart-felt sentiment, a conviction, an emotion that could only come with experience.

"Suffer her fury, cherish and love her ..." Jack read the line over and over again. There was truth in it and it made sense. Even his comparatively small Alaskan experience had taught him that with every action there is a reaction: love and pain, happiness and sadness. And in the Alaskan bush the pain and reality of her harshness and her fury was a daily occurrence, in the winter at least.

But, Jack reasoned, surely that was the point. No pain, no gain. Was it not impossible to attain self-truth, a real understanding of himself without the pain, the fury of the elements and the suffering outside of his comfort zone? Take his position now. Here he was alone, hundreds of miles from civilization, yet utterly complete, void of unnecessary material possessions, self-sufficient. Sure, he was often cold, sometimes a bit lonely, but he was in the most remarkably beautiful and pure environment, experiencing at first hand the last real frontier of the Americas, of the world even. Wasn't that worth the price, the price of solitude?

Robert Service, Jack concluded, was a believer in the philosophy that one does not choose the life of the far north, it chooses you. He couldn't have agreed more. Reuss, Beuys, and now Service, they all affirmed what Jack held to be true, personal growth through physical experience, surrendering to the call of the wild, the torment of the elements. Groub had often concurred, quoting Rothko and Gottlieb in their collaborative essay on primitivism during World War Two ... the constant awareness of powerful forces, the proximity of fear and an acceptance of "the brutality of the natural world as well as the eternal insecurity of life".

Jack's acceptance of the brutality of Alaska was the first stepping-stone into his mental tempering, a conditioning that would ensure, mentally at least, that he would survive the cruel winter. That mental toughness combined with a daily routine and physical exercise was to be key to his survival. But as the months went by and the sun began to break the horizon to the east in early February, Jack realized he hadn't just survived the winter, he had grown stronger, leaner, emerging with his sanity intact. "The bitch" had been kind. As the icicles started to form on the cabin porch and the sound of trickling water resounded throughout the creek, he knew it was time to move on once more, while the rivers were still iced over. Spring was coming and he had a long journey ahead. Again he had a plan: he was going to head toward the Brooks Range, the North Slope. He would try to follow the caribou to their summer pastures. There would be plenty of game food, and besides, he had had his fill of moose. In the spring he would be heading north, except that this time he was truly prepared, or so he thought.

★ ★ ★

Laura Wyler had had a tough Christmas. In fact, the entire year of Jack's disappearance had been an unbearable nightmare. First came the realization that with no word from him for almost five months there must be a serious problem. As a mother, Laura had for obvious reasons feared the worst. Jack was never one to lose contact, whatever madcap plan he had been hatching. She had read his note a thousand times over, the words "it's going to be a bit more than ... an expedition" constituting in her mind an absence of a few months and meaning just that, two to three months tops. She thought she knew Jack well. If she knew one thing to be true about her son it was the fact that he always got bored, sooner or later, and like most young, single men he needed to move on frequently to get a change of scenery.

With the advent of Thanksgiving Laura, in a desperate cry for help, had contacted Bob in New York. With the aid of Ollie Hanson they had registered Jack's disappearance with the FBI in Minneapolis, who in turn contacted the State Sheriff's department in Alaska and the local federal authorities. Bob had been her rock and had taken it all on, the liaison with the Feds, the police bureaucracy in Anchorage, and, after Laura's impassioned requests for help and assistance, with Sheriff Stetson too. The reward had been Bob's idea; money would be no object in searching for Jack, the board of Microstem would see to that, since Bob had not wanted Laura to spend her own precious capital. She would need that for the years ahead, for Holly's college fees, the occasional holiday, unexpected medical bills. Besides, both Hans Groub and Ingvar insisted they would front the capital for the search. That was non-negotiable.

Bob had found Sheriff Stetson pleasant enough to deal with, although he sensed that he hadn't really engaged with the concept of finding Jack alive. There was something about his phone manner, so unimpassioned, laid-back even, as if he had seen it all before and was almost beyond caring. Stetson's phone call had come as a surprise, the tone of his voice for once sounding positive, electrified with emotion, so early in the morning on such a bleak and bitterly cold January day. Needless to say the call had driven Laura wild with excitement. Bob had had to calm her down, long-distance from New York. After all, Stetson had only solved the riddle; there was still no evidence that Jack had survived the winter. Stetson had concluded that if Jack had taken to stealing the hunter's meat he would have been starving, unable to hunt for himself.

Although he had to admit that it made sense in the report, Bob didn't buy it, the hunger thing, he knew Jack too well. Jack was too industrious for such a coincidence, to be saved like that; the odds just didn't stack up, a trillion to one. Bob thought it was more like the spider in the web theory; Jack surviving just fine and then someone coming along and invading his space. Jack deciding to freak the hunter out, to frighten him away; Bob could relate to that. But he thought he would keep it to himself until he met Stetson and saw the look in his eyes, saw if he could trust him.

Bob's fears for Jack's safety lay elsewhere. Shortly after Jack had returned from Sredny he had sensed that he was planning something. Annie had felt it too, and Bob knew Jack well enough to know that when he planned something he planned it well, with almost military precision. After all, he had been hunting up there with his old man and had never had any problems. What worried Bob therefore wasn't Jack's physical ability to survive, his wilderness skills, he had too much respect for his friend's abilities. Besides, he knew, as every Minnesotan did, that Minnesota came close to an Alaskan winter, even colder some years. What worried Bob was something deeper, less easy to define. Something in Jack's mental make-up, his rational capacity, seemed to have altered. Dealing with the moment, surviving a calamity, was never going to be problem for Jack. Sredny had proved his theory: Jack was the original survivor. It was the lack of company, comradeship, of being so isolated, that concerned Bob, and also Jack's habit of drifting off. At least while growing up and later on in the city he'd had a constant cap to his mental wanderings, his moments and daydreams. But out there, alone and vulnerable, traumatized by recent events, Bob knew that could get to him. It could get to anyone.

Bob had understood and empathized with Jack's disappearance at first: with the trauma of Jim's death, the mounting stress at KLS, the guilt of it all coming to a head. But he knew the issue with Mikaela would have hurt him, broken his ego, really beaten him up. It could have even been the last straw, the deciding factor in his disappearance. Now, though, Bob had another reason to go and look for his friend, to uphold what they had always promised each other, Jack, Jim and Bob, the three musketeers. They had said they would look out for each other in the wilderness. Laura had agreed unreservedly, so proud but so saddened by the irony of the events of the year. Bob had to go in case the authorities found his friend first. He would be useful in the search, competent in the wild, highly incentivized. In light of the fact that Groub was paying, he needed to be there to make sure the game was played out, every angle was covered, no rock left unturned. Furthermore, Bob would be the first to hold him, hug him, a familiar face to be trusted and to tell him that he was to be a father in the fall. Tell him he had a reason to come home and work it out properly with his family, his mom, his friends and ultimately his child.

★ ★ ★

Mikaela had contacted Laura in the summer, the first three months of her pregnancy having passed, the danger period over, a baby growing steadily and healthily in her womb. Ursula had talked her into it, and she was right to have done it. Ethically at least Jack had the right to know, even if they were not to be together and to share a life on Mikaela's terms. He had the right to know he was to have a son and heir.

Mikaela had dreaded the call to Laura, who was in the dark about their relationship. Laura could scarcely hear the faint foreign voice traveling along the archaic copper lines of the Sredny party line. At first she wasn't sure that it hadn't been a crank caller. Then the Russian operator had confirmed the number that she had hurriedly scribbled down before the phone line went dead. The call had come from Russia, from Siberia, from the island of Sredny Zemelya.

Bob had got on to it the next day at Laura's request and all three of them had agreed to keep Jack's child a secret between themselves. Laura felt it was the right thing to do, out of respect for him, for his memory, for the hope that it would be Jack who would have the joy and pleasure of sharing his news with the world, as all fathers should. Bob believed in that, as did Laura. He had faith in his friendship from childhood and Laura had a deeper, unwavering belief that her son would be okay and he would come home to her one day soon. He would return to be with his baby, even with the mother of his child, as a family unit.

Laura decided that she wasn't going to push her faith and scare Mikaela off. To be happily married with wife and child was what she wanted for her son and for herself as a grandmother-to-be. It seemed so far off now, impossible nearly, and Laura decided to hide her dream in the place she reserved for miracles, in the deepest part of her mind under lock and key, in case the very thought of her fantasy could ruin the chance of her son's safe return.

It was Laura's sense of hope that had struck Bob, and as with Stetson she had infected him with her optimism. After all, the news was good. Jack had made it to November, to the hunter's sighting, the name in the tree, the snowshoes, the dark figure in the tree line. Laura agreed that Bob should be the one to go up to the Kuskokwim, it was where Joe had gone as a young man and where he had taken Jack hunting as a teenager. Now it was the origin of all her pain and sadness, Alaska and the writings of Reuss, a madman, a searcher, a known drifter and his romantic assumed identity and alter ego, that bastard Nemo. Laura prayed Bob would find him, overpower her son and bring him back to her. Laura needed him to replace the emptiness she felt, the terrible hole that her beloved plants and even her faith couldn't fill; the loss she felt without the two men in her life, the loss of her lifelong partner and best friend and the loss of her son.

★ ★ ★

By early March 2001, with all the normal distractions of Christmas over, Stetson had made a simple decision. He owed it to Laura – hell, he owed it to himself to follow up on that hunter's report. It was his only lead, and besides, he had the identity of the "wild man". There was no doubt in his mind that Wyler had been out there, it was just a question of whether he would still be alive after the winter and whether Stetson could find him before he did serious damage to himself. He had wanted to act sooner, in fact if it hadn't been for the severe winter storms rolling in off the Bering Sea he would have got out to Great Bear Lake as early as mid-February. But despite Laura's promise of funding, he had been unable to persuade the bean-counters at police HQ in Anchorage of the viability of the search. The Kuskokwim was a big area, and in winter, well, his bosses were just not convinced. They could lose a chopper and good men. The search was to be put on ice, no pun intended, pending improved weather.

Fortunately for Sheriff Stetson's personal aspirations, Laura Wyler wasn't going away and she had powerful friends. Not only had her late husband been a park ranger, part of the brotherhood, her son apparently had friends with money and serious connections. With the offer of increased private funding, Anchorage gave Stetson the thumbs-up. With the addition of a substantial reward for a successful operation, Laura made a sole condition to the deal: Bob Anders was to be allowed to assist in the search. Stetson had liked his phone manner and had ascertained from their regular conversations that Bob could handle himself in the bush. In fact he had decidedly more outdoors experience than he himself did. There was also another piece of good luck. With the advent of the Iditarod race, two search and rescue choppers had been posted to the Kuskokwim to the tiny native hamlet of Willow Creek and Anvik to the west.

Arriving in Alaska in early March, Bob had taken a room at the Hilton and spent most of the first day kitting himself out for the search. Like Jack he had always been a stickler for the right kit and a great believer that when in Rome . . . Stetson had arranged for Bob to be driven to Palmer the following day and they had spent an evening together poring over flight maps of the Kuskokwim. Bob was impressed by Jack's journey. The load-carries alone into the hidden valley were remarkable, and Bob noted the remoteness of the cabin's location, the high ranges to the north and the absence of lakes. Bob had liked Stetson immediately. There was something about the cop, something real, his face hard yet kind with a look of dependability. He was compact and stocky, and although he had gained a few pounds during this last winter he was far from fat. His broken nose and hooded eyes, the results of an impressive amateur boxing career as a teenager, made him look overly tough, as did his hunched shoulders, the shuffle in his gait, the altogether no-bullshit manner of a retired gunfighter.

Stetson was a man who had definitely lived, seen it all and was now more or less at peace with himself. But he might also have needed this case more than he let on. The fact that he had now become so involved with Jack's disappearance had impressed Bob. Initially Bob hadn't been convinced, and over a bottle of Jack Daniels Stetson had told him as much. They both agreed that Laura had got to them. Then Bob had told Stetson about the chain of events leading to Jack's disappearance, the deaths on Sredny, the details of Jim's death, the whole thing. Stetson hadn't managed to glean more than a smattering of Jack's mental profile from the FBI report. He even wondered if he hadn't been given the whole picture on purpose, if he'd been discouraged from getting too into what most believed to be a run-of-the-mill, drifter-gets-lost-and-dies scenario. But they both agreed that this case was different, that Jack was far more intriguing than most of the wasters who "bought it" out in the bush, unprepared dreamers lost in their suburban mess; for them, they both agreed, there was no chance. Jack was different.

Bob had been intrigued to hear how Stetson had landed up in Palmer, and his stories of life in Detroit broke the ice between them. Bob had turned in a little after midnight and he lay in Stetson's spare room listening to the Sheriff shuffling around his office until he fell asleep, his stomach knotted with anticipation of the search.

★ ★ ★

Having lived for most of his life in the lower 48, the Kuskokwim seemed like another world to Stetson. The massive patchwork of tributaries, mountain peaks and low-lying valleys bristled with black spruce, all frosted under many feet of snow. An inhospitable, beautiful, white nothingness; Bob was equally impressed with the magnitude and magnificence of the country. He watched Sheriff Stetson shivering inside his new down parka as the Twin Otter touched down on the frozen landing strip at Willow Creek.

Bob could tell Stetson was a city guy born and bred. He just wasn't comfortable with the remoteness of the place, perhaps even had a touch of agoraphobia. Air Deputy Bud Walker of the Alaska State Police had the swagger of a veteran bush pilot and the buzz cut of a GI. He escorted them both across the small airstrip to the Jet Ranger. There was to be no hanging around, since every minute airborne had the reciprocal maintenance time bill attached and the infamous "triple" remote region fuel tariff. The fuel caches were often dropped in along the Iditarod trail with marker beacons by parachute from the C130 out of Fairbanks, since flying in to drop fuel by chopper was a self-defeating exercise. Communities with more than a homestead of population were often supplied in this way, since the landing strips were restricted to loads of up to Twin Otters only.

Bud Walker liked to fly "tactically" as he called it out here in the west. Rumor had it he had flown in Grenada as part of the 82nd airborne's assault, and to Stetson he hadn't quite shrugged off the gung-ho military flyboy mentality. East of Anchorage, Bud explained, this "low level shit" wasn't "feasible". It was not permitted because of the relatively dense cable and aerial networks, but out in the Kuskokwim it was not a relevant consideration since there were no people. After twenty minutes, the chopper circled Great Bear Lake and navigated at treetop level over the pass and into the valley beyond. Contouring the slopes down toward the creek, Bud took a short detour to show his awe-struck passengers the steaming geothermic springs on the far side of the river.

"If there was a way to bottle that and sell it . . . I mean, that's the largest

Arctic hot tub in the world aside from Yellowstone and I've heard you can swim in it too."

Stetson wasn't impressed. "Not this man," he muttered gruffly into his headset. "This trooper baths strictly indoors."

Bob laughed out loud as Bud threw the chopper into a partial inversion, circling back round the spit of icy shale that separated the path of two tributaries. Flying the last twenty miles in minutes, Stetson, with his finger on the flight map, spotted a clearing and Jack's makeshift cabin. Looking down through the spindrift of the rotor wash, the cabin reminded Bob of a hut he had once made as a kid in the garden of his aunt's house in Duluth. In fact, the cabin was really more of a shack, the roof covered in a light dusting of snow and branches, mud and clods of earth. Bob craned for a better view and then, looking up to the horizon, he saw why Jack had done it, broken away and gone for himself.

The valley was perfect. It was exquisitely beautiful, and Bob imagined his friend alone down there in the clearing, cutting trees, carving joins, recrafting his life. The clearing was just wide enough for Bud to put her down but there was no need. From thirty-five feet Stetson could see that the cabin door was hanging off, probably the result of a hungry winter grizz. There were no tracks aside from moose spoor the other side of the tree line. Bud signed to Stetson that he was turning her around and spoke loudly into the intercom.

"No one home, guys, sorry 'bout that, Bob. Guess we could scout the area but in my opinion he's a goner, Stets. No way he could camp out all winter."

Stetson and Bob studied the map. "Is there anywhere else out here, Bud, say you needed to put down and could take shelter, a refuge, cabin, cave, whatever?"

"Negative, not in this valley. Only place is over forty miles from here, north of Hotspring Junction toward the trail system, the DeCourcy mine head. But that's some tough high country and not the sort of place you just happen upon."

"But what if he had it charted, planned even," probed Bob, "before he came in, as a Plan B location? I mean, Bud, Jack's got some balls, man, and he's bright. Isn't there a chance he could have hauled it out there?"

Bud gave Stetson the nod and banked the chopper north, nose down, full throttle. "Let's check out that mine then. Hold on, we'll see if we can't shave a moose on the way in . . ."

Bob laughed nervously, and Stetson gripped the passenger handle so tightly his knuckles turned white.

★ ★ ★

Jack was stoking the fire when he first heard the faint wash of rotors. The sound made him freeze, sickening him, fear balling in his gut like a wire knot. The report of the hunter's rifle at the old cabin had been enough to ensure he had the systems in place to move fast and evasively, as if his life depended on it. But an inbound chopper, that meant people, people possibly looking for him. There was no time. Jack grabbed his parka and the felt roll with the Samurai knife. He would have to come back for the sled. It had served its purpose, and when it boiled down to it he could improvise or even make another one. Although no substitute for the original Beuys sled, he would certainly be able to fashion an alternative mode of transport. Nothing mattered to him as much as his freedom, and the sled had given him that. Like a caged animal Jack kicked open the back door of the cabin as the chopper hovered overhead, the spindrift cutting into his eyes as he shielded his face to look skywards.

Stetson looked down through the spindrift as the bearded man looked up at him through the whirling snow. "Get me down, Bud, now! He's going to bolt for it, I can see it, quickly now. Kill those engines when you touch down too, okay. I'm going to need to talk this one through."

Bud pulled on the joystick in a well-practiced movement and hovered expertly, nudging the rear skids with a rakish flair before cutting the engines and coming to rest on the snow. Bob was frustrated. He had seen Jack look up at him, seen the look in his eyes, and he knew Jack wasn't going to be reasoned with, not by Stetson at any rate. He tried to speak to Stetson but this was police business and he gave him that look he always gave when he was serious. Bob backed away and watched as Stetson prepared himself, animated, adrenaline pumping as he jumped from the side door of the chopper and sank into the drift.

On seeing the police officer jump, Jack turned and loped effortlessly across the snowfield. Stetson attempted to run after him but the drifts were so deep he sank up to his waist at every move. Putting a good sixty yards between himself and Stetson, Jack turned to observe his pursuer, his eyes wild, weighing up his options. Beyond the snowfield there was just taiga, the bush, the entire Reindeer River flood plain. There was no way he could escape the chopper there, no cover, no gradient, no trees. As he turned toward the tree line Stetson, standing on harder snow now, shouted over to him, "Jack, please don't run! I'm here on behalf of your mother. Bob is in the chopper. He's come to take you home Jack. He's here for you..."

The spindrift had began to swirl again from the turbines and soon Sheriff Stetson had lost his track, deafened by the whine of the gyrating rotor blades as the stationary chopper began to wind up for takeoff. He couldn't believe what was happening. He had told Bud to hang slack until he gave the command. Bud had started the engines of his own accord, surveying the situation in an attempt to take the initiative; aware of the need to keep up with his would-be fugitive if he decided to bolt once more. The only problem with Bud Walker's plan was that Jack wasn't a fugitive, he was just a man trying to get away from the world, and now Stetson was trying to reason with him. He might as well have been calling in Chinese because over the twin turbines Jack couldn't hear a word.

Jack, of course, was oblivious to the entire goings-on. Somehow, though, he concluded that he was in trouble; the meat thing with the hunter, the wallet, not reporting his missing credit cards, shit, he had probably broken ten laws right there. But more importantly than that, he wasn't going to have the game dictated to him. Nemo ran it out here. Nemo called the shots, and a police chopper wasn't in his plans, let alone a candlelit dinner courtesy of the Sheriff's department. After all, what did he have to lose? His freedom was at stake and no one was going to take that away from him. He headed north in the direction he had been planning on going, running hard, as fast as his legs would take him, hurdling across the snowfield. Stetson was fuming. As he climbed back into the chopper his rage with Bud was such that he could barely speak.

"Don't fucking run him down, Bud, for Christ's sake! Just follow him, take it high and get me near, in front of him, got that? I just need to talk to the man, establish if it's Wyler, okay?"

It was then that Bob intervened. He had to, for Jack's sake, and anyhow in his mind there was no doubt as to the identity of the running man. He had seen his face looking into the Plexiglas footwells of the Jet Ranger. It was Jack. Stets was making a hash of it, and he sensed that things were getting out of control. He needed to take over. It was his friend down there. He took Stetson by the arm and in his calm manner looked Stetson in the eyes. "You got to let me talk to him, Stets. I'll get through to him, trust me. He's my best friend, and besides, I can make the ground to him quicker than you, Stets. I'm a lot lighter than you and I'm used to moving through this stuff."

Stetson fought it for a moment and then he realized Bob was making sense. What had he been thinking? It was as if he needed to prove himself to the younger, fitter man, and to himself, that not only could he find Jack, he could also bring him in. Just like he always had done back in Detroit, made the collar, his badge, put forward for the citation, his commendation. But now none of that had any relevance. This was between two friends. He had provided the means and he knew he had to leave it to Bob to talk to Jack, to make things right.

Stetson, his pride dented, gave the nod to Bud, who in turn dipped the nose down hard and banked the chopper away from Jack. Taking the bird to 100 feet, Bud followed Jack as he ran toward the far tree line. Banking again sharply, he hovered just ahead on a light impression in the snow. "Looks a bit deep and soft down there for a landing," he barked to Bob. "You'd better jump, you'll be fine."

Stetson opened the passenger door and stood to one side as Bob carefully stood on the skids. Shit, he hated heights, but there was no way he was going to lose face in front of Stetson, not after his pep talk. Pushing himself clear of the exit, Bob leaned out into the void. The six feet to the snow looked a short distance, but once airborne Bob realized it was closer to fifteen. The pack was soft, and as he landed he didn't stop on the surface but fell deep into the drift. Bud noticed the terrible mistake he had made and quickly veered the chopper toward more solid ground for landing.

Jack had seen the fall too, and he knew how deep the drift could be. In a decisive move he doubled back on himself and reached the place where Bob had disappeared in under a minute. The drift was deep. Crawling the last five yards toward the hole, Jack displaced his weight evenly across the pack and started to dig, his forearms like those of a mole shoveling large scoops of fresh snow, deeper and deeper.

Memories of Jim, the bear, of losing his friend due to inaction powered him on, forcing him down toward the fallen man. At last he felt Bob's body and gradually worked his way clear to his level. Bob was fine, a bit dazed and quiet. He had fallen on his back and had been winded. Wiping the light snow away from his face he reached out to Jack. "For Christ's sake, Jack," he puffed, "what does a friend have to do to have a quick chat with you?"

Before he could finish his introduction Jack, eyes wide in disbelief, stretched out his arm to his old friend. Grinning nervously from ear to ear, his thick beard parting to reveal a bright set of teeth, he leaned toward Bob, overcome with emotion, and braced himself on one knee in anticipation of counterbalancing his friend's weight. As he did so he appeared to stumble and slowly began to slip downwards, a faint look of confusion evident on his face. Bob, worried now, grabbed at his hand but as he moved toward him Jack, uttering only a faint gasp, suddenly and terribly slipped from view, a man-sized hole opening up just where moments before he had been standing.

Bob froze, and then it hit him: he wasn't standing in a drift and Bud hadn't dropped him on solid ground. The mound of snow had been formed not by a build-up of snow on a solid surface but by thermal activity beneath, energy from the ground, water movements to be more exact, and the spring had opened up right underneath him. Bob dared not move any further and slowly he began to crawl upwards away from the morass that had opened up only inches away. As he sat exhausted and in shock on the rim of the snowy impression, the violent sound of running water filled his ears. Peering over the edge, Bob watched in horror as the snow bridge he had been lying on only seconds before cracked and gave way, the snow and ice sucked fast into the underflow of freezing river water below.

"Jack!" shouted Bob in desperation and denial. "Jack!" he cried, lying back in the snow, tears welling in his eyes. "Jack, for Christ's sake ... what have I done?" He clenched his frozen fingers into the top crust of snow for support and began to edge toward the open maw of the hole. He could feel how precarious his position was on top of the crevasse, on the corniced lip of the broken snow bridge, and he froze once more, not daring to proceed further. Slowly he began to wail above the hole, above the sound of the tunneling water.

"I just wanted to see if you were okay, dude. To let you know that you're going to be a dad, that was all. I just wanted to tell you that, you crazy fucker ... "

Bob Anders, in the early stages of shock, remained in his prone position, his eyes fixed on the place of Jack's disappearance, until Stetson took him by the shoulders and held him tight while the full horror of what had just occurred began to dawn on him.

Jack was gone.

Chapter 4

Beuys stood at the bottom, looking up, his eyes piercing, liquid almost. He was smiling. After some time he turned, and, beckoning Jack forward, downward, walked methodically and in slow motion along the bed of rolling stones and weeds toward deeper, bluer water, his fur-lined greatcoat swirling and floating gracefully behind him. Sitting just beyond the bend in the river was Reuss. He was much younger than Beuys, twenty-something, with a good head of flowing golden hair. Even under water his skin seemed well tanned, brown and healthy-looking, in stark contrast to the older Beuys, his cheeks hollow, his forehead scarred, his head ever so slightly misshapen. There was a third man waiting for him down there in the greeny-blue glacial water. A man familiar to him in profile, and as he turned Jack gasped. It was Joe, his father. Jack, arms outstretched, duck-dived deeper; his head craned forward, eager for a better look. There was no mistaking Joe now as he turned to face his son.

The cold wasn't the worst thing. It was the fact that to talk to his dad or to any of them he would have had to breathe, take in the freezing liquid, deep into his lungs. And the water was so cold on his face, cold enough to stop him taking that fatal breath. Coming to rest on the river bottom, Jack felt somehow relieved. Relieved that the company was good and he was amongst his family. The initial shock, the speed of his descent, had at first caused him to panic and hyperventilate in the narrowing air pocket under the snow bridge and to fight against the surging power of the undertow. He had taken only one partial gulp of freezing meltwater and then it was as if he had just shut down. Many minutes later he began to feel warmer, at peace even; he was with his pop again, and finally his dad had found Reuss, his hero. How well it had all worked out.

He was with the people that mattered most, aside from his mother, but Jack was glad she was not there. However, there was someone missing, someone he missed so much. Rolling with the current, eyes open, mouth closed, Jack tried to find his friend. But Jim was nowhere to be seen. His father took him by the hand and together they hugged, warmth cloaking him as his dad squeezed him tight, the blood leaving his limbs and warming his very core. Beuys looked on, an unusual aura surrounding him, and as Jack observed him from the safety and warmth of his father's shoulder he realized he had probably never been happier, more complete and more loved. Both Reuss and Beuys seemed perfectly at one with each other. They were not hitting it off in the traditional fashion but their quiet acceptance of each other seemed to convey a mutual respect, down there in the deep river. The trout and Arctic char were also intrigued by these alien visitors to their underwater world but seemed on the most part unaffected by the strange congregation.

The touch of his father and the warmth of Beuys' spirit met with obvious approval from the lone, seated figure of Reuss. Of the three, there was no doubt that Reuss was the most idealistic and most romantic, but then he had youth on his side. After some time Jack glided onwards, taking a last look at the three ghost-like figures as he veered downstream toward a single fallen pine covered with river weeds. Standing at one end, propping up the log and prodding a playful finger at an inquisitive river trout was Jim, his friend, a beaming grin stretching from ear to ear. Jack took water again, the cold choking him, but soon he was able to float. Taking Jim's hand in his, they were now alone, kept together by a deep sense of love, a painful reunion but a good one. Now even the fish had gone and Jim seemed to grow uneasy, distraught even. As Jack slipped deeper into a torpor Jim gripped his hand firmer, as if seeking a response. Taking Jack's body in his arms he trailed his white hands along Jack's face and opened his eyes with thumb and forefinger. Jack was taken aback. Jim, his smile gone now, looked deep into him, his blue eyes piercing. In the clearest voice that he could summon, Jim spoke to his friend.

"Not now dude, not yet. You go now. We'll do this some other time."

Jack wanted to take Jim with him but he was unable to respond, unable to move. Frozen and weak, he began to feel himself being pushed aloft, drifting onwards, upwards, spinning, floating, as if in a dream. Jim soon became a distant apparition, fading behind him in the clear expanse of meltwaters. The new feeling of warmth was overwhelming, too warm almost. Jack began to move of his own accord. His consciousness and sense of motor control was returning as he floated faster, turned faster, drifted faster, spinning at a nauseating pace along the river bottom. He hit logs, bounced off underwater boulders, and as he went the color of the water changed. Emerald green, murky and milky, a new water system took him along until he reached the surface once more, barely conscious, wedged across a broad pine trunk at the far end of the pool in the steaming waters of the geothermic spring. For Jack there was peace at last, whiteness, perfect oneness with the water; the drifting had stopped, floating over, he was still and at rest. If this was death, then death wasn't so bad after all.

★ ★ ★

Bud Walker put in the high-frequency SOS call on emergency channel 16 to Anchorage, but being the primary response chopper the best they could hope for was support from number 2 chopper in Alekit. But with the Iditarod only forty-eight hours away from finishing, that just wasn't going to happen. They were on their own. Airborne once again, Bud flew south-south-west trying to anticipate the river's source, looking for an opening in its path. But flying over ten miles along and back down the stretch of topographical whiteness that was in summertime a roaring river, they found no openings in the snow at all. Without thermal imaging equipment, an ice dive team and ground support, the search was hopeless, rationalized Bud. Jack would have barely minutes to live in that kind of cold, assuming he had not drowned right away. Even taking into account bradycardia, the mammalian breathing reflex that has allowed humans to survive for many minutes in sub-zero immersion by concentrating the blood supply to the core and brain, allowing the peripheries to shut down, even in the hundreds of cases of this phenomenon being recorded each year, all the victims had to be physically rescued and manually resuscitated. Falling into a winter lake was one thing. A good team of brave divers can make informed rescue attempts based on a specific point of entry. In the Kuskokwim River the undercurrent was so fast the victim would be hundreds of yards away from the point of accident within minutes. If Stetson was honest, the search was utterly desperate and totally hopeless.

Bob stared out across the landscape, stunned by the chain of events, his breath causing the side window of the cockpit to mist up. Bud, turning the chopper around after an hour of low-level flights up and down the trajectory of the Kuskokwim, headed in silence back for Willow Creek.

"You okay, Bob?" offered Stetson.

Bob smiled weakly and turned to the Sheriff . "No, no, I'm not, Stets. But I'll tell you one thing, I'm better off than Jack, poor bastard."

"Shit happens, Stets," cut in Bud rather insensitively on the mike. "You've been around. Out here things can get so fucked up so quickly. It's not your fault. What were you going to do, jump in after him?"

Bob looked at the ground below him through the Plexiglas floor panel.

"He jumped in for me, didn't he, Bud? He didn't have to do that, and it sure as shit wasn't his fault, now was it?"

Bud focused on the horizon. To him it was just another case of accidental death. Bob would get over it, he thought to himself. Both he and Stetson had seen their fair share of death. Besides, he reasoned, the Wyler kid only had himself to blame. Shit, this country was a bitch. On that point at least the two police officers both agreed.

★ ★ ★

Bob was destroyed, and he blamed himself, absolutely. Maybe Stetson would have handled it differently, jumped at a different time, not been so impulsive. Of course Stetson knew there was nothing they could have done for Jack. It was a simple case of wrong place at the wrong time, but Bob wouldn't accept it. In his mind he was convinced Jack was dead because of his action and it was his fault alone. Jack was gone and Bob knew that with the rush of the water. At those temperatures, there was no way anyone would walk out of it, and the irony of the situation ate away at him. The irony that it was the search for him that had killed Jack, not the Alaskan winter, not starvation or the wildlife, it was Bob, sent by Jack's mother and friends to save him and together they had killed him. Why couldn't they just have let him be? He would have worked it out eventually, got the peace of mind he was looking for, found the answers and eventually gravitated to civilization, made the call to his mother. But now what? Nothing, it was all over, a pointless end to a young life.

Now Bob had tasted the same thing Jack had done, the helplessness at watching his friend die, going over it time and time again in his mind, the "what ifs". And he knew it to be useless, all of it, even the regret. It was as over for them as it was for Jack, and now he had to tell Laura, Holly, Mikaela, Groub, Jack's infant son, tell them all that Jack was lost to them. That he wouldn't be returning from the wild. That he was dead.

The killer of course was the kid, as if Jack's death wasn't unbearable enough. It burned inside Bob, and he promised himself that he would pay the price. After all, he was a dad and he knew as well as anyone what was needed, the cost of that commitment; the time, the energy and the love needed to raise a child. Bob promised his friend, as they had promised each other as teenagers back in Ely to look out for each other, that he would look after his kid. All Mikaela had to do was accept his offer. He would ensure that she could rely on him to help raise Jack's son. After all, who else was there to take it on? To pass on what Jack would have wanted his kid to know. No one knew Jack as well as he did, even Laura, and besides, she was getting on now. Of the three of them he was the last man standing, the sole survivor.

Chapter 5

The wolf pack waited, pacing with frosted steps in the tree line, their breath rising in warm eddying rings in the frigid air. The alpha male stood at their head, tense, alert and on edge. His intuition told him that something in the hotspring creek was different. The wolf didn't quite know what, or for that matter how he knew, but something was out of place. The very sense of the spring had altered, just marginally, and it was enough to spook him. The wolf trotted back and forth along the line of low spruce trees. Nose high, nose low, his alertness was heightened, hackles up, ears forward, eyes focused, darting left and right. The females and beta males began to yelp, high excitable coughs. His actions were exciting them; something unspoken, a sixth sense, brought them together as a unit and the alpha male began to howl, summoning and assembling the pack to a sense of alarmed excitement, a deep melancholy crooning wail that echoed deep into the forest. The rest of the pack instantly joined in the baying, signing into their natural roll-call. Shortly after their vocalization of attendance and their acknowledgement of a potential threat they began to fall into a defensive arrowhead formation behind their leader. In all they were eight individuals, 1,400 pounds of predator, eight mouths, a lethal, unstoppable, predatory pack.

The pack was fresh off a large moose kill and had gorged themselves during their first sitting, their muzzles now garish masks smeared crimson with drying, congealed blood. With their bellies full they should have been resting, but the strange presence in their creek meant their rest would have to wait. The dead ungulate was lying not 100 yards from the spring, its mauled, still warm, partly eaten carcass steaming in the midday sun. The wolves would stay near to the kill for the next two days, to feed fully and keep other wolves, wolverines and foxes off the kill. Only the wolves' symbiotic sentinel, the raven, was allowed to feed while the pack patrolled nearby. Only a large Alaskan brown bear could run them off the kill. But bears were not a problem in February, as they wouldn't be waking for many months.

The moose had taken to feeding on the young fresh shoots, and while still technically winter these had begun to sprout, due to the proximity of the warm mineral-rich waters. The springs in this part of western Alaska were temperate, non-saline, non-caustic and non-sulphurous. The combination of upwelling from the glacial stream and the merging of the geothermic spring had resulted in a temperature akin to that of a warm jacuzzi, no hotter at least.

The pack had taken moose here the winter before and the winter before that too; it was a perfect ambush point for relaxing prey. The old bull had been caught unawares, a careless and ultimately fatal move from an animal too wise to turn its back on the dark tree line. The noise of the bubbling spring hadn't helped, but a younger bull would never have made that mistake, there was too much at stake, too many seasons of rut to miss out on, too many battles to forgo. The fight had not been an epic one. With both of his huge femoral arteries gashed by the curved vice-like incisors of the attacking wolves, the moose had staggered for the short distance toward cover in the tree line before succumbing to the tactical supremacy of the pack. Unlike other large predators, the wolves were not concerned with a quick death. Lions and tigers are renowned for constricting, immobilizing and suffocating large prey, not attempting to devour their quarry until it is safe and of course dead. Wolves, pack predators, would not risk injury and lacked the individual muscle bulk to take down the 1,200-pound moose. Rather like their African cousins the wild dogs, the wolves allowed the moose to bleed to death slowly, marshaling its demise with lethal, biting, jabbing forays. The constant running down, nipping, slashing and ripping of flesh around the hind quarters and underbelly and the stress this causes mean older prey such as moose often succumb to cardiac arrest or hypovolemic shock due to severe blood loss. To be eaten by wolves, entrails first, can be a slow death.

As the alpha male proceeded across the melting snow flats toward the edge of the mist-covered creek, the three beta males retreated to guard the kill. The alpha female followed her mate in single file, step for step toward the hotspring. The wolf stopped. Next to the old tree trunk the wolf spotted the reason for his unease. Wedged alongside the trunk was a strange form, an animal he was unfamiliar with. The body was large, larger than himself, and appeared to be still. Something primal, a sense of a past relationship with a superior animal, persuaded the wolf it was okay to approach further. His mate waited, tense with anticipation. The form seemed still, dead almost, and he approached closer now, craning his neck forward to sniff and sense for any signs of life. The body was warm, and the wolf pushed the torso and then the head with his wet nose, listening now.

Somewhere deep inside, the wolf's DNA reassured him that the being was no threat. Not that the animal was dead, the wolf could sense it was not, but neither did the forlorn body constitute prey. Now the wolf's mate joined him at the side of the steaming pool, her sense of curiosity heightened by her leader's reaction. She too sniffed, careful not to infringe on her male's space, respectful of his every move. Tugging lightly on the forearm of the animal, she leant back and with a faint growl pulled at the damp clothing. The male stood back; he was intelligent and patient. Circling around, the wolf came from the right-hand side and nudged the bulk of the torso on to its side. Gently pushing the body and floating log toward the pool edge, the body came to rest in the shallows at the wolf's feet.

Suddenly the wolf yelped and hopped high in the air, the shock of movement visible in his eyes. The female ran away fast, sprinting to safety, but the male stood his ground, looking about him. The form was moving, slowly at first, then shuddering, coughing, spluttering, shaking violently. The wolf, now visibly alarmed, circled again, keeping his distance but slowly beginning to move forward toward the strange animal that had woken up. Jack tried to breathe but his lungs, still carrying a small quantity of water, burned and he was again racked by a fit of deep, watery, phlegm-filled coughing. The wolf had inadvertently managed to push him on to his side into a recovery position of sorts, the result of which had been to enable most of the warm water and surfactant fluid to be rejected in his sporadic fits of hacking. He slowly knelt on all fours and was now fully out of the warm spring water. He began to shiver. His underwater journey over the past fifteen minutes had meant his body had shut down, a classic case of a fit healthy individual's ability to survive cold water immersion and a testament to our aquatic mammalian past. But the key to his remarkable survival came in the fortuitous and accidental joining of the fast cold currents with the upwelling of the warm spring water. This had the effect of neutralizing any symptoms of hypothermia and immersion exposure.

The wolf's inquisitive nudging had also helped with the draining of any residual water, but victims who experience the mammalian diving response do not take on unnaturally large quantities. The cold serves to impose a restriction on the breathing reflex that can best be understood by illustrating the phenomenon with the regular occurrence most of us experience when standing under a cold shower. We simply gasp for breath. So in this way Jack Wyler had survived a near-fatal accident, but now he was confronted by an even greater challenge, surviving the bitter cold on the surface. The wind was biting, and his clothes were already beginning to ice over. As the wolves trotted back to their kill, Jack realized he needed to compose himself, get a grip quickly, if he was going to survive the next and only golden hour. The pack was now staggered across the flats, actively guarding the kill. Two of the females had started to feed again, their unborn pups demanding vital nutrition, their mates conscious of their maternal needs.

Jack was now fully conscious and emerging well from his previous state of shock. Later on there would be opportunity to muse about the mysterious luck of his survival, but now was not the time for such thoughts. The fall into the river had, however, already changed him, forged him almost, but there was a negative effect. The underwater experience meant that he couldn't quite relate to the surreal reality of his current predicament. He was standing dripping wet in the last of the mid-afternoon twilight, the valuable rays of sun already disappearing below the frosted tree line. Still somewhat slow and numb, Jack began to rip at his clothing, both eyes fixed on the pack of wolves not thirty yards from where he was standing. He knew from his training as a kid that he only had one choice. He had to strip off his clothes, get a fire going and seek warmth and shelter from the elements. Failing that, he had to generate enough heat to either dry his clothes or enable himself to regenerate his circulation and flagging energy so as to be able to establish and build shelter at a later time.

It was then that he saw the kill. The chest and ribcage of the large moose were still relatively intact, the wolves having concentrated on the meat-rich hindquarter and stomach offal. With one eye on the wolves, he reached down for his knife and the felt roll that he had tied off his belt as he had rushed from the cabin. The knife was still there, and Jack quickly drew it from its thick grey sheath, dropping the felt roll to the ground. Taking the large knife by the back of the blade, he crouched down and cut the laces off his boots, which had began to form with ice crystals into a solid icy block. Next came his pants, thermals and parka. Taking the knife in his right hand and the felt roll in the other, he walked toward the pack slowly, naked, exposed and utterly terrified. Somewhere inside himself he knew this was his only chance. He had to make a radical move and get inside the kill, warm himself up within the voluminous carcass before it too began to freeze. As Jack approached stealthily and with great purpose the wolves began to snarl and yelp. Only the alpha male stood calmly.

Jack was now yards from the kill and controlling his instinct to run. Eyes to the ground in an instinctive gesture of respect, he carefully went

247

down on to his knees and crawled down next to the fallen moose. Putting his arms into the chest cavity, he pulled out the offal and half-eaten stomach contents and threw the heart, kidneys and liver toward the wolves, an offering from one predator to another. The alpha male took the string of organs and withdrew with his mate to a safe distance as Jack shimmied feet first, slipping almost, into the bloody gore-filled cavity. The moose smelled strangely homely, as far as dead animals go. Probably, Jack concluded, on account of the dominant role moose had been playing in his diet for the past year. He owed them one for this, that was for sure. The smell was not at all bad, since the kill was fresh, but the most notable thing of all was that the moose was still warm, warm enough to slowly reinvigorate his numb and frozen limbs. Jack was inside the bulk of the beast, curled into a fetal position. The wind, whipping from the north against the moose's thick flanks, couldn't touch him. For the time being he was safe.

As the light began to fade, casting tall, eerie shadows across the creek, the pack came in close to the kill, resting just yards away, their bodies creating sheltered indents in the bloody and melted snow. The alpha male was last to rest. As if willing to share warmth with this new and alien member of his pack and to escape the mounting wind, he demonstrated the most remarkable display of submissive trust. The wolf turned twice clockwise, as if checking the ground was suitably clear, then nuzzled down, touching Jack, who by now had passed unconscious with exhaustion into a deep and troubled sleep.

Chapter 6

Jack's death had stayed with Sheriff Stetson, or rather the circumstances of it had. Stetson had put Bob up for the first few days after the accident and had been there for him, to listen mainly, and hold his hand through it. What else was there to do? Bob was surprisingly calm, and Stetson suspected he was bottling everything up. Stetson had sat with him as he had made the call to Jack's mother, and had held him tight, as he had done so many times before when it was he who had had to make those calls. There had been so many of them over the years. A shitty business, informing the next of kin. At the end of the call, Stetson had taken the phone from Bob, who was so overcome with grief he was struggling to hold it together.

Stetson had noted Laura's composure, as she sat alone in her large house. She had a secret, that woman, he was convinced of it. But he knew she would be destroyed by the news. He half-suspected that the elapsed time, the past year of Jack's disappearance, had helped, as if she had believed her son was dead already, protecting herself from the grim reality. But he couldn't be sure. Whatever the reason or rationale, it was a cluster-fuck, that's how he saw it anyway. The whole search had been handled wrongly, and he wanted Laura to know that, as if he owed it to her to be as honest as he knew she needed him to be.

Laura was as dismissive of Stetson's candor as she was impressed by his desire to be held accountable. She asked him to look after Bob, to keep an eye on him, and of course to tell her and her alone when they found the body. That was important to her, for closure and for peace of mind more than anything else. So she could say her farewell to her son, so she could believe once and for all that it was over, his short life.

Throughout the following summer months Stetson took a long overdue vacation and flew down the Aleutian chain to Hawaii with his wife. But despite the break, the warmth, the sea and sand, he just couldn't shake the guilt he felt. From his perspective the guilt was not without reason. Out of a sense of ego-driven duty, to fill his time and test his fading mettle, he had chosen to pursue a man who had done no wrong. That was his mantra, at least. The facts, however, were far less vindictive than his own self-imposed penance. Jack Wyler was the subject of a federally authorized missing persons directive. Stetson had, as far as the state of Alaska was concerned, done a commendable job putting the pieces together. After all, Jack wasn't the first idealistic drifter to fall foul of the last frontier. The rest of the story to date and his ensuing death was just a terrible, unfortunate accident. From a career and professional standpoint Sheriff Stetson was off the hook. But his guilt just wouldn't go away, even after an emotional union of unconditional forgiveness with Laura Wyler. The wake was a small and desperately sad affair, held at the DeCourcy mine head with a few friends and family. Worse still, and despite numerous sweeps along the winding banks of the Snake River, there was no body and with it no sense of final closure for the family.

On reflection, what Stetson and for that matter all Jack's friends and family couldn't quite come to terms with was the reason why. Why had Jack, the all-American boy, just dropped out and thrown it all away – his family, his wealth, his career, his life? The answers to this mystery lay in a series of personal losses, starting years before with his father and, more recently, Jim. But traumatic personal loss provides rational, reasonable explanations to alienation and various forms of ensuing clinical depression. While Jack's withdrawal from society was clearly not a black and white affair, he was not depressed. The intricacies of his decision to withdraw from society can be best understood by recognizing the importance of less obvious motives: attention to special possessions, passions and personal feelings that Jack kept hidden close to his heart and with few exceptions chose not to share with those traditionally close to him.

Alienation is not always a self-imposed state. The causes of loneness are not only psychological but are a reaction to an external circumstance outside the control of the afflicted individual. In simple terms, a chain of traumatic and stressful circumstances can affect anyone. In Jack's case they provided the catalyst for change, a total change, unconditional, irrational and, somewhat more relevantly, unconventional. Or was it? A closer look at society's obsession with individuality and the fantasy of the rebel, with chucking it all in, starting from fresh and social reinvention, is at the very epicenter of our value structure. It is the possibility rather than the reality of such a change that keeps many people going. Nowhere can this fantasy be more acutely observed than in the fast-track world of investment banking – an environment where high stress combines with the daily possibility of economic and personal reshuffle, and huge bonuses, to give real credibility to the possibility of the totally life-changing fantasy. If anyone could make the break, Wall Street high flyers could, and if nothing more they could afford it. "It could happen. I could take control of my destiny. I too can think outside the box, follow a dream, get away from it all." But could they handle the inherent risks attached when an individual's radical departure from conventional society becomes reality? The fact that Jack actually did what many of his peers only fantasized about was an illustration of the conviction of the man. Bob Anders summed up this philosophy in his commission of a plaque to be attached to the cabin at the DeCourcy mine. It simply stated:

Jack Wyler 1967–2001
This was a Man.

But as Stetson was later known to point out in regular drunken hypothesizing: "What type of man would want to live alone in the wild?" The concept, for Stetson and indeed for most people, is too alien to comprehend. The answer was, of course, hard to determine. But clearly Jack was one such person. Unwittingly, a combination of his love of the wild, of art, the controversial teachings of the shamanic Beuys and a searching for the kindred spirit of Everett Reuss had culminated in him inadvertently finding his own nirvana. These passions had culminated in a cocktail of antidotes to his pain and personal loss.

As Stetson and Bob had both discovered, searching, be it for oneself or of a more literal nature, can come at a price, a price that Jack felt was worth paying and they did not. But it is rarely the dead who pay the ultimate price. The pain and suffering of those left behind does not fade easily, and for Laura the stigma of surviving her first-born was, for the first few months, nearly too much to bear. Thankfully her friends were there for her. Bob Anders, true to his word, had become a lynchpin in her daily life; nothing was ever too much trouble, and his family were a constant support. But it was Mikaela and her decision to make her home in the USA for part of every year that had brought Laura back from the abyss.

Mikaela had, with Bob's support, managed to get a temporary work permit on account of being a "child-bearing dependant of a recently deceased citizen". Bob had friends in all the right places, including immigration, and Laura had covered the legal fees, flights and living expenses. Bob's help in the liaison and administration of Mikaela's seasonal translocation was all she required, and she refused point-blank to accept his money; after all, he had his own family to provide for. The way Laura saw it, Jack had left her a lot of money. What better way to spend it than on his son, her grandson, little Sasha.

Mikaela had realized some months after the affair that she had been unfair to Jack, cruel even. At the time she had seen no other way to end it and she knew she had to bring it to a close, for both their sakes. Viktor's death had hurt too much, and she had begun to question whether she had really known Jack at all, ever loved him. It had all been a bit of a blur, a whirlwind romance that had ended in the loss of her brother and Jack's friend. The pregnancy was just the icing on the cake, and she knew that if she had told him he would have wanted to do the right thing, which would have been the wrong thing for their relationship. Somewhat selfishly, back on Sredny Jack hadn't been what she wanted. Not at that time, not while her feelings were so raw.

The change had begun gradually, Teresa acting as the instigator, urging her to see some reason, to compromise, but as she began to gain weight and the pregnancy drew to its finale she yearned to see Jack once more. There was something maternal, the nest-building factor in her nature, that needed a man to protect and hold her, to tell her it would be okay. Teresa had been there for the birth and then Mikaela had made the call to Bob.

Bob had told her about Jack's disappearance in Alaska. At first she had thought it out of character, since he seemed to have so much going for him in the city, but she couldn't have read him more wrongly. Sure, she had seen him animated away from the office and his stress, but secretly she believed he thrived on it. Gradually her surprise had turned to guilt. She suspected that if she had thought more about him after the accident and told him about their child, maybe he wouldn't have gone. It was as if he had acted like a man with nothing to lose. Perhaps the knowledge that he was to be a father, regardless of his feelings for her, would have prevented him from doing something so rash, so irresponsible. It was then that she realized she had made a terrible mistake: there she was alone in Sredny, with little money, no future. She decided to go back to America, give it a go, meet with Jack's mother, take up Bob's offer of an air flight and a visit.

Mikaela had liked Ely. It reminded her of the countryside around St Petersburg, the hills and valleys of western Russia, the rich vitality of the land, the trees, the lakes, the remoteness of the place. The people were kind too, of Finnish stock mainly, and that felt familiar, the local sauna, the coffee shops, the references to the old country. She had stayed in a small rented house nearby Laura's, a good job organized at the local store. Her modeling career was over now, and besides, there wasn't the money in it up in northern Minnesota. A shoot for the occasional outward-bound catalog was fine, but to have a career and be a mother, that life was not for her.

Laura had been wonderful; like her mother would have been had she lived long enough to see her grandchild. She had hoped that Bob and the Alaska police would have been able to find Jack and let him know about his son, baby Sasha. She had asked Laura for her approval and Laura had loved the name, and that had made her feel good, loved, part of the family. When Bob had called from Alaska it was early evening and they had all just finished eating dinner. She could tell from Laura's tone, distant, composed, across the sitting room, that the news was bad and Jack was gone. In one sense she felt some relief in knowing for sure, but that was the only consolation she could glean from the whole terrible affair. She had tried to explain to Sasha as he lay wide-eyed and immobile in his cot, watching his mother cry, tears falling on to his tiny face. Sasha would have to wait to learn about his father, and then she, Mikaela, Bob, Laura, all of them, would tell him who his dad was and why he had gone away.

★ ★ ★

In addition to her new grandmotherly responsibilities and the joys inherent in caring for the young Sasha, the board and business of Microstem had become a vessel in which Laura could immerse herself and physically see the fruits of Jack's vision. The business gradually became her passion, and as Microstem grew in both respect and market value, the pain of her son's death began to blur in favor of pride. Along with Sasha, Microstem was Jack's legacy, the last gesture he had made before going himself. Microstem's unprecedented nine patents in "stem-cell development technology" and its complimentary neuro-inhibitor patent (the wonder-drug pioneered with Jack's initial capital) had, within a radical sixteen-month timeframe, become the most regarded and significant discovery in the history of Parkinson's pharmacology. For Laura, this unprecedented success had become a reason for her undiluted maternal pride. Of course, Laura's feelings for her son's posthumous successes were heightened by the demise of those she most despised; ultimately those she held most accountable for Jack's stress and his decision to drop out.

Lane Connor and Lou Jacobs, fresh from market ridicule for their shortsighted "writing off" of Microstem as an ongoing concern, were currently under investigation by the New York Attorney General's

253

Commission into Corporate Fraud. The charges of stock spinning and preferential treatment versus new business incentives, rife throughout the investment banking community, were to carry no leniency in the courts. Merrill's had taken the rap first and now the smaller boutiques were falling. As a result of public and shareholders' demands, the board of KLS wanted heads, as did the Securities and Exchange Commission (SEC), headed by the infamous Aaron Lek. There was no shortage of first-hand evidence and testimony to Lane and Lou's underhand dealings, but Lane's defense team provided a tough barrier to conviction due to the absence of hard copy evidence. Other testimonies for the prosecution told of midnight shredding sessions, but without the physical first-hand emails and memos the case would fall foul of technical evidence loopholes in the form of the "clear absence of concrete evidence detailing the said communications". The judge was clear: without any email proof the prosecutors would lose. Prosecuting New York attorney Pat Levine and SEC tsar Aaron Lek went ballistic on the grounds of the severity of the charges and were awarded forty-eight hours continuance.

As fate would have it, a brown manila envelope detailing a catalog of internal emails and memos from the two indicted directors, instructing their junior management to pump and dump stocks, was that day removed from its resting place in a New Jersey safety deposit box and delivered by an anonymous former KLS employee to the SEC in person. The reason for the anonymity was of a personal nature and the reason for the tardy arrival was that the case had, until the technicality, seemed a foregone conclusion. The contents subsequently provided the Commission with all the evidence it needed. With the advent of a climate of corporate distrust, the SEC and the Attorney General's office now had the heads they needed. Lane and Lou were found guilty on more than seventeen counts of fraud, deception and breaking the investment banking code. They were going away, a minimum sentence of three and five years respectively, assets impounded subject to investigation, the full enchilada! The aggrieved KLS clients, still licking their wounds late into 2002, had at last received their satisfaction, as had Laura. The KLS chapter was finally at an end.

It is said that time can be a great healer, but time alone cannot heal. Mental fortitude and a decision to move on are key to the healing process. Through the success of Microstem, all those affected by Jack's mysterious and ultimately tragic disappearance in May 2001 were given an opportunity to bring a positive sense of closure to his untimely demise, and in so doing change a small part of medical history. In January 2002, a commission from

Stockholm made the journey to New York City for a meeting with Dr Johan De Blevis. Their mission's objective was to deliver, in person, an invitation. It was an invitation to a most exclusive club, and De Blevis was to be encouraged to accept. Modesty would not be considered.

On the 10th of December 2002, the anniversary of Alfred Nobel's death, De Blevis was awarded the Nobel Prize for Medicine by the Nobel assembly of the Karolinska Institute. At fifty-two years old he became the youngest scientist and the first South African ever to receive the prize. In his acceptance speech he dedicated his team's success to the belief of one man, who, he explained, preferred to be known by an adopted name: "Nemo – No One, a true friend of science". How proud Jack would have been. As De Blevis stated in his oration to the society on the stage of Stockholm's Bla Hallen that crisp winter's evening, miracles really do happen. How prophetic he was.

Chapter 7

The cave was warm and musty aside from the occasional gust of cool, summer wind. A slight shaft of moonlight danced across the floor by the entrance to the den, reflecting a flash of teeth and the silvery glint of a watchful eye. The alpha male lay beside his mate close by the entrance of the cave, not quite resting, never quite asleep. He had sired a new litter in the late spring, and although not doting by nature, something in his spirit told him to protect his young; after all, they were of his seed.

Jack knew not to get too close, the other wolves had taught him that. They were an excellent gauge for him to follow, their intuition and responses honed so as not to incur the wrath of the lead dog. Ironically it was the rest of the pack, those lower down the hierarchy, that he knew to fear the most. To them, for the first few months, he had represented a direct threat to their ascension within the strict lineage of the wolf pack. But he had heeded their warnings: a stamping gait, agitated movements, ears back flat, the occasional snapping and bearing of curved incisors, muzzle drawn back, snapping and snarling. It was all the warning Jack needed, but he had also learned never to back down, not to the extent of appearing vulnerable, weak or prey-like. That would have been a real mistake, one he might not have walked away from.

In general, certain taboos were not to be broken, and the alpha male and his mate would make it clear when they would accept any interaction from the outsider. A mutual tolerance had led to a certain level of trust, but Jack suppressed the urge to pet the alpha pups, the new focal point of the pack. All in good time, he thought. After all, time was something of which he had plenty.

★ ★ ★

It wasn't just the dead moose carcass that had saved his life; it was also the knife, Beuys' Samurai knife, the new antler handle, and the things he had learned as a kid. Nothing much after that time had any relevance out here, which Jack thought reasonably ironic considering all the time he'd spent at school and on Wall Street. Now all he cared about was the basics and he needed to understand them totally, as if they were second nature to him.

Joe had drummed the fire thing in deep. The flint stick was kept as a rule in his parka pocket. This single stem of manmade strikeable magnesium core had enabled Jack, still in shock, hypothermic and scared, to create sparks, and the thousands of brilliantly heat-intensive charged thermal particles had in turn given him new life and new hope.

Jack was quite literally dead to his old world, dead to all he had known, his family, his friends, his career. He had gone too far, and any chance of returning to his former life had been dashed in the freezing currents in a remote Alaskan river. Now it was only Nemo who lived, and those closest to him, his mentors and the wolves. By his rationale he owed them all for his life: the wolf pack, his father, Beuys and Reuss too. But in the coming weeks Jack began to see his metamorphosis in a different light. He began to realize a deeper sense of responsibility. He didn't actually owe anyone anything any more, not if he got down to it. Everything he had learned, seen and done, his very winding up out here, naked and alone, next to a pack of wolves, that too was, when it came down to it, his own doing. He had created his destiny. He had made the bed, fluffed up the duvet and now, like it or not, he had to lie in it. But the flint had helped, as had the knife, so he was grateful, especially grateful for a second chance. He was happy to be alive.

The moose hadn't tasted too bad either. It was amazing what a man could eat if he had to, and Jack really had to. He had eaten his meal, bloody and raw, next to the wolves, hunkered down, covered in guts and shit, and it had tasted good. The hide had made a fine knee-length coat too. He hadn't bothered to make pants, there was no time for such work, but the roughly skinned cape, still waxy with the residue of epidermal fat, had helped. The wolves had been curious and very tolerant, but the fire had scared them. Soon, though, after he had erected his lean-to, the pit and makeshift drying horse from bowed willow branches, they had come back round, probably enjoying the warmth. Jack thought back to the story he had been told back in the backwoods about the hunter, frozen, broken, starving, who was allowed to feed next to a wolf pack. The story of the wolf scraping on the trapper's cabin door for warmth and for a place to die, so he wouldn't die alone. The historical evidence of man and wolf engaged in the hunt is a relationship as old as time, a precurser to the partnership of man and dog. But how would Jack ever truly come to terms with the responsibility of that trust, the wolf almost beckoning him, so tolerant and at one with an inferior two-legged predator, a wolf at one with a man. The first nation, the direct descendants of the roving hunter-gatherers who had passed over the Bering land bridge, across the far north and then down through the plains into the swamps and southern jungles in search of food and shelter, they had been right. At least today they had been right, the animals were his brothers that day. The day he had survived the river, there was no doubt about that.

The snow was still firm, and away from the hotspring it was hard and dry, so in the following days Jack made moose-hide mukluks bound with tendon and sinew. Using his dried socks as an insulating layer, they were soon worn supple and became comfy as hell, even though they needed some wearing in. Once the wolves had eaten all they could and Jack had taken as much of the hide as he could use, the alpha male led the pack back to the far trees. Jack had waited, out of respect more than anything else. Besides, it was probably best they parted company before anything got out of hand, since a human would surely only prove a hindrance and slow them down. But the alpha male just waited, he waited a whole night, and then at first light Jack realized he had been accepted. Tying the felt roll and the knife around his waist and gathering up the cape in a large bundle (he cut a hole for his head and slung the fleshy pelt over his back), Jack began to trudge toward the pack, who in turn moved northwards, climbing the nearby ridge. For the next two days the pack, trailed by an exhausted Jack, navigated the high ridgeline of the lower Alaskan ranges, descending into the rocky scree of a far and sheltered slope. The going had been slow for them but the wolves displayed the most remarkable sense of patience and care. The beta males would scout ahead of the trail and in the thicker sections of snow the alpha male would follow behind Jack's snail pace, resting when he rested, yelping with excitement when he moved on again. The nights had proved almost too much, the cold unbearable and shelter scarce, but Jack had used what energy he had to make a fire and keep the warmth coming. Once again, the fire saved him.

On the lower slopes of the scree the wolves came to rest in a densely wooded gully, sheltered from the north wind by high red spruce and sitka pine. It was there that Jack discovered the cave, the wolves' den and his summer home. Initially he had survived on spearing fish and on the abundance of antioxidant-rich bearberries and crowberries in the new valley. The river had an abundance of salmon pushing themselves upstream, manatrons on a one-way journey to lay eggs and die. Sometimes the pack was gone for a week or so, always returning, but never with food.

Jack understood. Wolves regularly regurgitate food for their young but he was seen as an equal, better than an equal, an alpha male, and Jack understood that he too must provide food if he was to be truly accepted.

After some weeks the rest of the pack had on the whole accepted him, their acceptance generally illustrated by a cool disregard. To the pack Jack had become a joint leader, but a leader who couldn't keep up with the chase. He was therefore seen as a mysterious member of the family, a novelty of little use. But at least he was now regarded as a member and the signs and signals of threat from the wolves had ceased. He had accepted that the wolves as a pack would always feel this way with him, a kind of accepting indifference, and he felt fine with it. The alpha male had changed too. Previously he had fronted the pack's interest and inquisitiveness with a sense of playful intrigue. Now the alpha began to look to Jack for leadership, observing him preparing himself for the hunt as he readied his equipment, visibly enthralled by his activity, tuned in to the action of his new hunting partner.

It was shortly after this time of acceptance, after only a few months in the cave, that the new dreaming began. It was as if over the past weeks the wolf pack had penetrated the membrane of Jack's subconscious as depicted by the great cave painters. Together they hunted now, flying through the forest, searching out prey to ambush and track down. Jack's dreams became a nightly occurrence, an essential ritual that he consulted before a hunt or journey from the cave, a mental map that would indicate the path of their potential prey. But it was the nature of flight in the dreams – flying low level over the forest floor, close enough to see the animal tracks – that caused Jack the greatest sense of joy and calm. There was no more stress, no regret, no guilt, no fear, all that negativity now vanished, and Jack remembered where and when he had last dreamed that way. It had been back in Ely as a kid, growing up in the bush with his family and his friends, happy and without a care in the world.

★ ★ ★

In contrast to the past winter the summer was pleasantly temperate, occasionally warm but most importantly bright, the days golden and never-ending. Jack had made an impressive array of spears, their points tempered black and hard in the fire. On occasion, he had knapped flint hand-axes, sitting for hours in the cave cross-legged, diligently chipping away at the edges of the stone until the ridge created was cutting sharp. Using the same

259

technique, he sharpened small flints to act as hunting hard-points for his spear. He lashed these with tendon from the moose vellum, cutting grooves into the young wood with the Samurai knife. Once he had even attempted to construct a bow, but to date this had proved totally ineffective as a hunting tool.

Soon after arriving at the cave, Jack, visibly thinner now, had contemplated returning to the DeCourcy mine to collect his rifle; but the likelihood of it still being there after the accident and the chances of being seen helped him to decide wisely against such a mission. Dead men walking in the forest have a way of creating their own bush telegraph, and Jack didn't want any further interaction with people. It was better to keep it that way. The sled, however, was still with him, mentally at least, but as time went by its relevance to his new life somehow began to diminish. After all, what did he need it for now? All he had was a moose-skin jacket, mukluks, a pair of worn jeans, a knife and a flint. The realization of his survival and complete reinvention pleased him. Before, even a well-packed rucksack had made him feel complete, materially economical even, but now with literally no possessions other than those he carried on his person, all he needed was either on a piece of sinew around his waist or in his head. To fill the days he fished, built basic noose snares and dug two massive deep stake-filled deadfalls for larger game close to the den along the east and west trails. The wolves had watched him build the deadfalls and Jack hoped they would remember their locales. He need not have feared. Their smell alone belied their presence, and wolves do not forget easily, they are too cunning and wise by far.

Soon he was tracking moose with the pack. Initially, he had attempted to drive the moose toward his deadfalls but this hadn't worked, and after two near-fatal charges from an obstinate bull, Jack had decided it was far safer to stalk and ambush the great beasts only once the pack had engaged in the attack. There was something about the intuition of the pack fanning out behind him, just as in his dreams, as he slowly crept up on the feeding ungulates. The alpha male and female would initiate an attack, working in perfect unison with the rest of the pack as they harried the moose until it was too exhausted to run any further. It was then that Jack learned to join in with the kill, bringing the final blow to the moose with a well-aimed thrust into the animal's pulsating exposed carotid with a sharpened spear. There was easier prey to kill. Lone territorial bull caribou were the easiest to fell, passing along ancient trails, never to venture north. The true migration began slowly, but as June grew old the caribou began to visit the valley with greater regularity, the sound of their large crescent hooves cantering through the narrow trails, sometimes barely yards from the unusual ambush party, echoing around the creek.

In the evenings, before his dreaming began, Jack would build a small centrally placed fire, which seemed to please his hosts. Using a blackened branch he drew on the walls, rubbing in soil and sometimes using softer porous rocks, imbuing his illustrations with rich ochres and charcoal. There was no real significance to his drawings: Jack had never before shown much interest in the physical activity of painting, but now it pleased him to make the marks, create patterns and annotate events. There was a certain therapy in the exercise. Reuss, before his disappearance in the canyon lands, had enjoyed drawing, illustrating articles about his journeys for the east-coast press, and Jack signed most of his drawings with his borrowed pseudonym, "Nemo". As for Beuys, drawing was a compulsion, a means of shamanic expression, storytelling, the conveyance of messages from the spirit world. For Jack, the activity was engaging, therapeutic at best. His daubs provided a physical document of his daily experience, evidence of unfolding events, however trivial. After all, what else was a man to do living in a cave?

★ ★ ★

One day in late summer the wolves began to act strangely: the wind had turned and with it came fresh messages. Again Jack felt welcome to follow the pack but there was something in the urgency of the wolves' movements that day that told him they might not be returning to the den. The pups were strong now, able to walk for miles at a time and certainly strong enough to make it to the next den site. Being suckled on protein-rich mothers' milk and on scraps from the kill, the pups had grown strong fast. The entire pack had been instrumental in their daily wellbeing, teaching them play, backtracking, ambush, the skills of the hunt and the constant importance of inter-sibling dominance and rivalry. The combination of a strong family bond and good nourishment had accelerated their strength and resistance to the elements dramatically, fifteen times quicker than a human child of the same age. A larger pack would be leaving the summer den site, the four pups increasing the scope and ability of the pack to be successful in the critical late winter hunts to a total of twelve wolves and one human, an odd complement to an awesome killing party.

Jack hastily gathered his few belongings together and, standing in the entrance of the cave, turned and looked back into the somber depths of his home, a last goodbye gesture more than anything else. His fire sat smouldering and the slivers of daylight revealed the extent of his drawings. Over the past months he had transformed the cave, enriching its walls with his drawing and signatures. Acknowledging his handiwork, he smiled, then turned and headed out into the brilliant daylight, his body silhouetted by the sun's rays, which cast long shadows on to the walls of the cave.

Traversing the far ridgeline, the wolves followed an ancient trail used for thousands of years by predators and their prey during migration from valley to valley. Jack carried across his shoulders his longest spear, to which he had bound his favorite flint-knapped point, and took up the rear, trailing the pack through the night. Exhausted, bruised and bleeding after a night of stumbling and pushing through dense low-lying willows, he came to rest high above the snaking plains of an unknown river. The river was huge, and as Jack laid his head down on the moose-skin roll he fell quickly asleep to the sound of the mighty waters crashing and roaring below.

At first light one of the younger wolves nudged him awake. The pack had made yet another kill and the male had brushed fresh aortal blood across Jack's cheek with his nose. Following the wolf, still half asleep, Jack descended the bank to find the pack devouring a large bull caribou, its head bobbing listlessly in the brook, trailing a thin slick of blood downstream. By the time Jack arrived at the kill the alpha male had gorged himself and Jack watched as the younger wolves fawned by him, creeping almost, at the last second snatching at the entrails of the caribou carcass. At first the alpha male went for the young thieves, pinning them down with his great forepaws, one after the other, asserting his dominance. Then, accepting their whimpering, submissive grimaces, he retreated to his indentation in the grasses, permitting the rest of the pack and Jack to come on to the kill and feed. Not since their first meeting had the wolves permitted Jack to approach the kill to partake in the offering. This was the largest caribou Jack had seen during his time in the Kuskokwim and its presence meant only one thing. The migration had begun in earnest, since the big bulls always flanked the females and young along the trail. The wolves would head north now, since the pups were growing ever stronger.

The Brooks Range lay over 300 miles to the north, but the summer was still young and Jack had wanted to go there. But it seemed so perfect here, a remote enclave without lakes or any possibility of uninvited visitors. Winter and summer, it was a secret haven for a secret man. If he was honest, this way north, out of the familiarity of his enclave in the

Kuskokwim, held a great fear for him, a crossing point from which there could be no return. The fear of hardships unknown enticed him and lured him onwards, just like the sled in Groub's gallery had done two years before. The distant mountains had become a profound and driving focus, a logical progression to assure his solitude. Jack had visited their remote rolling vastness in his dreams, injecting himself deep into the vast expanses that now seemed familiar to him. The lure of the northern mountains represented the catalyst for yet another change, and the thought of the journey ahead drew him ever closer in search of the truth, in search of himself, healing his wounds, numbing his guilt.

The journey would be worth it, Jack decided, and since his new family had accepted him he wasn't going to be left behind. Nemo had a new sense of purpose. He had survived all of it, the winter, the icy waters, the wildlife, all that Alaska could throw at him, and it felt good to have passed the initiation, to have been tested in the extreme and now to be more alive than he had ever been. He was heading north, moving on into the unknown, but this time he wasn't alone, the wolves were with him, guiding him. The sled had served its purpose, got him to where he was now. Its symbolism had given him a way of seeing, a way of traveling, a way ... the only way for him at least, free from the constraints of the city, the so-called civilized world. Maybe now he would come to be at peace with himself in the wild high country.

Epilogue

The report now sitting on the desk of the director of the Department of Fish and Game at number one Raspberry Avenue in Anchorage had been quite specific in its findings. The Willow Creek pack had moved north. Dr Wally P. Smith and his field assistant Bret Lile had spent a month on the trail that spring, and aside from one brief sighting had recorded no predation or pack activity since early July. The moose kill at the hotsprings had come as a complete surprise, since never before had they seen the hide removed from such a large ungulate. At first they had considered the culprit to be an opportunist – a large grizzly, for example, might have dragged it off, but that didn't explain the crude cut marks in the bone and surrounding tendon. On close inspection a large portion of the hide seemed to have been removed by a knife, perhaps by a hunter or visiting fly fisherman who might have taken it as a trophy. Anything was possible these days, they had both concluded.

Wally surmised that the den site had been used throughout the spring and early summer months. Moulted hair, urine traces, blood and scat were evidence of that, but Wally also concluded that the Willow Creek pack could not have stayed for their normal term, since there were remains of a series of manmade fires, possibly extinguished as recently as June. Wally had thought it strange, though, since normally local trappers informed the department of any new den site location and most hikers flying in to the Kuskokwim are fully briefed to give all known sites a wide berth. Most notably worrying in the report were the drawings they had found on the walls and roof of the den, especially the repeated signature of the artist. Both the research biologists had found them vaguely amusing, the scrawlings of a modern-day cave man, they joked, but they were deeply concerned that a trusted haven for the wolves had been compromised by a woodsman with too much time on his hands.

Wally Smith had been studying the Willow Creek pack for three years. Traditionally he spent six weeks each summer near them, both following them on the hunt and camping near the den site. With the assistance of the polar-shelf research chopper as drop-off, he had managed to trail the pack throughout their huge range by four-wheeler. The ongoing and controversial field research issue of "How far should one interact with the animals?" showed that Wally's hands-on approach to wolf behavior had resulted in the most extraordinary insights into their family behavior. In his adopted role of alpha male for the summer season, Wally had successfully tracked them on quad-bike until he realized his presence was having a negative effect on their hunting-to-kill ratio. Occasionally Wally had shot small game, Arctic hares, ptarmigan and muskrats for the young and the females, but the alpha male had seemed to disapprove of this alien taking any supportive role within his pack. Wally had observed the alpha male's reaction, a low confrontational cough, and had stopped the practice. The last thing he wanted was a confrontation with the wolf.

The early disappearance of the Willow Creek pack from the upper Kuskokwim range, however, did not cause Wally or Bret undue concern. With the summer passing of the caribou migration deep into the Brooks Range, the wolves had in previous summers been known to move far more in response to their surroundings than was previously thought. Wolves were killers and could always be relied upon to go where prey was bountiful. Wally knew he would catch up with the pack sooner or later, and when he did he would collar that alpha, then the tracking would be a lot easier.

Wally drove north to Palmer, top down, the warm Alaskan sun above him, the wind in his hair. He had the weekend off and his buddy Sheriff Stetson had invited him up for a barbecue, some well-earned R'n'R. He had far too many lies to tell and shit to shoot. No one enjoyed his backcountry bullshit more than his buddy Stets, and besides, Stets had enough urban warfare tales to keep him out of the lower 48 indefinitely. They were chalk and cheese and that was probably why they got on so well.

Stets as usual was late, burning the meat, spilling beer, but what did it matter since it was only Wally. Jenny, Stets' wife, enjoyed his company too. After all, there weren't many Wally Smiths in the world. His articles for *Geographic* made him one of the most revered field biologists in the States, and despite his rough and sometimes coarse exterior he was the original sweetheart. Wally threw his arms around his friend and his wife, giving them his biggest bear hug. Chucking his worn daypack on to the easyboy, he walked into the kitchen, straight up to the large fridge and cracked himself a cold one.

"Glad to see you lost your shy streak, Wally. Why don't you make yourself right at home!"

"Aw, fuck you, Stets. If I'd waited any longer I'd have died of thirst! Now, what you folks been up to?"

They talked, ate and drank long into the night and at around 2am Stets caught himself nodding off; too many war stories, too many near-fatal bear attacks and far too many shots of Jack Daniels.

"Well, Wally, I'm going to call it a night. You know where everything is. You know the score, make yourself at home but leave the wife alone. And I don't want to find you drawing in doodoo on the toilet wall. All that bush living is turning you into an animal."

Wally belly-laughed and Stets, waving his friend goodnight, walked toward the stairs.

"Hey, Stets," Wally added. "Talking of drawing shit on the wall, never guess what we found out in the den site last week? Cave drawings, man. Can you believe it? Cave drawings, graffiti actually, the whole of the den site full of the shit."

"What do you want, Wally, a fucking medal? Wal, I thought you said all these caves out west were full of native pictographs, or have you been forgetting your own lies?"

"No, Stets, this shit was different."

Stets turned, yawning. "Okay, Wally, make it quick, I'm exhausted..."

"Well, Stets, I tell you, these drawings were new, like this summer new. Definitely since the spring, because I was there doing scat analysis late March into April."

Stets was too drunk to care. "Okay, so what we got? A hiker who likes to graffiti in the wild ... Jesus, Wally, this is 2001. That's what kids do these days, they draw on anything, you know that. Whadaya want me to do, arrest him?"

"But Stets, this is some wild country. Not too many hikers or kids out in the Kuskokwim, and anyhow the kid left his name. Strange as shit, come to think of it."

"The Kuskokwim? Jesus, that is remote out there. So go on then, what was the name? Amaze me. Let me guess. Picasso..."

"No, Stets, it wasn't anything like that. It was...yes, it was Nemo. Yeah, like the captain in the movie. The kid had carved Nemo in bold letters on the wall of the cave. What d'ya make of that?"

Stetson stood motionless, his mouth dry, and turning to Jenny he motioned at the phone. "Jen!" he called across the room, "be a doll, run and get me my address book. On my desk in the study."

"Jesus, Stets, what's come over you? Look like you seen a ghost, man. You okay?"

Sheriff Stetson didn't answer but sat on the stairs, phone in hand, a smile breaking across his face.

The End